Julia Lisle is the pseudonym ̱ ̱ ̱ ̱ ̱ ̱ ̱ ̱ ̱ ̱ ̱ ̱ ̱ ̱ ̱ ̱ ̱ ̱
and cookery writer. She bega ̱ ̱ ̱ ̱ ̱ ̱ ̱ ̱ ̱ ̱ ̱ ̱ ̱ ̱ ̱ ̱
ing and public relations befo ̱ ̱ ̱ ̱ ̱ ̱ ̱ to Somerset
with her husband and taking up cookery. Her first Julia
Lisle novel, *The Changing Years*, is also available
from Headline.

Also by Julia Lisle

The Changing Years

A
Perfect Match

Julia Lisle

HEADLINE

First published in 1996
by HEADLINE BOOK PUBLISHING

First published in paperback in 1996
by HEADLINE BOOK PUBLISHING

10 9 8 7 6 5 4 3 2 1

ISBN 0 7472 5247 5

Printed and bound in Great Britain by
Cox & Wyman Ltd, Reading, Berks

HEADLINE BOOK PUBLISHING
A division of Hodder Headline PLC
338 Euston Road
London NW1 3BH

In memory of
Marjorie
with love and many thanks

ACKNOWLEDGEMENTS

I have had help with this book from a number of people, some in England and some in Provence. I would like to thank particularly Maggie Soulsby of Yeovil Hospital and Dr Audrey Dunlop for helping with medical details; Tessa, Shelley, Pat and Maggie of The Group for their valuable comments and advice during the writing; and my editor, Clare Going, for her perceptive remarks and suggestions. Many thanks also to Michael Thomas, my agent, for his encouragement and, most of all, to Keith, my husband, for his patience and support.

PART ONE

England

Chapter One

Olivia Warboys put papers into her briefcase and wished she was packing for a holiday. Somewhere with the sea or with mountains, with a terrace and a view, somewhere she could stretch out with a long, cool drink and forget about working in London in an August heatwave. The office was hot and airless and opening the windows merely increased the noise and the dust and the sense of breathlessness.

Olivia pulled her silk blouse away from her sticky shoulders and sighed. There was no prospect of a holiday for her in the foreseeable future. Too much work and, more important, no money.

She looked at the client proposal for a packaging exhibition in Paris that was still sitting in the middle of her desk. Her stand designs needed more work. Reluctantly she picked up the file.

'Forget it!' her colleague Margie Carmichael said assertively. 'You've slaved yourself to a standstill over that project.'

'Gavin will be mad as hell if my bit's not ready by tomorrow.'

'You know and I know our dear boss has got a long way to go before the rest of the proposal's ready.'

Olivia dropped the papers back on her desk. 'I do want tonight free for Tilly,' she confessed.

Margie raised an eyebrow. 'Her birthday? I thought that was in February.'

'It is. Today's the day the A level results come out.' Olivia looked at the telephone that had rung continuously throughout the day but never with a call from her daughter. 'She was supposed to let me know her grades.'

Margie dumped a load of papers into her own briefcase. 'Oh dear, bad sign, do you think?'

'Not really, she's worked very hard. No, she probably just hasn't been able to get through to me. This evening she'll want to talk about her plans – you know, what her choices are for university, whether she wants a year off, all that. I don't want to have to tell her to keep it all for the weekend. I hate it when work comes between us.' Olivia pushed back the stray strands of fair hair that had worked themselves out of her chignon (if she called it that rather than a bun, even if only in her mind, then somehow it seemed more of an actual hairstyle instead of a cheap way to keep her abundant hair in place).

3

'Tilly leaving school!' Margie exclaimed. All at once she straightened up and looked across at Olivia. 'Then you can start living again.'

'I live all the time, thank you very much.'

'You do not!' Margie screwed up her nose, accentuating the wide-eyed charm of her urchin face. 'When was the last time you went out? And I mean with a man, not with a crowd of friends.'

Olivia hesitated, wondering how to reply.

'See, you can't even remember!' Margie said with a note of triumph. 'All the time you've worked here, it's been the same thing: can't go out, have to get back to Tilly. What do you do with your weekends? Spend them visiting your parents or working or at some teenage-focused activity. Never anything for you, Olivia. My God, if I had your looks, I'd have men queuing up to take me out.'

'Come off it, Margie, I'm over the hill, middle-aged!'

'Only thirty-eight and you still look like Grace Kelly crossed with Michelle Pfeiffer on one of her better days. It's time you broke out, girl, and enjoyed a thoroughly decadent time.'

'Wait till you have children, Margie, then you'll know they can be just as much fun to be with as someone of the opposite sex. More, sometimes!'

'No way, I'm not saddling myself with that sort of baggage.' In her late-twenties and divorced from two husbands, Margie now declared marriage was not for her; she intended to be running her own design company within five years.

Olivia had no such ambitions. She was happy to have a job that she enjoyed and carried a salary that meant she could just about keep a roof over her and Tilly's heads. A job she needed to keep. She gave another anxious look at the sketches on her desk and her sense of unease deepened; she hated getting behind on a project, it only piled on the pressure. Then, 'Sod it,' she said and resolutely placed them in her in-tray. As she picked up the briefcase, the telephone on her desk rang and she reached for it eagerly. Tilly at last. 'Yes?' she said.

'Olivia?' asked a hesitant male voice.

For a moment she couldn't place it.

'Charles Frome,' the voice said apologetically. 'You remember, you said now would be a good time to ring you? I'm sorry it's so late but I've only just got out of a meeting. I was afraid you'd have gone home.'

Charles Frome! Olivia sat down at her desk, all of a sudden breathless with an unfamiliar excitement.

She'd last seen Charles three months ago, at the exhibition for which she'd designed his company stand. Both of them had been tense and exhausted from setting up the previous evening and Olivia had wanted nothing so much as to slide back to the office for a couple of calming hours of paperwork. Instead she'd agreed to be there for the press preview day to see the stand in action.

She'd watched Charles survey his little kingdom.

4

'Any moment now I shall have to give all my attention to business,' he'd said, turning to her, his gaze very straight. 'I've so enjoyed working with you and I'd hate us to lose touch. Would you come out to dinner with me after all this is over?' His gesture encompassed stand and exhibition hall; his eyes, the shade of a peat river, deep brown with light flecks, were wary but hopeful.

Olivia almost said, yes, she'd love to. Charles Frome's sense of humour had enlivened their sessions together and she'd appreciated the way he could be decisive without being aggressive, qualities that were rare in the men she usually worked with. But years of self-imposed resolution held. 'I'm sorry,' she said, 'I'm not free.'

Charles, with the exhibition about to open, important press about to arrive, looked at her carefully. 'What does that mean?'

She floundered, 'It means what it says, I'm not free to go out to dinner with you.'

'I know you're a widow and have been for years, your colleague told me.'

Olivia promised herself to have a word with Margie when she got back to the office. How dare she not tell her friend that Charles had been asking about her?

'So,' he continued patiently, 'are you living with another man? Or in a committed relationship?'

She couldn't lie so she shook her head.

Relief lit his square features. 'So what does not being free mean?'

Charles Frome seemed blissfully different from the other men who'd been interested in her since she'd been widowed. And, just for once, it would be wonderful to be taken out and made a fuss of. Tilly would soon be finished with school and have made her decision on her future. When that happened, perhaps Olivia would be free. The question that was beginning to occupy her was what was she going to be free for?

Her hesitation relaxed him. A hint of humour lit his eyes. 'Well, do I have to pass some sort of exam?'

She laughed. 'Nothing like that. It's just that I haven't time at the moment.'

'So when will you have time? I can't believe you never go out.'

She nearly said, only in a group or with girlfriends. Instead, 'If you like to give me a ring in three months' time, I should be free then.' Then she added quickly, 'I'm sorry, that sounds dreadful. Talk about a rain check, that's more of a snowstorm!'

But he didn't laugh and his brown eyes still held hers steadily. 'Three months? Right, I shall ring you in three months' time.'

Then someone had arrived at the stand and there'd been no more personal conversation.

She'd thought he'd forget, she almost had. Not quite, though. The possibility of his ringing had surfaced from time to time, giving her a frisson of excitement, something to cheer up the daily slog of working on demanding but far from exciting designs. She certainly hadn't imagined, though, that he would ring her exactly three months to the day, at a time when she was leaving to catch her train, when she was worried about not hearing from Tilly.

'Charles!' She heard the unguarded pleasure in her voice with a touch of surprise. 'How nice to hear from you.'

'I was wondering, have you anything on for tomorrow night? If not, perhaps we could have a meal somewhere?'

'Why not?' Everything suddenly seemed simple. 'Look, I can't talk now, could you ring me later at home?' She gave him the number then replaced the receiver and ignored Margie's interested look. Once again she picked up the briefcase.

Gavin Rickard thrust back the door of his office, his small figure imposing itself on the open space as he raked back his long, fair hair with an extravagant gesture. 'Ah, Olivia, leaving are you?' How did he manage to make going home nearly an hour after the day had officially ended sound as though she was skiving? Apart from Margie and her, the office was deserted. 'You'll have those sketches ready for me tomorrow morning, won't you?' He gave her a curt nod and strode back into his office.

'X-ray vision and X-ray ears, that's what that man's got,' Margie murmured, plonking a chic straw hat on her short, shining haircut.

Olivia yanked the project file back out of her in-tray and hurriedly forced it into her briefcase. 'I don't care who else rings or wants a word, I'm off!'

The two women left the office. Outside Margie flagged down a taxi and gave her Chelsea address. Olivia headed for the commuter train.

Chapter Two

At Surbiton station, Olivia alighted and walked quickly to the High Street Sainsbury's.

There she hesitated over the bewildering choice of salad ingredients on offer and the even more varied bottles of wine. Only steak was simple to snatch up. Outside once again after battling with bad-tempered shoppers and the check-out queue, she turned towards the river. Dusty-edged heat slammed against the hard grey pavements and ricocheted off the redbrick houses. The briefcase and the plastic shopping bag grew heavier.

Olivia felt hemmed in by the untidy drabness of Surbiton and the disgruntled faces that surrounded her. She felt deeply nostalgic for the large house in Richmond where she'd grown up. For the elegant drawing room where her mother had reigned over gatherings of smart friends, the large kitchen, warm in winter and cool in summer, where Barbara, the Polish housekeeper, had always had a cookie and glass of milk for her. And her bedroom, with its small, muslin-draped four poster bed, white-painted furniture and a line of teddy bears and dolls on a window seat that overlooked a street with leafy trees. In those days everything had seemed safe and life ahead an exciting adventure.

Sometimes Olivia also dreamed of a car that could take her to large supermarkets with huge parking areas, where the whole week's shopping could be piled into a capacious boot after a credit card had flexed itself to take the strain of the sort of sum that was way beyond her current resources. Her mother had offered to give her a small second-hand runabout but it wasn't only pride that had made Olivia turn the offer down. The running expenses of even a small car would eat too heavily into her budget. Tilly had her bicycle and Olivia managed on public transport.

She turned down a side street near the river and slid her key into the door of a small, early-nineteenth-century terraced cottage. 'I'm home!' she called as she let herself in.

There was no reply.

She walked through to the kitchen, dumped the shopping bag on the work surface by the sink, took out the bottle of white wine, the steak and saladings and placed them in the fridge. Automatically she ran a light hand over the polished yew units that an unexpected repeat royalty payment for one of her husband's scripts had financed a couple of years ago and felt, as

7

always, deep satisfaction. At least the kitchen now matched her idea of what an attractive home should look like.

Then she went and placed her briefcase beside the antique flat-topped desk in the open-plan living room. Once two small rooms, the previous owner had opened them out so that living space ran from the front of the cottage to the French windows at the rear. It was still quite a small area but a few good pieces of furniture that Olivia's parents had said they didn't need managed to lend a sense of style, helped by several nineteenth-century water colours from the same source.

Olivia glanced at the couple of letters sitting on her desk where Tilly must have put them; she recognised her mother's handwriting and the pristine anonymity of a piece of junk mail, sighed, picked up the first and dumped the other in the wastepaper basket.

The room was stuffy. Olivia unlocked the French windows, pushed them open, then stood and savoured the scents of the tiny garden. This was Tilly's domain. Olivia's daughter loved the roses that tangled along the dividing brick walls, fighting with clematis and jasmine for room to breathe, all of them offering an almost constant succession of flowers and fragrance. Tilly had filled terracotta tubs with flagrant displays of geraniums, begonias and petunias. 'Granny says they're hopelessly suburban,' she sadly told a visitor who commented on their colour and profusion. 'But there isn't much time for looking after anything that isn't pretty hardy.' It was Tilly who'd planted a variety of herbs in gaps in the paving stones, Tilly who'd mourned when the basil and the dill didn't come up and the mint encroached where it shouldn't.

It was Olivia who had found the old wrought iron table and chairs from a card in a local newsagent's, who'd stripped and painted them a sparkling white then found the time to make round squabs of blue and white striped canvas with matching blue piping. These were kept in a neat little garden shed in a corner of the terrace, together with Tilly's fork and trowel, potting compost, watering can and spare flower pots.

Olivia placed her letter on the table, opened the shed, fished out the cushions and placed them on the chairs. The evening was so warm, they could have supper out here, or at least a glass of the wine she'd bought to celebrate Tilly's results.

She glanced at her watch. Tilly should have been home some time ago. She couldn't have gone out straight from work, not today!

Olivia's daughter was working at a local restaurant, helping in the kitchen with lunches and teas. Run by a couple of enterprising housewives, it didn't open in the evenings.

When Tilly first told her about the job she'd found, Olivia had thought it sounded far too exhausting and she could just imagine what her mother would say when she learned her granddaughter was going to work as a kitchen maid. As Tilly had detailed her duties, Olivia's doubts had grown. All right, she looked sturdy enough; if anything, too sturdy. Olivia herself was slender and always had been while Tilly's frame was more generous. There was never any trouble about Tilly borrowing her mother's clothes. But, 'You look so pale, darling, it's all that hard work swotting for your exams. Why don't you go and stay a couple of weeks with Grandma and Grandpa in Sussex? They'd love to have you and it would do you so much good, all that country air.'

'Ma, I need to earn money! And you know I love cooking.'

It was true. A twelve-year-old Tilly had tried her hand at a cottage pie when Olivia had succumbed to 'flu, and revealed herself as a natural cook, far better than her mother.

'But you'll get so tired. I remember when I was waitressing in California, when your father and I were first married, it was killing!'

'You were pregnant, remember? Of course you got tired!' Tilly said irritably, biting the side of her thumb the way she always did when she and her mother disagreed about anything.

'Shouldn't you be trying something different? Something that would stretch your wings a bit?' Olivia tried a last protest.

'Jobs aren't that plentiful, Mum!' Tilly pushed back her long, mouse-brown hair with a sigh of exasperation. 'I've been to all the agencies, including the Job Shop, *and* all the newsagents' windows. Everyone wants people with experience. How do you get experience if no one will give you a job without it? Anyway, I don't get tired. It's like you and work – you know you can go on organising your exhibitions and conferences until you drop.'

For the first time Olivia heard resentment in Tilly's voice. She had always been grateful she and Tilly got on so well, that she didn't have to cope with a difficult daughter the way so many of her friends did. Was it all going to start now?

'Anyway,' Tilly continued in a rush, 'I'm only going to be the assistant and it's only for the summer until . . .' her round face with its small, straight nose and big, soft grey eyes looked suddenly alarmed '. . . until I start university.' Once again she pushed back the hair that was always falling over her eyes. One day Tilly was going to be beautiful, Olivia decided. When she had lost the puppy-fat softness that hid the strength of her facial bones and overfleshed her bust and hips, and she'd learned how to handle the thick hair and make the most of those lovely eyes and her good skin.

For now, though, she had only the fresh attractiveness of unsophisticated youth. At the moment a slightly belligerent youth. What lay behind her sudden rush for independence and impatience with her mother? 'Are you having second thoughts about college, darling? Would you rather do something else? Just because Grandma and Grandpa are so keen for you to go doesn't mean you have to.'

For a second something like hope had flared in Tilly's eyes and Olivia thought they were going to get to the bottom of whatever was troubling her. Then Tilly had swallowed hard and said with resolution, 'I just hope I've got the right grades.'

'I'm sure you'll do well, darling, you always work so hard.'

Tilly had got up from the table and picked up her plate, still loaded with half the smoked mackerel salad she'd prepared for their supper. 'You need more than just hard work,' she muttered, dunking the remains of her meal in the bin, then announced she was off out with some friends before Olivia could probe further.

It set a pattern for the next few weeks. Declaring the job was proving just what she wanted and wasn't tiring her at all, Tilly appeared determined to demonstrate she had plenty of energy by disappearing most evenings and weekends with friends from school. Released from the purdah of studying for exams, they were enjoying freedom with relentless enthusiasm.

Except that Olivia sensed that Tilly's involvement was more relentless than enthusiastic.

Olivia tied the last cushion to the last chair then glanced over the fence. Nobody was out on the little terrace of the house next door but she could see a figure moving behind the kitchen window. She went and rang the bell.

Clodagh Howard came to the door wearing rubber gloves and a bikini, her rangy figure slicked with sweat, her springy auburn hair tied with a piece of string on the top of her head. 'You've caught me cleaning the oven,' she declared, standing aside for Olivia to enter.

'You're impossible! Cleaning the oven on a day like today? Why not wait for the weather to break?'

'Because it's been this hot for three weeks and Michael's coming tomorrow evening. You know what a pernickety sod he can be, not to mention Caroline, my precious daughter-in-law. She's not beyond running a finger through the dust that so liberally coats my furniture. And you know how Michael expects a roast from his old mother no matter what the weather.'

'Honestly, Clodagh, you spoil that boy!'

Olivia and Clodagh had chummed up the moment Clodagh had moved in next door four years ago. Recently divorced, declaring her husband had fooled the courts into believing his income was half what it actually was and that the house was all she could afford, Clodagh attacked life head on. She'd always wanted to write, she said, and this was going to be her opportunity to find out whether she could make it or not. While her son finished his articles as a chartered accountant, and spent most of his spare time at his father's big house in St George's Hill, Weybridge, complete with swimming pool, gym and smart young stepmother, Clodagh struggled with her word processor.

It had been a relief for Olivia to find another single mother with similar financial problems to her own. But Clodagh had no lack of boyfriends and was always trying to arrange a date for Olivia. Until yet another of her relationships went wrong. Then she'd announce, 'I tell you, Olive, you're right not to have anything to do with men,' and open a bottle of wine. 'They're sods the lot of them. I'm writing this latest bastard into my book, that'll do for him!'

Clodagh had the warmest heart Olivia had ever met and she hated the way Michael so seldom came down to visit his mother. He'd married a real Sloane Ranger at an enormous wedding at her parents' estate in Gloucestershire. Clodagh had come back pale and tense. 'I've lost him,' she told Olivia that evening. 'Their entire wedding list was at the General Trading Company and her father's put down the deposit on a three-bedroomed house just off Clapham Common. She's getting the curtains from Osborne and Little!'

'Come on,' Olivia said gently. 'You bought cushions the other day from Designer's Guild and don't tell me you don't know what to do with every knife on any table.'

'But it isn't *important* to me,' Clodagh had mourned. 'And it is to them. Ah, well, better get back to my latest attempt to break into the bestseller list.'

Now she stripped off her rubber gloves and gave Olivia a relieved grin. 'At last, an excuse to break off. What will you have? I've a fine Sancerre chilling in the fridge.'

'I haven't come to stop, I just wondered if you'd seen Tilly this afternoon?'

Clodagh led the way straight through a Conran-modern room that had been opened out in the same way as Olivia's and into a well-designed minimalist steel kitchen. She took a bottle of wine from the fridge. 'Come on, have a glass. I need a reviver.' Without waiting, she opened the bottle, poured two glasses and took them out on to the small terrace.

The two women settled themselves on gaily cushioned garden chairs and sipped at the chilled wine.

'So, what's happened to Tilly?' asked Clodagh.

'She just doesn't seem to be around and today's the day the A level results came out.'

'Ah!' said Clodagh as if that explained it all.

'But she's bound to have done all right. I know she's not particularly brainy but she's always passed everything very respectably so far, she works very hard.'

'Does she?'

'Clodagh, what do you mean?' Olivia pushed her glass away from her. 'What do you know that I don't?'

'Well,' Clodagh bent her red head over her glass for a moment then looked up, 'I'd better tell you, I suppose. All the time you thought she was revising for her exams, she was entertaining a young man.'

'Tilly? Here?' Olivia waved in the direction of her house. 'Why on earth didn't you tell me? I thought you were supposed to be my friend!'

Clodagh refused to be disconcerted. Her long, narrow, yellow eyes

11

looked frankly back at Olivia. 'You know me. I mind my own business and let others get on with theirs.'

There was no point in remonstrating; Clodagh had her own standards. 'So,' Olivia said grimly, 'tell me more about this "young man".'

Clodagh thought for a moment. 'Early-twenties, I suppose, attractive, public school type, *very* smooth, from what I could see. He came here almost every afternoon over a period of about two to three weeks, I suppose, after Easter.'

'Easter! That'd be Mark. Tilly met him at some tennis party and brought him home for lunch Easter Sunday. He was studying at the Guildford Law School. I think his people live Yorkshire way.' Olivia remembered the young man extremely well. He'd been everything Clodagh had said, had teased Tilly like an elder brother and half flirted with Olivia, making her feel attractive, almost young again. Tilly had been sweet, puppyish in her delight at having him there, enjoying his praise of her food. Olivia had seen nothing to worry about, she'd told herself Mark was far too sophisticated to be interested in a child like Tilly. Had she really allowed the attentions of a young man fifteen years her junior to blind her to the true situation?

She finished her wine and stood up. 'Well, all I can do is wait for her to come home. Thanks for the drink.' She marched out of the house, feeling in less accord with Clodagh than at any time in their relationship.

Back in her own home, Olivia returned to the terrace and once again picked up the letter from her mother. The bold, black writing demanded attention.

Slowly she opened the envelope and drew out the heavy pieces of writing paper. Her mother was the last person she knew who used the expensive, Bond Street-bought, tissue-lined envelopes and paper with those hard, sharp, deckle edges.

Reluctantly she began to read. Letters from her mother were always a signal that Olivia had in some way failed. To Daphne Ferguson, words over the telephone were too fleeting to do justice to censure. Reprimands had to be tethered to paper, anchored down with ink so they could carry weight, could still be there for a second reading if the first hadn't struck sufficiently forcibly.

Such were the barriers Olivia had erected to defend herself against whatever attack was now to be aimed at her, it took a little while for the sense of the letter to penetrate. Then odd phrases reverberated: Incredible selfishness . . . your daughter's health . . . that ridiculous job you allowed her to take . . . get to the bottom of her unhappiness . . . exams are so important . . . we'll help with a crammer if necessary . . . ring me the moment you know the results.

The letter dropped on to the table as all Olivia's moments of unease over Tilly during the past few weeks joined with what Clodagh had told her and she knew with awful certainty that it wasn't because she couldn't get through that Tilly hadn't rung her today.

She glanced upwards. Her daughter's bedroom window was open.

Olivia ran up the stairs.

Tilly lay slumped on her bed, her arm over her eyes.

Olivia sat down beside her. 'What's the matter, darling? Is it your results?'

Tilly's arm fell down from her face, revealing red and swollen eyes. 'Ma, I've failed! I only got a D and two Es.' The words came out in a long wail then Olivia found her arms full of weeping daughter.

She held her tightly, murmuring soothing noises, telling her it didn't matter, exams weren't that important, that Tilly could never, ever fail.

Olivia's soul filled with the bitter realisation that her mother had been right. How could she have been so incredibly selfish? She'd allowed herself to become too caught up in the demands of her job. Because she'd been so used to Tilly spilling out her troubles, she'd blinded herself to the fact something was seriously wrong. Olivia felt a deep sense of failure and as she held Tilly, the raw and throbbing pain that she had tried to bury with her husband suddenly rose up and threatened to swamp her.

'Hush, darling, hush! It really doesn't matter.'

'It does!' Tilly said fiercely. She gave a hiccuping gulp and leaned back on the pillows, wiping away her tears with the heel of her hand. 'Everyone expected me to get a B and two Cs.'

Olivia looked at her daughter. She was wearing a T-shirt and matching jeans with pretty appliqued flowers, Olivia's Easter present, but there were stains on the shirt and her long hair could do with a wash. When had she last seen her dressed with care?

'What's happened to that nice Mark you brought home for Easter?' she asked gently.

Tilly stiffened, pushing herself back into the corner of the bed against the wall, as though she wanted to disappear, and the flush that had been on her cheeks died, leaving her face looking pale and pinched. Her soft mouth trembled and her stubborn chin dimpled with distress. 'He's gone back to London,' she jerked out. 'He – he hasn't rung me.'

'Oh, darling, I'm so sorry!' Olivia took a firm grip of her daughter's hand. 'Were you very fond of him?' Stupid question, she told herself. All the signs of desperate first love were there, how could she have missed them before?

The tears overflowed as Tilly nodded wordlessly. Then she burst out, 'He said he loved me and – and I believed him!'

'Of course you did, darling. I'd have done as well.' Olivia cursed Mark from the bottom of her heart. 'He's a rat, not worth one tear. But I know that doesn't make it any easier. Is this what upset you so much during your exams?'

Tilly's body shook suddenly. 'I . . . I thought I was pregnant!' she said in a long, shuddering whisper.

'Oh, darling, why didn't you tell me?' Olivia tried to hide her profound shock that Tilly had been to bed with Mark. Of course, she should have realised that from what Clodagh had said. She should even have expected it; seventeen these days was late still to be a virgin. But you couldn't be realistic about something like this. Her sweet little girl, played with and cast aside by a wretched youngster not fit to tie her shoelaces! But why hadn't Tilly told her before? They'd had long talks about sex, about love, when Olivia had tried to caution Tilly against passion without a solid foundation of respect and friendship. How stupid of her! Of course Tilly wasn't going to heed that sort of advice when someone like Mark was out to seduce her.

Olivia longed to sweep Tilly into her arms again but she still burrowed desperately into her corner.

'I – I was so ashamed. And afraid!'

Olivia's grip on Tilly's hand tightened. 'It's all my fault, I should have seen what was happening, been there for you.'

'When I was trying to revise, all I could think of was what was I going to do? Then when I went into the exams, I couldn't remember a thing. I just sat there, thinking about Mark, realising he didn't want anything more to do with me, and wondering how I was going to cope and what you and Grandma and Grandpa were going to say.' Tears flowed down Tilly's face. 'When I found I wasn't pregnant, the day after the exams finished, it was such a relief. I thought I'd be able to forget Mark. I found the job at the restaurant and I thought maybe everything would be all right. But . . . but I couldn't stop missing him and hoping he'd ring me.' Tilly gave a sobbing hiccup. 'How can you hate someone and love them at the same time?'

'Oh, quite easily! Love can be the most painful experience there is.'

Tilly gazed at Olivia. 'But you were happy with Dad, weren't you?'

Olivia bent forward, took a tissue from Tilly's bedside table and tried to wipe away the tears. It was like dealing with Niagara. This was a girl with a truly broken heart. Olivia drew her back into her arms and tried to be honest. 'Darling,' she said into her hair, 'no marriage is all joy and happiness. Living together with anyone is difficult, and just because you are in love doesn't mean the difficulties all disappear.'

Tilly drew away slightly from her mother. 'Isn't anyone happy, then?'

Olivia sighed. 'Yes, of course, lots of people are. But happiness isn't something you switch on like an electric blanket. It's, well, sometimes it sneaks up on you when you aren't expecting it, like when you first met Mark. And other times you have to work for it. And if you're the only person working at it, sometimes that isn't enough. That's when you get hurt.'

The big grey eyes never wavered in their stare. 'Will I ever forget Mark?'

'No, darling, you don't forget first love. But you will find that what you felt for him, deep as you now think it is, is nothing compared with what you will feel for someone else in the future.'

14

'Did you love anyone before Dad?'

Olivia swallowed hard and tried to think back. 'There was a boy I thought I loved. We went out together for a bit, then he found someone else and, like you, I thought my world had ended. But then I went to that party and met your father and I realised what I'd felt before had been nothing.' She'd forgotten all about that first boy until now. She couldn't remember his name – David? Donald? But she could remember the coming out dance he'd taken her to and kissing in his car after he'd brought her home. The following day they'd gone on a picnic. They'd lain in a field under a clear blue sky with a lark singing; he'd held her as though she was made of fragile glass and told her she was the most beautiful girl he'd ever seen. But they hadn't made love. Her husband Peter had been her first lover. Her only lover.

The ridiculous beep of the telephone in her bedroom came through the thin wall.

Tilly tensed, seemed about to leap off the bed and rush to answer it. Then she gave the faintest of smiles. 'It's probably for you.'

How long before she gave up hoping it was going to be Mark every time she heard the phone ring? Olivia went reluctantly into her room and picked up the receiver.

'Oh, Charles!' She held her breath, dismayed. She couldn't possibly go out with him now, not when Tilly needed her. 'About tomorrow, I'm sorry, I don't think I can make it after all.'

There was a short silence. 'I see,' he said, sounding hurt. 'I suppose something has come up. Well, some other time perhaps,' he ended firmly, and she knew there would be no other time.

Olivia felt a rush of deep disappointment and realised she really did want to see Charles Frome again. 'You wouldn't like to come to supper here, would you?' she suggested in breathless rush. 'With my daughter and me?'

'Tomorrow, you mean?' He sounded nervous. Olivia waited for him to find some excuse.

'I'd love to!' he said decisively, managing to sound delighted. 'What time and where do you live?'

Chapter Three

'Tilly, I said chicken salad, not turkey!' Beth Spade thumped the plate down on the counter, her round blue eyes clouded with irritation. 'What's the matter with you? Nothing but bishes all morning!' She didn't wait for an answer but bustled back into the main part of the small restaurant, her full cotton skirt swishing round her thick legs, a pleasant smile once again glued to her broad face.

'That one never knows what personal problems are!' Jemima's beaded hair clinked lightly as she whipped the plate out of Tilly's hands and started replacing the turkey meat with chicken and the avocado with strips of grilled red pepper. 'I'll do this. You get another cheesecake out of the fridge, that one's nearly finished.'

Tears stinging at the back of her eyes, Tilly went over to the other side of the small kitchen, carefully lifted a strawberry cheesecake out of the large fridge and brought it over to the counter.

Nothing had gone right this morning. She'd over-processed the pastry then put the quiches into too high an oven. And she'd forgotten about the peaches that she'd put to poach with chilli peppers for Jemima's speciality dessert and they'd almost disintegrated.

'You look like you lost the world and found a dog turd. Nothing's that bad.' Jemima took the cheesecake and set it on the side then went back to slicing up a roasted chicken, her knife flashing with easy skill. 'Set up more salad plates and don't overdo the radiccio. It's grand for colour but the punters don't like the flavour. Don't appreciate what a touch of bitterness can do. If life's all sweetness and light, what fun's that, eh?'

Tilly gave a small smile. 'Wouldn't mind a touch of sugar now and then.' At the moment she couldn't see how she would ever find life fun again.

'Just because you've failed an exam or two and lost a man it doesn't mean your life's over! What about your mum? When your dad died, did she turn her face to the wall, forget the beat of life? Did I when Jango walked out on me and the girls? And haven't I now found Duane?'

Jemima was six foot of coffee-coloured whirlwind. Tilly had never seen anyone move as quickly as she did. She'd taught Tilly how to chop vegetables in a blur of the knife and how to plan her preparation and cooking so that no second was wasted. 'My dad was a chef,' she'd said when Tilly had asked where she'd learned her skills. 'I was all set for a

17

career, up the ladder to the Roux brothers; Dad worked in one of their kitchens once, before he took to the bottle. Then I met Jango and he got me producing food for the group. All over the country we went, gigs here, there and everywhere. Then he finds that little black number and at the end, what did I have? Five hundred recipes for vegetarian sandwiches and my twins.'

Tilly had gone home with Jemima once, on the back of her ancient motor cycle to Tooting. She'd met Jemima's mother, Marsha, almost as tall as her daughter and just as attractive, with skin the same shade of coffee. And she'd met the three-year-old twins, two little girls, twice as dark as their mother, with fuzzy hair and inexhaustible energy. Jemima's dad, the chef, had disappeared several years earlier. Marsha looked after the twins during the day then worked in a local restaurant in the evening.

Was that what life was like for women? Find a man, get pregnant, lose a man and spend the best part of your life looking after children?

Tilly could just remember her father and living in a big house in the hills outside Hollywood. It had had a swimming pool. The sun had always shone and her mother had always been there. Not her father, though, he'd had to work at the studios in Hollywood, writing scripts. 'The sun comes free but that's about all,' he'd say, swinging Tilly round, making her dizzy, then placing her gently in one of the big wicker chairs by the pool. 'I gotta go and spin some dreams, you be a good girl.'

'Take me too, Daddy, I can help, I can spin dreams.'

'Sure you can, baby, but not today.' He'd been tall and dark, his hair worn caught back in a pony tail, his preferred wear jeans and a T-shirt.

'One chicken liver *salade tiède*, one leek quiche, two chilli peaches and a cheesecake,' sang out Judy Wilson, Beth's partner, as she dumped a tray of dirty crockery on the counter.

Tilly quickly junked the bits of left-over food, noting guiltily that most of it was overcooked quiche, stacked the dirty stuff into the washing machine then cut a fresh slice of quiche to put with a ready prepared plate of salad while Jemima added chunks of chicken liver to a sauté pan and started to stir fry them. Then Tilly spooned out the too-soft peaches into dishes and added a spray of coriander to try and hide the condition of the fruit.

'Like it!' Jemima said, her eyes taking in everything as she added dressing to her pan and swirled it around.

'For heaven's sake,' Judy protested as she came back for the dishes. 'I know we've got a name for being different but that's going too far!' She whipped the herb off the fruit, took a look at it, then put the green sprays back again. Her mouth compressed, she whisked the desserts out without further comment.

Jemima poured the just-cooked chicken livers over the plate of saladings Tilly had got ready earlier and handed it across for a final touch of chopped parsley, tarragon and chervil.

18

Beth swept in with another load of dirty plates and more orders. The pace of the restaurant rose to its highest pitch and Tilly and Jemima were soon working far too hard for chat.

By half-past two things had slowed down. 'Here, have a coffee. Wish it was wine but we want to keep our jobs, don't we?' Jemima handed a steaming mug over to Tilly, who placed it beside the washing machine while she finished stacking in the last pile of dirty crockery. Then she switched the machine on, took a grateful swig of the powerful liquid and fought her depression.

So, she'd failed some exams. Big deal! The world wasn't going to come to an end. Her mother had taken the news very well. Her grandparents' reaction, though, would be different. Tilly drank more coffee and fought a renewed sense of profound failure. Her grandmother was bound to insist that Tilly resat the exams. The thought of grappling once more with Shakespeare and themes of universality, the nutritional values of carrots or what led up to the Second World War (I mean, when you'd said Hitler, you'd said it all), appalled Tilly. But there was little chance her grandmother would be as understanding as Olivia.

It had been such a relief to tell her mother about everything. For a little while last night Tilly had thought perhaps her life was going to sort itself out again. She'd washed her hair and changed into a clean dress and they'd had steak and salad and wine. Tilly had spilled out everything, all her hurt and loneliness and despair. Olivia had told her this was just a little blip in a life that was going to get better and better and Tilly had tried to believe her.

But this morning it had all flooded over her again. Being with Mark had been like living in a dream. He was so attractive, Tilly had felt something in her melt every time she looked at him. It had been a constant miracle that he wanted to be with her, that he said he adored her silly little face and those big, big eyes. That he loved the way she was so restful, didn't ceaselessly chatter at him the way other girls did. Tilly had snorted at that and almost told him it was because she was terrified of making a fool of herself. Mark was so much older and more sophisticated than the other boys she knew.

She'd dreamed of going up to Yorkshire with him and meeting his parents. Of becoming part of his life. Even, perhaps, once he'd passed all his law exams, of getting engaged. He'd take care of her, introduce her to life, and in return she'd look after him, cook him delicious meals, make sure he had everything he wanted. School became an irritant, her friends seemed stupid and terribly young.

The day Mark had said he wouldn't be round any more, he was going back to London, Tilly had been sorry but she'd imagined that he would ring her, ask her up there. Of course they wouldn't be able to see each other so often but they'd have telephone calls and exciting weekends together.

But days had passed without his ringing. Days when Tilly had hung around the house waiting, unable to concentrate on her revision. Instead she wrote scenarios in her head to explain why he couldn't contact her and cursed herself for not asking for his address.

Finally, she faced the fact that Mark had only been interested in her as a diversion until he went back to London. And that she was so late with her normally regular period that she must be pregnant. What had been despair became nightmare. One of the girls in her class had had an abortion the previous term. Tilly knew she could never do that. Mark's baby would be far too precious. But how was she to cope and what would her mother and grandparents say?

She had sat her exams in a daze of misery and terror.

And as devastating as the realisation that she was never going to see Mark again was knowing that he hadn't meant any of the lovely things he'd said. She longed to see him again yet burned with humiliation that she could have been so deluded about anyone. Never again, she told herself, would she get involved with a man.

Then, the day after the last of her exams, her period came and one of her problems was solved. For a time it was almost enough.

Tilly straightened herself up and finished the coffee. Mark was yesterday's news, she told herself firmly. At least she wasn't having to cope with being pregnant. At least she wasn't being left to bring up a child on her own. Heavens, what if it had been twins like Jemima had to cope with!

'Tilly, help with clearing the tables, will you? Beth has to leave for a couple of hours.' Judy, small and determined, her hair a fair frizz, her face red with effort, dumped another tray of dirty crockery on the counter.

'Go on, girl, I'll see to this lot.' Jemima pushed her towards the restaurant.

Tray in hand, conscious of the odd stain on the T-shirt that had been clean on that morning, Tilly tried to look inconspicuous as she loaded abandoned crockery from empty tables. By now the restaurant was more than half-empty. Most of the clientele were local office workers and shoppers who didn't spend long over their meals. A few tables, though, had gossiping women lingering over cups of coffee and two were occupied by latecomers still eating.

'Excuse me!'

At a table by the window was a young man sitting alone. More casually dressed than the office workers, he still had an air of respectability, short thick fair hair was nicely brushed and he wore a striped short-sleeved shirt tucked into well-pressed chinos. His thin face, beaky nose and long mouth looked disgruntled. In front of him was a plate of quiche and salad.

Tilly looked around but Judy had disappeared.

'Are you or are you not part of the staff?' His tone had an edge to it.

Tilly went over, bracing herself. This was trouble, she knew it.

'Do you think it's fair to serve this to customers and expect them to pay for it?' A disdainful fork prodded at the overcooked quiche. 'The pastry is as tough as the Mafia and the filling's so curdled you could call it cheesecake and get away with it.'

Tilly flushed. 'I'm sorry, would you like to choose something else?'

'Any likelihood it'll be any better?' The long mouth with wide, clown's lips, was turned down.

'We have a very good reputation,' she said stiffly, hating the way his hazel eyes flicked their gaze over her, dismissing her as easily as he had the piece of quiche. He had Mark's air of self-confidence. That certainty the world would go his way. He looked about Mark's age, too.

'It was because of your reputation that I came,' he agreed.

'Ohmigod,' she gasped. 'You're not from one of the guides?'

He gave a shout of laughter that sounded genuinely amused. The laugh transformed his face, softening its angularity and air of disdain, turning up the long mouth into a delightful smile. 'Good God, do I look as though I am?'

'I don't know,' Tilly protested. The tray was getting heavy. 'They don't exactly wear labels, do they?' She adjusted her grip on the load of dirty crockery. 'Look, do you want something else or don't you?' She could sense other people in the restaurant looking at them. Any moment now Judy would be back wanting to know what was going on.

The young man transferred his attention to the menu card. 'Chicken and red pepper salad,' he read out. 'Is your chicken as overcooked as this?' Another disdainful flick of the fork.

'The chicken is fine,' Tilly said through gritted teeth. 'The chef cooked it herself. I'm afraid I was responsible for the quiche.' She balanced her tray on the corner of the table, picked up his plate and put it on the top of the pile of others she'd collected. 'I'll bring you some.' She turned to stalk off to the kitchen, but the second chair at the table hadn't been pushed in properly; she caught her foot in its leg, staggered and fell. The contents of the tray flew through the air, shattering as they fell to the ground.

'Are you hurt?' The young man leapt to his feet and helped Tilly up.

She was more concerned with the chaos she'd caused than her bruises. She retrieved her tray and started to pile it with broken pieces of china.

'Right, that's it!' An irate Judy stood there. 'I've just about had it with you, Tilly. Your mind's never on the job. You can take a week's notice.'

'It was an accident,' protested the young man, picking up bits of plate, putting them on the tray and removing it from Tilly's hands just before she dropped it again. 'All my fault, I pulled out that chair to put my briefcase on.'

Tilly couldn't feel grateful to him, she could only silently agree that it had, indeed, been his fault, and pray that perhaps Beth would change Judy's mind over firing her. After all, she wasn't often as stupid as she'd been today.

Twenty minutes later Tilly had cleaned up the debris and was laying up tables for tea while Judy dealt with the last luncheon customers. The young man asked for his bill. 'Delicious chicken salad,' he said, producing a wallet and dropping two crisp five-pound notes on the table.

'But I served you with quiche,' Judy said, her eyes narrowing.

'It was one of the casualties of the crash,' he said smoothly, not looking at Tilly. 'Your waitress replaced it with chicken and red pepper salad. And the chilli peaches I had to follow were sensational, even though a little too well-poached.' It was as though he couldn't bring himself to be less than honest.

Judy's mouth tightened as she picked up the money. 'I'm glad the meal was to your satisfaction. Perhaps we may hope to see you again?' It was said with no great expectation.

'I'm sure you will, keep the change.' A moment later he'd left the restaurant without so much as a glance in Tilly's direction.

Which suited her. Never would be too soon for her to see him again.

Beth was back by teatime and by the end of the afternoon had Judy soothed and Tilly reinstated. 'We all have our off days,' she said nonchalantly. 'We'll deduct the cost of the broken china from Tilly's wages and she'll buck her ideas up. Won't you, dear?'

Shattered by her day, Tilly finished clearing up the kitchen then left Jemima sorting out the supplies' order for the next day. She put her shoulder bag into the wicker basket on the front of her aged bicycle, unpadlocked it from the drainpipe outside the kitchen and wheeled it through the narrow passage that ran into the High Street. Waiting for her there was the young man who'd sent back the quiche.

Tilly ignored him and manoeuvred her bicycle on to the road.

He grabbed the handlebars.

'Will you please let go?' Tilly said with freezing politeness. 'I have to get home.'

'I only want to know if you're still fired. I found out the time you closed and waited specially.'

She could find nothing in the thin face with its wide mouth and hazel eyes but concern.

She ducked her head and whizzed the pedals round. 'No,' she muttered. 'I'm still there.'

'Good!' he said decisively. 'Look, there's a wine bar just opening, come and have a glass with me.'

He released his grip on the handlebars and Tilly could have ridden off if she'd wanted.

'I've got to get home,' she said and gave the pedal another turn.

'Come on, just one,' he wheedled. 'I do feel responsible for your dropping that tray this afternoon.'

When he smiled like that, his eyes crinkling at the corners, it was, Tilly found, impossible to refuse. She looked around for a convenient place to secure her bicycle.

'Here,' said the young man. He indicated a lamp post and helped her with the padlock.

Inside the dark and almost deserted wine bar he led the way to a corner table. 'How about this? Now, let me introduce myself, I'm Rory Wilde.'

Tilly slid into the chair he held out for her and muttered her name.

He gave her one of the wide grins that transformed his long face. 'Delighted to meet you, Tilly. Would you like red or white wine?'

'Er, white,' chose Tilly, feeling ill at ease. Her crowd couldn't afford wine bars, cans of Pepsi were their usual tipple.

'Dry or medium?' asked Rory.

All these decisions! Tilly had a sudden vision of the label on the bottle her mother had brought back last night that had been supposed to celebrate her exam results. 'Chardonnay would be nice,' she said, hoping she sounded as though she knew exactly what it was.

Rory flashed her a quick smile and was off to the bar then brought back two generous-sized glasses filled with golden liquid.

'Hope you like this, it's quite a decent one from New Zealand. They seem to know what they're on about here.' He put the two glasses carefully down on the table, flashed a glance around, settled himself then raised his glass in a salute. 'Here's to you and apologies again for this afternoon.'

Tilly followed Rory's lead, holding the glass up in front of her for a moment before sipping the wine. It was fragrantly fresh and, despite its flavour, not at all sweet.

'How is it?'

'Oh, lovely,' she said with swift sincerity, feeling the agony of her day start to recede.

'Good!' Rory sounded pleased. 'Now, tell me about you.'

'Me?' Tilly was dismayed. There was nothing about herself she wanted to tell this very self-possessed young man.

'For instance how long have you been working at that restaurant and where did you learn your cooking.'

'Oh, that!' Tilly was relieved he hadn't got personal but, after her disastrous day, not much happier to talk about her job. 'I don't do much cooking, I'm a sort of general kitchen assistant. But usually my pastry is much better than today and I've never overcooked the quiche before,' she added with a defiant note.

'So who does most of the cooking, then?'

Happy to move away from talking about herself, Tilly launched into an enthusiastic description of Jemima. 'And her mother's from the Caribbean and Jemima grew up with all these spices and wonderful ways of using them. That's why her cooking's so different.' She paused and looked across at Rory, who'd been listening to her with every appearance of deep interest. 'You said you'd come today because of our reputation. Where had you heard about the restaurant?'

For the first time he looked slightly disconcerted. 'Oh, I can't remember. Someone said had we – that is, had I eaten there, that the food was really good. So I thought I should give it a go.'

'And got my dreadful quiche!' Tilly gave a gurgle of laughter. 'You must have thought you'd been given a bum steer.'

'But the saladings were delicious, loved the rocket and those herbs. And then you brought me the chicken with red peppers and I knew I was on the right track.'

'Right track?' It seemed an odd phrase to use.

'To good eating!' Rory said triumphantly. 'Tell me, what does your Jemima use to roast the chicken with? There were all sorts of subtle flavours there.'

Apart from Jemima and the others at the restaurant, Tilly had never before met anyone who was interested in food. Her mother merely dealt with it as efficiently as she did everything else in her life. And, as for Tilly's grandparents, they seemed to think that showing an interest in what you ate displayed dangerous moral weakness. Now, at last, she'd found someone who was happy to talk about ingredients and flavour and different styles of cooking. Who obviously had a wide knowledge of food. He'd travelled, eaten at different restaurants, enjoyed experimenting.

Tilly was so entranced by all this, she didn't bother to wonder whether it wasn't slightly unusual for a young man to be interested in food to such an extent, or whether all his questions about Jemima and her cooking weren't slightly suspicious.

'Have another one?' he asked, picking up her glass.

She glanced at her watch and gasped, 'I can't! I'm late.'

'A date?' he suggested with a hint of a twinkle in his hazel eyes.

'Not really. My mum's got someone coming to dinner and I promised to help get the meal ready.' Tilly was dismayed. Any minute now her mother would be back with the food and Tilly should have showered and changed and laid the table.

'Sounds as though it's someone important.' Rory didn't sound too disappointed she couldn't stay. He hadn't asked for her telephone number, either. She wasn't interested in him anyway. He was the same height as Mark but his body was too thin. And whereas Mark's face had the open charm of a Hugh Grant, Rory's, unless he was smiling, was positively dour. And such a bony nose; it jutted out like the beak on a blackbird. His eyes were his best feature, hazel and expressive.

'I think this chap's just someone she works with,' Tilly said. Then added reflectively, 'She's never asked a man home on his own before, though.'

'Sounds as though it could be a heavy scene. Perhaps it would be better if you kept out of the way?' It wasn't exactly an invitation to spend the evening with him but Tilly thought if she was the sort of girl who knew how to manage men, it could turn into one.

Almost she wished she was that sort of girl. Part of her was more than a little apprehensive of meeting Charles Frome. Something about Olivia when she'd announced he was coming to dinner suggested that this was someone different. It was slightly scary thinking of her mother involved with someone. Of course, Tilly wanted Olivia to be happy and didn't being happy mean having someone to share life with? But Olivia shared her life with Tilly.

'I think she wants me to be there,' she said, a little sadly. 'Anyway, I need to see what he's like.'

'Check out whether he's good enough for your mum, eh? Spot of quality control?'

'Exactly!' Tilly stood up. 'After all, I'll be off doing my own thing soon, then she'll need somebody else.' But the thought of leaving home was scary. Before Mark, Tilly had been looking forward, not really so much to going to university, she'd been having doubts about that for some time, but to finding out more about life. Now she'd had a taste of that and it had been bitter.

Just what was she going to do with her future?

Chapter Four

Tilly had a struggle to get home through the rush-hour traffic. She arrived even later than she'd feared. She looked down at her dirty jeans and T-shirt and debated the choice between changing now or laying the table. She decided it was better that the room should look as if Charles Frome was expected.

As Tilly fished around the sideboard drawers looking for her mother's best embroidered Madeira linen mats, her sense of failure returned. Why on earth had Rory Wilde bothered to treat her to a glass of wine when he hadn't even asked for her telephone number? Not that she wanted to see him again but it would have been nice to have felt attractive.

Mats set on the round, mahogany table, their dark ecru stitching elegant against the polished wood, Tilly grabbed handfuls of the antique silver cutlery her mother had been given as a wedding present and laid three places. Next was china. She dashed into the kitchen and yanked out chintzy pink-flowered plates from the cupboard. In her haste, she knocked a casserole dish off the work surface and it shattered on the ceramic-tiled floor.

Tilly looked at the broken shards in dismay. The dish was one Olivia used constantly. Most of her entertaining involved a casserole cooked the night before, served simply with noodles and a salad. As she found the dustpan and brush and disposed of the mess, Tilly hoped desperately that her mother wouldn't need the dish tonight and tried to stop her hands shaking. Everything in her life was changing and she wasn't sure she could cope. What if every time she was faced with a new challenge all she could do was panic?

Then Tilly told herself fiercely that this was no way to deal with things, her father would have been disgusted. 'You have to grab life by the scruff of its neck, woman, and force it your way,' he'd shouted at Olivia just before he died. At five years old, Tilly hadn't known what he meant but the words had stuck, perhaps because her mother had been so upset.

Tilly finished sweeping the floor and reached again for the flowered china. Then opened the next cupboard and took out instead the Spode red and gold china that had been the Fergusons' wedding present to their daughter.

In another cupboard was the Baccarat glass bought after her father had

27

sold his first script. Far too precious to use normally, it was dull with dust. Tilly fetched a clean tea towel and, with infinite care, polished the tulip shapes until they shone with the clear transparency of water. She placed them on the table and thought how much more she liked them than her grandmother's ornate Waterford cut glass.

It had been Daphne Ferguson who had taught Tilly how to lay a table. Tilly sometimes thought the appearance of things mattered more to her than what the food tasted like.

Tilly stood back and checked if everything was on the table that should be. Water glasses were missing. More polishing, which was then extended to rubbing off the finger marks from the transparent set of salt and pepper mills. She placed a slice of unsalted butter on a small oblong porcelain dish and arrange it on the table with a silver butter knife.

Once again Tilly studied her handiwork. The centre of the table needed something. She wondered about cutting a geranium or two from the garden then had an inspiration and fetched a silver candelabra from the small sideboard. Another wedding present, it had nearly been sold a number of times as the Warboys struggled to make ends meet when they first went to California. 'But in the end something always turned up. Just as it has since we came back here. Now I think of it as our lucky emblem,' Olivia had said not long ago.

Tilly placed the candelabra in the centre of the table, found candles, inserted them in the five branches, then reckoned the table would do.

Just in time, she told herself as she heard her mother's key in the door. She waited for something to be said about the fact that she hadn't changed yet. But Olivia seemed far too concerned about other things.

'I'm late, I couldn't get away from the office, Gavin wanted this and then that. It was almost as though he knew I was desperate to leave and was doing it on purpose.'

'Of course he was! Honestly, Mum, I don't know why you let him rattle your cage like that. You know he needs you, why didn't you just say you had to go?' Tilly got exasperated at the way Olivia allowed herself to be taken advantage of. She acted as though she was terrified of losing her job when everyone knew she was terrific at it. At least, that's what Margie said. Tilly had a lot of time for Margie Carmichael, she did a great job keeping up her mother's morale.

'I know, darling, I know. But it's not quite as easy as that. Oh, you've got the table laid, that's great. And you've found some candles! I realised I'd forgotten to get any just as I reached the house.' Olivia moved into the kitchen and started unloading her plastic bag.

'They were at the back of the drawer. With the napkins that match those mats. What shall I do now?'

Olivia looked distractedly at her assortment of food. 'Oh, darling, I can't think! What's the time? Heavens, I shan't be able to change. Will I be all right like this?' Tilly looked at her mother. Olivia was wearing a short-sleeved Liberty print blouse with a round collar, a long, brown, pleated linen skirt and brown patent leather pumps. The overall effect was smart and sophisticated but rather severe, at odds with the excitement in her eyes and the slight flush on her cheeks. All at once Tilly felt years older than her mother.

'You look great but why don't you go and have a shower and change into something less formal? You don't want to look businesslike. I can get things organised here and then have my shower after you. It doesn't matter if I'm not ready when this chap arrives, does it?'

'He's called Charles, darling, Charles Frome. Are you sure you can manage?'

Tilly laughed and pushed her mother towards the stairs. 'After the restaurant it'll be a doddle.'

When she first opened the door to him, Charles Frome was a disappointment to Tilly. She didn't know what she'd expected but from her mother's distracted manner it had been someone more, well, more like her father had been. With his high cheekboned face, sparkling grey eyes, which her mother said Tilly had inherited, and slightly twisted, magnetic smile, he'd had instant charisma. Charles Frome was very different, a solid-looking man in his late-forties with sandy hair and a square, freckled face.

Then he smiled at her and his face came alive. 'Hello, you must be Tilly, I've been looking forward to meeting you.'

She found herself warming towards him. 'Come in, Mum will be down in a minute.'

He entered without fuss, his brown eyes inspecting her with lively interest. In the curve of his arm, cradled against his chest, was a brown paper bag. It looked heavy. 'I've got a daughter, a bit older than you, though, twenty-three last May.'

'I'm seventeen. What's your daughter doing?' Tilly found it unexpectedly easy to talk to him.

He put the bag down on Olivia's desk. 'Phyllida? She's in the city, working in the money markets, buying and selling currency. She says it's a great life if you don't weaken. I tell her she'll be burned out before she's thirty.'

'She sounds terrifying!' Tilly said, astonished.

A wry smile twisted Charles's mouth. 'Yes, she is rather. But great fun as well. I only wish I saw more of her.'

'Can I get you a drink?' She looked doubtfully towards the small cupboard that held Olivia's meagre supply of booze. 'We have whisky and some sherry, I think.'

He indicated the brown paper bag. 'I brought some wine, my contribution to the meal. I didn't know whether white or red would be appropriate so I brought some of each.' His voice was confident but not unpleasantly so. 'And if you have whisky, I'd love a small one.'

29

Tilly went to the cupboard and took out an unopened bottle. She'd bought it with her first pay from the restaurant, to replace the one Mark had finished during the afternoons they'd spent together while her mother was at work. She'd placed it in the cupboard, blindingly grateful Olivia hadn't discovered that the other bottle had disappeared. 'Water?' she asked.

Charles nodded and she brought in a small glass jug and watched him as he topped up his whisky, thinking he actually didn't seem dull after all. She liked the way he was dressed in grey well-cut trousers and a dark jacket of some very smooth, lightweight wool. His shirt was blue with apricot stripes. Mark had had one like that, she'd picked it up from where he'd dropped it on the floor one afternoon and read the label: Hilditch & Key of Jermyn Street. Charles's dark blue tie had a discreet rope pattern in gold and azure and looked like real silk.

Tilly lifted out a bottle from the paper bag. 'Meursault,' she read and wrinkled her nose. 'I've never heard of that, but I'm sure it'll be delicious,' she added quickly.

'The red's a burgundy, I prefer it to claret. All that tannin hits my teeth.' He gave her another of his easy smiles.

'I don't know an awful lot about wine,' Tilly confessed.

'Nor did I at your age, you've got a lot of fun ahead of you. I kept the white in a cool bag in the car so if you put it into the fridge, it should be all right for drinking with the meal, if that's what you'd like.'

Tilly took the bottles off to the kitchen thinking what a very practical man this was. When she returned, her mother was coming down the stairs and he was gazing up at her with an expression that made Tilly suddenly very glad she had persuaded Olivia to change.

She was wearing floating pants in dark blue cotton voile with a long matching top, slashed into panels that ran from her waist to below her knees. The outfit made her look taller than usual and emphasised her grace. Its colour, somewhere between azure and navy, was exactly the shade of her eyes. She'd done her hair into a soft knot that showed off her slender neck and she'd added the heavy silver necklace that had been the last present Tilly's father had given her. It had been made by Navaho Indians and had a primitive splendour that contrasted perfectly with Olivia's gentle loveliness. An aura of Penhaligan's Victorian Posy drifted around her as she moved down the stairs.

Tilly and her friends had once discussed their various mothers' looks. The one voted the prettiest had dark curly hair and a lively face. She worked in a local florist and wore casual shirts with leggings. Olivia never dressed in things like that. The most casual she got was jeans and a shirt. Someone had hesitantly said she thought Mrs Warboys was lovely. Tilly had been surprised but proud and for a moment the others had considered her mother's looks then someone else had said, 'I suppose she's got what you'd call classical looks but all that's gone out of fashion now,' and they'd moved on to discussing someone else.

Now Tilly realised that her mother was beautiful and, for the first time in her life, she wondered why she hadn't had a relationship since they'd returned to England. Surely Charles couldn't be the first man to admire her? Other girls in her class had single mothers. They were always going out with men. One girl had had three stepfathers. Had Olivia been mourning Tilly's father all this time? Would she, Tilly, take twelve years to get over Mark? A cold little shiver ran down her spine.

'Mr Frome has brought some lovely wine,' she said.

'How very kind.' Olivia smiled at him. 'Charles, it's so nice to see you again, I'm sorry I wasn't ready when you arrived.'

He took Olivia's hand in his and their eyes met. Tilly felt excluded. She had a moment's panic. Her mother had turned into someone else, the comfortable closeness she and Tilly enjoyed seeming to evaporate. She muttered something about going to change and scampered up the stairs. Then Charles called after her, 'Don't be too long,' and the feeling of being an outsider vanished.

It was the most enjoyable occasion Tilly could remember in a long time. She didn't feel jealous of Charles. Even as she realised she was seeing a new side of her mother and that Olivia was attracted to this solid, comfortable man almost as much as he was to her, she realised they both seemed to enjoy her presence as much as they enjoyed each other's. Perhaps everything was going to be all right after all.

The only awkward moment was when Charles asked Tilly whether she had finished school or not. A little silence fell then Olivia started to say something but Tilly swallowed hard, looked straight at Charles and said, 'It's awful, I've just failed my exams.' She saw her mother look proudly at her and realised that coming out with it like that hadn't been nearly as difficult as she'd thought it would be.

'That's tough,' Charles said sympathetically. 'I remember failing the first of my engineering exams. I thought the world had come to an end, that I'd never be able to hold my head up again.'

'What did you do?' asked Tilly, amazed that someone like Charles, who looked so successful, so in charge, could fail in any way.

'I discussed it with my father. He asked me if I thought I could retake the exam and pass. If I didn't think I had much of a chance, then perhaps my future didn't lie in engineering after all but that I shouldn't be too despondent, there was bound to be something else I could do.'

'But you decided you could make it?' Olivia asked, her head held slightly on one side as she watched him.

'Yup, I decided that if I really applied myself and worked a lot harder than I had up until then, I ought to be able to crack it. And that I really wanted to.'

'And so you did,' Tilly breathed.

He nodded. 'And is that what you're doing, assessing your resit chances?'

She shook her head, suddenly quite confident about one area of her life. 'No, I don't want anything more to do with education. I should have passed but even if I had, I wouldn't want to go to university.' She felt rather than saw her mother look at her.

'Are you quite sure, darling?' Olivia asked.

Tilly nodded and took another sip of the quite delicious white wine she was drinking. 'I'm not at all academic. Even to please you and Grandma and Grandpa, the thought of spending three more years studying is too awful!'

'That sounds pretty definite,' said Charles. 'So what are you going to do?'

Tilly shrugged her shoulders and lost her brief feeling of confidence. 'That's the problem, I don't know.'

'She's working in a local restaurant at the moment,' said Olivia, looking worried.

'Does food interest you?' asked Charles.

'A bit,' Tilly confessed. 'But I'm not sure I'd want a career in it.' Not after the mess she'd made of things today, she told herself. Being able to produce a nice meal at home was very different from working in a restaurant kitchen. She'd never be able to cope with that pressure.

'Well, your mother's a grand cook!' Charles finished his plate of stuffed chicken breast, *pommes dauphinoise* and green salad.

Tilly met Olivia's eyes across the table. 'She is,' she said, and willed Olivia not to say it had been her who'd stuffed the supremes with curd cheese, spring onions and green peppercorns and made the potato dish. After all, Olivia had actually cooked the meat and put the salad together. Tilly had come downstairs after she'd showered to find the two of them in the kitchen laughing together over Charles's account of the exhibition his firm had been involved in. It sounded as though it had been a wild success.

Olivia brought in a cheese board and a bowl of fresh fruit.

'Oh, how French!' exclaimed Charles happily.

'Is it?' Olivia looked at the table uncertainly.

'Don't you know France?'

'Only slightly. I went there from school once, years ago. On an exchange with a girl called Monique. She came and stayed with us in Richmond first and then I went to her family. They lived in Brittany. It was all quite dreadful!' She smiled reminiscently. 'All Monique was interested in was boys. She was mad as anything I didn't have brothers or go to a mixed school. Then I took her to the tennis club and she found lots of boys there. I hardly saw anything of her after that.'

'What happened when you went to Brittany?' Charles asked as he helped himself to cheese, efficiently separating a long sliver of brie from the main piece.

'I was miserable! None of the French boys Monique produced was at all interested in me – I thought it must be because I didn't have hair underneath my arms like her. And my French was appalling. Then we had a party one night and one of them kissed me. He tried to put his tongue into my mouth.' She gave a low laugh, full of amusement. 'I was terribly shocked and disgusted. I thought he must be a pervert.'

Tilly was fascinated, she'd never heard any of this before. She wondered what she would have done in her mother's place. Probably kicked him where it would hurt. Unless, of course, he'd been attractive, like Mark. She remembered the burning, leaping sensations that Mark's kisses and caresses had aroused in her.

'How old were you?' Charles asked, his voice indulgent.

'Oh, fifteen, I think. It put me off boys for ages.'

Charles ate his cheese with a knife and fork, cutting off neat bits and eating them just as if they were pieces of meat. 'I remember visiting Le Touquet when I was eighteen, with a school chum. We'd hitchhiked there just before going to university. There were two girls on the beach we thought looked terrific. They were wearing bikinis, had short hair and looked so French, it took ages for us to summon up our courage and sort out enough of the language to ask them out. Only to have them say they *no comprendez* and we discovered they were English!' Tilly and Olivia laughed with him. 'But that was the start of my love affair with France. I don't know what happened to those girls but I kept going back and back. When Phyllida was little we used to take a flat in Nice for three weeks every summer. She and her mother liked the beaches and I enjoyed looking round the markets and driving into the hills.' Tilly wondered what had happened to Charles's wife. Could she still be around? Did her mother know? 'And I loved the food, of course.' He looked across the table at Olivia. 'Where did you go for your holiday this year?'

She gave a light laugh, 'We haven't had one, too busy. We'll maybe think of going somewhere later.'

Would they? Tilly thought it was unlikely. There was never much in the budget for holidays. Usually they spent a week or two with her grandparents in Sussex, when the high spot for Tilly would be being taken up to London by her grandmother on a shopping spree. They'd go to Dickens & Jones and Laura Ashley in Regent Street, then on to Knightsbridge and Peter Jones. Tilly would be bought at least two or three outfits that were never quite as sharp as those her friends at school wore – her grandmother said leggings were for ballet dancers and looked ridiculous on the street – but the clothes were always very pretty. The long flowered pinafore dress she was wearing at the moment was one of the last set of gifts.

'I'll make some coffee,' she said, collecting the cheese plates.

'Thank you, darling,' said Olivia absently as she turned to Charles and asked him to tell her more about France.

Tilly cleared up the kitchen, taking her time, before she put the kettle on to boil.

When she took the coffee tray into the living room, she found her mother and Charles were still sitting at the table, talking quietly. The candlelight picked out silvery highlights in Olivia's blonde hair and deepened the gold in the last of the wine in Charles's glass as he turned it absently on the polished wood of the table.

He was telling Olivia about some contract his company had won. 'They just assumed I couldn't speak French and I didn't disillusion them. It made their little side comments to each other during the discussions very interesting!' Tilly thought the more she saw of Charles, the more impressive he seemed. As she poured out the coffee, thinking her mother looked more relaxed and happy than she had ever seen her before, it gave her a funny feeling because she knew it had nothing to do with her presence.

'I won't have any coffee, I'm quite tired. I think I'll go to bed,' she murmured, rising from the table.

But Charles got up as well. 'It's time I went,' he said. 'That is, unless you'll let me help with the washing up?'

'Certainly not,' Olivia said, laughing at him. 'Guests aren't allowed. But do you really have to go?'

His square face looked regretful as he reached for her hand. 'I'm afraid so, I live the other side of London and I've an important meeting in the morning.'

'On a Saturday?' exclaimed Olivia.

He nodded. 'It's a convenient time to get people together.' He paused, still holding her hand. 'Perhaps you'll let me take you both out to a meal soon?' His look encompassed Tilly, hovering by the bottom of the stairs, not sure whether she should disappear up them or stay to say goodbye as well. She gave him a cheeky smile back that she hoped said she appreciated the thought but, not to worry, she'd be doing something else when the invitation was actually issued.

'We'd love to,' said her mother.

Chapter Five

Saturday morning Olivia put Tilly's navy blue T-shirt in with the whites and then had to put sets of pale blue underwear, shirts, petticoats and the Madeira mats and napkins through several more washes to bleach them out.

Furious with her carelessness, she carried up polish, duster and vacuum cleaner to her bedroom full of good intentions. But after she found she was polishing her side table with hair spray, she gave up, went and sat outside with a cup of coffee and allowed herself to think about Charles.

The natural thing would have been to go next door and tell Clodagh all about him. But Olivia found it was too early to decide what her feelings were and they were far too fragile to be exposed to probing questions, however sympathetic.

So she sat in the sun and let its heat spill over her. But much more than sun was warming her spirit. How many years was it since she had enjoyed talking with a man who appeared to be seriously interested in her? One who didn't have his wife sitting on the other side of the room? She'd forgotten how delightful the experience could be. By the end of last evening she'd felt alive all over. Olivia stretched out her arms towards the pigeons strutting along the dividing fence and relished the unfamiliar tingling sensation along her limbs. The only thing she was sure of was that she would be desperately disappointed if Charles Frome didn't ring her again. But she was confident he would. After all, would he have come all the way out to Surbiton for an undistinguished supper with her and her daughter if he wasn't seriously interested? Olivia relaxed and let her thoughts drift.

Charles rang on Monday and asked her out to a show and dinner in London the following Friday. Best stalls seats at a musical then the Grill Room at the Savoy.

'I'm not very adventurous, I'm afraid,' Charles said as they were shown to their table. 'I don't know the smart little places that are "in". I prefer to come somewhere where I'm known and can rely on the food.'

Olivia couldn't think that anywhere else would have been a better choice. She loved looking at the other diners, a mixture of sophistication and the merely well-heeled, and felt pleased that the emerald silk dress she was wearing, her 'good' evening number bought second-hand from a shop that specialised in designer clothes, stood comparison with the other dresses on display.

She appreciated, too, the unobtrusive excellence of the service. Charles had merely to raise a finger and a waiter appeared ready to produce whatever it was they wanted. And the food was wonderful. She had smoked salmon and grilled sole. No doubt Tilly would say that was a grossly boring choice but she loved the quality and taste of the fish.

They talked about the show they'd seen, how they had both liked the music but thought the story pretty ridiculous, then Charles mentioned a new order that had just come through for his company as a result of their participation in the exhibition and they were back discussing business.

Right from the start, Olivia had found Charles easy to talk to. But she didn't want to dwell on business matters on what she thought of as their first proper date, so she asked about his daughter.

Charles was more than willing to talk about Phyllida, about how bright she was, how independent. 'I don't see enough of her these days. Not now she's got a flat of her own. She wheedled me into giving her the deposit but I agreed it was better for her to be paying into a mortgage than rent for some squalid place in Battersea. Every now and again she gives up one of her evenings to come and have dinner with me here but she's such a popular girl it isn't often.' Charles produced his wallet, fished out a snapshot and handed it to Olivia. 'That's her.'

Phyllida was blonde and extremely attractive. Her face was much narrower than Charles's, the bones smaller and more delicate, which gave her a slightly kittenish appearance. The eyes, though, were sharp and her smile had a touch of derision.

'What a pretty girl, did you take it?' asked Olivia, handing back the snapshot.

Charles nodded. 'It was a couple of months ago. I'd taken her to Paris for the day on Eurostar, thought it would be fun. And it was. We had a wonderful lunch at the Tour d'Argent, cost an arm and a leg but Phyllie said it was the only place to go, then we went up the Eiffel Tower. Phyllie had never done it, said it was too naff for words. I insisted, said she'd chosen one tower so I should be able to insist on another, and that I'd only accept that it was a totally worthless experience after she'd been up to the top. Of course, when she saw Paris all laid out before her, she had to admit it was quite a sight. Then she said, right, now she'd done the Eiffel Tower and once was enough but didn't I want to eat at the Tour d'Argent again? Which I had to admit I did!' He smiled at the memory.

'I've never been to Paris,' Olivia said a trifle wistfully. It had been something Peter had promised they would do, one day, when he was a success.

'That has to be put right,' said Charles decisively. 'I'll get something organised.'

Olivia didn't quite know what to say. To protest seemed gauche and

36

naive yet she wasn't sure she wanted to be swept up in a way that suggested here was a godfather to grant her every wish. 'One of these days that would be nice,' she said weakly. Then she asked, 'What about Phyllida's mother?'

'Veronica and I are divorced. Have been for several years,' said Charles shortly.

'I'm sorry,' Olivia said. She took a sip of wine and wondered what the right key was that would get Charles to open up and tell her more. She wanted to know what had happened to his marriage, who had left whom and how Phyllida had reacted. But she recognised the keep off signs and it was not her style to ignore such messages. Nor did she want to get on to the subject of her own marriage. So she changed the subject. The rest of the meal was spent discussing books and films they'd both seen. Safe subjects but ones that allowed exploration of each other's tastes.

At the end of the evening Charles drove Olivia home and refused to come in for a coffee. He took the key from her fingers, opened the door and stayed firmly on the step. 'It's been a wonderful evening. Can I give you a ring next week, perhaps arrange something for the weekend?' She nodded and waited for him to kiss her, aware for the first time in a very long while that it was something she wanted.

He gave her a warm smile and turned away, walking lightly back to his car, giving her a brief salute just before he got in. Olivia was left with a definite sense of anti-climax. Despite her enjoyment of the evening and Charles's company, she went up to bed with a feeling of unfinished business.

Once again he rang on the Monday. This time he invited her and Tilly for a trip on the river the following Sunday.

Tilly hadn't wanted to go, said she didn't relish the gooseberry role, but Charles had asked to speak to her and whatever he'd said had changed her mind.

Olivia asked what it had been. 'Oh, just something about how nice it would be for us to get to know each other,' Tilly said airily.

It was a good day. Charles had laid on a private launch to take them down to Greenwich. There was a guide to tell them all about the river, its history and the buildings they were passing. Both Tilly and Olivia were fascinated to see the new office blocks, rising in soaring splendour, stacked and angled so that each new perspective was another surprise, and the recent developments round the south side of Tower Bridge, where the new Globe Theatre jostled beside restaurants, art galleries and shopping malls.

'Once again,' said the guide, 'London is appreciating the scenic qualities of Old Father Thames. Two hundred years ago the river was the heart of the city, the main thoroughfare, the focus of all activity. Now it is regaining some of that role.'

Tilly looked at another resplendent building that offered balconies planted with green shrubs and small trees. 'How wonderful to live there!' she sighed. 'I'd love to have breakfast looking at the river.'

'That's where my daughter's apartment is,' said Charles, looking pleased.

Olivia looked more closely at the luxurious quality of the block. Putting down the deposit for an apartment there must have called for serious money.

'Good heavens,' said Tilly. 'She must be doing well.'

'She is,' agreed Charles. 'I suggested she join us today but unfortunately she had something else planned.'

Olivia couldn't be sorry. Somehow Phyllida didn't sound the sort of girl she'd find it easy to have around.

Lunch was provided on board, a lavish buffet with lobster and smoked salmon and chicken in a creamy sauce. Even Tilly had been impressed.

At Greenwich they admired the proportions of the Naval College and the small Queen Anne palace behind, then the boat continued to the Thames Barrage, the barriers standing proud above the calm waters like polished steel shells. At that point they turned and motored steadily back up river to the landing stage near Westminster Bridge.

Then Charles took them for tea at the Dorchester.

'Wow!' said Tilly, looking at the vaguely Egyptian splendour of the wide corridor lounge where they were served Earl Grey tea and delicious scones with jam and clotted cream. Olivia sat back in her comfortable chair and felt the ambience settle round her like a cashmere shawl, adjusting itself to her shape with gentle warmth and immense style.

Afterwards Charles drove them back to Surbiton.

It was Tilly who suggested he came in for a game of cards. She loved playing and never seemed to mind whether she won or lost. Charles joined in willingly and quickly picked up the nuances of Heart, bluffing his way to sweeping the board with the Queen and all of the tricks. 'You're a fraud!' Tilly accused him gleefully. 'You've played this before!'

'A very, very long time ago,' he confessed, a trifle shame-faced. 'I'd forgotten until you explained it.'

They played two more games, each of which Charles had no difficulty in winning, then Tilly made coffee and some tiny sandwiches, they were too full of food to want a proper supper, while Olivia showed Charles a Patience she was particularly fond of.

It was a casual, very successful evening. In fact, the whole day had been a delight, said Olivia, seeing off Charles towards midnight. Tilly had already gone upstairs to bed after thanking him enthusiastically for her day. Once again, Olivia waited for him to make a move towards her; once again he gave her no more than a smile and a promise to ring her.

'It's so frustrating,' she exploded to Clodagh the next evening. 'All these years I've worked at putting out the keep off signals. Now, when I'd like a little physical approach, the man appears to be uninterested!'

'Then why is he going to so much trouble to entertain you?' Clodagh asked. They were in her living room, a bottle of white wine open on the table, Clodagh's latest manuscript abandoned. When Olivia had knocked on her door immediately after getting back from work, she'd been more than happy to leave her work. This was her fifth attempt at writing a novel someone would publish and she was, she said, getting pretty cheesed off with rejection slips.

'Perhaps all he wants is a reasonably attractive woman around him, someone to be seen out with, laugh at his jokes and share his interests,' Olivia suggested gloomily.

Clodagh got up and found a packet of Kettle chips. 'Here, you need something more sensible to chew on. I've never heard anything more ridiculous! You told him to wait three months before asking you out. If all he wanted was a decorative arm piece he'd have gone elsewhere, not counted the days and then rung you immediately time was up.'

'So, what do *you* think? Come on, you're the author, you understand motives, what are his?'

Clodagh stuck the pencil that seemed permanently attached to her fingers when she wasn't at her word processor into her tangle of hair then thrust her hand in as well, as though that would help her sort out her thoughts. 'Well, since what he did was actually wait rather than bombard you with flowers and phone calls, I think this Charles Frome is a careful sort of bloke who plans long-term strategy. The fact that he's followed your lead and made a major attempt to involve Tilly as well as yourself suggests to me his intentions are serious.'

'So why hasn't he even tried to kiss me?' wailed Olivia.

'He's waiting for the time to be ripe,' announced Clodagh. 'This man is great at waiting.'

'I'd rather he was great at doing.'

'Ah, but he is. Look at what he's achieved – more than any man you've met since you moved here, what was it, ten or twelve years ago? Long before I arrived, certainly. Remember all the men I tried to fit you up with? The parties you spent brushing off attractive chaps?'

'Most of them married,' Olivia said tartly.

'Never mind. You weren't interested in any of them, married *or* single. For as long as I've known you and, I'd be prepared to take a pretty large bet, years before that as well, you've fought shy of any entanglement with the opposite sex.' Clodagh laughed suddenly. 'Do you know, at one stage I began to wonder if you were a lesbian?'

'Clodagh!' exclaimed Olivia, sitting bolt upright.

'OK, OK! I reckoned quite soon you weren't because you didn't proposition me.'

'Clodagh!' Olivia repeated on a rising note.

Clodagh grinned at her, hair now all over the place. 'You want me to tell you how many times I've had to reject my own sex? Never mind, I've got nothing against lesbianism, you understand, it just isn't my scene.'

'Nor mine!'

'And then I heard from Tilly about your perfect marriage and its tragic end when her father was killed when she was five and I worked out that you were looking for something that would be equally as perfect. And that's why you've never wanted to talk about it with anyone, even me.'

'My perfect marriage,' repeated Olivia expressionlessly.

Clodagh looked at her with suddenly narrowed eyes. 'You telling me it wasn't perfect?'

Olivia shrugged her shoulders. 'What marriage is?'

'Don't tell me my dream of your fairytale romance has no foundation!' Clodagh hesitated for a moment then plunged on. 'Tilly told me once you met at a party, that it was love at first sight and he whisked you into marriage and off to California, despite all parental opposition. That wasn't true?'

Olivia smiled softly. 'Oh, yes, every last word of it. It could have come straight from a Mills and Boon, or just like that song, "Some Enchanted Evening". I came into the room and saw Peter with two girls. I looked at him and I knew that if he didn't come and talk to me, the rest of my life would be like a desert and I would always be parched for water.'

'Boy!' said Clodagh in awe.

'It's the only time I've known exactly what I wanted in life. And the only time in my life I got what I wanted without waiting.'

'You mean he came straight over?' Clodagh poured more wine into their glasses and Olivia sat clutching hers, back in that evening.

She saw again Peter's crooked smile and the alert way his sparkling grey eyes searched the room even while he was talking to the two pretty girls. She saw his dark pony tail, the long line of his back in the creased T-shirt tucked into jeans and how one shoulder was held higher than the other. She saw his eyes widen ever so slightly as they met hers, the way he detached himself and walked over to her with that rapid, jerky gait she got to know so well and leaned one hand against the wall above her head, bending down so that his face was close to hers.

'He said, "Hi. My name's Peter Warboys and I've been looking for you all my life." And,' she added to Clodagh, 'before you say, what a corny line, let me tell you he made it sound as though he was the first person ever to use it.'

'He should have been *in* films, not writing them. So it really was love at first sight?'

Olivia nodded, still back in the magic of that moment. 'I've never felt anything so intensely in my life, except when Tilly was born. He was the sun, moon, stars, the entire universe as far as I was concerned.'

Clodagh's sharp eyes softened. 'No wonder no other man has ever stood a chance with you.'

Olivia drank deeply of her wine. 'After he died, Tilly was my world. I closed the door on marriage. And after an unfortunate couple of episodes, I decided I wasn't going to consider any sort of a relationship with a man. Not while Tilly was growing up, anyway.'

40

Clodagh snorted. 'Bloody unnatural if you ask me! So, now when Tilly is just about to fly the nest, along comes this Charles fellow and all of a sudden you're all dewy-eyed again.'

'I am not dewy-eyed,' Olivia said hotly. 'It's just that I don't understand him.'

'You mean you're not ready to fall into his arms?'

'Of course I'm not! It would just be nice if he wanted to kiss me, that's all!'

'Hoo hoo! Methinks the lady doth protest too much and all that.'

'Clodagh!' Olivia flung a cushion at her friend. She ducked, caught it and placed it firmly behind her back. After a moment or two Olivia said quietly, 'Honestly, I'm not dying to go to bed with him, it's just that, after all this time, it's – well, it's exciting to feel something when I'm with a man. You can understand that, can't you?'

'You bet I can, Olive! Just wish I was in your place.'

'But you've never stopped having relationships! You're always complaining your life's too complicated.'

'Wish it was a bit more complicated at the moment. Look, this isn't solving your problem. Except I don't think you've got one. All you have to do is wait, unless . . .'

'Unless what?'

'Unless you want to take the initiative. You're too passive, Olive, you should seek to control situations more.'

'Throw myself at him, you mean?'

'Well, you could try a little come on.'

Olivia felt a sudden moment of panic. This wasn't for her! After all those years of combining looking after Tilly with making a career for herself, she felt way out of her depth.

'And there's another thing, what on earth am I going to do with Tilly?'

'When you swan off into the night with Charles whatshisname?' Clodagh reached again for the bottle of wine, saw it was empty, got up and went into the kitchen.

'Clodagh! I'm not swanning off into any night, with or without Charles,' Olivia called after her in exasperation. Clodagh reappeared, inserting the corkscrew into another bottle of wine. 'It's just that Tilly seems to have decided not to resit her exams and doesn't have a clue what she's going to do with her life. I want to help her but I don't know how.'

'Give her space,' Clodagh advised. 'I always wished Michael had taken time to think instead of plunging straight into accountancy. What a straightjacket of a career!' She refilled their glasses.

'You mean, let her go on working at that wretched restaurant?' Olivia felt strangely relieved to have got away from the subject of Charles Frome. Talking about him with Clodagh hadn't straightened out any of her feelings for him. They remained as ambiguous as before, if not more so.

'What's wretched about it? It's got style and the food's excellent.'

41

'I don't know, it's just . . .'

'Just that you think working in the kitchen isn't good enough for Tilly,' said Clodagh shrewdly.

'You make me sound a snob,' Olivia complained.

Clodagh said nothing.

'I just think she should be doing something more, well . . .'

'Intellectual?' asked Clodagh with a big grin. It was Olivia's turn to be silent. 'Just let her be, things will sort themselves out.'

Chapter Six

A couple of days after Olivia had had her chat with Clodagh, Tilly arrived at the restaurant to find that instead of Jemima in the kitchen there was an elderly woman with a face like a boot, dressed in a pristine white overall with a high neck. She was stuffing a chicken with a lemon and two shallots.

'Where's Jemima?' asked Tilly sharply. 'Are the twins ill?'

'Twins? What are you talking about?' the boot-faced woman said irritably. 'If you're referring to that coloured cook you had here, she's left. I'm standing in until the girls have found somebody else. I'm Judy's mother,' she added after a moment as Tilly stood and stared at her.

'What do you mean, Jemima's left?' she asked stupidly. Jemima had said nothing to her the previous evening. Except, now that she thought about it, she had given her a hug as Tilly had said goodnight. But then Jemima often gave her a hug, it being Jemima's opinion the world could do with a lot more hugging.

'Apparently she's got another job,' she was told shortly. The hands finished shoving the lemon and the shallots up the bird's back end and placed it with several others in a large roasting pan. There was a quick sigh as the cooking oils were surveyed. 'No corn oil, I see.'

'Jemima always used olive, said it gave the best flavour,' Tilly explained, still thinking about her having got another job and remembering that there had been something more than the usual air of excitement about her over the last few weeks. She'd thought it had had something to do with Duane, her new boyfriend.

'Olive oil! No wonder this place isn't making any money. Well, I'll soon see what we can do about that. If you're Tilly, and I can't think who else you'd be, you'd better get your jacket off and start preparing those vegetables. Come on, chop, chop! There are no dawdlers in my kitchen.'

Tilly swallowed hard, hung up her jacket and started to scrub potatoes.

Two minutes later Judy swept in. 'Ah, Tilly, you've met my mother, Mrs Major, have you?'

Tilly swallowed a gurgle of laughter at the appropriateness of the name. A sergeant major, not a major general nor even a prime minister. No, Mrs Major would have a field day ordering the troops about on the parade ground.

'Now that Jemima's left us in the lurch, we're terribly lucky to have Mummy. She used to be a domestic science teacher, you can learn a lot from her, Tilly.'

She let this comment pass. 'Where's Jemima gone?' she asked.

'If you want to keep your job, you won't mention her name again,' said Judy sharply.

'Haven't you finished those potatoes yet?' Mrs Major asked. 'You need to get a move on, my girl.'

Get a move on Tilly did but everything took her longer than usual because Mrs Major's style was very different from Jemima's. Mrs Major didn't like herbs added to the salads. Mrs Major decided it was a waste of time and energy roasting the red peppers. Tilly tried one protest then shut up and stuck the stiff raw pepper slivers between the slices of cooked chicken as instructed and thought the result looked as unpleasant as brand new jeans before they were washed. Out went the spicy dressing for the *salade tiède* and Tilly just knew that by the time the dish reached the customer, the chicken livers would be horribly grey and overcooked instead of meltingly soft and pink. If Rory Wilde ever came back, he'd be very disappointed.

For several days she'd had a pleasurable feeling of expectation as lunchtime approached. She wasn't attracted to Rory, she told herself. But there'd been something about the way he'd seemed so interested in what she said that had made her feel he'd want to get in touch again. And Jemima had teased her about the way she was constantly finding excuses to pop into the restaurant so she could check who was there.

Today she found herself doing it again. Not a sign of Rory, but instead two of her old schoolfriends. 'Hi, Clare, Kate,' Tilly said. 'I thought this place was too expensive for you.'

'Celebratory lunch,' said Kate, an exuberant girl, her hair full of curls, her long body wearing a collection of antique garments that managed to look as though they'd all been intended to be worn together.

'I've got a place at Manchester!' burst out Clare, her fair hair caught back in a tortoise-shell alice band. Her neat figure was dressed in a skinny rib sweater and suede waistcoat, mini skirt and long boots. Her exam results hadn't been as good as she'd hoped and she'd been worried she wouldn't be accepted.

'That's wonderful, Clare.' Tilly was genuinely pleased for her friend.

'Even more wonderful, I've got a job!' Kate said, the excitement about her so tangible, electric sparks seemed to fly off her hair.

'Not on a magazine!' Tilly exclaimed. Kate wanted to be a journalist and everyone had told her she had to go to college and then work for a provincial newspaper. Kate said that she wanted to go straight from school on to a magazine; she didn't care how lowly a position it was, she could work her way up once she was inside. 'How did you do it?'

'I got fed up sending off letters so last week I made up a portfolio of everything I've written – things from the school magazine, that article that was printed in the local paper and the letter I had published in that teenage magazine plus other things that haven't been published – and I went up to London with a list of mags for the young.' Her lively voice was full of triumph.

'You mean you just walked in and asked for a job?'

'Sure!'

'How?' Tilly was deeply envious of Kate's chutzpah.

'Oh, I went up to reception and asked for the features editor by name. I'd checked who they were from the front pages of the magazines. If they said she wasn't available, I said I'd wait, that I'd got something important to show her. It didn't work the first couple of times then I struck lucky and several editors saw me. And the third one talked to me for ages then said that actually they were looking for a dogsbody in the fashion department and I appeared to know something about clothes and would I like to see the fashion editor!'

'And you got the job?'

Kate nodded. 'I start on Monday.' She sat back from the table, a huge smile on her monkey face.

Tilly didn't know whether she was more envious of Kate's job or of the single-mindedness that had got her the position. If only *she* knew what she wanted to do the way Kate did!

Then Judy came up and said was there anything anybody wanted, and would Tilly please get back to the kitchen? She was surprised at her socialising when her help, such as it was, was needed by Mrs Major. The girls exchanged derisive looks as Judy stalked off and Tilly said she'd talk to them later.

As the lunchtime rush subsided, Mrs Major gave a great sigh. 'Well, we've survived!' She gave a triumphant grin that held all the hilarity of a death's head and sat down on the kitchen stool. Tilly suddenly realised that she had been far from confident of her ability to cope. It was probably years since she'd had to work so hard. She felt a surprising rush of sympathy. 'Let me make some coffee,' she said. 'Jemima and I always have one – had one about this time. She said we deserved it.' Tilly put the kettle on then reached for the packet of ground coffee that was kept on the shelf above the preparation counter and put it beside the cafetière Jemima always used.

Mrs Major's eyes widened in horror. 'You're never making real coffee! No wonder my daughter never knows where the money goes here.' She levered herself off the stool and snatched the packet out of Tilly's hand. 'Where's the instant?'

Tilly gulped. 'There isn't any. Jemima always said it wasn't worth the price of heating the water to pour on it.'

Mrs Major clicked her tongue in exasperation. 'I've never heard anything like it.' She fished out a handbag from the back of the saucepan cupboard, took out a purse and handed a couple of pound coins to Tilly. 'Just you get down the High Street and buy a jar of instant, the cheapest they have.'

It was dreadful stuff. Even Olivia, who didn't seem able to tell breakfast from dinner coffee, let alone Mysore from Mocha, didn't sink that low. Not after Tilly had complained and threatened to throw the next jar in the dustbin.

Under strict instructions not to use more than one level teaspoon of the fine powder, Tilly made a mug of coffee and Mrs Major drank it with every appearance of deep appreciation. Then she staggered once more to her feet. 'Now, what's to do for these teas, then? Scones, is it?'

At the end of the afternoon, Tilly could hardly wait to finish clearing up the kitchen so she could leave.

She found a public call box and dialled Jemima's number. Only to be told the number was unobtainable. No doubt disconnected, Jemima and her mother were always having trouble finding the money to pay the bill.

Tilly got on her bicycle and rode off towards Tooting, trying to remember exactly which route Jemima had taken on her motorbike. It took some time through the rush-hour traffic and one or two wrong turns but at last she dismounted with a sigh of thankfulness outside a shabby house with sparkling clean windows. She could hear the twins screaming with delight and gave thanks that someone was in.

Marsha opened the door, holding one of the twins in her arms while the other pulled at her skirt.

'Why, if it isn't Tilly! Come in, girl. You'll be wanting to know what happened with Jemima, yes?'

Tilly nodded, trying to catch her breath.

'It's marvellous, you know? And all thanks to you! Come along now, let me make you some coffee, you look all done in. Girls, go off and play, Gran's got to talk to Tilly.' Marsha put down the small child she was carrying and gave her a pat on the fat little behind. The little girl somersaulted over, picked herself up and repeated the motion, shrieking with excitement. Followed by her sister, she disappeared into the front room.

Marsha led the way into the kitchen, a tiny, galley-shaped room with a free-standing stove, a sink and various cupboards, none matching but all organised and spotlessly clean. By the stove was a magnetic holder with a set of assorted knives, their blades fiercely sharp. In the window were several flower pots with tiny, pointed peppers hanging red and yellow amongst the green leaves.

Tilly leant against a twintub washing machine and watched as Marsha put on the kettle and ground some coffee beans. The rich, deep aroma spread pervasively, overlaying the background spiciness.

'So, what's happened to Jemima, then?' she asked eagerly.

46

Marsha tipped the coffee grounds into a jug and poured on the hot water. 'Let's take this through to the front room so we can sit and be comfortable. You bring the mugs and that milk.'

In the living room the twins were busy jumping off the arm of the fake leather settee on to a large cushion, now splitting at one of its seams. Feathers drifted around the room.

'Oh, you kids, never happy unless you destroy something!' Marsha said happily. She picked up the cushion and put it on top of the television set. 'Now let me see you play with that nice set of bricks your mammy gave you. Build your old gran a castle, a castle with dreams coming out the tower.'

'My father used to spin dreams,' said Tilly. She picked up several of the brightly coloured bricks and started fitting them together. Sharon picked up a blue one and put it on top of the first row. Noleen followed suit with a yellow one.

'What's dreams?' asked Sharon, squinting up at Tilly.

'Dreams are things you want,' she said, adding another couple of bricks to the first row.

'There's nothing Sharon wants,' said Sharon.

'Noleen wants a daddy,' said Noleen.

'We got Mum and Gran,' insisted Sharon. 'No room for a daddy.'

This appeared to satisfy Noleen, who got on with adding bricks, lifting them one by one with enormous care and positioning them precisely. Sharon was more slap-dash, adding them higher and higher until, inevitably, the structure wobbled and fell.

With more shrieks of laughter the girls began to build again.

'So?' asked Tilly, taking the mug of coffee Marsha held out to her. 'Tell me what's happened with Jemima?'

'She got a better job. A much, much better job.'

'No! Where?' Tilly was thrilled. A better job meant more money and she knew just how much that would mean to Jemima and Marsha.

'There's this chain of restaurants, all over London. All *Frère* something: *Frère Jacques, Frère Pierre, Frère Claude,* and I don't know how many others. And they're opening a new one, *Frère Marcus,* with a Martinique theme. Lots of spices and cooking with fruit and things. Don't suppose it's really authentic, because otherwise why they get a chef who cooks from Jamaica? Eh, tell me that, girl?'

'And you mean *Jemima* is going to be the chef?' Tilly could hardly believe it. She'd read something about the *Frère* chain of restaurants; they were fashionable and popular, combining imaginative food with value for money.

'You better believe it, girl! She's working as sous-chef in one of the other restaurants for a couple of months, so she can learn the ropes, how they like things done, the systems and all that, and then she gets to be chef at the new one. Already she's on twice what she was making at your place and when she gets her own restaurant it'll be over three times plus a bonus scheme!' Marsha beamed triumphantly at Tilly.

'That's wonderful. Oh, I'm so pleased!' Tilly got up and hugged her.

'And it's you we have to thank!' Marsha added, the wattage of her smile rising even higher.

'Me?' squeaked Tilly, sitting down again. 'I haven't done anything!'

'Who was it spoke to that young man? Who was it told him what a wonderful chef my Jemima was? How she knew it all, was such a professional? How I'd taught her all about Jamaican spices and cooking an' all? That wasn't you?'

'What young man?' But even as she asked the question, Tilly knew the answer. 'You mean Rory Wilde?'

'That's the one! He's old man Wilde's son, the Wilde what owns all the *Frère* restaurants!'

'He said he'd heard we'd got a reputation,' Tilly said slowly, as it all came back to her. 'And that was the day I overcooked the quiche and the pastry was heavy as iron. Ohmigod, I nearly blew it for her!' She buried her face in her hands as she realised just how disastrous it could have been.

'You didn't, girl! Haven't I just been telling you how you sold my Jemima to the man?'

'And the rat never said a thing!' Tilly exclaimed. She'd been conned by an industrial spy! Rory Wilde hadn't been interested in her at all. That was why he never came back to the restaurant. He'd no need to, he'd got everything he wanted. First Mark ditched her then this slimebag came along and used her to pinch the restaurant's chef. If Judy and Beth ever found out, she'd be out on her ear.

'Why didn't she tell me?' Tilly demanded, some of her resentment spilling over on to Jemima.

'I'm sorry, pet. She wanted to give two weeks' notice, told the Wildes that was only fair. Only when she told that Judy last night, she was told to go right then and there. Called my Jemima an ungrateful cow! Said she'd given her a job when nobody else would have and now she was leaving her in the lurch! As if Jemima hadn't done them a favour by working for the ridiculous sum they was paying her.' Marsha sounded resentful herself.

'It's Jemima's cooking that's built up all their trade,' Tilly said wisely. 'It's all going to go down the pan with her gone. Neither Judy nor Beth has a clue. You've no idea what it's like there now, Judy's mother is doing the cooking. She's dreadful! She's thrown out all the spices and most of the herbs. All she uses is a sprig of parsley on top of a twist of tomato peel. Calls it a garnish!' She threw herself back in the chair and gave a hoot of laughter.

'Well, Tilly, Jemima was really sorry she couldn't tell you herself what had happened. But, see, the phone got cut off yesterday,' Marsha said matter-of-factly. 'Well, couldn't expect them to wait forever for their money, could we?'

Tilly found the ride home long and exhausting; hills she'd hardly noticed before now appeared daunting.

More depressing than the slog of keeping the pedals of her bicycle turning, though, was the realisation of how stupid she had been over Rory Wilde. Thinking he'd been enjoying their discussion when all the time he was finding out whether it was worth poaching Jemima for his father's new restaurant. That was what made Tilly so mad. Why hadn't she seen through him? Was she really that stupid?

By the time she reached home, Tilly was too tired to care any more. Olivia was away for several nights, helping to set up some exhibition in Birmingham. Tilly tried to ring Clare and then Kate to hear more about their plans for the future but they were both out, still celebrating no doubt. She made herself some scrambled eggs, watched an old film on television and then crawled into bed, still feeling angry and not knowing what she could do about it

The next day at the restaurant was no better than the previous one had been. Judy's mother simplified more of the menu, shouted louder at Tilly and announced she was instituting a new stock control system. This seemed to consist of going through the vegetable peelings and complaining that Tilly had wasted too much.

Tilly unlocked her bicycle at the end of the day feeling she wouldn't really care if Judy did sack her again. There must be a better way of earning some money than this. Then, as she emerged from the passage, she saw Rory Wilde.

He was standing on the pavement and appeared to be waiting for her because as soon as she came into the High Street, his wide mouth lifted in a broad grin and he came towards her, bouncing slightly, his hands in the pockets of a pair of Levis worn with a short-sleeved patchwork shirt that Tilly would have given her eye teeth for.

'Come and have another glass of wine,' he said, reaching for her bicycle. 'I owe you a lot.'

She snatched back her handlebars from his grasp. 'How dare you! You, you . . . traitor!'

His eyes crinkled. She'd forgotten how engaging they could look. 'Come on, now! You're making rather a thing of this, aren't you?'

Tilly drew herself up. 'You took advantage of me! If Judy and Beth knew, I'd lose my job!' No matter that a couple of minutes earlier she'd been feeling she wouldn't care if she did.

'And if I hadn't found us a tip-top chef, my father would have fired me!'

Tilly hesitated for a moment, wondering if he had a point. Then, 'But why didn't you tell me? I'd probably still have told you all about Jemima. I mean, it's wonderful she's got such a good job.'

Rory's mouth turned down slightly, his face assuming its lugubrious look. 'But you were chatting away so hard, I could hardly get a word in!'

'That's nonsense!' Tilly flared at him. 'You were asking me all sorts of questions.'

'Which you answered beautifully. I was enjoying our conversation so much, I didn't want to break the flow.'

Tilly looked at him coldly. The wide mouth was still turned down, the hazel eyes were limpid and sincere, but lurking in their depths was an irrepressible humour. He was laughing at her!

'That's it,' she said, yanked her bicycle on to the road and pedalled furiously off.

'Hey, Tilly!' Rory shouted after her.

She ignored him and pedalled as hard as she could for home.

As Tilly was unlocking the front door, a voice behind her said, 'You're late!'

It was her grandmother.

'I've been waiting for you.' Over Daphne's shoulder Tilly could see her car parked a little way down the road. She gulped nervously.

Soon after the exam results had been announced, she had received a letter from her grandmother offering to pay the fees for a crammer to prepare her for a resit. It had been a long letter emphasising the need for creditable results and the importance of a university degree. So far Tilly hadn't replied. She hadn't even shown it to her mother.

'I'm sorry,' she said, opening the door and wheeling the bike inside. 'There was more clearing up at the restaurant than usual and then, well, I ran into somebody.' Thank heavens she hadn't gone with Rory for a drink. Tilly couldn't imagine what her grandmother would have said if she'd had to wait an hour or more for her to get home.

Tilly put the bike in its accustomed place under the stairs. 'Mum is away at the moment, in Birmingham,' she said as Daphne Ferguson entered.

'It's you I want to see,' her grandmother replied, closing the door, her upright figure dressed in navy blue linen with a white polka-dotted silk scarf tied in the neck of the tailored dress, her thick, straight and glossy dark hair cut in a razor sharp asymmetrical bob that did good things for her strong face with its classical nose, tucked away mouth and slightly protuberant blue eyes.

Daphne Ferguson had had a high-flying career culminating in an executive directorship of a by-no-means small advertising agency. The day she retired she started gathering a selection of charitable and political appointments that three years later kept her almost as busy as her former professional life had. Never too busy, though, that she didn't have time for her daughter and granddaughter. Up until now, Tilly had always enjoyed visiting her grandparents, finding her grandmother a stimulating companion. Now she sensed matters between them could be heading for rough water.

'Would you like a coffee or a tea, or we've got sherry and whisky?' Tilly offered, removing her jacket and hanging it over the end of the banisters.

Daphne gave a small, gracious nod. 'A sherry would be pleasant, thank you.'

Tilly got out the bottle and two glasses and poured a generous amount into each.

'They don't seem to have taught you standard measures in that place where you work,' her grandmother commented sardonically.

'We don't have a licence,' Tilly said, handing over one of the glasses.

Daphne Ferguson sat in one of the armchairs and indicated the other.

Tilly sat. She didn't actually like sherry but it hadn't seemed right to pour a glass out for her grandmother and not take one herself. She braced herself as she watched Daphne's liver-spotted hand raise the glass of sherry to her pale lips.

'I've been waiting for a reply to my letter. Didn't it merit the courtesy of a response?'

Ouch! thought Tilly. She could think of nothing to say.

Her grandmother settled herself well back in the chair, disposed her legs in a neat slant and stretched out her arms. She smiled at Tilly. 'I know how disappointing your results were for you but your mother has explained you had something of an emotional upset at the time you sat the exams.' Tilly wondered just what her mother had said; she'd promised not to divulge that Tilly had been afraid she was pregnant.

Her grandmother leaned forward slightly. 'Darling, I know how wretched men can make you feel. But you have to learn to wipe all such emotions from your mind, concentrate on the job in hand. Afterwards, that's when you can allow yourself to be upset.'

Tilly stared at her. Had Daphne Ferguson ever allowed herself to get upset over a man? Tilly's grandfather was a professor of English. Daphne always guarded his privacy fiercely. 'Your grandfather is working,' she'd say when meeting Tilly and her mother at the station for their regular visits to Sussex, meaning they weren't to expect him to appear before lunch. Never had Tilly seen anything that suggested passion was a factor in the marriage and she couldn't imagine that her grandmother's heart could ever have been broken the way Mark had broken hers.

Mrs Ferguson gave a small, sardonic smile. 'You probably think I can't possibly know what you've been through and I'm not going to try and persuade you otherwise. What matters,' a touch of iron entered her voice, 'is that you get your A levels. Time's getting on and term will soon be starting again.' She reached down for her navy leather handbag. Out came a gold-cornered leather notepad. 'I've rung . . .' she mentioned the name of a leading London tutorial establishment '. . . and they say they may be able to take you. I've promised to escort you to an interview with them tomorrow. I can't imagine you'll have any problem getting off work for something like this.'

Tilly clasped her hands tightly together. 'Grandma, it's really terribly, terribly kind of you but I'm not going.'

Daphne Ferguson's face remained unmoved. 'Of course you're going. Your grandfather agrees with me that it's much the best thing. You know what hopes he has for you.'

That was blatant blackmail. Tilly was very fond of both her grandparents but it was her grandfather who had her heart. He'd used imaginative approaches to interest her in classic English literature. He'd taught her revision techniques and how to approach exams. And he'd taught her how to play chess, showing her you had to look several moves ahead and try to understand what your opponent was likely to do so you could work out answering moves. Tilly once told her mother she thought her grandfather used similar tactics to deal with his powerful wife, defusing situations before they could erupt, making sure life proceeded smoothly for himself.

Olivia stifled a laugh and said, 'You're a wicked girl!'

Not answering her grandmother's letter had been a major error. She should have applied her chess lessons. Now she was going to have to fight if she wasn't to find herself consigned to another year's study.

'I'm sorry, Grandma, but I don't want to retake my exams. I know it's a disappointment to you and Grandpa but, you see, I'm not really academic,' she said apologetically.

'That's nonsense,' Daphne said sharply. 'And your mother agrees with us.'

Now that was a major tactical error on her grandmother's part. 'Mum has left it up to me,' Tilly said gently.

Daphne's gaze fell. The hands with their arthritis-thickened knuckles played with the gold-cornered notepad. 'What are you going to do if you don't retake the exams? Hmmm?' The tone was reasonable but her eyes were very sharp as they fixed on Tilly again.

'I've got a job that I'm enjoying,' she said with a hint of defiance.

'Skivvy in a soup kitchen! No one can call that a job worth the name.'

'Jemima, the cook I was working with, has just been appointed head chef of a new restaurant in the *Frère* chain.' Tilly couldn't help sounding triumphant as she brought out this nugget.

'I neither know nor care what the *Frère* chain might be. No granddaughter of mine is going to condemn herself to a lifetime's skivvying.'

'Cooking isn't skivvying!' Tilly burst out. 'Cooking's important!'

Her grandmother stared at her, her back ramrod straight. 'I see.' Daphne paused and her expression became more open. 'Do you think a career in food is what you want?'

Tilly felt bewildered. She didn't know what she wanted. She had enjoyed working with Jemima. Even with ratty old Mrs Major who reduced food to utter dullness, the restaurant was still a lot more fun than studying at school had ever been.

'I want to go on working where I am,' she repeated with as much confidence as she could muster.

'Then you must study home economics,' pursued Daphne Ferguson, handing down the verdict with the sort of assurance that must have accompanied the stones when Moses had received them from God.

'Grandma!' Tilly gasped incredulously. 'That's got nothing to do with food!'

'Any career starts with qualifications,' pursued her grandmother relentlessly. 'You must understand that. The days are gone when you can bungle your way through life picking things up as you go.'

'I'm not bungling my way!' burst out Tilly. 'I'm working hard, gaining experience, that's what everybody needs these days. What do all the ads ask for? People with experience!'

Her grandmother allowed herself a small smile, 'You have a point there, experience is important. But first of all you need – I'm sorry to have to keep harping on this but you don't seem able to take the point in – you need qualifications. I'd never have got where I did without my Oxford degree. And look at how difficult your mother found it when she came back to England after your father died. She'd never completed her graphic design course, despite my strongest recommendation that she do so before she married, so, of course, she wasn't properly qualified.'

'But she found a job,' Tilly pointed out. 'And look how well she's doing.'

'She was taken on as an assistant at a very low rate of pay. Had she had her degree that man would never have dared to offer her such a ridiculous salary. Even now she's not earning anywhere near what she's worth.'

Tilly couldn't argue with her grandmother, she didn't know what the facts were. It was certainly true that Olivia managed their lives on a very tight budget.

'Look, why don't we go and have something to eat? I noticed a pizza place on my way here.' Daphne rose.

Tilly got up as well. 'I'd love that, Grandma. Only,' she looked her grandmother straight in the eye, 'don't think you can persuade me because you can't. I'm not going to any crammer's. I don't want to go to university and I'm not going to.'

Her grandmother looked at Tilly for a long moment then gave a small sigh. 'How like your mother you look now, and your grandfather. Stubborn to the death, the lot of you. Don't worry, I know when I'm defeated. We'll have a nice meal and you can tell me all about this place you're working at.'

Tilly came and gave her a warm kiss, slipping her arm round the rigid shoulders in a quick hug. 'We all love you, Grandma.' But she was under no illusions. Her grandmother may have lost the first battle, she was not giving up the war. She just knew when a feint was advisable. Tilly was going to have to be on her guard. And she was going to have to give her

53

future some serious thought if she was going to be able to come up with the right counter moves when necessary.

Chapter Seven

'Is the roof open too much for you?' asked Charles as he handed Olivia into his car.

'It's lovely,' she said. 'Autumn's here and we need all the fresh air we can get before winter sets in.'

Charles closed her door and slipped into the driver's seat. 'It's hard to think of September as autumn when the weather is still so lovely.'

As he started the car's engine, Olivia sniffed appreciatively at the leather of the seats and ran a hand over the burled walnut of the fascia. 'What a treat to be going out in a Jaguar.'

Charles negotiated the busy streets of Surbiton towards the A3. They were going for a walk on the Sussex Downs followed by lunch at a pub somewhere. Olivia had dressed in a pair of tailored brown culottes with a cream silk shirt, its small collar and the short-sleeved cuffs self-embroidered. The shirt was open at the throat, showing her skin still faintly golden after the good summer. Over her shoulders she'd thrown a loosely knitted cardigan in shades of brown and gold. Lacy brown tights and tongued brogues completed the outfit.

'You look the spirit of autumn,' Charles had said when she'd opened the door, his eyes warm as they surveyed her. He was dressed in cream corduroy slacks and a blue check shirt underneath a navy sweatshirt, comfortable but with more than a hint of style.

The Jaguar slipped on to the dual carriageway of the A3 and picked up speed. The sun shone through the open roof and the air was pleasant around Olivia's head.

Charles switched on his CD system and Beethoven's Pastoral Symphony flooded the car.

'All right?' he enquired, sneaking a glance at her.

Olivia nodded, her face alive with delight. 'It's one of my favourites.'

'I thought it suited the day.'

They didn't talk as the car ate up the miles to Sussex. Charles turned off the main road after Singleton and killed the engine in a chalky clearing on the side of the Downs. The symphony was just coming to an end and they sat and waited until the last notes had died away before turning to smile at each other.

'Come on,' he said, releasing his seat belt. 'It's the most perfect day for a walk.' He reached into the back of the car and brought out a sturdy stick.

The air was warm but with that touch of crispness that says summer is definitely over. Birds were singing and the short grass was springy underfoot.

'One of these days I've promised myself to walk the whole of the South Downs Way,' said Olivia. She held out her arms, raising her face to the sky. 'Oh, isn't it wonderful? Working and living in London you forget what proper air is like. This is champagne. Vintage at that.'

'You look like someone who's just been given Christmas,' Charles said, amused.

'I feel like it.' Olivia started along a faint path that led up the slope. 'I can't believe how heavenly this all is.'

She set a fast pace, energy surging through her, fired by the perfection of the day. The temperature was just right, warm but not so warm walking briskly was uncomfortable. The leaves on the trees were all shades of gold and tobacco. The brambles still had succulent blackberries that Olivia stopped every now and then to savour, relishing their sweet darkness. Clumps of long grasses had turned pale cream and off the short turf drifted an ineffable aroma, the sweetness of the last of the wild flowers, woody hints borne on the breeze, all mixed with the scent of the warm chalk.

They climbed to the top of a ridge and stood for a moment looking at the glorious country spread out before them. 'Perfection,' said Charles. 'Such a gentle landscape, so civilised, and yet so natural as well. Look at the swell of the land, like the curve of a hip – no wonder Nature is supposed to be a woman.'

'Ah, that's because she's so fertile!' Olivia anchored back a piece of hair that had slipped out of her chignon on the climb up. 'Look at those fields, all the harvest has been gathered in and already they've started ploughing. Maybe they've even been sowing winter wheat to start the cycle all over again.'

'You're making me hungry! If my memory isn't failing, there should be a pub with decent food a couple of miles in that direction.'

Still walking briskly, they strode out the way he'd indicated, commenting on the scenery, on the birds and evidence of animals all around them.

'How do you know all that?' Olivia exclaimed after Charles had explained the difference between various birds of prey, pointing out a buzzard and then a kestrel, laying a hand on her arm to keep her still while they watched the hawk hover high above the landscape, until it stooped thrillingly down with astonishing speed, hardly pausing as it flattened out its flight just above the ground then rose into the air again. Olivia gasped as she just made out a tiny creature in its claws.

'Lunch,' said Charles matter-of-factly. 'Come on, we need ours as well.'

'Yes, but you haven't answered my question. Where did you learn all that about birds of prey?'

'I think it was *The Once and Future King*, T. H. White's book about the young King Arthur, that got me going,' Charles said, striding out again. 'Have you ever read it? You must, it's magic, full of fascinating details about nature as well as a damn' good story. Then I read White's autobiography and that got me interested in hawking. When I was a boy there were hardly any hawks left in the wild, nor were there all the demonstrations you see today. But I heard about a course in Gloucestershire and I cleaned cars and mowed lawns and mended bicycle punctures, anything that would earn me a couple of bob, and put it all in a post office savings account. It took me two years but I got there in the end and learned how to handle the smaller birds, kestrels and peregrine falcons. I wanted to keep one but my mother put her foot down. Said she couldn't be doing with all those chicken heads and having a bird around the place even if it was hooded most of the time. She wouldn't be moved. I swore then that if any child of mine wanted to keep a pet, no matter what it was, they could.'

'What pets has Phyllida had?' Olivia was panting slightly now. Charles was obviously in better shape than she was.

He gave a short laugh. 'Isn't it typical? She hasn't even wanted a puppy! We had a dog for a time but I was the only one who took it for walks and after a bit I couldn't find the time. Eventually I found a family who were desperate for a well-trained animal and gave it to them.'

He sounded amused but underneath Olivia thought she could recognise real despair.

'Did Tilly want a puppy?' he asked her.

'Oh, yes, desperately! It was no use, of course, we didn't have the room or anywhere proper to take it for walks. I bought her a kitten and that was a great success. It's quite untrue that all cats are standoffish, Tomtom was marvellously affectionate.' She stopped for a moment, both to catch her breath and because she still got upset when she had to explain the next bit. 'But two years ago he was run over and neither of us could bear to replace him.'

Charles slipped his arm round Olivia's shoulders. 'That's the hell of animals. They have such a short life and you mourn so desperately when they go.'

They walked in silence for a little and Olivia liked the feeling of his arm around her, solid and warm, anchoring her firmly at his side.

'Look.' Charles pointed with his stick. 'There's the pub.'

They quickened their step, Olivia realising just how hungry the walk had made her.

Inside it was all low beams and bright brass and a mixture of customers: local workers, teenagers, smart London types and the odd foreigner. There was a blackboard listing daily specials. Both Olivia and Charles chose steak and kidney pie. All the tables outside had gone but Charles secured a small one in a quiet corner.

When they'd finished the pies, he put a hand on Olivia's. 'Have you any idea how much I'm enjoying our times together?' he said quietly, his eyes watching her face.

Olivia felt herself flush and a little flare of anticipation lit itself somewhere in the pit of her stomach. The bustle of the pub around them faded, as though the two of them were enclosed in a bubble that protected against outside interference. 'Oh, I'm so glad,' she said unselfconsciously.

Some of the watchfulness in his eyes eased. 'You're always so calm, so controlled,' he said. 'I never know whether you are being polite or really happy to be with me. Today is the first time I've felt I'm starting to know you.'

Her eyes widened in surprise. 'But I haven't held anything back.'

'Haven't you?' he asked quizzically.

She flushed again.

After a moment he said, 'I'm taking some holiday in a couple of weeks' time. I thought I'd go over to France, down to the South. I'm hoping very much that perhaps you will come too?' He stopped, then, as she didn't say anything, added, 'I haven't hoped anything so much for a very long time.'

For a moment she wondered if she'd heard him correctly. 'France?' she said in a small gasp. 'Go to France with you? Just us?'

He smiled at that but his eyes were anxious. 'It's certainly not going to be a party. I want to get to know you. God, Olivia, you don't know how much I want to spend time with you, learn about you, enjoy things together. You'll love the South of France. If you think walking the Sussex Downs is wonderful, wait till you get to Provence! The air there is fabulous, full of the smell of thyme and marjoram. There are mountains of all sizes, big and small. And forests and rivers and lakes and the sea.' He'd caught hold of her hand and was holding it tightly as his words came faster and faster. Olivia could feel warmth flowing out of his hand and into hers. She could feel his pulse throbbing with life. She looked into the brown eyes and noted how they flickered, as though they were scanning her face, trying to monitor her reactions.

'Come with me, darling Olivia, please do!' he said urgently.

Neither of them was aware of anyone else in their vicinity. They could have been on a mountain top.

'Oh, Charles, I'd love to!' she burst out, conscious of just how wonderful it would be. France, a real holiday, with Charles. Someone who wanted just her. Someone with whom she could forget the past. Someone with whom she could be a woman again. Then the impossibility of it rushed in on her. 'But there's so much on in the office at the moment, I don't think Gavin would give me the time off.'

He gripped her hand even more tightly, delight flooding his face. 'Bugger Gavin! Look, you said you hadn't had any holiday, surely he owes you weeks and weeks?'

'Yes, but all of us are working as hard as we can just to keep up.'

'Come on, you can organise things better than that. I know you, you check everything at least three times. Cut it down to once and you'll soon have saved enough time to take a week or two out.'

'But you said you were going in a fortnight?'

'All right, make it three weeks. Will that be long enough for you?'

Suddenly Olivia laughed. 'What on earth am I hesitating for? Of course it will. If Gavin doesn't like it, he can stuff it!' Underneath her joy she felt a jolt of unease, as though the plates along an earthquake fault line had rubbed together, disturbing the equilibrium of the land around. 'I think it can only be one week, though. I really don't think I can swing two.'

'As long as you'll come, I don't care if it's only one day. Yes, I do,' he corrected himself swiftly. 'One day wouldn't do at all.' His face was as open and pleased as a schoolboy's who has just been awarded captaincy of the First Eleven. He rubbed his free hand over his mouth as though he couldn't bring himself to show just how thrilled he was. 'Look, do you want coffee or shall we start back?'

Olivia smiled; she could sense how impossible he felt it to remain sitting there any longer. She wanted to get outside herself, shout to the heavens how happy she was. 'No, let's get going.'

He paid for the meal and they left the pub, clutching hands.

Outside, Charles gave Olivia one triumphant glance then set off up the path to the ridge of the hill almost pulling her along behind him.

The path flattened out just below the top of the hill and ran alongside a gentle bank. A large bramble bush hid the pub below them. Charles stopped, turned round to face Olivia, dropped his stick and drew her into his arms.

'I've wanted to do this ever since the first time I met you,' he said, slowly drawing her close against his sturdy body.

Olivia just caught a glimpse of his half-closed eyes before his mouth met hers.

Long-forgotten sensations coursed through her body. She found urgency rising; her arms locked themselves behind his neck, then her hands pressed his head towards hers as her parched mouth opened.

They sank down on the springy turf easing out their bodies on the fragrant grass. Charles gently unfastened the top two buttons of her blouse and pressed his lips to the soft skin that led down to her breasts. Olivia lay back, her breath coming fast, joy flashing through her; from finger tip to finger tip, from the top of her head to the end of her toes, she felt alive in a way she hadn't for years.

Charles drew back and lay beside her. His eyes fastened on hers, he traced the line of her cheekbone, down to her mouth, then along her lips, his face serious and intent. 'Oh, Olivia,' he breathed. 'I want you all. I want to take you now, here, under the sun and the sky.'

She smiled at him 'And I was beginning to wonder if I didn't attract you after all.'

'Because I hadn't kissed you?' His face was still serious. 'But I couldn't trust myself and you were so beautiful but so remote. I thought I might frighten you off.' He laid his hand on her breast, over the blouse. 'I can't wait to see all of you. But I want it to be perfect, just right, the way I know it will be. That's why I want us to go to France together.'

Olivia gave a small cry of distress. 'You want to wait until then?'

He sat up and gave a triumphant grin. 'Ah, all defences down at last! It's not going to be as bad as all that, my darling. I have to go up north next week, to see our factory there. After that I've got to go to the States, so I shan't be here for nearly two weeks. I wanted to go to France on my return but if you can't arrange to get off for another week, then I'd much rather contain my impatience than make some no doubt hole-in-the-corner arrangement.'

A tiny doubt burrowed its way inside her. But when Olivia saw the look in his eyes, she felt ashamed. This was a man who was paying her an enormous compliment.

'I think it all sounds wonderful. It's just such a long time away,' she said softly.

He reached forward and carefully did up the two buttons he'd unfastened then smoothed back her hair, picking out a dead leaf and a piece of stalk. 'It'll pass like lightning,' he promised. With the ease and grace of a much younger man, he leapt to his feet and pulled Olivia to hers. 'Come on, let's enjoy the rest of our walk.'

His arm around her shoulders, they ambled along the ridge back to the car, talking in short bursts but most of the time content to be close to each other.

They reached the car and Charles said, 'What now? It's half-past three. I want to take you out to supper. Shall we do some exploring around here and find somewhere on the way back?'

Olivia thought for a moment. They were so near and it seemed such a perfect opportunity. 'My parents live within ten minutes' drive of here. Would you mind if we called in on them? I'm sure Mother would give us a cup of tea,' she suggested.

Charles looked slightly startled. 'Your parents?' Then he collected himself. 'Sure, why not? I'd love to meet them.' He put a hand to her face, holding it lightly against her cheek. 'You know, you're as old fashioned as I am. You don't want to tell your parents you're going away with a man without their having met him, do you?'

'How did you guess?' Olivia said demurely as she opened the car door and slipped into the passenger seat. Charles got out his mobile phone and she rang her mother.

'She'd love to see us,' she told him after a brief conversation. 'Head towards Chichester.'

Charles turned the car and started down the lane back towards the main road.

'Are your parents alive?' Olivia asked him, suddenly aware how little she knew about his personal life.

He shook his head. 'Dad died nine years ago and Mum just six months ago. She came and lived with me after the divorce. She said I needed someone looking after me – and Phyllida when she was home from school.'

'Was that difficult for you?' Olivia couldn't imagine having Daphne come and live with her, the tensions would be unbearable, but perhaps it was different with men and their mothers.

'I'll say!' Charles's exclamation was heartfelt. 'As far as she was concerned, I still needed being told about clean pants and wearing a vest if the temperature wasn't in the eighties. And she needed to know when I was coming home each evening.'

'With lectures if you were too late? And still no pets?'

He nodded. 'But I loved her and she hadn't been any too well since before Dad died. I organised a very good local girl to come and help with the cleaning and cooking, except that Mum thought her ideas on food were strange. Meat and two veg was Mum's idea of a proper meal for growing chaps, not salads and pasta. Followed by a steamed pudding. I don't know how I managed not to blow up.' But Charles sounded pleasantly exasperated by the memory.

'Your divorce must have upset her,' suggested Olivia, building up a picture of a bustling woman devoted to her home and family. Quite different from her own, powerful mother.

'Mum said that was the best day of her life! She and Veronica started fighting the day I introduced them and never let up.'

It was the first thing Charles had said about his ex-wife. 'Was it you they fought over?' asked Olivia, trying to reconcile this with the family-loving woman she'd pictured.

Charles gave a quick shrug of his shoulders, his eyes firmly on the twisting, narrow lane that took them back to the main road. 'Poles apart, they were. Until Dad died, he and Mum lived in a two up, two down in Leeds. Dad was a railwayman, Mum worked in the shop at the local bakery. Veronica's father was a clergyman and they lived in a huge, decaying Georgian rectory.'

As he talked, Olivia heard for the first time the slight Yorkshire burr in Charles's voice, as though talking about his parents had unconsciously sent him back in time. He didn't have much of any sort of accent usually, she supposed 'classless' was the word for it. But now she realised that it was that hint of Yorkshire that give his voice its warmth and directness. Gave him that quality she thought of as 'Charles'.

'How did you meet Veronica?' she ventured.

'She worked for me as my secretary. She was good, too. Gave style to the office, got us organised. I didn't understand until well after we were married that her plans for me didn't include my parents. Not until she'd persuaded me to set up our main office near London. Commercially she was right but it was for all the wrong reasons. Things began to go wrong between us soon after that.' Charles's voice was expressionless.

They reached the main road and turned down towards Chichester. Olivia put her hand on the top of Charles's thigh, felt the muscles tighten. 'I'm sorry,' she said. 'It must have been very difficult for you.'

He flashed her a warm smile. 'Worse things happen at sea. How about you, did you get on with your parents-in-law?'

'Peter was an orphan when we married.' She gave a brief laugh. 'In-laws were something I never had to worry about.'

'You were well out of it,' Charles said. 'Which way is it now?'

Chapter Eight

Olivia's mother was out in the garden weeding when the phone rang. She stripped off one of her gardening gloves and picked the mobile receiver out of the pocket of her green apron.

'Daphne Ferguson,' she said crisply. 'Olivia, how nice to hear from you, darling. What, in the area? Of course you can come, we shall be delighted to see you and – who did you say was with you? Charles Frome? Well, we shall look forward to seeing you both. About fifteen minutes, did you say? I'll put the kettle on.' She replaced the receiver in the coarse gardening apron and used her trowel to help lever herself to her feet. The weeding would have to wait.

She went upstairs and took off the pair of old trousers and shirt she was wearing and exchanged them for tights, a light tweed skirt, a cashmere sweater and a pair of low-heeled leather shoes buckled across the front. She added her pearls before brushing the thick straight hair back into place. Then she got out a powder compact and touched up her face before slicking fresh lipstick on to her thin mouth. She gave herself a quick, efficient glance and went downstairs again, her mind turning over the surprising news that Olivia was bringing a male friend to visit her parents. Except, was it so surprising?

Over the pizza the other night Tilly had been full of the man who'd entered her mother's life. 'And he's nice, Grandma, really nice,' she'd said, leaning forward eagerly.

So, Daphne had thought, Olivia's met a man with enough savvy to get Tilly on his side, has she? She'd asked Tilly for more details and what she heard made her thoughtful.

Just past the stairs was the door to her husband's study. Daphne knocked gently on the heavy wood then opened the door and put her head round it. 'Olivia's just rung, she's bringing a friend for tea,' she told her husband.

Thomas Ferguson looked up. His too-long, thinning grey hair was awry, as though he'd constantly pushed a hand through it, his glasses, as usual, were down his nose but at least he was wearing a halfway decent shirt and he hadn't put on the sweater with all the holes that he kept rescuing from the Oxfam parcels. For a moment the eyes behind the glasses remained unfocused, then he seemed to absorb what she'd said. 'That's good, dear,' he said absently. 'Clodagh, I suppose?' He looked down again at his work

63

and scratched out a word on the handwritten page, inserting another in its place.

Daphne gave a quick snort. 'Why do you like that girl? A most unhealthy influence on Olivia, I always think. No, it's a man.'

'Mmm? Really?' Thomas made another correction to his manuscript then reached for a book on top of one of the piles that were stacked around his desk.

Once Daphne had been charmed by her husband's inability to concentrate on anything but his work. Once she'd thought it was symptomatic of his great intelligence. Once she'd tiptoe away and leave him so that the latest magnum opus could continue undisturbed.

Now she advanced further into the study. 'Thomas, I said that Olivia is bringing a man to see us.' She looked at her watch. 'They'll be here any minute.'

'Good, good.' He had the book open now and was searching through the pages.

Daphne gave up. She went out, closing the door behind her with a controlled click that wasn't quite a bang.

In the kitchen she put the kettle on the Aga hot plate and got out a tray. Then stood in a rare moment of contemplation, looking through the window at the garden she'd been working in.

Daphne and Thomas Ferguson lived in three knocked together old Sussex cottages nestling into the foothills of the Downs. The house had low ceilings and rooms that led out of rooms. They had originally bought it for weekends, coming down late on Friday nights, being greeted by the smell of damp as the front door was pushed open, creaking its protests, the swollen wood scraping on the flagstoned floor.

The garden had been a wilderness of old roses, thick brambles, laurels and long grass. It had taken Daphne many years of patient toil to convert it into the plantsman's paradise it now was, with chalk-loving plants drifting in and out of each other in waves of skilfully blended colours and textures. The main work had been done after she'd retired and they'd sold the Richmond house and moved down here permanently. Daphne watched a couple of late butterflies alight on a rust-coloured sedum and remembered the fun and excitement she'd had planning everything. It had helped her get over the shock of realising her career was at an end at a time when she'd never felt more in control.

There was the sound of a car on the gravel drive and then a gleaming Jaguar emerged in front of the window. Daphne removed the kettle from the Aga hot plate, closed the lid and went to the front door before Olivia could follow her usual practice and come in the back way.

Daphne stood on the broad stone step, regularly scrubbed by Betty, and waited for her daughter and her friend to approach.

Olivia came up to her mother and gave her cheek a brief kiss. 'This is Charles Frome,' she said. 'Charles, my mother, Daphne Ferguson.'

Daphne held out her hand and gave him a smile. 'I'm delighted to meet you, Mr Frome.'

He shook it gravely. 'And I you, Mrs Ferguson. What a charming place this is.' He looked up at the flintstone exterior of the converted cottages. 'And what a wonderful view,' he added, turning to see beyond the garden to the undulating line of the Downs.

Over the years Daphne had perfected the art of scrutinising people unobtrusively. 'Come inside,' she said. 'Tea's nearly ready.' While she led the way into the cottage, her mind was mentally clicking up her impressions. Good figure, not tall but managing to top Olivia by several inches. Clothes acceptable; that sweatshirt was a little casual, perhaps, but it was good quality. The car a little suspect, perhaps? A BMW or a Mercedes would have indicated a more sophisticated outlook on life. Daphne associated Jaguar motors with self-made men who liked to flash money around. Still, the car wasn't this year's model.

More worrying was that touch of Yorkshire her quick ear had picked up. She hoped he wasn't the sort who talked about 'brass'.

'Tilly has given you an enthusiastic report,' she said, leading the way down the passage and into the main room.

'Has she indeed?' Charles Frome sounded gratified.

'When did you talk to Tilly?' asked Olivia, surprised.

'Oh, we had a pizza together the other night, while you were in Birmingham. I don't suppose you've had time to talk to her since you got back. What with her being so busy in that restaurant and you with your work.'

Daphne sailed into the main living area of the cottage. 'We knocked down a couple of walls to make this one big room,' she said. 'I hate poky rooms, don't you, Mr Frome?'

'Won't you call me Charles?' he murmured, his gaze travelling over the antique furniture, all of it polished and gleaming, thanks to twice-a-week Betty.

'We don't entertain much these days but it's nice to be able to do it properly when we want,' Daphne found herself saying. 'We can seat twenty over there.' She gestured towards the dining table that at present lacked the three leaves that could be inserted between each of its D ends. 'And can easily throw drinks for forty if we push back those sofas and that table.' She indicated the Regency sofa table that carried a large Chinese bowl. Inside the bowl was a huge white pelargonium, its butterfly-winged petals luminous in the shadowed room with its small windows. On either side of the bowl were piles of *Country Life* and *Vogue*.

'Where's Father?' asked Olivia.

'Working, darling, as usual,' said Daphne lightly. 'Why don't you tell him you're here?'

She noticed how Charles's gaze followed her daughter from the room. 'When we bought this place,' she continued, 'everyone was ripping out their flagstoned floors but we kept ours and now, of course, fashion has swung round to our way of thinking. It cost a small fortune to get hold of enough extra ones to fill in the gaps when we knocked down the walls. Won't you sit down, Mr Frome?' She waved a hand towards one of the chintz-covered sofas.

For a moment it seemed as though he would, then Olivia reappeared followed by her father and Charles went forward to meet him.

The immediate impression Thomas Ferguson always gave was of height. He was tall and very thin, with a wiry tautness. When she'd first met him, Daphne had been reminded of the etiolated figures in an El Greco painting, an impression increased by his high forehead and the remoteness of his expression.

'Thomas, this is Mr Frome, a friend of Olivia's.' Daphne could see Olivia was irritated by the way she insisted on calling Charles by his surname. Well, a little formality never hurt anyone.

'Good afternoon, sir.' Charles held out his hand and Thomas took it with an air of mild enquiry, as though he wasn't quite sure what he should do with it.

'We've been walking, Father, up on the Downs,' said Olivia, and Daphne noticed with a slight sinking of her heart the soft, shining quality about her as she looked at Charles Frome.

'Thomas, we're going to have tea on the terrace. Take Mr Frome out there and Olivia can help me with the tea.'

Daphne led the way back to the kitchen knowing that Olivia would follow.

She put the kettle back on the hot plate. 'Could you put cups and saucers on a tray, darling? And there are some biscuits in that tin.'

Daphne watched as Olivia took down the fragile Worcester china from the open shelves and she felt her heart give a painful squeeze as she recognised how beautiful her daughter was today. Before her teens, Olivia had been a thin girl with over-large eyes and the flowering of her looks had come as a revelation to Daphne. She herself had been held to be very attractive as a girl and she was unexpectedly susceptible to physical beauty in others. It had been the piercing blue of Thomas's eyes as much as his equally piercing intelligence that had drawn her to him.

With Olivia's emergent beauty and her undoubted talent for design, Daphne had dreamed of both a great career and a great marriage for her only child.

What a disappointment the advent of Peter Warboys had been! For Olivia to throw everything away for an irreverent, good-for-nothing, hippy scribbler with a dubious background! Daphne had distrusted his charm, thought his ability with words facile and his determination to take her daughter to California culpable.

She knew many people believed Olivia's marriage had been far from disastrous. After all, Peter Warboys may have made a shaky start but he'd achieved a certain success before he died in that appalling car crash.

If only Olivia hadn't insisted on abandoning the four-year graphic design course she was only halfway through. What had she said? That her talent was, at best, limited? Daphne had retorted it wasn't talent that mattered in life, it was what you did with it. Olivia replied that she was far better suited to being a wife and mother. Daphne had panicked then and asked if she was pregnant. No, said Olivia, but she hoped she soon would be.

Daphne had embarked on a series of lunches to introduce her to high-flying young female art directors so she could hear about their enviable life styles. It had made no difference.

Thomas had declared himself disappointed. He'd never made the mistake of thinking Olivia had a first-class brain or great creative gifts, he said, but she had seemed to have the makings of a sensible woman. Why, then, he asked, was she abandoning her education for the sake of someone without a steady job, prospects or background? He had put Peter through a comprehensive catechism when Olivia first produced him and revealed that this boy with the long hair had been educated at some unknown private school and had scraped a second-class degree in a third-class university. Peter Warboys was not what the Fergusons had wanted for their only child.

Their distress at his death had been purely on Olivia's and Tilly's behalf. Daphne would naturally have preferred a gentler end to the marriage but she welcomed the fact that it was at an end and her daughter and granddaughter were back in England.

Only gradually had she realised that Olivia, seemingly so gentle and compliant, was determined to march to her own tune. There had, for instance, been the matter of a home for the two of them and then a job for Olivia.

Daphne had offered to share the Richmond house with Olivia and Tilly. But Olivia said Thomas would never be able to continue his writing with a child in the house. She'd also refused the offer of help with a mortgage so she could buy somewhere decent. Instead, she'd insisted on buying that wretched terraced house in Surbiton, all she could afford on what she'd been left by her husband, calmly announcing that the local schooling was excellent and she preferred not to have the pressures of a mortgage.

What Olivia meant, as Daphne had no trouble understanding, was that she refused to be beholden to the mother who had fought so hard against her marriage.

The same thing had happened to Daphne's offer of a small car.

It had taken a devious subtlety Daphne hadn't known she possessed (her usual business style was up front and confrontational) to arrange for Olivia to be offered an interview with Gavin Rickards at *Designs Unlimited* without her daughter realising the strings that had been pulled behind the scenes. But at least she had the satisfaction of knowing that at last Olivia had a job in which she could use her talents and achieve a certain independence.

After that, Daphne had imagined Olivia would meet a respectable man (by which Daphne meant one with the right background, income and career, preferably something in banking or perhaps the Foreign Office) and achieve the sort of marriage she should have had in the first place. Then there would be more grandchildren and Daphne could play her part in guiding their footsteps and Olivia's proper destiny could be fulfilled.

Nothing like that had happened and Daphne had gradually grown to believe that her daughter would remain single.

Now, just when Daphne had taken on the battle for Tilly's future, Olivia had turned up with a man for whom she showed every sign of having fallen, hook, line and sinker. A man Daphne was far from sure was at all suitable.

'It always amuses me, Mother,' said Olivia, arranging the fragile porcelain on a tray, 'how you insist on using for everyday china what most people would keep in a display cabinet.'

'When you inherit as much of it as I did, it seems stupid to spend money on buying something vastly inferior that offends your lips to drink out of and your eyes to eat off.' Daphne reached for the old, embossed tin that her mother had always used for tea. 'Tilly is very concerned about this man,' she said, spooning dusty tea leaves into the large silver teapot she always used, its patina soft with constant polishing.

Out of the corner of her eye, Daphne saw Olivia stiffen.

'His name is Charles, Mother, and he's asked you to call him by it. And what do you mean, Tilly is concerned about him? You've just said she gave him a good report.'

Daphne dropped the wide spoon back into the tin and snapped it shut. 'Well, this is the first man you have brought home to meet her. She seems to think he could be important.'

'I met Charles through work,' Olivia said quietly. 'He has an engineering company, they make cog wheels and things like that.'

Nothing about this bit of background gave Daphne any confidence. 'I suppose he's married,' she said, pouring boiling water straight on to the tea. She never saw any point in warming a silver pot, it absorbed heat so quickly.

'He's divorced,' Olivia said in a tight tone.

'Children?'

'A daughter, in her early-twenties, works in the city. I believe she has a very good job.' Olivia put digestive biscuits on a Worcestershire plate and added, 'Charles and I are off to France soon on a short holiday.'

'With Tilly?' Daphne rapped out, trying to hide her sense of shock. She had no idea things had advanced so rapidly.

'Mother, of course not.'

'Hmmph!' Daphne placed the teapot on the tray, picked it up and walked determinedly out of the kitchen.

On the terrace Charles was listening with every appearance of deep interest to Thomas outlining his current project, a history of English dictionaries. 'Glossaries predated the earliest efforts at dictionaries, you know,' Thomas was saying, in a manner which suggested Charles was one of the students he no longer lectured to. 'And the first authors to write in the English language had only Latin grammars to aid their efforts.'

Daphne placed the tray on the garden table.

'But consider that those authors included Chaucer, Spenser and Shakespeare,' Thomas continued, taking no notice of the arrival of tea. 'Now we clutter our children with dictionaries and assume they are essential to the control and correct handling of the language. Yet what author writing since, for instance, the publication of the full *Oxford English Dictionary* has Shakespeare's breadth of vocabulary, let alone the same subtlety of language?'

Charles leant forward. 'Could you draw an analogy with the early architects? They had no slide rules, let alone computers, but they understood so many load-bearing principles and tensile strengths, and what has our modern age built that can match the beauty of so many medieval churches and cathedrals?'

Too often Thomas listened to guests with half an ear, lost in his own world, unable to connect with those around him. Now he looked alert. 'Interesting idea, yes!'

'Olivia tells me you are an engineer, Mr Frome,' Daphne said, handing him a cup of tea.

He accepted the cup and said easily that, yes, that was his line.

'Mother,' Olivia began, then subsided, taking her cup of tea and sitting in a chair beside Charles, a resigned expression on her face.

Daphne ignored the slight interruption and proceeded to quiz her guest, drawing from her capacious memory the names of various luminaries who held or, more often, had held, positions of power in the engineering world, Managing Director or Chairman of this, President of that.

While Thomas retreated once more into the sanctuary of his mind and Olivia sat throwing bits of biscuit to inquisitive birds, Daphne absorbed Charles's expression of polite attention as he occasionally agreed that, yes, he knew that person or had had contact with this.

Daphne was not impressed.

'What an interesting life you must lead, Mr Frome,' she said finally. 'So refreshing to meet someone engaged in actual production of an essential product. Down here we usually meet the financial wizards or those responsible for ordering our political affairs. I miss my encounters with what one might call the coal face of industry.'

His face remained politely interested but Olivia got up abruptly. 'More tea, Charles?' she asked, taking his cup.

He looked up at her and his smile was very warm. 'Nay, thanks, lass. That were fine.'

Daphne flushed. Charles Frome, she suddenly realised, had more

69

intelligence and personality than she had given him credit for.

'Then we should be on our way.' Olivia said firmly.

Daphne rose. 'It's been so nice to see you both,' she said smoothly.

Charles turned to Thomas. 'I very much enjoyed our discussion earlier, sir. I hope we can continue it on another occasion.'

Thomas blinked briefly then offered his hand. 'I would like that, Charles. Bring Olivia down for a meal next time, then we can have a proper chat.'

Thomas issuing such an invitation was so unusual, Daphne caught herself staring at him. Then said, 'You won't mind if I have a quick word with my daughter, will you, Charles?' and swept Olivia into the living room. 'I need to talk to you about Tilly,' she said authoritatively. 'It's quite ridiculous she isn't resitting those wretched exams. She'll regret it for the rest of her life if she doesn't.'

'I don't think so, Mother,' Olivia said, and Daphne could see she was holding on to her temper by the thinnest of threads. 'She has never been academic, you know, and I was more or less expecting her to turn down the idea of university whatever her results.' She went back on to the terrace and slipped her arm through Charles's.

Daphne followed her out. 'You're a professional man, Charles,' she appealed to him. 'Tell this poor daughter of mine how important qualifications are.'

'Ah, I'm not sure I can.' He smiled at Daphne with the same, easy charm he had displayed throughout their meeting. 'My daughter's earning more than most men, with hardly a certificate to her name. Seems to me charm, common sense and knowing what you want can be more important than bits of paper. Ready, darling?'

With inward consternation, Daphne watched the slight flush that rose on Olivia's face at the endearment.

As soon as she'd waved goodbye, Daphne went to her desk and got out her master address book. This contained all the contacts she had amassed during a successful advertising career. She began to go through it, making notes. On Monday she'd find out more about Mr Charles Frome.

Monday evening Daphne rang her daughter. 'Darling, I've been calling one or two people about your Mr Frome,' she said without preamble.

There was a quick sigh from the other end of the phone. 'Mother, he's not *my* Mr Frome and I thought you were going to call him Charles?'

'His company has found a nice little niche market, apparently, and has a good reputation. But I gather your friend Charles isn't exactly a leader in his profession. Not on any committees, no other directorships, never present at any of the conferences. Indeed, no one has ever *seen* him at any of the conferences.'

'I'm really glad to hear that, Mother.' Olivia's voice was tight. 'It must mean he has time for a private life.'

Daphne sighed. 'Darling,' she said, 'if you are thinking of forming a relationship, you need to know where he's going, don't you?'

'Mother, I can't believe you're doing this!' came back down the line. 'This is the first man I've done more than say hello to in, what is it, ten years? Shouldn't you be pleased someone's interested in me as a woman? That your ice-maiden of a daughter has found a man whose company she enjoys?'

'Now don't get on your high horse, darling, I've only your best interests at heart.'

'No, Mother, you haven't.' Daphne heard the anger in Olivia's voice with shock. 'You are only concerned with your own ideas of a suitable escort for your daughter. You can't look beyond your nose or understand that Charles has more poise than any of the succession of pretentious men you've tried to interest me in over the years. How many have managed to get through to Father on a first meeting?' Daphne found herself speechless at this unexpected attack. 'You don't care anything about what I, your daughter, actually want. You never have. I am going to France with Charles. When we come back whether or not I see more of him will have nothing to do with what you think. And don't try and bully Tilly while I'm away.'

Daphne gave a small bleat.

'Mother?' said Olivia, her voice suddenly hesitant. Daphne found herself unable to speak. 'Mother, I'm sorry, I know you love me but please believe I know what's best for me and for Tilly. I'm not a teenager any more. Think back to when you were my age, would you have tolerated your mother interfering in your life?'

'I, I . . . I can't talk any more,' said Daphne and put down the phone, the receiver rattling as she missed settling it back in its cradle; the last time Olivia had spoken to her like that had been when she'd announced that Peter and she had been married that morning and they were leaving for California immediately.

'If you're not careful, you're going to drive Olivia away again,' said Thomas from the doorway behind her.

Daphne whirled round in her chair. 'How long have you been standing there?' she asked.

'Long enough.' He came into the room, his tall figure scraping the beamed ceiling. He was, she suddenly realised, very upset. He took off his glasses with a hand that trembled. 'We did a terrible thing, you and I, all those years ago when we set our faces against her marrying that young man. Don't let's repeat our mistake.'

Daphne gazed up at her husband. 'But you agreed Peter was totally unsuitable.'

Thomas sat down heavily in a chair beside her desk and rubbed his eyes. 'This man isn't,' he said.

'Oh, as to that, he's nothing very much. A small-time industrialist from Yorkshire.' Daphne began to recover herself.

'He's an intelligent man who has made something of himself. He also seems to be an unusually kind man and is obviously very much in love with our daughter. And she seems to be extremely fond of him.'

Daphne bit back a comment to the effect that Thomas never saw anything of what went on around him so how could he know, and said instead, 'Are you telling me you wouldn't mind if she married him?'

'I think it'd be an excellent thing if she did. Olivia needs someone like that – and Tilly could do with a father as well.'

'Well, he's only asked her to go on holiday with him,' Daphne said waspishly. 'Don't start counting any chickens!' She rose and closed her desk. 'I'd better see if I can find something for supper.'

Chapter Nine

Monday started badly for Olivia.

The washing machine, put on overnight had failed. Instead of clean clothes ready for the tumble drier, Olivia discovered them sitting in a mess of dirty water. A faint metallic odour hung about the machine and suggested some vital part had burned out. Unless some miracle happened, she was going to be faced with either a large repair bill or the cost of replacing the machine.

The weather had broken and Olivia had to hunt for warmer clothes than she'd been wearing for the past weeks. All the delay meant she missed her normal train. While she waited for the next, she opened the post and found that the insurance premium for the house was being raised dramatically and that the telephone bill was more than she was expecting. She'd have to have a word with Tilly about not spending hours calling her chums.

Unable to find a seat on the crowded commuter train, Olivia stood swaying as it rattled along and tried to work out how she was going to pay for everything. Even abandoning the thought of something new to wear for winter wasn't going to help much.

'So glad you decided to join us today,' Gavin said as she walked in. 'Do you think you could manage to find time to drop by my office for an update on the ball bearing job?'

'Sure, Gavin. In five minutes?' Once Olivia had tried to deflect her boss's sarcasm with the same sort of sassy comment that Margie managed so successfully. But she lacked Margie's blithe disregard for any sort of authority and merely succeeded in stimulating even more unpleasant comments. She quickly returned to her previous tactic of ignoring the sarcasm.

At the end of a quick run through the current state of the exhibition contract, Olivia said, 'So you can see that everything is well in hand.' She then produced her sketches for the proposed stand.

'Hmm,' Gavin said as he cast an eye over the designs. 'Pretty rough, wouldn't you say?'

Olivia forbore to respond to this standard Gavin approach. He believed anything suggesting approval would be interpreted as an indication that a salary rise could be demanded. Instead she said, 'I've got an appointment to show the Managing Director finished sketches in two weeks' time.'

'Cutting things a bit fine, aren't we?' Gavin sat back in his chair and pushed a hand through his heavily bleached hair, his small mouth drooping in petulant fashion.

'I don't think so,' Olivia said quietly. 'But I am going to ring this morning and ask if we can bring the meeting forward, to the end of this week.'

Gavin raised a surprised eyebrow. 'Oh? Will you be ready?'

Olivia swallowed an impatient sigh. Why did Gavin always find it impossible to express any sort of enthusiasm, or even satisfaction, for the work his staff produced? 'Of course I shall be ready.' She took a deep breath, there was no point in delaying this moment. 'I'm bringing the meeting forward because I'm taking a holiday.'

Gavin's eyes bulged. 'Holiday?' he asked in a tone that suggested she'd proposed a trip to the moon.

'Yes. I'll be off for a week three weeks from today.'

He sat up straight. 'I'm not at all sure that'll be possible,' he started, and reached for his diary.

'There's nothing scheduled for then that requires me,' Olivia stated firmly. 'I've been through everything I've got on hand and there's no reason I can't take one week of the several that you owe me.'

Gavin looked at her with astonished eyes. 'I think we need to go through things very carefully together before I can be convinced of that,' he said repressively.

Olivia wished she could throw his job in his face. How dare he treat her like a schoolgirl who had a habit of handing her prep in late? She thought of the broken washing machine and the horrendous telephone bill and bit her lip. 'Let me itemise what I have on hand, Gavin,' she said, controlling herself, and began to enumerate her current schedule.

Quarter of an hour later she let herself out of his office and took several deep breaths.

'I'll bring you a coffee,' said the office secretary sympathetically as she passed on her way to the photocopier. Everyone knew about the effect a meeting with Gavin had.

Margie raised a questioning eyebrow as Olivia went back to her drawing board.

'I've just won myself a week's badly overdue holiday,' she said calmly, setting up the plans she had to work on. 'That is if I can pack into the next three weeks what I would normally be expected to produce in two months.'

'Stuff that!' Margie said, her eyes sparkling with anticipation. 'You know how Gavin likes to pile things on. Tell me more about the holiday? You didn't say anything about it last week.'

Olivia felt a lightening of her heart. 'I didn't know about it last week.' She paused provocatively, her head held on one side.

Margie's eyes narrowed suddenly. 'It's Charles, isn't it?' she hissed rapidly. 'My God, you're going off with him!' She gave a sudden whoop.

'At last!' Then her face broke into a broad grin. 'I knew something was going on, you sly old thing! You can't fool your Auntie Margie, not when you've been going round the office like the cat that's swallowed the cream.'

Olivia laughed and lined up the design sheet.

'Come on,' Margie urged. 'You've got to tell me all about it.'

'If you're free for lunch, maybe. Now I've got to get working.'

'You're on! We'll go to that nice place that's just opened round the corner and you'll tell me every last little detail.'

Margie not only paid for lunch, she insisted on taking Olivia off afterwards and buying her an incredibly expensive nightie. 'Don't say anything,' she insisted over Olivia's protests. 'This is an early Christmas present. Just lie back and enjoy it,' she added with a leer and an outsize wink as the heavy silk and lace confection was carefully folded into sheets of tissue paper and installed in a glossy cardboard box.

Olivia thought it was as well Gavin was having a long business lunch and wasn't in the office when they got back. Both their late arrival and the box would have called for comment.

She also took advantage of his absence to ring Charles to say she had her holiday organised. He sounded so delighted she found the rest of the afternoon flew by, even the extra couple of hours she worked.

The telephone was ringing as she let herself into the house. She hurried to pick up the receiver, hoping it was Charles. It was her mother.

By the time Olivia severed the connection, her hand was shaking and her spine felt like jelly. She tried to tell herself not to be such a wimp. Her mother didn't mean to be quite so domineering, it was just that she was used to organising people, including her family.

Olivia dialled Charles's number. 'Hi,' he said. 'You're not ringing to say you've changed your mind, are you?' he asked, sounding worried.

'No, silly, I just thought it would be nice to have a chat. How was your day?'

Ten minutes later she put down the phone once again feeling relaxed and happy. She was making the right decision, she knew she was. She went and rang Clodagh's bell.

'Thought you'd like to know you got it spot on,' she said when her friend answered the door dressed in jeans and an elaborately patterned sweater.

Clodagh looked at her for a moment, frowning, then she gave a little crow of triumph. 'You've done it! Come in, come in, this calls for a drink.'

Olivia followed her into the living room, laughing. 'No, no, I haven't done it, as you call it! At least, not yet! Your mind!'

'Is the mind of any normal, red-blooded female, thank heaven. Come on, have a glass of wine and tell little Clodagh all.'

Olivia gave her a swift resumé of her Saturday outing. 'Then, on Sunday, we took Tilly into the country for a wonderful lunch and another walk, followed by a quiet evening playing cards. They seem to get on really well.'

'And why not?' asked Clodagh rhetorically. 'She's a darling girl and he's in love with her mother.'

'She could be jealous,' suggested Olivia.

Clodagh regarded her, holding her head on one side. 'I don't think so. She's at the right stage, finding out about her own life. If you want my opinion, she's delighted you've found a man and one she can relate to. Now tell me more about this French trip.'

'I've told you all I know,' Olivia confessed.

'And when am I going to meet your Charles?'

Once again Olivia protested that he wasn't her Charles. 'And he's going to be in the States almost until we go off to France, so I don't think I can get you together until afterwards. If we're still speaking then.'

'Don't be so pessimistic.'

'Clodagh, what if he's disappointed in me? What if we bore each other silly after the first twenty-four hours?'

'Good heavens, where's the girl who says everything's for the best in this best of all possible worlds?'

Olivia couldn't help laughing. 'You are ridiculous, I've never been like that.'

'Then you should be. What is life for but for living? And you go off and live, girl.'

'Funny, Margie said something just like that several weeks ago. Clodagh, will you keep an eye on Tilly while I'm away?'

'Rather than turning a blind one when she brings home a young man, eh?' Clodagh asked wryly.

'I'm not asking you to spy on her, just to be here in case she needs anything.'

'Of course, Olive, you know that.'

'Oh, and can you do me a great favour tomorrow?' Olivia started on the saga of the washing machine.

Two and a half weeks later, Olivia sat in her living room waiting for Charles. By the front door stood her case. Three times she'd changed her mind over what she should take.

She looked at the size of the suitcase and felt a moment's doubt. Had she enough clothes? Unless they ran into a real heatwave, she must have. For the journey she was wearing a pair of tailored fawn trousers with a cream polo neck in very fine cotton jersey, worn with a tan suede jacket she'd bought in a sale the previous January. She ran a hand over her hair, checking that her chignon was in place, that no pins were coming adrift. She felt serene, she felt in control.

No, she didn't, she felt like a teenager waiting for her first date, all tumultuous uncertainty. She hadn't seen Charles since their Sunday with Tilly. They'd talked practically every day on the telephone but it wasn't the same thing. It wasn't the same thing at all. She knew, none better, how treacherous memory could be. What if her memory had built up a picture reality couldn't match?

The front door opened and Tilly came in, pushing her bicycle, her cheeks glowing. 'Hi, Mum!' She wheeled the bike to its home underneath the stairs, came and kissed her mother, then flung herself on to the small sofa.

Olivia dragged her mind back from wondering just when Charles was going to arrive and concentrated on her daughter. 'Are you going to be all right while I'm away?'

Tilly grinned at her. 'I've got five rave ups and an orgy planned. But I promise you we'll get the house together again before you return. Carpets cleaned, furniture repolished and the kitchen washed down.'

'No, seriously, darling!'

'What makes you think I'm not being serious?' Tilly leaned over and hugged Olivia. 'Look, you're going to be away nine days, right? Back a week on Sunday? Think I can't manage on my own that long?'

Olivia laughed and shook her head. 'Of course you can. And, remember, Clodagh's only next door and she'll be delighted to help if you do need something.' She opened the Mulberry tan leather shoulder bag that her mother had given her for her last birthday. 'I got you a little money so you can go out with your friends in the evenings sometimes.' She pushed fifty pounds across the table towards Tilly.

'Mum! That's far too much, I don't need all that!' Tilly looked at the notes in awe.

'It'll make me happy knowing you've got something to spend,' Olivia said, refusing to think about the state of her bank balance and thanking heaven for credit cards. Hers had just taken the strain of a new washing machine.

The doorbell rang.

Tilly jumped to her feet. 'That's Charles, I'll get it.' She ran to the door as Olivia rose eagerly.

Charles gave Tilly a quick smile but his eyes were on Olivia.

He seemed larger than she remembered, his shoulders broader. Or perhaps it was the casual, slightly padded jacket he was wearing. Stone-coloured poplin, it swung open over a polo neck and corduroy trousers, both in dark brown.

'Ready?' he asked exuberantly.

'All packed.' She indicated the case by the door.

He picked it up, hefting its weight experimentally. 'Should be enough in here for a four-month trip.'

'That's outrageous!' Tilly laughed at him. 'Mum's taking almost nothing. Now, you both have a wonderful time and bring me back a bottle of olive oil.'

She gave a shy peck at Charles's cheek, then squeaked as he dropped the case and threw his arms around her. 'You look after yourself,' he said, releasing her. 'Your mother will ring on Sunday, just to check everything's all right.'

Olivia hugged Tilly herself. 'Don't let Grandma persuade you into anything you don't want to do while I'm away,' she pleaded, looking into Tilly's eyes.

'The drawbridge is up, all boarders will be repelled. Don't worry, Mum, I can look after myself!'

'Sure you can,' said Charles. 'Come on, darling, let's go.'

He handed Olivia into the car, put her case in the boot, gave a wave to Tilly standing at the door, slipped into the driving seat and started the car.

Then, with the engine idling, he looked across at Olivia. 'Happy holiday,' he said softly.

'Happy holiday.' She smiled back at him, all her vague doubts and tensions gone.

They went through the Channel tunnel, Olivia for the first time. She couldn't believe how easy the whole experience was or what a short time it took. She sat holding Charles's hand tightly but, really, she wasn't nervous at all. It was all just as the advertisements said it would be!

Almost more thrilling was watching the car being loaded on to the train that would take them down to the South of France from Lille. 'It's a long way to drive and time's too precious,' Charles had said.

Olivia could only agree.

As they watched, she was conscious she hadn't had time for lunch that day and that she couldn't see a restaurant car.

'Come on,' Charles said, 'let's go and find our *wagon lit*.'

Inside the little compartment, where the upper bunk hadn't yet been lowered, he put down a wicker basket, then stowed their cases.

Olivia inspected the hanging space and the small basin, admiring the way everything had been so neatly fitted in, then the train started with a jerk that sat her abruptly on to the bunk.

Charles opened the wicker basket. 'I hope you didn't think I was going to let you starve,' he said.

Inside was a picnic, complete with plates, knives, forks and glasses.

There were rolls of smoked salmon stuffed with succulent-looking prawns in some sort of cream. There was cold grouse with redcurrant jelly, and a pasta salad with mushrooms, bacon and skinned segments of tomato, spring onions and lots of parsley in a red wine sauce. There were brown bread and walnut rolls, with pats of unsalted butter. There was a Stilton cheese that looked perfectly mature, accompanied by the Prince of Wales's Duchy oatmeal biscuits. And there was a small bowl of trifle for pudding.

'You serve whilst I look after the wine,' said Charles, taking out a bottle of Krug champagne wrapped in an insulated jacket.

'Heavens!' exclaimed Olivia.

'We don't have to drive so we can enjoy ourselves.'

'Who did all this?' she asked, carefully arranging rolls of smoked salmon on two plates, placing the ready-cut segments of lemon beside them while he undid the wire from around the champagne cork.

'Oh, a little firm I know. The days are gone when you could dine in luxury in a restaurant car. Can you hold the glasses?' He twisted the bottle while holding on to the cork, there was a subdued 'pop' and a tiny drift of spray came out of the neck. Then he swiftly filled the two glasses, allowing the fizz to subside before topping them up.

'It's all marvellous,' sighed Olivia happily, handing him one.

He held up his glass. 'Here's to us.'

The food was some of the best Olivia had ever tasted. Was it because of the occasion? Or because of the champagne?

She tried to control a rising feeling of anticipation. 'Tell me about your trip to America,' she suggested.

Charles made a small face as though this was a totally boring subject but as the train rattled along at an ever-increasing pace, he made Olivia laugh with his descriptions of the hustle and bustle of meetings in Chicago and New York that seemed to consist mostly of missing documents and unimportant interruptions. 'We had breakfast meetings and morning meetings, lunchtime meetings and afternoon meetings, meetings over dinner and meetings after dinner. The food was lousy, their mobile telephones never stopped ringing, and I reckoned we could have got the whole thing organised in half the time with no indigestion at all.' He helped himself to more grouse. 'How did the Americans ever get a reputation for efficiency?'

'What was it all about?' asked Olivia curiously.

He reached down for more champagne. 'We won't talk about that now. Hold out your glass.'

There was something about picnicking, decided Olivia, feeling the sway and rattle of the train, something that was definitely aphrodisiacal. Perhaps it was all the constant shifting of one's body that was required. She caught the gleam of Charles's eye and knew he felt the same.

They were both holding on to anticipation but Olivia was suddenly frightened. What if fulfilment didn't bring the rapture it had promised? Why, oh why, hadn't Charles cast aside all his stupid reservations and made love to her on that sunny slope of the Downs? Or why hadn't she followed Clodagh's advice and cast herself at him, then perhaps they could be relaxed together.

Instead tension grew tighter and tighter. As she started to pack the dirty plates and left-over food back inside the wicker basket, Olivia realised her hands were trembling. Charles poured out the last of the champagne and she saw that his hand, too, was not quite steady.

It was something of a shock to realise that he was as nervous as she.

The basket was repacked, refastened, and stood on the floor.

'I'm sorry,' Charles said, his voice not quite under control. 'I forgot, there should have been a thermos of coffee in there somewhere. And a small bottle of liqueur brandy.

'I think all I need is this last bit of champagne,' Olivia said unsteadily. Over his shoulder she could see lights rushing past the train window. They seemed to underline her vulnerability. All those people out there, safe in their homes, perhaps preparing for bed in their comfortable, accustomed rooms. Whilst she and Charles were whizzing along suspended on two thin rails, cut off from everything that was familiar.

Suddenly that very fact gave her strength and released her from all constraints. It was like being reborn.

'Why don't we draw the blind down?' she suggested.

Without a word Charles turned and pulled at the cord, blanking out the world that was rushing past them. No, that wasn't right, it was they who were rushing past the world. Hurrying on their journey – to what?

'I didn't think . . . I wasn't sure . . .' he said, his voice hesitant, vibrating. 'I thought we'd wait, until we reached the South, had found a hotel. But, God, Olivia, I don't think I can . . .'

His shoulders even without the jacket were very broad in the small *wagon lit*. His square, open face had an expression that sent the blood racing through her body. Olivia sat on the narrow bunk and felt something inside her swell and offer itself, like a flower caught by a slow action camera, its growth speeded up so that petals unfolded at the pace of a ballet until all was open. It was a long-forgotten sensation.

Charles leaned across and drew her to him. His breathing was fast and ragged. 'Oh, Olivia,' he murmured. He said something else but it was crushed between the meeting of their mouths.

It was the light that woke Olivia. It insinuated itself round the blind with a clarity that was irresistible.

Carefully she disentangled herself from Charles's arms, wondering how they could have managed to spend the night together in such a narrow space without one of them ending up on the floor, and sent the blind rolling up from the window. She sat staring entranced at the landscape that flashed past. It was so different, so dry yet with so much green, with those pine trees like umbrellas, those thick, shrubby bushes. It was so rocky, so untamed. And the light! Nothing could hide in that light, it cut through the air as though humidity had never been heard of. It reminded her of the dry, harsh light of California. But here there was more colour, more depth. And more history. The Romans had been here, and, before them, the Greeks. California was too new, scratch its surface and all you found was dirt. Here there were surely layers and layers of time and experience to be peeled back.

Behind her Charles woke, stirred, then pulled himself up. He slipped his arms around her waist and nestled his chin in the hollow of her shoulder, sharing her view of the world that was unfolding outside their window.

'Happy?' he asked.

Happy was too small a word for what Olivia felt. It was as though a whole new life was out there just waiting for her. The sun cut through the window and it was as though it lit parts she had guarded too carefully for too many years. And she didn't care. She was willing to open herself to whatever lay ahead of them for the next nine days.

Chapter Ten

At Nice station Charles reclaimed his car. They put their bags back in the boot and then found their way out of the big city.

'We need breakfast but let's get away from here first,' said Charles.

'Where are we going?' asked Olivia, not really caring, content to turn her face up to the sun and that incredible light.

'Into the hills, I think. Not very far, we don't want to spend all day in the car.' Stopped at traffic lights, Charles fished out a map of the Côte d'Azur. 'You any good at navigating?' he asked.

'Not bad,' said Olivia, studying his face and making no move to open out the map.

'What's wrong, have I got a smut on my nose? I did the best I could with that tiny basin.'

'You look perfect,' Olivia reassured him. 'Only, different somehow.'

'Different? How different?' The lights went green and he pulled away in the wake of the car in front.

'That's what I'm trying to work out.'

He flashed her a broad smile and reached for her hand. 'I'm happy, that's what it is.' Then had to drop her hand to change gear.

'Right,' agreed Olivia, privately coming to the conclusion that she had never seen Charles look so relaxed, or so confident. Not even on that Saturday on the Sussex Downs. There was a new tilt to his head, he held his shoulders a little straighter, and the wide mouth wasn't tucked away quite so tidily. She decided it suited him, gave him a look of authority that compensated for the sandy hair and freckled face.

They drove along the *Promenade des Anglais*, that remnant of a leisured age when English society adopted the Côte d'Azur as its playground. Now it was packed with traffic and modern buildings had been slotted in between the rococo elegance of fin de siècle constructions. There was the Negresco with its big pink dome, still oozing luxury, still redolent of that earlier time when to live elegantly required not only money but a great many people to look after your clothes, your hair, your food, all your comforts.

'Wish we were staying there?' asked Charles in amusement. 'You can if you like?'

Olivia stopped looking over her shoulder at the last of the hotel.

'Certainly not! I'd hate to be somewhere that large. I'm hoping we're going to a small place where we can be people, not cogs in one of your wheels.'

'Right,' agreed Charles, 'what we do not need is crowds. This is going to be a time just for us.' He reached out for Olivia's hand and placed it firmly on his upper thigh.

For the next few days it was indeed a time just for them. Charles took Olivia up into the hills above Grasse, to one of the perched villages, its bleached stone houses blending in with the rock on which they were built, so much a part of their landscape they seemed to have grown there.

They stayed in a small hotel. Their room had an eagle's eye view of dark forests and sparkling rivers. Olivia found herself leaving a sleeping Charles to sit by the window and gaze at the scenery, awed by its beauty, content to take in the tiny speck of a hovering hawk, the sounds of country life going about its early-morning business, and watch the light gain in intensity.

After leisurely breakfasts, Charles and Olivia explored, visiting other villages perched on other hills, lunching on picnics garnered from various *charcuteries* and eaten beside gorges of incredible magnificence. In the evening they enjoyed meals that displayed a typical French flair for food and went to bed somnolent – but not too somnolent.

Olivia had forgotten just what fun sex could be. Charles was considerate but exuberant. She lost years of inhibitions in a single night. 'Heavens, what I've been missing all this time!' she said on their second night together, now totally relaxed with him.

He grinned at her. 'Me too. Where have we been all each other's lives?'

She lifted her head from his chest, twisting and supporting herself on her elbow so she could look down at him. 'Are you trying to tell me you haven't been having affair after affair ever since your divorce?'

He tangled his hand in the long hair that hung down her back. 'Nary a one.'

'Not even *one*!'

He frowned, his sandy eyebrows drawing together. 'Actually, I lie. Just after the divorce I allowed myself to be seduced by a girl who sold office copiers.'

Olivia laughed, lowering her head so her hair swung forward and covered his face.

The third day they left the hills and came down to Antibes for a look at life on the Côte d'Azur itself. They stayed in an old-fashioned hotel on the front and explored the old town. It was quite different from the wild countryside they'd enjoyed up to now but Olivia found herself enchanted with the narrow streets that offered mouth-watering shopping, the restaurants that spilled out on to pavements and squares, the marina with its huge yachts that represented enough capital to float a small country, and the promenade along the front. She and Charles had fun watching the men playing boules, the middle-aged and elderly women walking their little dogs, the sailing boats that bobbed about in the bay. They walked round the Cap to Juan-les Pins, admiring the glimpses they caught of wealthy villas and looking at the private beaches, where there were still people enjoying the warm sun on brightly canvassed loungers under matching umbrellas. Juan was smaller, more touristy than Antibes, and already it had a look that said the season was nearly over. Many shops had Sale notices, some of them were already closed.

Charles and Olivia found a café and ordered icecreams. 'Where would you like to go next?' he asked, digging deep into a chocolate and vanilla sundae with white chocolate sauce. 'Do you want to explore Cannes or do you think we've done the gilded coast bit?'

'Oh, yes, let's go inland again, where we can get away from people,' said Olivia, relishing her vanilla icecream with butterscotch sauce. She felt supremely content. Being with Charles was wonderful. He was so easy to talk to, such fun to share things with. And being down here in the South of France was bliss. Even in October the sun was as warm as an English summer. The restaurants were amazing and there were so many interesting sights. The contrast between the crowded coast and the still unspoilt scenery up in the hills was extraordinary.

Best of all, Olivia felt, she had got away from work and from family problems. The infuriating Gavin and how she could continue to cope with him, the tensions between her and her mother, her worries about Tilly and her future, all had receded. It was as though crossing the channel had enabled her to place them in a better perspective.

And what a relief to be able to forget for a few days the awful reality of the new washing machine, the worrisome total of the telephone bill, the ongoing battle of how to make sure Tilly had everything she needed, and how Olivia herself could dress like an executive on a budget most secretaries would consider derisory.

Being taken around as though money presented no problems was dangerously seductive. Charles seemed to choose where they'd stay and which restaurant they'd eat at as though cost was the least of his concerns. It was such a joy to be able to order exactly what one wanted from a menu without worrying about its price and to sample wines one had only read about.

Yes, Charles made everything so easy.

That night they dined in a restaurant on the ramparts of Antibes, where the windows looked out on to the sea. There was a wind blowing and little white caps laced the waves that angled themselves into a relentlessly rhythmic dive towards the shore.

After they'd ordered, Charles said, 'You know,' then he hesitated. He pushed his set of wine glasses out of their neat line. Olivia waited.

'You know,' he began again, squinting at her, his face unusually guarded, 'you haven't told me anything about your husband.'

'No,' responded Olivia slowly, 'I haven't, have I?'

'But, then, I haven't told you much about Veronica. We've both acted as though our first marriages hardly existed.'

Charles fiddled again with his wine glasses. 'It's different for you, your marriage must be something you look back on with nostalgia and sadness. If it weren't for Phyllida, I'd say I wish I'd never met Veronica.' He reached over and took Olivia's hand. 'What I feel for you has no connection with anything else. It's not that I want to exclude you from my past, more that I'd like us to concentrate on the present. What do you feel?'

Something had closed in Charles's face and Olivia wondered just what Veronica had done to him. She did want to know about his first marriage. Divorce wasn't as final as death. As long as the person with whom you'd shared so much still lived, surely parts of your relationship did too?

But did death really end a relationship? Even as she asked herself the question, Olivia realised she didn't want memories of her life with Peter to complicate her time with Charles. She owed it to him to treat this holiday as something apart.

So she said, 'Why don't we both forget about the past?' then immediately felt an enormous sense of relief.

Chapter Eleven

The following day they packed up their bags and drove once again away from the coast, up into Grasse. But they decided the famous perfumery centre was too big to stay in.

'I'd like to find somewhere small, like that hill village we spent our first nights in,' said Olivia. 'But not too far away, I'd love to tour one of the factories and see how scent is made.'

Just below Grasse, off the main road, they found a tiny town with narrow streets tumbling down a hill, the buildings festooned with flower baskets. They parked the car and wandered through the streets, finally ending up in a small square. Tables spilled over the pavements and they stopped for a late lunch, ordering *salade niçoise* because Olivia wanted to save herself for dinner and Charles was fascinated by the number of variations restaurants made with ingredients.

They sat on after they'd eaten, drinking strong, aromatic coffee and watching the locals buying their bread from the *boulangerie*, walking through the square intent on their business or sitting around like them, drinking. Olivia compared the scene to Surbiton. There all was hustle and bustle and bad temper. People elbowed each other out of the way, rushed to get everything as quickly as possible so they could move on to the next area of stress. This place exuded a sense of quiet purpose, of being at peace with itself.

Look,' said Charles. 'That's a hotel over there.' The building had the same medieval look as the rest of the place, its grey solidity lightened by gaily coloured geraniums. Olivia could imagine carriages down the centuries drawing up in front of the heavy door.

'Shall we see if they've got a room?' Charles waved to attract the attention of the waiter.

'Oh, yes, please!' Olivia loved the thought of staying there. She followed him across the square.

Yes, there was a room, one with a huge bed and an *en suite* bathroom, decorated in best French flock style. The hotel didn't have a restaurant but they were assured there were any number of excellent places to eat round about.

They decided to stay there for the last few days of their holiday.

The area was delightful, offering small towns with picturesque streets and scenic countryside. They found narrow roads that led them away from the more populated areas and up into hills covered in farmland with grazing cattle, groves of olive trees and fields that in springtime would be heady with the scent of violets.

Two days before their departure, Charles and Olivia drove up one of these small roads, parked the car and walked along a well-worn path over springy turf that brought back memories of the Sussex Downs. They were high enough to see over the tops of hills to the Mediterranean. The blues of the sky and the sea were hazy, like the green of the trees and the surrounding countryside. But the sun was warm on their backs and Olivia was glad she'd put short-sleeved shirts in her bag. No need for even a cardigan today.

They scrambled down a bank and on to another path, then came to a metalled lane. 'Shall we go back?' suggested Olivia. 'We're getting quite a long way from the car.'

She got no response from Charles. He'd climbed up the bank again and was craning his head, trying to see over a high laurel hedge.

Olivia climbed up beside him.

'Look,' he said, waving a hand in the air in front of him, 'isn't that perfect?'

Olivia looked. Over the hedge, through a tangle of trees and hanging vines, she could make out a crumbling stone property with long green shutters closed over windows, their paintwork peeling and faded. There was a small tower at one end of the property, roofed, like the rest of the house, in slate with the odd one missing. The place looked deserted.

'Do you think Sleeping Beauty is inside, waiting for her prince?' Olivia clutched at Charles's arm as her feet slipped on the steep bank.

'That's it!' he exclaimed. 'It looks as though it's been sleeping here for years, waiting for someone to come along and bring it back to life.'

Olivia hung on to his arm, trying to regain her footing. 'Another few years and it will be too late!'

Charles gave a brief sigh. 'Well, we'd better find our way back. Poor darling, you're almost slipping down into the road.' He grabbed Olivia's hand and pulled her up the slope. Hand in hand they walked back to the car, Charles giving one last look at the old house before it was completely hidden by trees.

They returned to the square in front of their hotel for a light lunch.

Later they wandered around the small town, Olivia fascinated by the local shops and the old doorways with brass knockers, many in the shape of hands. Then she went into a shop offering souvenirs. It was time to think of something to take back to Tilly. She looked at large, soft zipped bags made from attractive Provençal prints and thought they were just the sort of thing her daughter would appreciate. Perhaps Charles might like to take one back to Phyllida as well? She looked round for him but he had disappeared.

She went out into the narrow street and saw him transfixed in front of an estate agent's window which displayed numerous photographs of properties for sale accompanied by the briefest of descriptions.

'Look,' he breathed as Olivia slipped a hand through his arm. 'Look at that!'

It was, it had to be, the house that had caught his interest that morning. In the photograph the shutters were shown open and the house managed to suggest it was in rather better condition than when they'd looked at it.

'Let's go inside,' said Charles, grabbing Olivia's hand and making for the entrance.

M. Garnier spoke reasonable English and was more than happy to tell them about the house.

When the previous owner had died some ten years ago, it had passed, as so often in the way of French property, to several family members, who had disagreed on what to do with it. Apart from odd holiday visitations from one or another of them, the property had stood unused.

At the end of last year another death had removed the most obdurate of the heirs and the remainder had finally come to an agreement that the house should be sold.

'It looks in terrible condition,' said Olivia sadly.

'*Ah, non, madame*. It looks, 'ow you say, a leetle not all there but in reality it is in fine shape. You come and see?'

'Yes,' said Charles before Olivia could venture an opinion. 'We might like to see what it looks like. Not that I'm really thinking of buying, you understand, but it seems an interesting property and, well, you never know,' he finished lamely.

'*Bien sûr*,' said M. Garnier with a broad smile on his face.

He took Charles and Olivia in his car. They went a completely different route from the one Charles had followed that morning, coming up to the property from a road lower down the hill.

There was a rusty iron gate with a chain and padlock, overhung with trees on either side. Olivia decided they were mimosa trees and thought how lovely they'd look in spring.

M. Garnier got out of the car, undid the padlock and chain, opened the iron gates, pushing them back against the long grass that encroached on the weed-filled gravel path, then got back into the car and drove in.

The gravel drive was several hundred yards long, winding in a broad curve through overgrown lawn and uninteresting shrubs. Then it swung round a large clump of trees into a courtyard and Olivia gasped.

The house was an L-shape with the tower in the corner of the L. There was a low outbuilding in very poor condition facing the long arm. The courtyard itself was paved in brick with a well in the centre. The well's stone surround was set into a number of wide steps and had a rusty iron arch that still sported a piece of equally rusty chain hanging from a cross bar. Virginia creeper, flaming an autumnal red, wound itself round the well and crept over the stonework of the house and outbuilding. It married together the warm stone of the walls, the grey slate of the roof and the terracotta of the brick courtyard, creating an air of enchantment. It really did seem as though Sleeping Beauty could be waiting for them inside the house. In one corner of the courtyard, beside the drive, was an enormous oak tree.

M. Garnier waved a hand towards it. 'The property is called *La Chênais*,' he said. He produced a large, ancient key and approached the heavy, iron-studded main door. Inside, dim light showed a sizeable, square hall. The estate agent bustled round opening windows and pushing back shutters like a theatre electrician bringing up stage lights. The dusty glass of the long, graceful windows filtered daylight into softness, gently illuminating first a black and white tiled floor, then an old chest that stood in the curve of a stone staircase and finally the narrow, elegant wrought iron balustrade that led up the stairs to a galleried landing and more darkness.

As Garnier proceeded to other rooms, Olivia and Charles slowly circled, letting their eyes adjust to the gloom, absorbing the atmosphere. Then, clutching hands, they followed their guide into the main salon.

There were cobwebs suspended between tattered curtains hanging on heavy brass poles and dust was thick on the parquet flooring. In the huge stone grate were ashes and a couple of discarded cigarette packets. M. Garnier had said that members of the family had stayed there from time to time but Olivia thought no one could have been for ages. She couldn't see how anyone could inhabit the house in its present state. There was a minimal amount of furniture. A couple of spindly couches were covered in faded and rotting silk and the walnut veneer of a sideboard and corner cupboard had dropped off leaving large bare patches as ugly as scar tissue.

There were three sizeable salons on the ground floor together with a rather smaller room that Olivia mentally tagged a study. All of them had plaster ceilings with moulded cornices. The walls in two of the rooms were decorated with graceful panels outlined with plaster curlicues. Dados ran round the walls at chairback level. All the plasterwork was damaged and incredibly dirty.

The domestic offices were on the other side of the hall, in the short arm of the L.

The kitchen seemed older than the rest of the house. It had a heavily beamed, smoke-stained ceiling studded with huge meat hooks. There was an ancient, rusty range, a scrubbed table and an old, green-painted dresser with tarnished brass handles. Off the kitchen were various larders and pantries. A pump over a deep wooden sink appeared to be the only source of water.

Charles said nothing, merely looked hard at everything. After they'd explored the back regions, picking their way through dirt and soot, he led the way to the main salon. 'Lovely proportions,' he said at last.

M. Garnier immediately went into raptures over the plasterwork and drew attention to the coat of arms carved over the fireplace.

Olivia went over to the long windows and rubbed at the glass with her hand. Then, impatient with the grime that obscured the view, she tried the catch. After an initial hesitation the bolts slid smoothly and she could push the window open and step outside.

After the shadowy interior, the sun dazzled her eyes. Then she saw she was standing on a narrow terrace that ran the length of the house and edged an expanse of shaggy grass that sloped down into an overgrown secretiveness of shrubs and trees. Over the tops of the trees could be seen grey-blue hills and, beyond them, the deep, dazzling blue of the sea.

Olivia stepped off the terrace and started walking down the slope, feeling the long grass brush against her ankles. To her left was the high laurel hedge over which they'd initially seen the house. In front of her the grass gracefully flattened out before the shrubbery. What a place for a swimming pool! The thought came unbidden and Olivia didn't develop it. Amongst the shrubs a rose bush sported a few pink blossoms. Memory flooded back, of her parents' Sussex house and childhood weekends spent playing in its then neglected garden. There'd been a rose bush just like this one, the blossoms blowsy and scented. The garden in those days had seemed an enchanted place, somewhere safe from the ordinary world.

'There you are, darling! Don't you want to come upstairs and see the bedrooms?' Charles came up beside her, slipped an arm around her shoulders and drew her against his side.

'Isn't that the most heavenly view?' Olivia asked as they went back up the slope. 'I can imagine a Greek classical villa here, or perhaps a Roman one, and some Frenchman coming along, finding a pile of ruins, deciding there couldn't be a better place for a house, and starting all over again.' They both turned and looked out towards the hills and sea.

'Yes,' said Charles. 'You'd have to go a long, long way to beat that view.'

Upstairs were half a dozen large bedrooms and no bathroom. The rooms were anonymous spaces containing little more than beds and the odd chest of drawers. Then they found a door to the tower. A spiral staircase brought them up to a small round room with windows that offered a panoramic view of all the countryside. Like children, Charles and Olivia ran from one to another, exclaiming at what they could see, identifying places they had visited, guessing at the names of others, marvelling at the extent of the view.

Then they fell quiet and looked at each other. Olivia didn't feel she could say a word. Nor, it seemed, could Charles.

Puffing slightly, M. Garnier reached the tower room.

'*C'est bien, n'est-ce-pas*, eh?' He took out a handkerchief and wiped his brow. '*La vue panoramique*.' He gestured with a flamboyant hand towards the windows. 'Do you wish to see more?'

Charles shook his head. 'You've been very kind, monsieur, we won't take up more of your time. Just one thing, how much land did you say came with the house?'

M. Garnier's eyes narrowed slightly. He opened his briefcase and whipped out a page of particulars. 'Four hectares,' he said as he handed it over to Charles.

It was late-afternoon by the time M. Garnier dropped Charles and Olivia beside the market square. Charles thanked him again for his kindness and said that if they wanted to take the matter any further, they'd call him the following day.

Nothing was said as they left the estate agent's office.

Back in their hotel room Charles said, 'I feel like going somewhere really good for dinner tonight. A chum gave me the name of a restaurant not far from here. I was going to save it for tomorrow but I think I'll see if we can get a table for tonight instead.' He fished out his electronic notebook, flashed up a name and telephone number then made the call.

'That's OK, we've got a booking. Now let's have a long soak and get rid of the dust. Nobody can have been in that house for months! Still, despite the odd slate off the roof, it did seem dry enough.'

'Charles,' said Olivia slowly, starting to undo her shirt and trousers, 'you're not really thinking of buying that place, are you?'

'Let's save talking about that until we're at dinner. Right now I reckon I should help you with that bra.' He reached out and drew her towards him and Olivia forgot about the house.

Later that evening they were sitting at a table for two in a delightful restaurant in Mougins, another small town huddled on a rock inside the remains of fifteenth-century ramparts that were approached by a bridge spanning a deep gorge. 'My friend said Roger Vergé's restaurant is the smart one to go to but that the food here is every bit as good if not better,' said Charles as the waiter handed them menus.

Olivia, feeling totally relaxed and happy, wearing black crêpe trousers and matching top with a fuchsia pink silk overshirt, chose quickly.

Charles relayed their order and asked for the white wine he'd selected to be brought to them immediately. Underneath his evident contentment with the situation, Olivia sensed something akin to the excitement he'd shown that first night, on the train.

'Come on, Charles, tell me, are you really thinking of buying that house?' Olivia took a mouthful of bread and enjoyed the contrast of the sweet crumb with the crusty exterior.

'What did you think of it?' he asked, his eyes anxious.

'What did *I* think?' Olivia repeated. She looked at him and knew that her response was important. She took a deep breath and said, 'I thought it was marvellous. The size of those rooms, and the atmosphere. And what a stunning view! But,' she went on hurriedly, 'it's in terrible condition. No running water, no proper drainage, there's damp in the kitchen and I wouldn't be at all surprised if there wasn't dry rot or wood worm in the upstairs beams. Did you see the little piles of sawdust on the floor? It would need a bomb spent on it and they're not exactly giving it away.' She'd been shocked by the price that was being asked.

'But could you live there?'

Olivia felt excitement begin to build inside her. She tried to quell it. 'Are you asking if I think you could live there?'

'No,' he said slowly, clearly. 'I mean could *you* live there? I already know I could.'

'Charles,' said Olivia faintly, 'what exactly are you saying?'

'What I'm saying,' he said, speaking rapidly and taking hold of her hand across the table in a painfully strong grasp. 'What I'm saying is that these have been the best days of my life since more years than I can remember. Will you marry me and come and live in that house?'

'But, Charles,' Olivia felt she would never be able to regain her breath, 'do you mean give up England and everything?'

He nodded, never taking his eyes off her.

'But what about your company, your new product, all those orders?' It was more than she could absorb. There must have been something she'd missed or hadn't understood.

'Ah, now, remember I said I had some news I wanted to tell you?' An exultant light came into Charles's eyes. 'Just over three weeks ago I had an offer for the firm. From an American company.'

'That's why you went to America?'

Charles nodded. 'And why I had to go up north. I had to show the company directors around and open up all the books, let their accountants go through them like bag ladies searching through dustbins.' He gave a small smile that was full of triumph. 'They reckon they drove a hard bargain but I can tell you, lass, that they're paying twice what I ever thought I'd be able to get for the company.'

'But,' Olivia was flabbergasted, 'didn't you start it and build it up? Didn't you take that exhibition stand so you could expand?'

'That company's taken nearly every thinking moment of my time for the last twenty years. And before that I slaved for someone else for five. That's long enough. Life's for living, isn't that what they say? Ever since I first came to France, I've dreamed of living here. They've such a sensible attitude to life. They enjoy the important things: good food, good wine, good company, the land. England's full of pretentious ponces who care more about style than substance. I tell you, I'm fair sick of it.

'When I saw that house today, I knew this was my chance to realise my dream. I want it, not for a *résidence secondaire*, somewhere you never have enough time to visit, but a place to settle and put down roots.' He paused and tightened his grip on Olivia's hand till she felt that the blood would be stopped from circulating. 'I can restore that place, give it life again, make it beautiful. But I know it won't mean anything if you can't share it with me.'

For a long moment Olivia looked at him and felt his gaze holding hers. The tremendous surge of excitement that had been building up inside her seemed to have flowered and dissipated itself. Now she felt detached, remote from what was happening.

'I'm in love with you,' said Charles, releasing her hand as if he didn't want to impose himself on her, didn't want to seem to be forcing her in any way. He clasped both of his hands together and sat looking down at them resting on the table.

It was the first time the word 'love' had been spoken. They'd called each other, 'darling', the word 'adore' had been used and phrases of passion, but never before had either of them said: 'I love you.'

'I love your gentleness, the way you don't feel you have to challenge everything I say but come out with funny, interesting comments that make me see things in a different way. Like thinking of people through history that could have wanted to live on that site. And I love the way your eyes light up when you laugh and that little chuckle you give sometimes. And,' his voice stumbled slightly then he continued on a firmer note. 'And I think you're the most beautiful woman I've ever met.'

Charles looked at Olivia again and there was a look in his eyes she couldn't remember seeing in anyone's before. Not even in Peter's. She saw love there and commitment and a terrible uncertainty over what her reaction was going to be.

Deep inside herself, Olivia felt frightened. She felt as though she was on a bridge like the one that had brought them to this place. The bridge was very slender and she knew that one false step would send her over the edge, down, down, down into the gorge with its terrifyingly unknown depths.

She forced herself back to the feeling of peace she had experienced in the garden that afternoon and her delight in the house: the way the rooms had folded themselves around her, the stunning view from the top of its tower. She thought of the care Charles had taken of her during the days they'd spent together down here and the fun they'd had. How the sun had constantly shone and the living had been easy without any of the strains that waited for her back in England.

Too easy, of course. They'd been on holiday, staying in hotels without any chores, nothing to pressurise them. Normal life wasn't like that, couldn't be like that, not when you had responsibilities.

'There's Tilly,' Olivia whispered.

Charles's eyes sparkled, as though that oblique answer gave him confidence. 'Of course there's Tilly,' he said, his voice warm and understanding. 'We'll help her find what it is she wants to do. Maybe she'd like to come and live with us here while she finds out what it is.'

Tilly, in France! Olivia drew in a deep breath. At least that would be an answer to her mother's concerns over her granddaughter's future. Even Daphne Ferguson would be able to see that living in France, learning the language and becoming a European, had to be an advantage.

Olivia looked at Charles, her eyes shining. 'Oh, darling, yes! I'd love to marry you and live here.'

Chapter Twelve

The moment Tilly saw her mother and Charles after they came back from France, she knew that something had happened. The announcement that they were engaged did not come as a surprise but the news that they had bought a house in France and were going to live there was something of a shock.

In odd moments, Tilly had wondered if her mother would marry Charles. They hadn't known each other long but men in her mother's life were so unusual she couldn't help thinking that he must represent something serious. She had indulged in a daydream of a life with Charles to fill the missing gap her father's death had left. Nothing could replace her memories of him but she could see Charles as someone who could love her as a daughter, advise her, and give her mother happiness.

This daydream was cloudy around the edges, Tilly never filled out the details: where they would live, whether her mother would continue to work or what she herself would be doing. The daydream exploded into nothing when she heard about the French plans.

She suspected her grandparents weren't happy with the news either. Soon after the engagement had been announced, Tilly visited them in Sussex. Her opinion of the situation was asked. Tilly said stoutly that she was delighted. 'They'll be terribly happy, Charles is wonderful and I think Mum's very lucky.'

'But what about living in France?' asked her grandmother in an exasperated tone.

'It sounds great fun. I'm longing to go and see the house, I've always wanted to go to the South of France,' Tilly asserted, knowing that to offer the slightest hint she found the idea unsettling would mean that Daphne wouldn't rest until she'd enrolled her in a campaign to sabotage the plan. After all, Tilly told herself, she'd probably have been leaving home in a year or two anyway and it was time she learned to stand on her own feet. And, yes, she was really pleased about gaining Charles as a stepfather and it was fun thinking about going out to France.

Her grandmother shot her a keen look but was apparently convinced because she said nothing more.

Charles was eager to introduce Phyllida to Olivia and Tilly. Twice he arranged dinner for them all at the Savoy. Twice he, Olivia and Tilly sat in the American Bar there waiting for her to join them. And twice she telephoned to say that she couldn't make it. The second time it happened, Charles looked so sad that Tilly had jumped up to kiss him on the cheek. 'What a shame. Never mind, we'll meet one of these days and then I'm sure we'll all get on.'

Charles brightened. 'You're right, of course, Tilly. It's this job, you see. The money markets never close, there's always somewhere in the world they're open and Phyllie has to keep on top of things.' He gave Tilly a big smile. 'You're going to have lots of fun together, you'll like having an older sister.'

Tilly couldn't share his confidence. The more she heard about Phyllida Frome, the more frightening she sounded. Beautiful, bright and high-powered, all the things Tilly knew she wasn't and never would be. And obviously hating the idea of her father marrying again so much she couldn't bring herself to meet her future stepmother and sister.

Apparently it was Phyllida who suggested she and Charles spend Christmas together. The happy couple had decided to get married just before the New Year. Phyllida said it was going to be the last opportunity they would have to be together, just the two of them. Charles told Olivia and Tilly this one Sunday night in December shortly after the second attempt to get them together had failed.

Tilly was very disappointed. She'd hoped they could all spend Christmas together. But Olivia said brightly, 'What a good idea, then Tilly and I can spend Christmas with my parents as usual. It's our last opportunity as well.'

It might be traditional but Tilly didn't feel it was one of their most successful Christmasses. Judy and Beth had decided to close the restaurant over the holiday and open again in the New Year, so Tilly was able to take over the cooking of the Christmas meal. Presents were opened beforehand. Olivia already wore the pearl necklace and earrings Charles had given her the night before he set off with Phyllida to the smart hotel they were staying at in Gloucestershire but there was a golden cashmere sweater for her from him under the tree. Daphne raised her eyebrows when Olivia opened the parcel but she said nothing. Tilly's parcel from Charles was a pair of knotted gold earrings plus a book on wine. She'd given him a book of cartoons on the same subject. From her grandparents she had a generous cheque and from Olivia a set of cassettes of her favourite group together with the long skirt and ribbed top she'd said she wanted. Altogether, it was a most satisfactory haul. When all the presents had been opened, Tilly cleared up the wrappings, inserted her new earrings and went off to finish the meal. She'd been really worried about the turkey but they all said what a good job she'd made of it. Somehow, though, festive gaiety had never got going.

Afterwards Tilly played a game of chess with her grandfather while Daphne and Olivia cleared up.

It was very peaceful in front of the open fire. Her grandfather opened up the antique games table and Tilly helped arrange the carved ivory chessmen at either end of the marquetry chessboard. She chose black, Thomas advanced one of his pawns and Tilly settled down to concentrating hard.

Ten minutes later Thomas captured her pawn and asked, 'When will you go to France, Tilly?'

She bit the side of her thumb and looked at the board, trying to see where her grandfather's strategy would lead him. 'I'm not sure,' she said carefully. 'The house needs a lot of work done on it and, well, I'm enjoying working in the restaurant. I do most of the cooking now, Mrs Major just supervises and tells me what I'm doing wrong.' She gave her grandfather a grin that said she had the situation well in hand and moved her bishop into play, threatening his queen.

He raised his eyebrows slightly at the move. 'Are you intending to continue living in Surbiton then?' he asked. 'On your own?'

'There's a schoolfriend who might be interested in sharing with me. Kate's working in London and her family lives much further away than we do. She's sick of living at home, anyway.'

Later, after Thomas had, with a little struggle, won the game, and Daphne and Olivia had brought in coffee and Christmas cake, he asked his daughter about the arrangement.

'I've been telling Mother,' Olivia said calmly. 'Tilly has decided that she's going to stay in Surbiton for the moment. We've had a long discussion and she knows she can come and join us at any time.'

'I've said it's ridiculous,' Daphne announced loudly, her mouth tight with disapproval. 'I can understand Tilly's not wanting to go to France, leaving us and her friends, everyone she knows, but if she's to stay in England, she should come and live here.'

'What about it, Tilly?' asked Thomas, his eyes lighting up.

Tilly put the last of the chessmen into their drawer and gave him a kiss. 'I couldn't work in the restaurant if I lived with you,' she said gently.

'You can easily get another job round here,' Daphne said firmly.

'But I like the one I've got,' Tilly insisted. 'I'll come and see you but I want to stay in Surbiton.'

Later, when they were back home, Olivia expressed reservations about the plan then asked, 'Darling, are you sure you don't mind about my marrying Charles? Because if you do . . .' She wasn't allowed to finish the sentence.

'Mum, I think marrying Charles is the most sensible thing you've done since, well, since we came back from California,' Tilly said firmly. 'I think he's really great. My only worry . . .' She hesitated.

'Yes, what is it?' asked Olivia.

'Is that I won't be able to get on with Phyllida.'

'I don't suppose you'll have much to do with her, darling,' Olivia said.

She rose and started clearing coffee mugs. 'And I'm sure when we meet her she won't be nearly as daunting as she sounds.'

Olivia and Charles were married on a cold winter's day.

Tilly had helped her mother choose a gold silk dress and jacket from Caroline Charles (Olivia had announced she was going to do Charles proud and didn't care if she used every penny she could lay her hands on). With it came a matching pill box hat with a burst of spotted veil. Olivia tilted it over one eye and said, 'It makes me look slightly wicked.'

'I think it suits you,' said Tilly. She had a new outfit, too, a long navy blue skirt topped by a navy blue and white houndstooth jacket with a nipped in waist worn with the skinny rib polo-necked sweater Olivia had given her for Christmas. Tilly thought it was incredibly smart. With it she wore Charles's earrings.

For her wedding present, Charles had given Olivia a pair of diamond earrings and she wore these with her gold outfit. She carried a small bouquet of yellow roses.

The wedding party gathered in an ante-room to the Register Office and waited to be called for the ceremony. There were the happy couple, Tilly, Daphne and Thomas Ferguson, Clodagh, Margie, Charles's best man, an old friend called David Watson with his wife, Angela, and a couple of his other friends.

Every few seconds Charles glanced first at his watch and then at the door of the ante-room. Olivia, too, seemed nervous. Tilly saw her lay a hand on Charles's arm and whisper some words into his ear. He smiled at her. 'Phyllie's just got delayed, that's all. I wonder if we can get the ceremony put back if she doesn't get here soon?'

At that moment the door opened and Phyllida entered.

She was a small girl, slender, with tiny wrists and fragile hands. She wore a very short, double-breasted scarlet coat, almost transparent stockings with a high sheen, black patent boots and bag. She made Tilly instantly feel her own outfit was dowdy and unfashionable. Phyllida's copper hair was cut like a boy's, emphasising the vulnerable quality of her bone structure; her skin was pale and finely textured. Her amber eyes had a Slavic slant, her nose a very slight bump at its middle. Somehow this minor blemish increased her attractiveness. Her mouth was small and neat. She wore the merest hint of makeup, looked exquisite and held all eyes.

Phyllida glanced briefly at the assembled company then moved swiftly towards her father, who had immediately gone forward to greet her. She twined an arm around the back of his neck, kissed him on the cheek and whispered something in his ear. Then she turned to look enquiringly at Olivia.

'This is Phyllida,' said Charles, his air of anxiety vanished into beaming joy. 'Phyllie, this is Olivia.'

The slavic eyes looked Olivia carefully up and down. 'Hi,' said Phyllida, still holding on to Charles's arm.

Tilly was proud of the warmth with which her mother kissed her soon-to-be stepdaughter. 'I'm so pleased to meet you, Phyllida. We've been looking forward to it so much. This is Tilly, I'm sure you're going to be great friends.'

Tilly's approbation of her mother vanished. How could she say anything so crass? Olivia stretched out a hand towards her and Tilly came forward reluctantly. Obviously there was no way Phyllida was going to be detached from Charles, would take even one step in her direction. Any more than there was the faintest glimmering of hope she herself would ever have any sort of relationship with this spoiled and golden figure.

Tilly summoned up a smile and held out her hand. 'Great to meet you,' she said in a small husky voice that strained for enthusiasm.

'Yah,' said Phyllida, flicking her gaze over Tilly in a dismissive fashion. 'Dad, when's this show getting on the road? I promised you I'd be here but I can't stay long.'

Charles looked dismayed and Tilly found herself hating this new stepsister. 'But you're going to eat with us afterwards, aren't you, darling?' he said anxiously. 'We're going to a wonderful restaurant. There's going to be a cake and – and everything.'

'God, not speeches?'

Olivia gave her another warm smile. 'No, Phyllida, I've put my foot down, nobody wants to listen to speeches. We're just going to have a good time. If you can stay on, we'd love you to be with us. But the important thing is that you're here to see us married.'

Tilly held her breath. Part of her wanted this poisonous girl to walk away after the ceremony. They would have much more fun without her. But another part of her knew that for Charles it would mean something very important was missing from his wedding day.

Phyllida looked from Olivia to her father. Her mouth opened, a tiny, cat-like tongue flickered for a moment, wetting her lips. She looked as though she was calculating some secret odds. But before she could speak, the registrar poked her head round the door and said they were ready for the Frome/Warboys party.

It was a lovely ceremony. There was music and the registrar sounded as though she was really enjoying her task. The large room had lovely flowers decorating the highly polished official desk and another arrangement on a pedestal. The atmosphere wasn't as solemn as in a church, it was friendly but also conscious of the importance of the occasion. The bride and groom were whole-hearted in their responses and the look they gave each other after they had been pronounced man and wife made Tilly's eyes prickle.

Afterwards Phyllida came with them to the restaurant as easily as though she'd intended to all along. They had a round table in a private room with an open fire burning in a huge grate.

101

Tilly expected Phyllida to hog all her father's attention. Instead she was beautifully behaved, chatting to David Watson, on her left (Charles was on her right), and making him laugh, leaning across her father to direct the odd remark to Olivia on his other side, just occasionally putting a small hand on her father's arm as she smiled up at him and listened to some remark of his.

'Strange, is it?' asked Margie after they'd eaten their smoked salmon and were being served with Boeuf Wellington, 'to find yourself with a stepfather – not to mention a stepsister?'

Her dark, bright eyes sparkled, as though the whole thing was a huge joke.

'It's great,' Tilly responded.

'Sure, but isn't it strange?' Margie pressed.

Tilly didn't really want to think about how strange it was. It had only just come home to her that her mother was no longer exclusively hers. That not only had she given herself to Charles but she was going to live in France. Her mother hadn't deserted her, Tilly could never feel that, but she had moved on. That was the funny feeling; it was all upside down. Tilly should have been the one moving on, her mother the one left behind.

'Yup, it's strange, but a nice strange, you know? Mum's so happy and I love Charles.' She felt rather than saw Phyllida's gaze fall on her across the table.

Margie looked at the happy couple. 'She's lucky and so's he. They should be fine. Things should work out.'

'Of course,' Tilly squawked, amazed Margie should raise even the possibility that they mightn't.

'But I'm going to miss her in the office. Gavin hasn't found anyone yet to replace her and it's going to be hell until he does.'

Later Tilly went to the ladies' cloakroom. When she came out of the loo, Phyllida was leaning over the basin, inspecting her makeup in the mirror.

'Hi,' said Tilly nervously. Her eyes met Phyllida's in the mirror.

Phyllida smoothed the almost invisible plum-coloured eyeshadow over her right eyelid with a slender finger, gave her appearance a final glance, turned round and leant against the basin, folding her arms across her chest. 'Well, it's my dear stepsister,' she said softly, expressionlessly.

Tilly said nothing. She'd made a reasonably friendly overture, now it was up to Phyllida. She envied the poise of that slender figure leaning against the basin, those slim legs emerging from the scarlet coat, and wondered for a moment if the girl was wearing anything underneath it.

'No doubt you and your mother think you've landed yourselves a soft little number in my father,' Phyllida said in a clear voice, her slanted eyes narrowed. 'Got yourselves the easy life. Don't you believe it. Dad's no pushover and I shall make sure you don't get a penny that's mine.'

Tilly's heart almost stopped. She couldn't believe what she was hearing. She'd expected jealousy, animosity perhaps, but never anything like this.

'What a pity all you can think about is money,' she said, her voice steady. 'No wonder Charles fell in love with my mother.' She swept out of the cloakroom, unable to trust herself to say anything more, betraying tears pricking at the back of her eyes. She couldn't face going back into the private room so she went outside and stood in the gloom of the winter afternoon, the cold freezing her face, the wind blowing round her ankles, the small amount of self-confidence she'd managed to build up over the last few months destroyed by Phyllida's unpleasantness.

How could anyone say those things?

Thomas Ferguson put his arm around her shoulders. 'A cake's just been produced and your mother doesn't want to cut it until you're there,' he said. 'I said I'd find you.'

'I just needed a spot of air,' Tilly said, her throat constricted.

'All right now?' he asked.

She nodded and they went back inside.

Charles and Olivia left for a honeymoon in the Seychelles. After that they went off to France.

Tilly tried to settle down once more to life in Surbiton. But it was difficult.

Mrs Major's criticisms began to make working at the restaurant depressing. Tilly told herself she didn't deserve such harshness, that she was becoming more and more competent and certainly wouldn't have been allowed to do so much cooking if she was as stupid as Mrs Major made out, but it was difficult. The effort needed to ignore what she said and concentrate on learning everything the woman could teach her became greater and greater.

Sharing with Kate wasn't as much fun as she'd thought it would be, either. Kate was working and playing hard, coming back to the house late at night or not at all. At the weekends she flopped exhaustedly or went to see her family. Tilly's other schoolfriends were either away at university, working in London, and getting back too tired to want to do much in the evenings, or unemployed. Those out of work were all too ready to come round to Tilly's and bitch about life. 'Don't know how you can stick that job,' they'd say, helping themselves to another Coke. 'It's not as though it pays you much either. Got a fag, have you?' Soon Tilly decided she'd have to tell them she couldn't afford to have them around any more.

Only Clodagh offered optimism and a sense of fun but she was deep in another book and Tilly didn't like to disturb her too much.

Olivia rang frequently, describing with enthusiasm everything that was happening at the house where, it seemed, Charles had got numerous French workmen repairing decades of neglect. She sounded blissfully happy, full of searches for authentic panelling and stonework and French furniture, the difficulties of deciding on paint and wallpaper. 'You must come out very soon,' she kept saying to Tilly.

One Sunday in mid-February Tilly went to visit Jemima in Tooting.

'Life is great,' Jemima said, pouring coffee in the small front room, one twin on her lap, the other climbing around the sofa, over and under cushions. She looked wonderful. The beads had gone from her hair. Instead it was dressed in a rich profusion of tight little plaits. Her skin glowed with health and her long body was lithe and limber.

'Duane asked you to marry him?' Tilly grasped her mug of aromatic coffee and felt tired and washed out beside her.

'Nah!' The voice was full of scorn. 'That layabout son-of-a-bitch faded out of the picture a long time ago. Soon as I wasn't around evenings to fill his stomach, he took off. But not before he tried to make up to Mum instead!'

'Jemima, he didn't!'

Her eyes sparkled. 'That man was only interested in one thing and it wasn't sex either. All he wanted was food, food and more food.'

'Oh, Jemima, I'm so sorry, I thought you were happy with him.'

'Listen, Tilly, it was the best thing for me. Now I can concentrate on my girls and my career. I don't need a man, they're just a nuisance.' Jemima dunked a cookie in her coffee and fed it to the twin on her lap. Then dunked another one for the other twin. Nothing about her suggested she was missing the delinquent Duane.

'So how's the restaurant going?'

'Opens in two weeks' time,' said Jemima proudly. 'You must come along.'

'Don't be silly, I couldn't afford it. Anyway, I'd hate to go on my own.'

'No boyfriend? You're not still pining after that Mark fella?'

'Good heavens, no! I'm like you, I don't need men,' Tilly said valiantly, trying not to think of how happy her mother had looked as she'd set off with Charles after their wedding.

Jemima didn't look convinced. 'Well, why don't you come along one evening and have a look behind the scenes? Might get you interested in going for the big time, not wasting your talents in that itty-bitty café.'

'You didn't call it that when you worked there,' retorted Tilly.

Jemima put down her daughter from her lap. 'Go play with your bricks, Noleen. Both of you, show me how high you can build them.' Then she leaned forward. 'What do you want to do, Tilly? You want to mess around in places that are never going to go anywhere, or do you want to make a career for yourself?' Her dark eyes were serious for once and Tilly felt panic-stricken. Where she'd been able to fend off her grandmother and her mother, somehow Jemima's questioning her was different.

'You've got talent, you know that?' Jemima continued earnestly. 'You want to, you can make it.'

Did she want a career in cooking? To be a proper chef like Jemima? That would mean apprenticing herself to a major kitchen or enrolling at a catering college. It would be a big commitment. The prospect was scary and Tilly wasn't sure she'd be up to it.

'You'd hire me, would you?' she said as a joke.

But Jemima put her head on one side and looked at her. 'You need a job, girl, you come to me. At the moment I ain't got no openings. But if you're interested – and prepared to work your butt off – you let me know.'

That made Tilly feel even more panic-stricken. She wasn't ready yet to make decisions about her future. As long as she was working in the restaurant, she felt her life had some sort of purpose. She didn't want to think beyond that. Not yet.

A few days after that, the telephone rang one evening and it was Rory Wilde. 'I wondered if you might like to come to the opening of Jemima's restaurant?' he said, his voice bright and breezy.

Tilly was stunned. She'd mentally written Rory out of her life. Not that he had ever really been in it. And she still smarted at the way he'd laughed at her, still felt angry at how he'd wheedled all those details about Jemima and her cooking out of her, all the while making her feel he was actually interested in her. His perfidy was somehow connected in her mind with the way Mark had betrayed her.

'No thanks,' she said baldly.

'Oh, do come,' he pleaded, his voice warm and conciliatory. 'I'm making up a table, we want some young people in the restaurant. There'll be several of us.'

Tilly wavered for a moment. She badly wanted to see what Jemima's restaurant was like and to be there on the first night would be really special.

'Jemima suggested I ask you,' Rory's voice continued. 'She'd love it if you were there.'

Well, that at least told Tilly exactly where she stood as far as Rory was concerned. It meant she didn't have to worry about his trying to get her to forgive his unbelievably awful behaviour.

'OK,' she said grudgingly.

'Great!' He sounded really pleased. 'I'll pick you up at seven on Thursday, just give me your address.'

Tilly told Kate and asked her what she should wear.

'Fantastic!' Kate said. 'You'll need something really snazzy. Not your usual Laura Ashley stuff.'

She looked through Tilly's small wardrobe and shook her head. 'Nothing's really right. Can't you get something new?'

Tilly shook her head. She couldn't afford it. And she wouldn't feel comfortable in the short shift dress Kate was saying would be just right. She liked long skirts and blouses with sleeves. It was all right when you were reed thin like Kate, not when you were big like her.

She rang Jemima. 'Anything goes, girl, the more outrageous the better!'

105

she laughed. 'Tremendous you're coming, need all the moral support I can get. Marsha will be there too.'

'That's wonderful!' Tilly felt better about the evening. 'On our table?'

'Don't know about that. It's Rory who's organising all that side. That boy's a little wonder when it comes to marketing and promotion. The opening night is all his responsibility.'

That made it sound as though he'd be really busy. Tilly wondered how he could find the time to come all the way out to Surbiton and pick her up. The question was answered when a hired car arrived at seven o'clock on the Thursday.

In the end she'd decided to wear a pair of navy culottes that came almost to her ankles, a matching, fringed waistcoat and a white silk blouse with a drooping collar that she'd bought with some of her Christmas money. It wasn't outrageous but it had a certain style.

For ten minutes or so Tilly had the car to herself, then it stopped at a house in Richmond and out came a girl in her early-twenties, wearing the sort of dress Kate had said was just the thing, a mini-shift in some shiny material. It showed off legs that went on forever before finishing in high-heeled strappy sandals. Over the dress she wore a scarlet suede bomber jacket, brightly studded. Her short platinum blonde hair stuck up in spikes and looked as though it had been cut with blunt garden shears. As she got in the car, Tilly saw a flash of pale makeup, dark-fringed eyes and bright red lipstick.

'Hi,' drawled the blonde. 'You one of the young lot Rory's rounded up?'

'Well, yes, I suppose I am. I'm Tilly, Tilly Warboys.'

'Yah, right! Maddy Harman.' With that she fell silent. Tilly was relieved when the car pulled up outside a restaurant in Battersea with a vinyl blind that read: *Frère Marcus*.

Inside Rory greeted them with enthusiasm, smacking a big kiss on Maddy's cheek but just saying hello to Tilly. He did look pleased to see her, though.

The restaurant decor was simplicity itself: white walls, black bentwood chairs, round tables covered in long white tablecloths. The only decoration was a set of fabulous colour photographs of Martinique scenes on the walls and black vases with orange marigold-like flowers on the tables. The tables themselves were set with plain white octagonal plates with a beaded edge, modern stainless steel cutlery and white napkins. The huge menu cards were plain white also with the name in bold black lettering. Tilly thought the effect was incredibly restrained and chic.

The decor might have been restrained, the company was not.

Rory took the two girls over to a table for eight where three young men and two other girls were already sitting. All the chaps were wearing suits with outsize jackets. Rory's was a very pale grey and with it he was wearing a black shirt with a buttoned down collar and a white tie. One of the girls had on a shift dress, like Maddy's, but in electric blue with a matching jacket. The other was in tiny black velvet shorts and a huge white shirt with drop sleeves. Tilly felt totally unsuitably dressed.

Rory made introductions but she couldn't catch any of the names, the restaurant was full and everybody was making so much noise. Then, over the other side, she saw Marsha, looking terrific in a very short black, sequined dress with a black overshirt. She was with another exuberant party of people of mixed ages and colour. Tilly went across. 'Jemima's so pleased you're here this evening,' Marsha said after she'd kissed her on both cheeks. 'That girl is so uptight about it all you wouldn't believe.'

There was the sound of champagne corks popping and a cheer went up from Tilly's table. Rory appeared at her elbow and took her back to her seat. 'We want to start taking orders,' he said.

Tilly wasn't sitting next to him, he was between Maddy and the girl in the shorts. Tilly managed to sort out that David was on her right and Dexter on her left. They were in advertising, Dexter told her. And they'd been at school with Rory, said David, flinging a bread roll across the table at him.

'Behave yourself, guys, unless you never want a *Frère* meal again.'

The waiters and waitresses were dressed in white shirts and black waistcoats with tight black trousers over which were tied small grey aprons with large pockets. They were all young and good-looking.

'Hi, I'm Sally,' said the girl who came to their table. 'Have you decided what you'd like to eat yet or would you like a little longer?'

'Tell us something about the food, Sally,' suggested Rory, giving her a great smile, his wide mouth splitting his face apart.

The waitress gave him a smile back, smoothed her wild dark hair, took a deep breath and said, 'The food at *Frère Marcus* comes from the beautiful island of Martinique.' She gestured to one of the photographs on the wall behind Rory's head, a stunning view of blue sea crashing on rocks under a blazing sun. 'The influences are French and Malay, and the food uses subtle spices. Now, for this evening, can I recommend sea bass with lemon grass and fresh ginger or entrecôte Martinique with its blend of peppers.'

The food was indeed fabulous, layers of flavour yielding a complex taste experience. With her first taste of a curried coconut milk soup, Tilly started to enjoy herself. David and Dexter were boisterous but friendly. They were fascinated to know more about the restaurant she worked in, declared they'd come down to Surrey and try it out, and spent most of their time teasing all the girls, who seemed to have a whole vocabulary of shrieks.

Halfway through the meal a photographer appeared and started taking shots of all the tables. 'If nothing else, we'll get one in the local rag,' Rory said.

'You promised *Tatler*!' complained Maddy with a pout. 'That's the only reason I came!'

'Could be, darling, could be, if you look beautiful enough. There, give a great big smile for the man.'

Maddy licked her lips, leaned towards Rory, looked straight at the

107

camera and murmured 'lesbian' just before the flash went off. 'Does fabulous things for the lips,' she tossed off at a startled-looking Tilly. 'Much better than "cheese".'

All the time Tilly couldn't help wondering how Jemima was faring in the kitchen. She looked round the restaurant, full of happily talking and eating diners, and was relieved to see that everyone seemed to be enjoying themselves. But if it was free, they would, wouldn't they?

'The "buzz" level rating is very satisfactory,' said Rory, leaning across to her.

'What?'

'The "buzz" level. It's what I use as a measure of success. A quiet restaurant is an unsuccessful restaurant, at least so far as the *Frère* chain is concerned.'

'Are your parents here?'

He nodded. 'Over at that table.'

Tilly saw a quietly mannered man of about fifty with thin grey hair sitting with a comfortable-looking woman of about the same age and an older couple. Tilly noticed how Mr Wilde's eyes never ceased scanning every aspect of the restaurant: the waiters, the food that was being carried to other tables, the way wine was poured and orders taken. 'Does he ever just enjoy his meal?' she whispered to Rory, though there was no way her voice could have carried to the other table.

'Never!' he said, almost proudly. 'The business is his life, he couldn't live without it.'

By the time coffee arrived, the restaurant had settled slightly and the excited chatter had fallen to a contented hum. David and Dexter were competing to see how many bread pellets they could lob into the cleavage of the girl sitting across the table and Maddy had forgotten about looking bored.

Rory got up and came round behind Tilly's chair. 'Would you like to pay Jemima a visit in the kitchens?' he asked her.

'Oh, I'd love to. Do you think she'd mind?'

'On the contrary, about now's the time she'll be looking to hear how things have gone. You ready with your compliments?'

'You bet!' Tilly got up and followed him to the back of the restaurant and through a pair of black swing doors with porthole windows.

The atmosphere in the kitchens was hot and steamy and had the air of a typhoon area just after the worst of the storm had passed. Except that all was orderly. There were four white-coated chefs with wild eyes and exhausted faces still organising plates of food as waiters swung through one door with trays of dirty crockery, and swung out the other with a freshly loaded tray. In the centre of it all was the tall figure of Jemima, eyes ceaselessly checking everything in her little kingdom while her deft fingers arranged a dessert plate. A coffee and cumin parfait was topped with a large disc of almond pastry dusted with cocoa powder and surrounded by a sea of vanilla custard studded with spots of melted chocolate that Jemima

108

was drawing out into decorative commas. Gradually everyone in the kitchen stopped to watch her.

With easy rapidity she drew out the last little comma, lifted the plate and gave it to a waiter, who whisked it out with another couple. 'The last dessert!' She gave them all a triumphant smile. 'We did it!' She raised her hands above her plaited hair and shook them in a boxer's salute. 'We did it!'

The exhausted faces around her broke into smiles and someone gave a small cheer. 'Thank you, everyone,' she said. 'You gave me everything I asked for and more.' Then Rory stepped forward and kissed Jemima before turning to them all and saying, '*Mes hommages*. It was brilliant.'

Tilly remained just inside the swing doors and watched the broad smile that lit Jemima's face, the exhilaration that lifted the tired brigade, all young people, none of them more than in their mid-twenties. One of them clapped his neighbour on the shoulder; a girl ran fingers through her hair, easing it back from a face that glistened with sweat and was naked of makeup.

'It was really good?' Jemima asked Rory, still grinning widely.

He answered her grin with his own. 'Sublime. Everyone's having a marvellous time and saying how wonderful the food is. Time for you to come and table walk.'

'Ooof, let me get into clean whites first.' Then she saw Tilly standing by the door and swooped down on her. 'Fantastic to see you, girl! You had a good time? Enjoyed the food?'

Tilly kissed her a little shyly. This triumphant amazon wasn't the girl she had worked with and visited in Tooting. She tried to tell Jemima how good she thought the food had been. Rory went round the brigade, congratulating each member. There was a powerful air of excitement in the kitchen as Jemima gave them a stern reminder about clearing up their stations and turning up on time the following day. 'Remember, girls and boys, the punters will be paying then.' She turned back to Tilly, 'Must go and get ready to face the audience now. See you later, girl. I'm so glad you came!' she ended on a squeak of exhilaration.

Tilly went back to the table. Rory started walking behind her but stopped to table hop, talking with first one group and then another. He was as excited as Jemima, she could tell, no trace of the sad clown about him at the moment. This was a man surging with adrenaline, high on the success of the restaurant and the evening.

She sat in her chair and could feel the electricity that was running high in Rory and Jemima. Half of her was still back in the kitchen with its atmosphere of exhaustion and elation. What a thing to be part of all that!

She tried to explain it to Clodagh the next evening. 'There was such . . . I suppose "camaraderie" is the only word I can think of. They were all so excited and, I don't know, it was as if something just fizzed between them all. And it was all due to Jemima.'

'She'd made them into a team, you mean?' That was one of the nice things about Clodagh, she always seemed to understand what you were trying to say.

Clodagh poured some more coffee into their mugs. She had made a pasta supper for them both and now they were relaxing before watching the ten o'clock news on television.

Tilly nodded. 'It was much more than just cooking.'

'And you think that's what you'd like to do?'

'Me? I couldn't run a restaurant!'

'I don't see why not,' Clodagh said in a very matter-of-fact way. She sat back in her chair and crossed one jeans-clad leg over the other. She was wearing one of the ornate knitted sweaters she favoured and her hair for once was brushed back and tied with a black velvet fastener. 'Aren't you doing most of the cooking in that café you work in?'

'But that's nothing compared with what Jemima does, and I don't have to do any of the ordering or checking supplies or costings or . . . well, any of the other things you have to do to run a restaurant.'

'Yes, I can see it's all more than just cooking but that's something you could learn. I suppose even Escoffier started as a lowly kitchen boy somewhere and he finished up running the cuisine at the Ritz.'

'And the other thing is you have to create recipes, make up your own dishes, you can't just copy other people's.'

'Ah, yes. Don't you think you could do that? I mean, isn't it a matter of just using your imagination? I didn't follow a recipe tonight, just chucked things together, and I thought it came out rather well.' Clodagh had served a smoked salmon, basil and *crème fraîche* sauce with tagliatelle.

'It was delicious,' Tilly assured her. 'And you really didn't find it in a book?'

Clodagh shook her head. 'After you've been cooking for a bit, you just get a feel for what will go with what. You're not always right, I have to say, and sometimes you realise a few changes could improve the dish, but the basic bones are often there.'

'I think you're terribly clever, I don't think I could do that.'

'You think about it,' Clodagh picked up the cafetière. 'More coffee?'

The more Tilly thought about her future, the more depressed she became about it. Yes, she enjoyed working in the restaurant but she was sure she didn't have what it took to become a proper chef like Jemima.

Yet the memory of that first-night meal at *Frère Marcus* resonated like a bell constantly calling a congregation to church. Time and again Tilly remembered Jemima's progress round the restaurant in brand new whites with her name embroidered over the breast pocket, exchanging a few words with each table, obviously receiving more compliments in one night than she had probably had in her life before. Everybody had wanted to congratulate her. Even Mr Wilde had stood up when she came to his table and shaken

110

her hand. She had ended up sitting at Rory's table, between Tilly and Dexter, not saying much but drinking a malt whisky and allowing herself to wind down a little. Marsha had come over and joined them as well.

It really had been a wonderful evening. The same car that had driven Tilly and Maddy to the restaurant came for them just after midnight. 'I'm sorry I can't drive you back,' Rory said. 'I've drunk far too much and daren't touch a car. We're all going home by taxi.'

Tilly had wondered about that. Rory hadn't seemed a particularly sensible young man at the table; he'd been as lighthearted as any of them, telling silly jokes and teasing Tilly about her serious attitude to the food. Perhaps it was just an excuse not to have to drive her? Then she thought he hardly needed an excuse, it wasn't as if he'd pretended she was going to be his date. And she wouldn't have come if he had, she reminded herself.

No, it wasn't Rory himself that she kept remembering, it was the whole ambience of the restaurant.

Tilly's depression wasn't helped by the level of business at Judy and Beth's place. By the end of February they were still only doing a quarter of what they'd been used to when Jemima had been with them. Tilly suggested to Mrs Major that they go back to some of Jemima's dishes, she knew exactly how they should be done, but Mrs Major wouldn't hear of it. 'Foreign food!' she barked. 'Don't you know traditional British is the "in" thing these days?'

Not the way Mrs Major produced it. Her latest innovation had been roast beef and Yorkshire pudding, with the pre-roasted, overcooked slices reheated in the microwave then served with soggy individual puddings.

Olivia's regular telephone calls only increased Tilly's sense of disorientation. She had a firm sense that the new marriage should not be invaded by others.

Then early in March Tilly had her eighteenth birthday and her mother and Charles flew back for it. She was taken out with her grandparents to a wonderful meal at The Waterside Inn at Bray. 'Do come out,' her mother kept on saying during it. 'The house is beginning to look wonderful, you'll love it. And Charles wonders if he's offended you in some way. Come for Easter, he's trying to get Phyllida to come out as well. It would be such fun to get all the family together.'

To visit France with her stepsister on the face of it bore all the attractions of a holiday spent with Hitler's SS. But the notion that Phyllida might see the house and experience life in the South of France before *she* could was insupportable.

Towards the middle of March, Judy and Beth decided they couldn't afford to employ Tilly any longer. 'If business picks up after Easter, perhaps we may be able to take you on again,' Judy said briskly one Saturday afternoon. Beth was silent.

To Tilly the news came as a relief. At last a decision had been taken out of her hands.

A week later she was in an aeroplane looking down through clear air at arid brown mountains topped with white. Their sides were deeply riven, as though acid had been poured down them like gravy on a mound of mashed potato.

Tilly sat back in her seat, her heart thudding.

This was so different from Surbiton. It took her back to California and their house in the hills above Hollywood.

Her memories of that time were jumbled, like a box of snapshots, with only bits of different pictures appearing from underneath bits of others. Clear as anything were sunlit days with her mother and the glorious technicoloured occasions when Daddy was there as well. But there were odd corners of others: of the sound of her mother crying, of an unrecognisable male voice that she somehow knew to be her father's, sometimes shouting, sometimes begging and pleading.

Tilly's heart gave a little jump. Where had that memory come from? Why had it suddenly come back now? Her parents' marriage had been a fairy tale of happiness, everyone said so.

The instruction to fasten seat belts for landing came over the intercom. Tilly scrabbled for her shoulder bag under the seat. A whole new phase of her life was about to begin.

PART TWO

France

Chapter Thirteen

It was mid-January by the time Olivia saw her new home. After the balmy warmth of her Seychelles honeymoon, coming down to the Côte d'Azur was an unpleasant shock. Mediterranean blue had disappeared behind grey clouds and a chill wind was blowing. The dreams of sunshine with which she and Charles had buoyed themselves up during their brief stopover in a damp and cold England disappeared.

Once again they had put the car on the train to Nice. Driving up towards Grasse in the chilly morning air, Charles had the heater on full.

'Do we check into the hotel first or go straight to the house?' he asked.

'Oh, the house,' said Olivia. She was still trying to forget parting from Tilly. A look at how the builders were getting on might give her an idea of when they could offer a proper home to her daughter.

Charles gave her a smile. 'I can't wait to see what they've done.' He turned up the side road that led towards the house. Then stopped. A flood streamed down the small lane, the water gathering bits of leaves, twigs and other debris at its edges, swirling them along at a fast and furious pace, rushing down the hill and across the junction where Charles had stopped, disappearing through a small hedge into a field of olive trees where several goats were grazing. Their bony heads adorned with tufty beards of pale hair ignored the pond that was gathering around several of the twisted trunks.

'Heavens!' said Olivia. 'It must have been pouring here.'

'Hardly this much,' Charles said grimly. 'I think this is man-made.' He started the car again and drove slowly up the hill, the Jaguar stoically moving at a careful pace through the waters.

Behind them came the clang of a fire engine. Charles edged into the drive of a neighbouring house to let the vehicle pass.

'You don't think it's something to do with us?' Olivia asked anxiously.

'Something tells me it's more than possible,' Charles said in the same grim voice. He moved out into the road again and followed the fire engine up the hill.

At the top they saw the engine swing into the drive of *La Chênais* then stop. It was immediately surrounded by workmen. Blue-uniformed firemen jumped down on to the road and then, together with the workmen, gathered on the grass verge outside the gates. Above that point Olivia and

Charles could see that the road was clear of water.

Charles stopped the car just past the fire engine and they got out. He approached one of the workmen and there was a rapid exchange of French. Olivia waited.

After a few minutes Charles came back to her, his square face creased in irritation. 'Apparently a lorry carrying a load of materials for the swimming pool swung too hard into the drive and damaged a water stanchion. That's where all the flooding has come from.' Over his shoulder Olivia could see firemen working on the damaged pipe. 'I'm going to have a word with the driver who caused this mess.' He strode off back to the little group, extracted one of the workmen and took him up the drive to the house.

Olivia pulled her light coat more tightly around her against the chill wind that whipped down the lane and leant against the car. The firemen bustled about with a great sense of purpose and incomprehensible shouts. Wrenches were produced, brute force applied and gradually the flood reduced to a trickle. So did the bustle. Cigarettes appeared and conversation as opposed to staccato commands developed. She gathered that the worst of the problem had been solved.

The wind grew worse. Olivia pulled up her collar, thought about getting back in the car, then decided to follow Charles up to the house. Halfway there she met her husband coming back, face frowning and body rigid with annoyance.

'Have you sorted anything out?' Olivia asked, slipping her arm through his, trying to achieve a sense of warmth.

'It's hopeless! The driver says the pipe never should have been sited there and there isn't enough room for the lorries to swing into the drive. He says they'd clipped it twice before and the foreman had complained to the *Mairie*. I have to go down there and try and sort something out.'

'What a shame,' Olivia said consolingly. 'Just when we were looking forward to finding out how much has been done.' She couldn't get any response from Charles's body, stiff and implacable beside her. She felt as though she had her arm through a statue's and drew it back. He didn't seem to notice.

'It looks as though they're way behind. I haven't been inside but they've only done half the roof and the swimming pool's hardly started! I shall have to have words with M. Pontevrault.'

Between their initial trip and their marriage, Charles had been over several times. On his first visit he'd found a local architect, Michel Pontevrault, and briefed him. He'd also organised a swimming pool manufacturer. Olivia had accompanied him on the second trip, when they'd signed all the papers for the purchase of the house and Charles had handed over the final payment. They'd met the architect on site, gone over the plans and estimates he'd obtained from local *entrepreneurs* and decided which should be accepted. Then Charles had made two more visits, the last time just before Christmas, to check that everything was proceeding as it should.

'I'll be glad when we're on the spot,' he'd said to Olivia after that last trip. 'I can see they need someone behind them all the time.'

Excited to have Charles back again, involved in the final preparations for Christmas and their wedding, Olivia hadn't really taken in what he'd said. Now she realised with a sense of depression that it was going to be some time before they could move into their new home. 'I'm sure you'll get them properly organised, darling.' She tried to sound reassuring.

'I'm going to have my work cut out here,' he said grimly. 'Do you want to come with me to the *Mairie* or would you like to start checking what stage the building work's reached?'

Olivia looked at his preoccupied face and tried to decide which he'd prefer her to do. The small frown of irritation between his brows deepened. 'It won't be much fun for you at the *Mairie*, much better if you start making notes here,' he said abruptly and turned towards the gates.

Olivia remained where she was for a moment. She felt chilled to the bone and not only by the wind. The kind, considerate man she'd married seemed to have disappeared.

Suddenly Charles was beside her again. 'Darling, I'm sorry, this must be a wretched homecoming for you. Don't worry, we'll work everything out. Are you sure you're happy to stay here, you wouldn't rather come with me?'

Olivia smiled and kissed his cheek. 'Of course not. You go off, I'll be quite all right.'

She watched his sturdy figure disappear out of the gates then stop to have a word with the chief fireman. She started once again to walk up to the house but had to scamper on to the grass verge as a construction lorry, driven far too fast, came down the drive. No doubt, she thought grimly, the driver who had done the damage with the water pipe!

The remainder of the walk up to the house was depressing. The shrubs and grass seemed to have grown even more unruly since her last visit. The garden had an air of desolation that was compounded by the huge hole that had been dug at the bottom of the sloping bank, just where she had initially pictured a swimming pool. The cleanly cut sides of the kidney-shaped hole were edged round with huge mounds of earth. No one was working on the pool but bags of cement and pallets of other construction materials had been dumped on the lawn. Olivia tried to visualise the pool completed, the garden around it tamed and she and Tilly and Charles swimming under a brilliant Mediterranean sun.

After a moment she gave up and continued towards the house. A light drizzle started to fall.

As she approached the courtyard, she looked up at the roof where two workmen were working at astonishing speed fixing the new slates, piles of the dark grey rectangles strategically to hand. Olivia wondered why this house hadn't used the red Roman clay tiles that were on most of the other buildings in the region. Ostentation, perhaps? One of the workmen shouted a greeting down at her and she threw up a hand in acknowledgement. She noticed there were several vans in the courtyard and wondered if things were really as bad as Charles seemed to think.

Inside, she realised they were. The damp course had been installed and drains leading to a *fosse septique*, the septic tank now installed in the garden, but the bathrooms and cloakrooms were empty apart from the gaping ends of naked sewage pipes. None of the electrical works had been started, water still wasn't connected and there was a considerable amount of plastering to be done. The only workmen around seemed to be on the roof. There was, though, a stack of breeze blocks and insulation board in the kitchen where the partition walls between the main area and the service rooms had been torn down. It was now one huge, chilly space. The blocks were no doubt intended to be used for new walls that would provide a small larder and a sizeable utility room. Looking more closely, Olivia found that a foundation line of blocks had in fact already been started.

One of the workmen who had been down by the road appeared. He grinned at Olivia and directed a stream of rapid, strangulated French at her.

'*Je suis désolée, mais je ne comprends pas,*' she said apologetically, using the phrase that was her standby. She had been studying books but, without time to go to classes, was finding it very difficult to make much progress with the language. Perhaps now that she was here permanently, it would be different.

The workman shrugged his shoulders, turned towards the outside door and roared, 'Jacques! Claude!' Two more workmen arrived and the breeze-block wall was restarted.

Olivia reached into her handbag for the notebook she always carried.

After two hours she had made a list of all the outstanding work and her hands had become so cold she could hardly hold the pencil. She returned her notebook to her bag and negotiated the narrow spiral staircase from the tower room. Going down the main staircase, she attempted to picture an elegantly furnished house. But all she could see were scarred walls and debris-littered floors.

Then the front door opened and Charles was there. He looked so gloomy that her heart sank and instead of rushing down into his arms, she paused on the stairs. 'How did it go, darling?'

He looked up and his face was transformed as he smiled at her. 'Oh, I got it sorted, mainly by writing a cheque for some incredible sum. Look, I'm starving. Is there anything we should do here or shall we go and find something to eat?'

Olivia ran down the rest of the stairs and slipped her arm through his, hugging it to her side, snuggling into the warmth of his body. 'Oh, do let's go,' she said fervently.

Later, sitting in a small restaurant not far from their hotel, whisky starting to circulate central heating through her veins, Olivia asked, 'It is going to be all right, Charles, isn't it?'

He put down the menu. 'What do you mean?' he asked, his voice cautious and cagey.

Once again she had this sense he was a stranger.

Olivia fought a sense of panic. 'It's just, well, there's such a lot to do with the house.' Then she pulled herself together and gave a small laugh. 'I can't help remembering when Tilly and I moved into the Surbiton house. It took me forever to do all the decorating. I want us to be living there tomorrow!' She looked at him expectantly.

He gave her an indulgent smile and suddenly there was her Charles again. 'Don't worry, my darling, you're not going to have to do the decorating this time.' He squared his shoulders unconsciously and reached a hand across the table. 'And we're going to have fun chasing the builders and making our dream come true. Then we can relax and have a wonderful time.'

Olivia gazed into his warm brown eyes and was comforted.

Their days soon settled into a pattern. Breakfast in their bedroom at the hotel, then a drive down to the house where Charles checked progress. Twice a week he insisted on meeting the architect on site and going through the work. He soon made friends with each of the *entrepreneurs*, taking an interest in what they were doing and encouraging them. Olivia thought that his colloquial French improved every day. With his help, she acquired enough command of the language to shop in the local *charcuterie* and *boulangerie* for cold meats and bread for lunch and began to enjoy the grave politeness of French shopping: the greeting everyone gave everyone else, the frequent use of *s'il vous plaît*, the importance each shopkeeper attached to satisfying his customers. After Surbiton it was a revelation.

While Charles checked the builders or, armed with a large billhook and wearing wellington boots, assaulted the shrubberies, Olivia would wander through the house absorbing its atmosphere and trying to decide what to do with each of the rooms. *La Chênais* was so different from any house she'd known before and found it difficult to visualise a decorative scheme.

By mid-afternoon, they would abandon the house and go shopping, checking out door furniture, bathroom fittings, lights, kitchen cupboards, and all the other bits and pieces a house required. Olivia bought French magazines on interior decoration and haunted bookshops looking for illustrated volumes on period design. Michel Pontevrault, the architect, said that though parts of the house went back to the fifteenth or sixteenth century, the main rooms had been built in the eighteenth and that was the period she concentrated on.

She bought large sheets of cartridge paper and, back at the hotel, sketched out various designs, using chalks to add colour. The next stage was hunting for curtain and carpet materials.

119

Every moment seemed to be taken up with organising the house. Saturdays were spent searching out useful suppliers and checking on antique shops. Even on Sundays they spent most of their time at *La Chênais*, wandering through rooms deserted by workmen, deciding on more and more details, going out for lunch somewhere, then coming back for more decisions.

One evening about three weeks after they'd arrived they were having dinner in what had become their favourite local restaurant when Olivia said, 'Charles, I've been wondering.'

'Yes, darling?' he said and stroked her hand as it lay on top of a pile of swatches she had brought with them.

She smiled at him and felt languorously relaxed. The weather hadn't improved but somehow it had ceased to matter. The physical relationship between them continued to develop and bed had become a place where they could forget the frustrations of the day and devote themselves to each other. There Charles never disappeared into what Olivia had begun to think of as his stern-faced industrialist look. That was reserved for moments when the building wasn't going to his satisfaction. She hoped it would disappear altogether when the house was ready.

Olivia gently squeezed his hand then picked up the pile of swatches. 'The prices are absolutely horrendous! I'm sure Gavin would allow me to use the firm's trade discount, which would mean we could buy in England for much less than here. We know what we want now, why don't I go back to London and see what I can find?' Much as Olivia hated the idea of leaving Charles, at least she would be able to see something of Tilly and she was certain the trip would more than pay for itself.

Charles frowned. 'I don't want to leave the builders, the work is badly behind as it is.'

'I quite understand, darling.' Olivia had never for one moment imagined that he would come with her.

'And I hate the thought of your going. I need you here.' Once again he squeezed her hand and Olivia felt a surge of happiness at being wanted in this way. But she couldn't see writing to Peter Jones and asking them to send samples was going to be satisfactory. There were other suppliers that needed to be checked and it was more than possible that some of the trade contacts she'd used for furnishing various exhibitions could be useful. The thought gave her an inspiration. 'Why don't I ring Margie? Ask her to help?'

The waiter arrived to take their order and for a moment they both concentrated on food. When he'd gone, Charles said, 'Darling, that's a brilliant idea. Ring her tonight and ask her to come out. Tell her we'll make it worth her while; with all the carpeting that house needs, we'll still be saving a bomb.'

Margie was enchanted to be asked for her help. She immediately cleared her diary for the following weekend. Olivia and Charles met her at Nice airport on the Friday night and drove her back to the hotel. Over dinner they showed her photographs of the house and enthusiastically related their plans. Margie listened to them, her dark head held on one side like a sparrow faced with unruly fledglings. With the arrival of dessert she waved elegant hands in the air and laughed. 'I can see I'm going to have the time of my life with this project. But if you tell me any more, my head's going to spill over with details. I'd love to know something about the area round here. Will there be time to do any sightseeing?'

'Sightseeing!' Olivia cried. 'We never have time for sightseeing!'

Charles laughed. 'Forgive us, Margie, we get far too involved. Of course we're going to show you around. We'll enjoy taking some time off.'

They should have people out more often, Olivia thought. What they were doing with the house was very important but the thought of abandoning it for a day to do something totally different was invigorating. She launched enthusiastically into a description of some of the places they could visit.

When they took Margie to the house the following day, her mobile face became still as she was taken through the rooms and Olivia produced what she called her story boards and the swatches of French materials she had chosen.

'Leave it all to me,' Margie said at the end. 'I know exactly where to go. And you're quite right,' she added, looking at the prices Olivia had noted on the backs of the swatches, 'it'll be much, much cheaper than buying over here.'

'Splendid,' said Charles with satisfaction and Olivia almost expected him to rub his hands together. 'Now, let's see something of the countryside. I've booked a table at a marvellous place for dinner and tomorrow it's Sunday lunch out. Olivia and I love seeing the French families enjoying themselves.'

Margie looked amused. 'Your lives seem to revolve around the house and food. What are you going to do when the project's complete?'

'Relax and eat some more,' said Charles promptly.

Before Margie left, she found the opportunity to say to Olivia, 'Marriage isn't for me, darling, but you've found yourself a wonderful man there. Look after him.'

'Oh, I do,' Olivia said quickly. 'And he looks after me as well.'

'Just as it should be,' Margie said approvingly.

'Tell me about the office,' Olivia suggested. 'How are things at Designs Unlimited?' She had a moment of homesickness for her work there. 'It all seems so far away!'

'It's business as usual,' Margie said with a small grimace. 'Gavin grows less and less ambitious. He wants to stick to the markets he knows. He doesn't seem to realise we can't stand still, we've got to keep exploring new possibilities.' Her dark eyes sparkled with relish. Olivia could just imagine the arguments the two of them must have. For a startling moment, she wanted to be back there, designing exhibition stands, absorbing herself in client requirements, seeing her ideas take shape. Then feelings of nostalgia vanished as she remembered how tired the backbiting had always made her feel. Designs Unlimited had nothing to do with her life now. She refused to be excited by the news that Gavin had had to hire two people to take on the work she'd handled.

Margie didn't take long to arrange for a large parcel filled with swatches of curtain and carpet samples to be sent by special messenger.

Olivia took everything down to the house and spent a whole day sorting out the materials while Charles was arranging for the water and electricity to be connected.

'Margie's found everything we need,' she reported that evening over dinner. 'We'll go through it together tomorrow then I can fax her the order.' They'd discovered this could be done through the post office.

'Marvellous. Everything seems to be coming together at last,' he said with great satisfaction.

Olivia looked at him curiously. 'You really seem to be enjoying this. Don't you miss your firm at all?'

He looked surprised. 'Why should I?'

'Well, you spent all that time building it up. A lot of men I know would start getting withdrawal symptoms without having their business to organise, subordinates to order around, ambitious plans to dream about.'

He waved an impatient hand. 'I'm not that sort of bloke. I don't need the adrenaline of business success. I used to meet chaps like that, never happier than when they were making a deal, preferably one that did someone else down. Hard dealing in smoke filled rooms wasn't me. I produced a good product and reckoned it should sell on merit. I only wanted to make money in order to give my family a good life. When everything went sour with Veronica, I still wanted to be able to give Phyllie the best possible start. Now she's launched and I've found you. When that offer came in for the company, I realised I didn't need to keep going with it any more. I had enough to buy and restore *La Chênais* and provide a good income for us both.' He reached for her hand, 'You are my ambitious plan now! You and the house.'

'Will you start bossing me about instead of your staff?' She smiled at him.

'Never! We're a team.' His grin was warm with a lively humour.

'And when we've got the house ready, what then?'

'Then we start enjoying ourselves,' he said exuberantly. 'We'll have the girls out, friends down, explore all the sights of the Côte d'Azur together. Our life here is just beginning.'

Olivia smiled at his enthusiasm but a daunting sense of responsibility began to niggle at her. What if she couldn't live up to Charles's golden vision of married life for them? She looked at his square, dependable face that until now had always been so reassuring. She remembered his enthusiasm for his business when they'd first met. Could he really let go of all that so easily? Her own brief moment of nostalgia for Designs Unlimited came back to her.

'Penny for them? Or should that be a centime?' Charles gave her another bouyant smile.

'They aren't worth a sou,' Olivia said briskly and dismissed her unease with a resolute attempt at confidence. 'How long do you think before we're ready to start entertaining?'

'I reckon we can get everything done in time for Easter. I've told Phyllie she's got to come out then.'

Olivia stared at him 'You never told me that!'

'Didn't I? Don't you want Tilly to come out then too?'

'Well, yes, but I was going to discuss it with you first, see how the house was going.' Olivia felt she'd been put at a disadvantage. 'There's so much to be done. I mean, we haven't even been able to move in ourselves yet and Easter is . . . what?' Olivia calculated frantically.

'Just under eight weeks away,' Charles said calmly. 'Plenty of time to get everything done. If we pile on a bit more pressure and get moving ourselves.'

Olivia wondered what they'd been doing since they'd arrived if it wasn't moving! She gazed at Charles and felt as though she'd been struck by one of the jet planes from Nice airport. 'But we haven't even got any furniture yet!'

He struck the table with a forceful hand. 'That's true! We'd better start looking. It shouldn't take long; after all, thanks to all your work, we know what we want now.'

Olivia doubted it was going to be that easy but it was impossible to argue with Charles in this mood and she found she didn't want to anyway, his enthusiasm was so infectious.

However she soon found Charles and she had very different ideas about how to shop. Olivia liked to look, noting possible pieces but continuing to find others. Charles preferred to say. That's it, we'll get that. It was true that his eye was good and the pieces he wanted were always fine quality but Olivia felt that if only they spent a bit more time looking, they could find equally nice ones at half the price. 'Don't worry,' he told her the first time she questioned the cost. 'If they're good pieces, they'll maintain their value.' He wrote out a cheque for what Olivia considered was an incredible sum for two console tables with marble tops and carved, gilded legs that, she had to admit, were perfect to set between the long windows in the salon.

Gradually the reroofed outhouses began to be filled with furniture carefully covered with dustsheets.

They searched as well for upholsterers and curtain makers who could produce what they wanted by Easter. Charles negotiated with them, juggling prices against delivery dates. He seemed to revel in pitching his wits against theirs. Olivia could hardly believe his temerity in pressing for shorter working times and lower costs but each session seemed to end in mutual respect.

'It's all part of the French psyche,' he explained one day after a piece of particularly long and arduous negotiation. 'Accept what they first offer and they'll think very little of you. Now that woman is going to put her all into producing what we want. She knows that she'll have to wait a long time for her money if she doesn't.'

Night after night Olivia and Charles fell into bed exhausted by all their activities.

Five weeks before Easter, just after their flying visit back to England for Tilly's eighteenth birthday, Charles and Olivia moved into their house. By then two of the planned three bathrooms had been installed, water and electricity had been connected and the kitchen was under construction. A big double bed had been purchased and placed in the room they'd chosen as theirs. Large and airy, it had a heavenly view of the sea over the tops of trees and hills. Charles organised a clothes rail so they'd have somewhere to hang things while the built-in cupboards that had been planned for the room were installed. The decorators hadn't arrived yet and it was more like camping than living but Olivia was overwhelmingly relieved to be in a home again. Perhaps, now, life would begin to settle down and she'd feel more like a proper wife rather than some kind of cross between a kept woman and an interior decorator.

Their first meal in their new home was a dish from the local *charcuterie* heated up in the microwave oven that was their sole means of cooking. It was eaten at a refectory table they'd decided was ideal for the kitchen. Its long top, scarred from the years but polished to a high shine, had a decidedly snooty air as it stood amongst the mess of half-constructed cupboards; it looked like a pedigree hound that had found itself amongst a rabble of mongrels. An impression heightened by the assorted set of ladder back chairs Olivia had found at a second hand bric-a-brac place not far from *La Chênais*. Charles had been scornfully dismissive but she'd said firmly that they would be very useful. The rush seating was in good condition and by the time she'd stripped the dark varnish off the wood and given it a more natural finish, they'd look perfect.

Empty wine bottles served as candlesticks and for the first time they were able to use the earthenware service they'd chosen for daily use. It had a pattern of huge yellow sunflowers spilling over a bright, Provençal blue background. 'I really like these,' Charles said as he placed them on the table and added the yellow-handled stainless steel cutlery they'd also bought. Olivia was finding he was helpful around the house. Such a change from her father, who seemed to think meals arrived out of thin air, and from Peter, her first husband, who'd claimed he had work to do whenever she'd suggested he might lay a table or wash up.

124

Charles finished his task and stood back to assess the effect. He moved the wine bottles slightly closer to each other then gave a grunt of satisfaction. 'We'll find proper silver for the dining room later, and a decent dinner service,' he added as he started to open the bottle of excellent burgundy he'd found to accompany the meal. 'I saw a very nice Herend one in Antibes the other day, remind me to show it to you next time we're down there.'

The candlelight softened the bare plaster walls and the builder's mess and even the table seemed to settle down and accept that things could only get better. Charles and Olivia toasted the house, the builders, their daughters and themselves. It was a happy meal and by the time they went up to their disordered bedroom, Olivia had forgotten her exhaustion.

Chapter Fourteen

'I've got to get something done about those gates,' Charles announced the next morning. 'If we leave them all rusted like that much longer, they're going to fall off the posts. And the posts aren't any too sound either. Michel's given me the name of an ironworker near Nice. I think I'll go down there now. Do you want to come?'

Olivia shook her head. 'I wish I could, I saw a poster in the village for an art exhibition there that I'd love to see, but I still haven't decided on the curtains for the main salon. Margie says that unless I can give her the details today, there won't be a hope of getting them here with the rest of the stuff.' A special van was being arranged to bring out their order.

Charles didn't seem too upset. 'Well, there wouldn't be time for art exhibitions anyway. I'll see you for lunch. I'll pick something up on my way back, shall I?' That was another nice thing about Charles, he was never fussed about shopping for food. In fact, he never seemed to worry about what Olivia asked him to do. They were in this together, he'd said after she'd apologised one day for giving him a shopping list.

After he'd left, Olivia went into the big salon with the long French windows opening out on to the terrace. It was the one room she hadn't decided on what to do for curtains yet. Was she to choose an elaborately draped effect in a plain silk, or straightforward, triple pleated ones in a pattern? Or a combination of both? The windows were an important feature of the room and she needed to be sure whatever she chose looked right.

She started to sellotape material samples on the walls beside the windows, cursing the cloudy weather that still showed little sign of clearing up into the bright sunshine they'd been expecting ever since they'd arrived.

Just as she finished and was about to step back and assess the effect, the door opened and the room was invaded by workmen in white overalls carrying ladders, dustsheets, brushes and pots of paint. She'd forgotten the decorators were starting today!

She stared in dismay as they greeted her courteously. These were men she hadn't seen before. Gradually Olivia had got to know each of the Frenchmen who were working on the house and found that her very limited vocabulary was no bar to establishing friendly relations. Now she'd have to start from scratch with this lot.

The workmen laid dustsheets on the restored parquet flooring, erected ladders and started work on the ornately plastered ceiling. It was soon apparent that if she remained where she was, she'd need an umbrella. Olivia removed the samples from the far end of the room, where the light was best, and reaffixed them at the other end. Unobtrusively she set about memorising each of the workmen at the same time as she studied the effect of her samples. Soon, though, her concentration was focused solely on the windows. Imagining swathes of silk fantastically draped, richly patterned brocades and cut velvets, Olivia was so deep in her work she never noticed the door opening until an English voice said, 'Good heavens!'

A tall girl in her mid-thirties stood in the doorway. Hands thrust into the pockets of well-tailored slacks, a soft suede jacket open over a silk polo-necked sweater, a scarf tied at her neck, she looked stylishly casual in a way not quite in keeping with her thick plait of dark hair and strong, plain face with its bushy dark eyebrows and thin mouth. Jeans and sweatshirt would have been more in keeping with her no-nonsense appearance.

'Hello?' Olivia said enquiringly as she went forward.

The newcomer remained where she was, relaxed but unforthcoming. 'I couldn't find a bell and the front door was open. I'm Liz Ratcliffe. We're your next-door neighbours, just down the lane. Someone told us English people had moved in here so I came to introduce myself.'

'How lovely!' Olivia forgot about her curtain samples. 'We haven't met anyone yet.' For the first time she was aware of how dependent on Charles she had become. Apart from the architect and the workmen, the only social contact she and Charles had had since arriving in France had been Margie's fleeting visit. And their own conversation these days seemed to concentrate exclusively on the house. Olivia found herself overwhelmingly pleased to see this rangy-looking girl with her abrupt manner. 'We can just about boil a kettle in the kitchen, come and have a cup of coffee.'

'I ought to invite you back to our place but I'd really like to see the house.' Liz looked apologetic, as though the confession betrayed a major weakness. Olivia warmed towards her.

'Would you like a tour first?'

'Coffee, please, then I can find out about you,' she said without apology.

'Only if you reciprocate,' Olivia insisted with a laugh as she led the way into the half-constructed kitchen.

'Ever since we moved here,' Liz said as she settled herself, surveying the kitchen and her hostess with frank curiosity, 'we've wondered about this house. We came and looked round when it was first put on the market, I think half the village did. I admire your courage in taking it on.'

'Not mine, Charles's.' Olivia switched on the coffee filter machine that had been one of Charles's first purchases. He loved freshly made coffee.

'Your husband? Is he working out here?'

Olivia shook her head. 'He's just sold his company and taken early retirement. It's always been his dream to live in France. We found this house on a trip last October and suddenly everything seemed to fall into place.' She heard herself saying the words and thought how strange they sounded. To throw up a well-organised life in the country of your birth and start again somewhere foreign. Why had she never questioned the decision? Had it had something to do with the fact that this was the second time she had turned her back on her family and England without questioning the advisability of her actions? She pushed away the thought of that time in California with Peter. 'How long have you lived here?' she asked, thinking how very English her guest looked with her unmade-up face and yet how French with the way the brightly patterned, Hermès silk scarf had been tied in such a way it sat perfectly on the polo-necked sweater.

Liz placed her hands together on the table and looked down at her long, strong fingers lying interlaced on the polished wood. They could have come from a Holbein drawing. Her eyelids hid the hazel eyes that had looked around with such curiosity. 'Patrick was promoted here about twelve years ago. He's in property, working for an international firm. They deal in houses, apartments and business premises all along the Côte d'Azur and into Italy and Switzerland. Only the very rich need apply,' she added, raising her head and looking at Olivia with lurking humour.

'My!' said Olivia ironically, then wondered if Liz felt she and Charles fell into that category.

She needn't have worried; Liz gave her a broad smile that said they understood each other. 'It's meat and drink to Patrick. When the new job came up he didn't even ask me what I thought. We'd been married just over three years, living in a Cotswold cottage that I'd rescued from complete collapse.' She glanced around the bare kitchen with its open beams. 'So I have some idea what you're coping with here. I put my heart and soul into that cottage. So far as I was concerned life there was perfect.'

'And you had to give it all up to come out here?' Olivia noted the way that, even after all these years, the well-shaped fingers clenched themselves as Liz talked about her lost home.

Her face softened indulgently. 'Yes, well, that's what being married's all about, isn't it? And Patrick was so excited about the move. The house came with the job. I didn't like it much when we arrived, but then at that stage I don't suppose any property would have met with my approval.' It was said with wry self-knowledge.

'I expect you settled in after a bit,' Olivia suggested. The filter machine gave a last gurgle, she poured out two cups and placed one in front of her guest.

Liz gave a moue of distaste. 'I couldn't speak French, Patrick went off for days at a time, sometimes staying overnight, leaving me alone in a house I didn't like, shopping in a language I didn't understand. If I hadn't had my work, I think I would have gone crazy.'

'What is your work?' Olivia asked with real interest. She felt an immediate affinity with this straight-speaking girl who obviously

129

understood her own sense of bewilderment as she grappled with all the new challenges facing her in this foreign country.

Liz's expression was closed. 'I paint,' she said briefly.

Olivia refused to recognise the keep off sign. 'Oh, how interesting! I trained as a graphic designer and I used to design exhibitions. That's how I met Charles, in fact.'

Liz allowed herself to open up sightly. 'Do you paint as well?'

Olivia shook her head. 'I have no talent for that sort of creativity. But I love looking at paintings. I wanted to go with Charles this morning and see the exhibition that's on in Nice. But I have to decide on the salon curtains and, anyway, Charles said there wouldn't be time to look at pictures. I'm longing to have the house finished so we'll have time to relax and look around,' she added a little wistfully.

'Take a day off and we'll go into Nice together,' Liz suggested. 'That exhibition's marvellous and I'd love to go again.'

Olivia was delighted with the assumption that they could do things together and decided questions about Liz's own painting should wait. 'Have some more coffee,' she offered.

'I'd rather see the house,' Liz said in her direct way.

Olivia collected her design boards from the corner where she kept them in a large cardboard box. 'I'm aiming for a look that's sympathetic rather than faithful to period,' she said as they left the kitchen. 'The house is a combination of periods anyway. This hall is earlier than the main salons, our architect thinks it's sixteenth-century.' The two girls stood on the black and white marble tiles and surveyed the space. 'All this heavy stonework and those rather small windows are a bit of a problem to do anything with so I thought we'd leave the hall to make its own statement. Just a large round table in the centre and perhaps one of those huge Provençal *armoires* against that wall. Charles wants a tapestry on the wall going up the stairs. What do you think? Too much?'

'Depends on the tapestry,' Liz said with authority, looking around her with interest. 'You've had pediments mounted above the doors, haven't you? I'm sure those weren't here when we came round.'

'Absolutely right!' Olivia realised that here was someone with a true painter's eye for detail. An assessment that was proved true time and again as the tour proceeded.

At the end Liz expressed approbation of everything Olivia and Charles were doing with the house. 'I can't wait to see it finished,' she said as she took her leave.

'I've found a friend,' Olivia announced when Charles got home with lunch, a *blanquette de veau* he'd picked up at the local *traiteur*, together with salad from the vegetable shop. 'She wants us to go to supper tomorrow night and meet her husband,' she added, starting to wash the lettuce.

'Sounds good,' said Charles absently as he assessed the lack of progress in the kitchen. 'I suppose Michel didn't call this morning?'

Olivia hoped that this lack of interest didn't mean he wasn't going to get on with Liz and Patrick. Which he certainly wouldn't if Liz's husband turned out to be one of those pushy estate agents who were always trying to sell you properties you didn't want. She hoped he wouldn't be, it would make friendship with Liz more difficult and Olivia realised she wanted very much to be real friends with her neighbour.

So it was with anticipation edged with a certain amount of anxiety that Olivia waited with Charles outside the Ratcliffes' front door the following evening.

It was opened by a very tall man who topped Charles by at least five inches. He had a lean body and a long face, deep lines running down beside the nose and mouth and across his forehead, giving him the look of a bloodhound who'd had good news, for his mouth curved upwards and his blue eyes sparkled cheerfully. 'Come in,' he said welcomingly. 'I'm Patrick and I'm so pleased to meet you, Liz says you're doing wonderful things with *La Chênais*.' He took their coats. 'Isn't this weather the end? The Mistral this year has been really wicked. Come on in and get warm, I've lit a fire. The central heating is adequate but there's nothing like real flames, is there?' He led the way into a large room furnished in unobtrusively modern pieces that provided a low-key background to a stunning collection of modern art.

Olivia wanted to look at all of the paintings and the bronze and wooden sculptures that sat on every flat surface, including the stone surround of the raised fireplace where a cheerful fire blazed out. Charles, though, hardly gave the art a look, he headed straight for the fire.

'This is wonderful,' he said, rubbing his hands. 'We're beginning to regret moving from our hotel. I've bought two convection heaters but the only room we can get to any sort of comfortable temperature is the bedroom. The kitchen just swallows the heat up, I think it's warming the beams. I thought the Côte d'Azur was meant to be warm!'

'Not in winter!' said Liz entering the room. 'But usually we get lots of bright sun. This year you've struck it unlucky, I've never known such a gloomy winter. Hello, you must be Charles, I'm Liz Ratcliffe.'

Olivia saw with relief that Charles liked both Liz and Patrick. The warmth of the room seeped through to her bones, thoroughly chilled by living in their unheated house, and her spirits were equally warmed by the company.

As the evening wore on, though, she began to wonder just how successful Patrick Ratcliffe was in business. The quiet luxury of their home suggested he was extremely good at his job but he showed none of the upfront cheekiness that she associated with property wheeler dealers. But maybe Patrick's rich and high-powered clients preferred his quietly sympathetic approach and undoubted intelligence to the bullshit so often peddled by salesmen. Talking with Charles about European economics and politics he sounded as though he knew exactly what he was talking about and that always inspired confidence.

'Would you like to look at the paintings?' asked Liz as Olivia found her attention wandering to the walls rather than concentrating on a debate over the advisability of the single European currency. 'I'll only say something I'll regret if I don't get away,' she added as she took Olivia over to the other side of the room. 'I'm fiercely against and Patrick believes Europe will only really go forward when they've got rid of any sort of exchange rate mechanism. I gather Charles tends towards my view.'

'They seem to be discussing it all quite amicably,' Olivia observed, glancing back towards the men.

'That's because they're both male and not married to each other,' Liz said caustically.

Meeting the Ratcliffes brought a new element to Olivia's and Charles's lives – socialising. No doubt due to Patrick's job, the Ratcliffes had a wide circle of friends on the Riviera, many of them English. Liz said she wouldn't let Olivia in for an all-French-speaking occasion just yet, but that there were many English-speaking people they should meet. She launched into a series of dinner and luncheon parties for them.

Olivia was taken back to the formal parties her mother gave and the entertaining she and Peter had occasionally been involved with in Hollywood after he'd made the big time. Guests were sophisticated and beautifully dressed and happy to talk on a wide range of subjects. The food was as sophisticated as the company. Drinks before the meal would be accompanied by delicious little eats. For the meal itself, course followed course. Never less than two and often three wines were served. Conversation was both civilised and gossipy. Soon Olivia began to recognise certain names, then found she was meeting the owners of the names. Those who met the Fromes at the Ratcliffes' extended invitations to their places. Soon each week involved three or more events. It seemed everyone was eager to share in the new couple.

Olivia found she enjoyed it all hugely. It was many years since she'd been a shy teenager, desperately nervous of her ability to entertain the people she met, but never before had she felt able to meet people on a level of equality. Being married to Charles seemed to have given her a new confidence. And it was delightful to be able to get away from the hard work of getting the house together and to wear the pretty clothes Charles had insisted on buying her before their wedding. She exuded a sparkling enjoyment of each occasion and charmed all she met.

The English on the Riviera they were introduced to were a mixed bunch. Many were retired businessmen, often back in Europe from a life spent working in Africa or the Middle East and unable to face the rigours of the English weather. Their wives had been well trained by a lifetime of entertaining and being entertained and had no trouble in pitching their conversation and their flirtatiousness at precisely the right level for each occasion. Then there were others who came from privileged backgrounds but had led chequered careers and now found the laissez-faire attitudes of the South of France to their taste. Even without the funds others found essential, they managed to hack an entertaining path through the Riviera expatriate crowds, indulged for their wit and style.

Brought up by Daphne to remember details about people she met and involve herself in their concerns, trained by her time with Designs Unlimited in drawing out clients to discover their exact needs for exhibition or conference stands, occasionally having to steer them tactfully in a different direction, Olivia was well equipped to hold her own on these occasions. With Charles by her side, no longer a vulnerable single woman, she could enjoy being flirted with without giving any wife or partner cause to regard her as a danger. She was a social success.

Charles, however, did not enjoy the parties as much as Olivia. While she was involved in lively exchanges with new acquaintances, he would be sitting quietly listening without great interest to someone holding forth on some subject or other. Only with the Ratcliffes did he appear able to relax.

'We never seem to have time to ourselves these days,' he grumbled one evening after a day spent trying to clean out part of the outhouses to give more room to store the furniture they were still acquiring. 'Olivia, haven't I got a clean shirt?' He banged shut the drawers of their recently acquired chest then rattled the hangers on the clothes rail. The built-in cupboards were still only half-completed.

She paused in the business of choosing earrings. 'I thought you had lots of shirts.'

'I did have,' he said irritably, 'before we started going out every night. Don't we have an iron?'

Olivia felt guilty. 'Darling, there just hasn't been time for ironing. And it's not because we've been out every day, this is the first party this week. Look, give me a moment and I'll find you a shirt.' She dropped the earrings and ran downstairs.

She'd put up the ironing board and had begun to iron one of Charles's smartest shirts when he came up behind her and slipped his arms round her waist. 'Tell you what, let's ring and say we can't make it.'

'Don't be an idiot,' Olivia laughed. 'We can't let our hostess down. Be careful,' she yelped as he tightened his grasp on her and buried his mouth in the back of her neck. 'You don't want the sleeves all creased!' He withdrew his arms, went to lean against one of the now completed kitchen cupboards and watched her as she smoothed the crisp cotton.

Olivia paused for a moment, holding the iron in her hand. 'Do you really not want to go? I get the feeling you aren't enjoying all this meeting new people.'

'Are you?' he countered.

She nodded slowly. 'Am I being very selfish?'

133

He gave her a suddenly warm smile. 'No, I'm the selfish one. My trouble is I'm jealous of every man who looks at you.' He advanced towards her. 'Put that damn iron down and come and make love to me.'

'Charles!' Olivia squealed as he removed the iron from her hands. 'I've nearly finished. Please, give it back to me.'

Reluctantly he handed over the iron and watched her while she finished the fronts.

'There,' Olivia held up the shirt. 'You'll be smart as paint and I'll attack the rest tomorrow, promise.'

'Get a woman in to do it, I don't want you tied to an ironing board,' Charles said as he took the striped shirt from her. 'Now come with me.'

'We haven't time,' Olivia protested as he unplugged the iron and then took her hand firmly in his, ignoring her weakening feeble protests as he led her upstairs.

They arrived late at the house of yet another set of new acquaintances and Olivia had to apologise prettily for trouble in finding the way.

'You do realise,' Charles said the next day as they surveyed the salon, complete except for carpet and curtains, 'that we now have a list a mile long of people we have to invite back? Saying we have nowhere to entertain them soon won't be true any more.'

Suddenly Olivia forgot her excitement at meeting all her new friends. Up until now she'd been able to say, laughing, that they were sorry but return invitations would have to wait until the house was ready. Now it nearly was.

She'd never be able to cope! Cooking was not her forte and so far in her life the only entertaining she'd done had been informal, a few friends in for a casserole or pasta. The only big party Peter and she had given in Hollywood, they'd had caterers to provide the food.

'Perhaps we can take people out to a restaurant?' she suggested hopefully.

They'd already done this once with Liz and Patrick. At the end of the evening Liz had said, 'Charles, we've really appreciated the evening but, please, once is enough. Let us have the pleasure of feeding you until your house is ready. I promise you, then we'll be round every night.' Charles had had to agree but Olivia knew he'd been uncomfortable with the amount of hospitality they'd been given by the Ratcliffes and he didn't consider presenting them with cases of wine was sufficient return.

'It's not the same,' he said now. 'Nothing beats home cooking. I keep on remembering the marvellous meal you gave me that first evening.' Olivia's heart sank. 'Anyway,' he continued, 'everyone's dying to see this place. Don't worry,' he added reassuringly. 'The house is looking great and we've got everything we need: the silver, the china, the glassware. After Easter we'll start entertaining.'

Easter! Olivia confided to Liz over one of their regular cups of coffee that the very thought of it was beginning to terrify her. 'There's still so much to be done and I don't understand the rush. I mean, it's not as though we've got the Queen coming.'

'But didn't you say Charles's daughter is?' Liz asked quietly, refilling her coffee cup from the jug on the kitchen table.

'Yes,' Olivia agreed expressionlessly.

After weeks of prevaricating, Phyllida had finally rung to say that she was coming. With a boyfriend. And they'd be staying for a fortnight. In one way Olivia was pleased because she'd be able to get to know Phyllida properly. But she was also terrified. From meeting her at the wedding, she knew theirs was not going to be an easy relationship. She also knew how important Charles's daughter was to him. She had to make the visit a success.

'He must be so excited,' Liz continued, her gaze fixed on Olivia's face.

'Oh, he is,' Olivia agreed.

Charles had been ecstatic. 'Now we know that Tilly is coming out as well, we can look forward to being a proper family.' He'd grabbed Olivia and given her an enormous hug. 'Oh, darling, it's going to be great. And you've done such a fantastic job on the house, it's going to knock their eyes out.'

When Olivia remembered how pleased Charles had been to hear that Tilly wanted to join them, she felt mean at not being able to feel equally delighted at the prospect of Phyllida's coming out.

'When's she arriving?' Liz asked.

'The morning of Easter Saturday,' said Olivia without enthusiasm.

'Well, at least you'll have Tilly to yourself for a few days.'

Olivia immediately felt more cheeful.

'And the weather's brightened up,' said Liz encouragingly.

For the last few weeks the mimosa trees had turned the hills golden and made it seem as if the sun was shining. Even though the chill wind had continued, at least it had started to feel more like the sunny Mediterranean. Then the wind had died down, the rain clouds had disappeared and the sun itself had emerged.

By the time Olivia went to meet Tilly, there was a distinct feeling of warmth in the air and she found herself humming happily as she parked the car outside the arrival hall.

Olivia had never been parted from Tilly this long before. Driving to the airport, she felt slightly schizophrenic. So much had changed in her life. She was now two different persons, Charles's wife and Tilly's mother. Would one interfere with the other?

As soon as Tilly came through from the plane, Olivia flung her arms around her and fought back tears. 'Oh, darling, it's marvellous to see you again!'

Tilly returned her hug. 'I can hardly believe I'm actually here!' She looked around. 'Where's Charles?'

'Chasing up the electricians. Some plugs haven't been put in right and the painters haven't finished yet. You know what builders are like. Anyway, I thought it would be nice to meet you on my own.'

'Right,' Tilly said equably. She gave her mother a brilliant smile. 'It's so good to see you again.'

Driving back was taken up with hearing about Tilly's life and telling her something of their struggles with the house.

'Sounds as though you've had quite a job,' she said as they drove into the courtyard. 'Gosh, isn't it big!' She stood looking at the house with an expression of awe, then flung her arms round Charles as he came down the steps.

'I'll take your things, you show her inside, darling,' he said, releasing himself from the bear hug.

'I expect you'd like to see the kitchen first.' Olivia led the way through the hall.

Tilly's face lit up. 'Mum, it's fantastic,' she said after she'd inspected the split-level oven and cooker, the island unit complete with electrical points and small sink and an iron hoop above hung about with the *batterie de cuisine*, plus the double sink under the window, the polished light wood cupboards and the sealed terracotta Provençal tiles on the floor. 'For a non-cook you've really gone to town.'

'Charles got a specialist to plan everything. It was finished a few days ago but I haven't dared use it yet. I feel like a dinghy owner who's been given an America's Cup boat! I shall have to learn, though, everybody entertains like mad here.'

'Oh, good, I'll be able to help,' said Tilly happily.

She loved her room too. It had a view of the sea and, with feelings of nostalgia for her own childhood room, Olivia had found a four poster bed and hung it with white muslin. Charles had found the painted Empire furniture decorated with carved ribbons and bows. 'There's a bathroom here,' said Olivia, opening a door off the bedroom. 'But I'm afraid you have to share it with Phyllida. Her room's the other side.' She showed Tilly. Charles had been thrilled to find a rosewood double bed in the shape of a shell. 'Phyllie will love it,' he'd said, writing another cheque that made Olivia blanch. The room was furnished in rosewood to match with a white lace bedcover and curtains.

When they came downstairs again, Charles handed Tilly an oblong package. 'I found this the other day,' he said. 'And I thought you might like it.'

Inside was a lace fan with beautifully painted sticks. 'Oh, Charles, it's one of the loveliest things I've ever had. Thank you!' She gave him an enormous hug and kissed both his cheeks.

'Now,' he said, flushed with pleasure, 'I'm going to take both my lovely women out to dinner, so get spruced up.'

The next day Tilly helped prepare a salad to eat with meat bought from the local *charcuterie* and asked what they were going to cook for supper?

'I have no idea,' confessed Olivia. She looked round the kitchen. 'I can't continue being such a coward, can I? It's so stupid to be terrified of fancy equipment but I can't even work out which button turns the oven on! I daren't tell Charles, he'll think me such an idiot.'

'Don't worry, Mum, you've got me to help you now,' Tilly said confidently, inspecting the oven's dials.

The weather was warm enough that day to eat out in the garden. Seated on the terrace, at a brand new garden table and chairs, Olivia felt content. The house was nearly finished, Tilly was with her, and Charles and she were together. After all, Phyllida couldn't possibly be as difficult as she feared, especially if she had a boyfriend with her. Olivia would make friends with her and they'd be able to be a family together, just as Charles wanted.

'I know,' she said, passing the cheese to her husband. 'Why don't I give Liz a ring and see if she and Patrick would like to come to dinner tonight? Tilly and I can christen the kitchen.'

'At last!' he said heartily. 'I wondered when we were going to start repaying some of their hospitality.'

For a moment Olivia felt resentment. It was hardly her fault they hadn't been able to do so before. Then he smiled at her and she relaxed again.

After lunch, Olivia and Tilly went shopping in the nearby town. 'We'll blow the expense and get a leg of lamb,' Olivia said, and thought how easily one got used to spending money. Tilly added chicken livers for a pâté to start the meal, haricots verts and new potatoes plus saladings. Then they bought cheese and fresh fruit and a big apple tart from the *patisserie*. Their final purchase was two long *baguettes* of bread.

The Ratcliffes arrived with a beautiful bouquet of flowers and a house warming present of an antique earthenware dish in cream pottery scattered with small green flowers. 'Oh, it's lovely,' said Olivia, admiring the way the old glaze had cracked into an interesting pattern.

'My,' said Patrick, looking round the salon. 'This really is something.'

The panelling had been painted a soft grey and several eighteenth-century landscapes had been hung on the walls. The plastered ceiling was white and the room had been furnished in shades of cream and gold, with draped, straw-coloured silk curtains and off-white brocade upholstery. A softly shaded Aubusson carpet covered much of the polished parquet flooring and more colour was added by the faded tapestry on a set of Louis Quinze chairs and bowls of fresh flowers reflected in the gilt-framed mirrors hung over the console tables set between the windows. The room was elegant but light-hearted. Olivia was pleased with the finished effect and knew Charles loved it.

'What are you going to do with yourself?' Patrick asked Tilly, settling his long body down beside her on one of the new sofas.

She grinned at him, at ease in a way Olivia hadn't seen before. 'I'm not going to think about work or the future for a bit. I know everybody thinks I should be deciding on a career but how can I when there's all this to enjoy?' She waved a hand at the elegance that surrounded them.

Patrick smiled back at her. 'That's the spirit! Youth never comes again. You can decide about a career later. Now, tell me what you think about your mother's new husband?' He shot a mischievous glance at Charles, pouring out Kirs at the drinks table in the far corner of the salon. 'Do you think he shapes up as a properly wicked stepfather?'

Liz threw one of Olivia's new cushions at her husband. 'Behave yourself or we'll never be asked again.'

'You forget,' said Olivia, 'it's the step*mother* who's wicked.'

'You couldn't be,' said Charles simply as he brought the drinks over on a silver tray.

The dining room wasn't finished yet so they ate in the kitchen. Quilted Provençal print mats were laid on the refectory table plus the sunflower plates and yellow-handled cutlery.

'Didn't you bring anything from your previous house with you?' asked Liz curiously after Charles had detailed where they had found everything.

'It was modern, nothing would have fitted here. But, also, it was my past,' he said, serving a Côtes du Rhône wine with the pâté. 'Olivia is my future. I didn't want the two to get confused.'

'I wasn't even allowed to see it,' she said.

'You can't divorce past from future,' Liz said lightly, smiling up at Charles as he filled her glass. 'If I'd been Olivia, I would have insisted on being taken there.'

'Why?' asked Charles curiously as he filled wine glasses.

'Because you can find out so much about a person by looking at how they live.'

'I knew enough about Charles,' Olivia said stoutly but inwardly regretting that she hadn't insisted on seeing his previous home.

Charles glanced round the kitchen, the dimmed lights in the working section emphasising its cavernous quality. 'What can you tell about us from this house?'

'Darling!' protested Olivia. 'This isn't some sort of party game.'

'Come on, Liz,' Charles insisted.

'I've put myself on the line, now, haven't I?' she said, but didn't appear at all discomposed. 'All right, no punches pulled?'

'No,' agreed Charles, sitting down at the head of the table.

'Now, watch yourself,' warned Patrick. 'Don't get carried away.'

Olivia felt a small knot of apprehension gather in her stomach, then remembered that Liz was her friend.

'OK, here goes. Both of you love beauty but for Olivia it lies in line, in texture, in colour. For Charles it is in order and quality. He says his previous home was modern. I imagine it was Scandinavian in atmosphere with precisely ordered, minimalist furniture and perhaps one rather uninspiring painting by someone who exhibits at the Royal Academy every year, chosen because it picked up the colour of the upholstery.' Her eyes regarded him wryly. 'Right?'

Charles nodded in a reserved way.

'If you'd done this house on your own, I think you would have got hold of a specialist and told them you wanted everything perfectly in period. Olivia has met your demand for quality and order but she's added her own lively talent for the unexpected, mixing different periods to achieve something that seems just right. On her own, I don't think she would have spent half as much but the effect would have been equally delightful.' She paused. 'How am I doing?'

'But isn't that using what you know of Mum and Charles to analyse what they've done, not the other way round?' objected Tilly, who'd been listening with close attention.

Patrick laughed. 'Hoist with your own petard, my dove!'

'And my first wife was in charge of my last house.' Charles grinned at her. 'It wasn't my taste at all.'

Liz flung up her hands. 'I surrender!'

'Tilly made the pâté,' said Olivia quickly. 'She's been working in a restaurant for the last nine months or so.' The conversation was successfully deflected into other channels and the evening developed pleasantly, involving a considerable amount of teasing of Tilly by Patrick and Charles. She accepted it with equanimity, helping to clear plates and serve food. The cooking was extravagantly praised and Tilly glowed happily.

'I really liked the Ratcliffes,' she said as she helped Charles and Olivia to clear up after the guests had left. 'Liz is a bit powerful, though.'

'Powerful?' queried Olivia.

'You feel she assesses everything you say. She doesn't let anything just slide by her. I feel I have to think before I open my mouth.'

'Not a bad habit to get into,' suggested Charles, loading the big dishwasher.

'I suppose so,' said Tilly a trifle doubtfully. 'But isn't it a bit exhausting all the time? I preferred Patrick. He was interested in talking to me without being judgemental, I really enjoyed our conversation.'

Later, as Olivia and Charles were getting into bed, he said, 'She's quite sharp, your Tilly. She summed up Liz and Patrick perfectly.'

'Not just my Tilly,' said Olivia, taking off her makeup. 'Our Tilly now.'

'You're right, my love,' Charles agreed enthusiastically. 'And soon we'll have our Phyllie with us as well.'

Olivia wiped away the last of her cleansing cream and tried to feel excited about the prospect.

Chapter Fifteen

Phyllida and her boyfriend, James Whistler, set off from England on Good Friday, stopped overnight just north of Lyons and arrived at *La Chênais* in time for lunch on Easter Saturday. Once again the sun was shining splendidly and James had the roof of his sports car down as they drove into the courtyard.

Phyllida, in skintight jeans and a close-fitting ribbed T-shirt, looked as chic and in control as she had at the wedding. James was a pleasant-faced young man with straight fair hair just skimming the collar of his checked shirt. He wore his sleeves rolled up and his lower arms displayed the beginnings of a suntan. He greeted Olivia and Charles with easy, public school charm.

Phyllida gave her father an extravagant hug.

Olivia came forward. 'Phyllida, we're so pleased to see you.' She kissed an unresponsive cheek.

Phyllida's eyes opened wide as she looked at the house. 'My, my, Dad, haven't you done well!'

'Olivia's designed it all,' he said, slipping his arm through hers. 'If it had been left to me, it would all have been done in repro.'

'Nonsense, Dad, don't underestimate yourself.' She gave his arm a squeeze.

'Take Phyllie upstairs, darling,' suggested Charles to Olivia. 'James and I will organise the baggage. If I know my daughter, she'll have brought enough cases for several months.'

Olivia took her stepdaughter up. 'We've given you and Tilly your own rooms, we hope you'll think of this as home. Your father found the bed,' she added. The girl said nothing but her hand caressed the top of the shell carving.

'I thought James would be comfortable in our guest room just along the corridor,' Olivia continued, chilled by Phyllida's cool control. 'The room has its own bathroom.'

'Oh, Jimmy sleeps with me,' she said carelessly as James came in carrying several bags. 'You can sling your stuff over there,' she said to him, waving at a corner of the room.

The young man's face remained as bland as it had been since their arrival. 'Right ho,' he said and disappeared for more luggage.

Charles's mouth tightened when Olivia told him of the arrangement but all he said was, 'She's an adult, we have to accept her decisions.'

After lunch, Phyllida and James said they wanted to do a bit of exploring on their own and disappeared, leaving Tilly and Olivia to clear up while a disappointed Charles went out to attack the garden.

Phyllida and James returned about six o'clock and announced they would have a quick snooze before dinner.

Olivia and Tilly prepared the meal and just had time for a shower before they all gathered in the salon at eight o'clock for drinks. Phyllida arrived bearing a box of Fortnum and Mason champagne truffles for Olivia and handed it over with a pretty speech of thanks for making her and James so welcome. Olivia's heart rose. Perhaps they were going to get on after all? Then she saw the sidelong glance Phyllida gave her father.

Dinner was served in the dining room for the first time. Dark red walls and matching curtains, lavishly trimmed with gold braid, and rococo bronze lighting sconces provided a rich background to the gleaming mahogany furniture and Olivia felt proud of the effect she'd created, enhanced by three branching candelabra set on the long table. Phyllida appeared to take the room for granted and James didn't comment. Olivia realised he would always take his cue from Phyllida and recognised somebody who, like her, disliked making waves. How long, she wondered, would he be happy to accept her belligerent attitude to life?

After the meal Charles produced a trolley and started to stack it while Olivia and Tilly carried out serving dishes. 'Not got staff organised yet?' commented Phyllida, making no move to help. 'Come on, Jimmy, let's have a look at the garden by moonlight before coffee's served.'

On Easter Day Liz and Patrick arrived for luncheon. 'How's it going?' Liz asked Olivia in the kitchen.

'OK so far,' she said, 'but we haven't seen Phyllida or James this morning yet. Charles took them up breakfast and said he couldn't see a sign of life from either of them. No doubt they'll appear at some stage.'

Phyllida and James drifted into the salon without apology just as Charles was opening a bottle of champagne. James struck up a conversation with Patrick about property values but Phyllida arranged herself decoratively in a corner of a sofa and looked bored.

The centrepiece of the meal was turkey. 'Where's the flavour of France, Dad?' Phyllida asked sardonically as Charles carved. 'I thought that was what you came for?'

'We'll go to some of the great restaurants we've got round here, Phyllie, then you'll eat French. Meanwhile, this *dinde* is delicious and the French also think it's great,' Charles said cheerfully.

'I've done a really French pudding,' Tilly said gamely. 'It's the first time I've tried it so I hope it's come out all right.'

Phyllida said nothing but Olivia caught her giving James a kick under the table.

The pudding was *Oeufs à la Neige*, ovals of poached meringue floating on a sea of *crème Anglaise* and laced with golden caramel. Charles was extravagant in his praise. 'One of my favourite puddings,' he said.

Phyllida said, 'Not bad,' her tone awarding somewhere around six out of ten.

'Really great,' James exclaimed, losing a little of his sophisticated detachment as he helped himself to more of the dish.

'*Formidable*,' Patrick announced. 'You've really got a tremendous talent for cooking, Tilly.'

She flushed with pleasure and Phyllida looked fixedly at her plate.

After lunch Liz chased Tilly into the garden with the others. 'I bet you did most of the cooking,' she said. 'Now it's my turn to help.'

'I think it's warm enough for the pool,' suggested Olivia.

Loud splashes from outside said that Phyllida and James had already decided that.

Tilly allowed herself to be shooed out of the kitchen.

'Phyllida seems a right little madam,' said Liz, stacking the dishwasher as Olivia put away food. 'I asked her about her work and she more or less told me I wouldn't understand.'

Olivia giggled. 'She's probably right. Charles tried to explain it to me one time and I gave up.'

'Surely it's just a simple matter of buying and selling at the right prices? Just because it's money, it doesn't mean it's different from any other commodity,' Liz said dryly.

'I suppose not,' agreed Olivia doubtfully. 'Charles made it sound terribly high-pressured though.'

'She looks as though she lives on a knife edge,' said Liz as she placed the last plates in the dishwasher. 'Her eyes are never still and have you noticed her finger nails? They're false. I bet she bites them ragged.'

Olivia paused in wrapping the remains of the ham in tin foil to think about a twenty-three year old living on her nerves. It wasn't a pleasant thought. She resolved to be kind and understanding towards her step-daughter.

'Great meal, darling,' Charles said, popping his head round the kitchen door. 'Patrick and I will go and keep an eye on the swimmers.'

'Men!' snorted Liz. 'They think things clear themselves up.'

'Well, we've just about finished,' said Olivia. 'Thanks, Liz, you're a treasure. We can go and join the others now.'

Later Olivia came in and made tea then took a tray out to the pool. 'Anyone for a cuppa?' she called.

In the kidney-shaped pool Phyllida and James, both wearing dark glasses, were reclining on inflatable chairs, heads thrown back, drinking in the sun. They flapped idle hands in a gesture that could have meant anything.

143

'Lovely,' murmured Liz, raising herself from a prone position on a lounger, pushing back its sun shade and reaching underneath for her large straw hat. 'You spoil us.'

Olivia handed her a cup of tea. 'Patrick?'

'Right,' he murmured, lying stomach down on another lounger and hardly moving his long body that swimming trunks revealed was surprisingly well shaped and muscular. Olivia placed his cup on the small table beside him.

She looked around. 'Where's Charles?'

'Gardening,' said Liz. She picked up her cup of tea. 'Oh, that's delicious. Where's Tilly? I thought she was going to swim as well.'

'She's just coming,' Olivia said. Tilly hadn't been in the pool yet and Olivia suspected that Phyllida and James had been less than welcoming to her.

Patrick looked towards the house and shifted himself upright. 'Here she is.'

Tilly came down the lawn carrying two plates, one loaded with biscuits, the other bearing a cake. 'Any takers?' she asked, putting them on the table.

'If it's one of your cakes, yes, please,' said Liz.

'And me,' agreed Patrick.

There was a shower of water as James hauled himself out of the pool and reached for a towel. He sat on the edge of a lounger next to the tea tray as he towelled off the worst of the wet then helped himself to a couple of biscuits. 'God, this is good,' he said, leaning back and raising his sleek face to the sun again. 'Bet it's raining in England. It always does at Easter.'

Phyllida paddled her inflatable chair gently to the side of the pool, neatly levered herself on to the stone paving and padded up to James. 'Pig, that's what you are,' she said in a light, expressionless voice. She deftly removed one of the biscuits from his hand and ate it herself while he reached for a replacement. With her eyes hidden behind large, silvered sunglasses, it was impossible to tell what she was thinking. Her neat little body was decorated with a minuscule silver bikini. Already her skin was a pale gold. Olivia wondered if she'd been on a sunbed before she'd come out.

Tilly cut the cake. Her much taller and altogether more substantial body was encased in a plain black one-piece swimsuit, her long, seldom seen legs unattractively pale.

Olivia looked around to see if she could discover where Charles was. Now that the house had been more or less completed, the wilderness of so much of the garden seemed to be a constant reproach to him. No doubt soon he'd start hiring men to bring the grounds under control. Already terracotta pots had been organised along the edge of the terrace.

Olivia rather liked the sprawling shrubs and lush grass. They reminded her of the Sleeping Beauty quality of the property.

Phyllida picked up her watch and glanced at it. 'I'm going to find Dad,' she announced. 'Come on, James!'

144

He reluctantly levered himself to his feet, slipped on a pair of flipflops and obediently followed her bare-footed figure down a path that led into the heart of the shrubbery.

Five minutes later the two of them reappeared with Charles.

'Have a cup of tea, darling,' offered Olivia. 'You look as though you could do with it.'

'I'm exhausted,' he pronounced, dropping on to a lounger and taking off his sunhat. Sweat ran down his face, his arms were scratched and so were his legs.

'You should have worn trousers, Dad, not those shorts,' said Phyllida severely. 'Make sure you get all that blood off before you go in the swimming pool.' Then she took another look at her watch and glanced towards the gates at the end of the drive.

A few moments later her face brightened and Olivia realised that a van had stopped outside.

Phyllida smiled at her father. 'I've got a surprise for you,' she said. 'Stay there!'

She darted off across the lawn towards the gates where a small Frenchman was now waiting and opened the door at the side. A moment later something brown and hairy streaked across the lawn and flung itself at Liz. She shrieked in what sounded like genuine panic. 'Get him off me! Patrick, Patrick, do something!'

Olivia rushed to her aid. But Charles was there first, got a hand in the dog's collar and pulled him off.

'Oh, God,' said Liz, collapsing back on to the lounger, 'I'm sorry.' She was shaking, her face white and drawn. She sat, eyes tightly closed, her arms hugging herself, as though she feared she might otherwise fall apart.

Olivia could hardly believe that strong, sensible Liz could so totally lose control. It was only a dog, after all.

Charles retreated, hauling the animal with him until they were well back from the pool. 'It's all right, Liz,' he said, 'I've got him, he won't come near you again.'

Liz opened her eyes and gave a shuddering sigh. 'I was badly bitten by a dog when I was child,' she said, a suspicious wobble still in her voice. 'I've been terrified of them ever since. And they always choose me to come at. It's as if they know.'

Charles took a firmer grip on the dog's collar and sat down on the sloping lawn. 'Now, perhaps someone will tell me where this mutt has come from?'

'It's a present for you,' said Phyllida, loping back towards them. The van and the Frenchman had disappeared. 'He wasn't meant to streak off like that, I was going to present him properly.' For once cool, possessed Phyllida appeared to have lost a little of her composure.

'A present?' repeated Charles. They all looked at the panting animal he was holding.

The dog had a fine head but a large and heavy body, legs that ended in massive paws, a matted, dark red coat and a tail like a feather duster. Ignoring everyone else, warm brown eyes fixed themselves on Charles, the big body pushed itself against his legs, a pink tongue hung out of a well-toothed mouth, the lips were drawn back in what seemed like a smile and the feather duster waved backwards and forwards. The attitude was ingratiating.

'I'll get a bowl of water,' Tilly said. 'If he's been in the back of that van in this hot weather, he'll be thirsty.' She set off in the direction of the kitchen.

Charles began stroking the animal, who tried to lick his face.

'I know you've always been crazy about dogs,' Phyllida said rapidly. 'James and I saw an ad for this one in the local *tabac* yesterday afternoon. We went and had a look at it and thought it would be a perfect present for you. He's a cross,' she added proudly. 'Half-Irish Setter, half-Great Dane.'

'Which means he'll eat you out of hearth and home,' said Patrick, looking at the animal admiringly. He clicked his fingers, the head slewed round and looked in his direction. Patrick clicked his fingers again, Charles let go of the collar and the dog trotted over to Patrick and shoved his head between his legs. Patrick pushed his hands down the dog's body in steady strokes then pulled at his long, floppy ears. The dog loved it. 'Fully grown,' Patrick announced. 'Could be two or three years old. Did they say why he was for sale?' he asked Phyllida.

She shook her head. It was obvious she hadn't thought to ask.

'Could be he was too much for them.' He continued firmly stroking the dog, who half-closed his eyes in appreciation. 'Needs a really good brush,' he said. Liz drew up her legs as though to make herself as small a target as possible for any renewed interest by the animal. She looked at Patrick with an expression of distaste.

With a quick twist of his wrist in the dog's collar, Patrick got it lying on its side, then moved his upper back leg and revealed a tattooed number on the pale, inside skin. 'He's had his anti-rabies jab,' he said. Liz shuddered.

Tilly returned with a bowl of water and put it on the stone paving. The dog immediately righted himself and started to lap it up with an eager tongue.

'Does he have a name, Phyllie?' asked Charles, regarding the scene with a fascinated eye.

'Juno,' said Phyllida eagerly.

'But it's a dog!' protested Patrick.

She shrugged her shoulders. 'That's what the man said. He said something about not many Js available. I don't know what he meant.'

'As far as dogs are concerned, each year in France is given a letter. When you register your animal you have to choose its name from a list all beginning with that letter.'

'Just like English cars,' exclaimed James, who'd been watching the scene with a somewhat jaundiced eye. Not a dog lover, decided Olivia. She wondered whether he'd tried to dissuade Phyllida from buying the animal for her father.

'Juno,' called Charles experimentally. The dog continued to lap up the water.

'Juno!' he called again with more authority. The dog raised his head, looked at Charles then loped over to him, pushing his head against his hand. Charles caressed him. 'Juno,' he said again with a note of possession.

Olivia realised that there would be no question of refusing this present. The Frome household had been increased by one dog. Phyllida might only be staying with them for two weeks but she had made sure her visit wouldn't be forgotten after she left.

Chapter Sixteen

Tilly struggled to snap on Juno's lead. The excited dog slithered on the hall's marble floor and barked with short, sharp yelps.

'Quiet!' she commanded – to no effect. She managed to manoeuvre the dog in between her legs and hold him still for long enough to get the lead in place. Juno shot off towards the front door.

More or less pulled down the drive, Tilly laughed with exhilaration. Walking Juno was proving a first-class way of escaping from the tensions of *La Chênais*.

Phyllida and James had been staying for a week now. Neither had displayed the slightest inclination towards helping with the household tasks. 'Well, they are on holiday,' Olivia had said in a tired voice when Tilly had suggested installing a rota to share the clearing up.

She turned down the hill outside the gate and tried to get Juno to walk to heel.

As she passed the Ratcliffe house, Patrick came out and his face lit up at the sight of them. 'Going for a walk?' he called.

'More of a trot,' Tilly called back.

Patrick came down the drive. 'Why don't you take him up into the hills for a real run? That's what he needs.'

'Charles has taken Phyllida and James off for a drink somewhere.'

'So you haven't a car! Look, Liz has sent me out to get some bread. Why don't I drive you up there? I'd love a walk, I've been stuck in the office ever since last weekend.'

'That'd be lovely,' Tilly said gratefully.

Patrick turned towards the garage and opened the back of his Volvo estate car. 'Here, Juno,' he said. 'Up you get.' Tilly let Juno go and he leapt into the baggage area, arranging himself on the carpeted floor like an emperor on his throne, tongue hanging out, panting. 'He is a handsome animal,' Patrick said admiringly before closing the tailgate.

'Handsome is as handsome does,' said Tilly, a trifle severely.

'Ah, what's he been up to?' Patrick opened the passenger door for Tilly, helped her in and handed her the end of the seat belt.

'Only stole half a leg of lamb that I was going to make shepherd's pie out of.'

'Oh, dear!' Patrick sounded amused. He started the engine.

Juno got up and braced himself against the motion of the car. Then he took a neat leap over the back seat and arranged himself comfortably on the leather upholstery.

'Get back, Juno!' Tilly ordered, turning round.

Juno liked it where he was.

Patrick laughed. 'You'll never get him to move. When I had a dog, I installed a proper meshed guard to keep him in the luggage area. He didn't like it one bit and most of the time I let him occupy the seat. It made life easier. That was before I was married, of course. As you saw last Sunday, Liz has a real terror of dogs.' At the top of the hill he took the small road that led up the mountain. 'Do you drive?'

Tilly nodded. 'My grandmother gave me lessons for my seventeenth birthday present. I passed the test last summer. First time,' she added proudly. 'I haven't had much practice though and I'd hate to take out Charles's Jaguar.'

'He really needs something more sensible for the everyday driving, especially now he's got Juno.'

It only took ten minutes to reach open land where they could let Juno out.

The dog took off over the short grass and stony ground, his long legs powering him at increasing speed until he'd vanished from sight, through the rocks and trees that stood soaking up the warm sun, undisturbed by any wind. No one else seemed to be around.

'Hope he won't get into trouble,' said Tilly in a worried tone.

'He'll be fine,' Patrick assured her, setting off at a comfortable pace in the direction the dog had taken.

'What if he gets in a fight?'

'Large dogs are rarely fighters, it's usually the smaller ones who are aggressive. So, didn't you want to go for a drink as well?'

'Mum said she needed to cook Sunday lunch so I thought I would help her. There wasn't room for Juno in the Jaguar, anyway, and he needs a walk. Just running around the garden isn't enough for him.'

'And Phyllida and James aren't the best of companions, anyway,' suggested Patrick amiably.

Tilly said nothing.

'I expect she's a model guest,' Patrick continued. 'Lays the table, helps with the clearing up, takes the dog for walks?'

Tilly laughed, she couldn't help it.

'No, I see she isn't. Nor James, I expect.'

'Mum says they're on holiday and shouldn't be expected to help.'

'Bet you don't behave like that when you're on holiday?'

Tilly remembered staying with her grandmother, helping as much as she could. But her grandmother was old, it was natural Tilly should want to help her. Perhaps Phyllida would help if she was staying with a grandmother. 'I just don't like the way she treats Mum like a housekeeper,' she burst out suddenly and stood stock still, feeling too emotional to continue walking.

Patrick stopped too. 'Let's sit down,' he suggested. A little way from where they were standing there was a grassy hollow backed by smooth rock. Tilly and Patrick arranged themselves comfortably and Tilly pulled at the thyme that grew round about, letting the tiny leaves drift through her fingers, inhaling the aroma that then clung to them.

Patrick watched her. 'I should think it's difficult for Phyllida,' he said gently. 'You've gained a father but she doesn't need a mother. As I understand it, hers is still around.'

Tilly nodded, tears pricking at the back of her eyes. 'I've tried to be friends with her but she hates me.'

'She might think she does but I'm sure she doesn't know you well enough to hate either you or your mother. She's just terrified of losing her father.'

Tilly looked at him. 'Do you have to know someone to hate them?'

'I think so. Oh, you can have an irrational dislike of someone you've only just met but in my experience it's usually because you feel threatened by them in some way or they remind you of someone you do hate.'

'Do you hate lots of people?' she asked doubtfully.

Patrick laughed and eased himself into a more comfortable position. 'I don't think so. In fact, I can't think of anybody I hate. Do you?'

Tilly shook her head. 'I'm like Mum, I try to get on with people and I get really upset if someone doesn't seem to like me.'

'Such as Phyllida?'

Tilly nodded reluctantly.

'She needs time. Probably you'll never be great friends because she doesn't strike me as the sort of girl you would enjoy having a deep relationship with. But if you work at it, I'm sure you'll eventually establish common ground.'

'You make it sound easy,' Tilly said gloomily, grasping the soles of her sandalled feet and pulling them towards her shins, feeling the tension in her muscles.

'I know it won't be,' Patrick said gently. 'Just remember that you have the position of strength.'

'I have?' Tilly looked up at him in surprise.

'It's your mother Charles loves, Phyllida's mother he is divorced from. And you're not jealous of Charles the way she is of your mother. At least, you aren't jealous of him, are you?' He looked suddenly anxious, the bright blue eyes in the thin face concerned. Thick dark hair fell over his forehead making him look much younger than she knew he was.

'No, definitely not!' Tilly assured him. 'I love Charles, I think Mum's terribly lucky to have found him. And he her, of course.'

'Of course,' murmured Patrick. 'And you wouldn't mind if they had a child?'

Tilly stopped pulling at her feet and gazed at him in astonishment. 'A child?'

Patrick flushed suddenly and looked even younger. 'I'm sorry, I probably shouldn't even have suggested it. But, don't you see, Phyllida could be really anxious that a new sister or brother could deflect her father's attention? I know one always thinks one's parents are ancient but your mother isn't that old, you know.'

Tilly picked some more thyme and thought about the possible advent of a small baby. 'I wouldn't mind,' she said eventually. 'But I don't think Mum's really interested.' She gave a little chuckle. 'I suppose that means that actually I'd prefer her not to. I have no idea what she thinks!'

'I think a baby would be wonderful,' Patrick said softly.

'Really?' Tilly looked at him. 'I thought most men didn't like babies.'

'I don't know where you get that idea from.'

'Oh, just someone I went out with once,' Tilly blushed. We were talking one day and he said he supposed he'd like to have a son some time but he hated the thought of nappies and a screaming kid.' Tilly could remember exactly the expression on Mark's face as he said this; it had been full of distaste, even revulsion. Then he'd told her that his mother was on her second marriage and he had a young stepbrother. 'I think, though, he could have been jealous.'

'Well, I love little babies,' Patrick said.

'But you and Liz don't have any children,' Tilly blurted out without thinking.

'No,' Patrick said quietly.

'I'm sorry,' Tilly said, 'I shouldn't have said that.'

'No, it's all right. We just don't seem able to have any. We've had all sorts of tests and there doesn't seem to be any real reason. Liz just doesn't get pregnant.'

'How awful for you,' Tilly sighed.

Patrick threw a small stone down the slope in front of them. 'Oh, I've sort of got used to the idea. And Liz has her painting. Sometimes,' he hesitated for a moment, 'sometimes I think a child would interfere with that too much.'

Tilly said nothing. She found it difficult to imagine Liz with a small baby. Poor Patrick, he obviously wanted children very much and his wife couldn't have them. Not only that, she was terrified of dogs and he adored them as well. Which reminded her. 'Where do you think Juno's got to?' she asked him. 'Do you think he's got lost?'

Patrick chuckled. 'Most unlikely. That dog knows when he is on to a good thing. But I think we should try and locate him.' He stood up and reached down to pull Tilly up. They started to walk in the direction Juno had taken, Tilly calling him.

No Juno appeared. 'Charles will be desperate if we can't find him,' she cried ten minutes later.

'Don't worry,' Patrick comforted her. 'I know dogs. He'll be down some rabbit hole or other. He'll come when he's a mind to. Now, tell me what you've seen of the Riviera so far.'

Keeping her eyes peeled for a sight of the dog, Tilly told Patrick she'd been to one of the perfume houses at Grasse and visited Antibes. They'd all crowded into the car and walked round the yacht basin, then Phyllida had found a dress shop and insisted on trying on a linen dress and jacket and getting Charles to buy them for her. The rest of them had had a coffee in one of the open-air cafés while they waited. It hadn't amounted to much of a sightseeing experience but Tilly had enjoyed herself and Charles had seemed happy. 'I expect when Phyllida and James have gone back, Charles will take Mum and me about a bit more. We're supposed to be going up the coast, to see Cannes and St Raphael, perhaps to St Tropez.'

'What about Nice, have you been there yet?'

Tilly shook her head. 'I'm dying to go and see the markets, I hear the food there is wonderful.'

'Look,' Patrick smiled down at her, 'I've got to go there on Tuesday. Why don't you come with me?'

'Are you sure you wouldn't mind taking me?'

The next moment she staggered and fell, pushed to the ground by an enthusiastic Juno, who had appeared from the opposite direction he'd disappeared in.

'Are you all right?' Patrick helped her up.

'Yes, fine, it was the shock!'

Patrick grabbed Juno by the collar. 'You'd better put his lead on. He's certainly had a gallop, he must have done a great big half-circle.' Juno stood panting proudly, wagging a happy tail. 'Come on, we've done hardly any walking ourselves, let's step out a bit before we find the *boulangerie* and get the bread Liz wants.'

At lunch Phyllida announced that what she and James really wanted was to visit the Casino at Monte Carlo.

'It's quite a long way,' said Olivia doubtfully.

'Less than an hour on the motorway,' Charles declared. He looked fondly at his daughter. 'You want to gamble away your inheritance at the tables, do you? Well, why don't we all go? Make an evening of it. We can eat at the Hôtel de Paris, that's where *crêpes suzettes* were invented,' he said to Tilly, 'and afterwards we'll visit the Casino. Have you brought some glad rags with you?' he asked his daughter. 'Not that you'd ever let me down. I know, we'll go on Friday, your last night, that'll give you something to remember.'

Phyllida gave a pretty little pout. 'Can't we go before then, Dad?'

Which meant, thought Tilly, that Charles would then be persuaded to take them out again for a farewell dinner. She had to admire the way Phyllida manipulated things.

Charles beamed again at his daughter. 'Can't wait, eh? Don't you know that things are all the better for waiting?'

'I didn't notice you hanging around before you married Olivia,' said Phyllida in a silky little voice.

Charles laughed. 'Nor I did, you little baggage. OK, we'll see if we can go earlier.'

Tilly hoped he wasn't going to suggest they went on Tuesday night because that would mean having to ask Patrick if they could be back in time for her to get ready.

But Phyllida pressed for going the very next day, Monday.

Charles rang up and found he could make a booking at the Hôtel de Paris and everything was set. 'Not my chosen entertainment,' he said to Olivia, putting down the telephone as she brought coffee into the salon, 'but it should be quite fun.'

'I think it sounds delightful,' she declared heartily. 'I'm so glad you suggested it, Phyllida, it'll be a wonderful treat.'

Phyllida hardly seemed to hear her. 'Let's go for a stroll in the garden, Jimmy,' she said. 'And Juno can come too.' She opened one of the long French windows and stepped out on to the terrace, clicking her fingers at the dog, who was lying on the floor at Tilly's feet. He raised his handsome head, looked at Phyllida standing in the window, gave a big sigh and returned his head to its resting place. 'He's tired,' Tilly said, trying to sound apologetic. 'I took him for a really long walk this morning.'

For a moment it seemed as though Phyllida would say something but she thought better of it, turned and went out into the dark garden. Jimmy followed.

Tilly patted the dog and felt inordinately pleased that he hadn't wanted to go with Phyllida.

'What are you going to wear tomorrow night, Tilly?' asked Charles.

She looked anxious. 'Will it be very smart?' Stupid question, she told herself, of course it would.

'You'd better take her somewhere tomorrow morning and buy her a nice outfit,' Charles said to Olivia. 'If I know Phyllie, she'll have brought something that'll knock our eyes out.'

While Charles took Phyllida and James off to the art colony of St Paul de Vence, Olivia and Tilly went shopping.

It proved difficult. Though the shop was well stocked, Tilly hated most of the dresses, all the skirts were too short, she said. 'Why can't I just wear my Laura Ashley?' she complained to Olivia.

'Darling, we're going to one of the smartest restaurants on the whole of the Riviera. Why do you hate displaying your legs so much? There's nothing wrong with them.'

'Too much of them,' said Tilly crossly.

'Well, how about a trouser outfit?'

'They show my big behind.'

The assistant who had been helping them made a comment and disappeared from the cubicle with an armful of rejected clothes.

'What did she say?' asked Tilly. But the French had been too rapid for Olivia to understand.

Then the assistant was back with a little sleeveless shift dress that Tilly had already passed over as not being her style. Beaming, the girl indicated that she should try it on.

Feeling far too large and bad-tempered, Tilly thought it was easier to obey than refuse. Then stood looking at herself in wonder.

The shift was in white piqué cotton; the A-line skirt skimmed the tops of Tilly's knees, the plain top went straight across her shoulders, the sleeveless armholes were superbly cut. The assistant made Tilly turn round and look in the mirror at the demure white bow that trimmed the dipping back. The dress was utterly simple but made Tilly feel marvellous. And her mother was right, her legs really were quite good.

Olivia smiled and said they would take the dress. But the assistant hadn't finished. She brought out a little black bomber jacket in some sort of ciré material that fastened down the front with silver studs. Again, totally simple, it suited the dress perfectly. 'And it'll be very useful,' asserted Olivia as Tilly protested it must surely be too expensive. 'The days can be warm at the moment but the nights tend to be chilly.' Then they went and bought a pair of strappy black patent leather high-heeled sandals and a black patent leather bag on a long gold chain. 'There's no point in not having the right accessories,' Olivia insisted. 'Charles told me to spend whatever you needed.' She paused then added, 'It'll all be a fraction of what tonight will cost him.'

Tilly told Patrick all about the Monte Carlo trip as he drove her to Nice on the Tuesday morning.

'It was sensational!' she said with a sigh. 'The restaurant at the Hôtel de Paris is out of this world. I've never eaten food like it. The sauces had a texture like silk and layers, just layers, of flavour. I had scallops to start with and the sauce had lobster in it and there was a dear little salad with all sorts of tiny leaves.'

'And after?' asked Patrick as he swung on to the coast road. Tilly couldn't help thinking as they drove alongside the Mediterranean that, compared with the autoroute, the road looked jolly scruffy. Small shops, commercial developments, too many cars, the beach just a narrow strip of sand right by the road. 'Oh, then I had more fish, I think they called it a *rendezvous*! Three different kinds in another fabulous sauce.'

'No,' Patrick laughed, 'I meant after the meal.'

'Oh, but I have to tell you how wonderful the dining room was! Like something out of a fairytale! Charles took Mum and me to the Ritz just before Christmas but its restaurant is nothing compared to the Hôtel de

Paris. And the service was fabulous, you hardly noticed the waiters.'

'And did Phyllie enjoy herself as much as you?'

'Well, she doesn't eat much, you know. But she loved the way everyone looked at her.'

'Now, Tilly, is that worthy of you?' Patrick shot her a glance of mock reproof.

Tilly giggled. 'Well, she did. And you could see James was delighted to be with her.'

'What about Charles and your mother?'

'Oh, they enjoyed themselves as well.' Tilly giggled again. 'Charles was like a sultan with his harem. Apart from James, of course.'

'Perhaps he stood in for a Eunuch.'

'Patrick! He'd kill you if he heard that. He loves to parade up and down the swimming pool showing off his body.'

'You know, I don't think you're the quiet girl everybody thinks you are at all.' Patrick sounded delighted by this conclusion. 'I think you keep a wicked eye on us all and are just waiting your time.'

'For what?' It was the first time anybody had ever suggested Tilly might be anything but a nice, not too bright, well-brought-up girl and she was enchanted. Especially since it was Patrick who'd said it. If it had been somebody sophisticated who was used to chatting girls up and putting it about, it wouldn't have had nearly the same effect.

'Ah,' he said, 'that's what I don't know. I'll just have to wait and see. But I shall be on my guard around you! Now, tell me all about the casino. Did you lose lots of money?'

'Well.' Tilly laced her hands over her knees, enjoying herself. It was incredible. I couldn't believe my luck; all the others lost but I won about eight thousand francs. So I'm going to treat you to lunch and I'm not going to take any argument,' she said firmly.

'All right,' Patrick agreed gravely. 'Since you're such a rich young lady, I'll accept. Now, here's the *Promenade des Anglais* where the rich Milords used to stay.'

'Mum's told me about the *Promenade*. Isn't this where the Negresco hotel is? Is it true it's got a fantastic chandelier?'

'Baccarat crystal.' Patrick assured her. 'We've just passed it, I'll point it out when we go back.' He turned off to the left, made his way to a graceful square and stopped the car. He reached behind him for his briefcase, got out a map of Nice and gave it to Tilly. 'Look, we're here, at the *Place du Palais*. I should be through with my business by twelve, so where shall we meet?' He thought for a moment, his face creased in an anxious frown.

'Why not over there?' Tilly pointed to a large building that looked as though the columns and pediment of the Parthenon had been slapped on to an Italian Renaissance palace. A wide flight of steps led up to the entrance and in front of them was a huge paved area. 'I could wait for you on those steps. Or have a coffee at that little café there.'

Patrick's face cleared. 'Excellent idea. Let's say on the steps of the *Palais de Justice* at twelve-twenty, OK?'

Tilly nodded, folded up the map, picked up her shoulder bag and slipped out of the car. She waved as Patrick moved back into the stream of traffic and felt a marvellous feeling of release. He was very nice but it was suddenly great to be on her own. Not to have to cope with Phyllida's animosity or James's indifference that were making her feel like some sort of housemaid. And the fact that Charles didn't seem to notice what was going on or that Olivia looked worried so much of the time was also wearing. But Phyllida and James weren't staying much longer and then it would all go back to the delightful way it had been before they arrived.

Tilly attacked the vegetable market like a fashion junkie at her first Paris couture show. All too soon the time melted away and she realised with a shock that it was a quarter past twelve and she was a long way from the *Palais de Justice*.

In fact it only took her ten minutes to get there but Patrick was standing on the steps of the impressive building looking even more worried than usual. Then he saw her hurrying towards him and his face lit up. 'Thank heavens, I thought you'd got lost,' he said, running down the steps to meet her.

'I'm sorry, I lost count of the time. Have you been waiting long?' Tilly gasped, trying to catch her breath again.

He shook his head. 'Not very long. The car's down here.'

'Where shall we go for lunch? Remember it's on me. How about the Negresco?'

'After dinner at the Hôtel de Paris last night? I'm surprised you can even face the idea of it!'

'Oh, I can always eat.' Tilly grinned at him.

'I thought we should go from the sublime to the ridiculous. There are some nice cafés at the old port.' He opened the door of his car and helped her into the passenger seat.

'Doesn't sound very special to me,' grumbled Tilly.

The old port sliced into the eastern part of Nice. A small *quai* was lined with old-fashioned bars and restaurants and the odd shop, all looking out on a mish-mash of small yachts and fishing vessels.

The restaurant Patrick chose was small and the decor ordinary. But Tilly could see that the other clients looked French and it had an atmosphere that said here was somewhere people came to eat enjoyably but not extravagantly. She felt at home after the glamour of the Hôtel de Paris.

They had fish soup, a marvellously satisfying burnt orange purée with round croutons that Patrick showed her how to spread with *rouille*, a tangy mayonnaise, and top with grated cheese. Then she ordered *merlan* with ratatouille.

'Don't you like meat?' Patrick asked.

'Yes, I do, but I love fish almost better. The texture is so much more interesting and the flavour more subtle.'

'I'm a meat man myself,' he said, tucking into his veal escalope. 'This is a real treat. The only time we have proper food at home is when we're entertaining. When she's working, Liz hardly notices what she eats. You could feed her on brown paper and she'd think it was ham.'

'Come on!'

'No, seriously. She gets so immersed in what she's painting – the shapes, the images, the colours – hardly anything else exists for her.'

'Mum says she's been really helpful,' Tilly said, feeling in some obscure way that she needed to stand up for Liz. Which was odd because she found it difficult to understand how gentle Patrick, who was so kind and understanding, could be married to someone who seemed so independent and, well, inconsiderate. She certainly didn't seem to worry much about looking after him.

'Oh, Liz likes Olivia very much. She can be very charming when she's interested in someone. And she's a tremendous help to me with my business, always willing to entertain clients and contacts.' Patrick sounded eager to defend her now and Tilly thought again what a nice person he was.

'How did your business go today? Sell any penthouses or luxury villas?'

'Ah, today was preliminary discussions on a new development along the road towards Villefranche. Luxury maisonettes, all with a view of the sea. The developers are hoping to sell most of them before the building is finished. They think they'll prove ideal *résidence secondaire* properties.'

'And will they?'

Patrick gave a little shrug to his shoulders. 'We're hoping to get the Germans and the Swiss interested. Maybe some Dutch and some Austrians.'

'No English?'

'Perhaps one or two but the days when the English were buying up French properties like, well, like maiden aunts bedsocks, are over. The franc's too strong, the pound too weak, and nobody has sufficient confidence in the economy yet.'

'But the others will buy all the flats up?'

'Certainly hope so. Be a nice little project to sink my teeth into, anyway.'

'Don't you have lots of projects like that, then?'

He looked amused. 'Not too many, no. If I told you what the commission will be if we manage to move all the maisonettes, you'd give up thinking about making money at the casino. Selling luxury property is rather like placing your chips on the numbers. The market's small with too many agents chasing too few customers, so the chances of selling are not great but the returns are worth the hassle *if* you succeed.'

They had apple tart for pudding then Patrick pointed out where there was a sign saying *Toilettes* over a door in the corner of the restaurant. Tilly thanked him, picked up her bag and said she'd be back in a few minutes.

There was only the one loo for men and women but it seemed clean enough. There was a tiny mirror as well and she brushed through her long hair, untangling it from having been blown about by the wind, and studied her face. It was, she decided, unremarkable, nothing like Liz's strong look. Olivia had called Liz plain but Tilly didn't think so; to her eyes Liz was memorable. She renewed her pink lipstick and decided that she'd start wearing mascara during the day as well as for special occasions, it added definition to her eyes. After all, Charles was always saying they were her best feature and they were large and a nice shade of grey. She adjusted the set of her shirt under the fringed waistcoat and retied her Doc Martens.

When Tilly got back to the table she found that Patrick had paid the bill. 'That's grossly unfair,' she flared at him. 'I said this was going to be my treat.'

'Darling Tilly,' he said, standing up and looking down at her, 'I know you wanted to and it was such a sweet thought but I couldn't possibly have accepted. Keep your quite splendid winnings and guard them well. I'm sure you're going to need them for something important one of these days. I shall treasure the fact that you wanted to take me out.' It was so sweetly said, Tilly couldn't continue to be cross.

They walked up the quay towards where Patrick had left his car. Tilly stopped suddenly and sniffed the air. 'What's that wonderful smell?' she asked. It was pungently sugary, citrus strong and coming from a shop ahead of them.

It was a sweet factory and open to the public. 'Do let's go in,' cried Tilly and pushed open the heavy glass door. A big, open space was divided into different areas. On the left was a boy tending a moulding machine decanting long sausages of striped boiled sweet mixture. He cut it into oblong cushions, said, '*Bergamot*,' and gave one to Tilly. Sucking the deliciously scented sweet, she wandered over to the other side where tangerines were being crystallised in small copper kettles of boiling syrup. Upstairs were rows of jars of different varieties of boiled sweets and boxes of crystallised fruits. Tilly bought two jars of the bergamot sweets and gave one to Patrick. 'That's for you and Liz and this is for us.' When they got back to the car she added the bottle of sweets to the olive oil and lavender honey and hazelnut confit she had already bought.

'Now, I promised you a little sightseeing but I got the impression you aren't particularly interested in the museums,' Patrick said. 'Where would you like to go?'

'Can you show me where your luxury maisonettes will be?'

He looked startled. 'You can't be interested in them!'

'I am, then I'll know what you're talking about,' Tilly said firmly and knew from his face that Patrick was delighted with her request.

They drove a little way along the coast to Villefranche. The development was above the main road in what seemed to be the garden of a large villa. The site itself was boarded up with an artist's impression of the finished building. It certainly looked as if it would be luxurious, with yellow sunblinds to all the apartments and green shrubs tumbling over the balconies. Tilly looked at the view the apartments would have and gasped as she saw umbrella pines, glimpses of opulent, *fin de siècle* villas and the picturesque port of Villefranche with the blue of the Mediterranean beyond. 'Oh, I'd love to live here,' she said with a deep sigh.

'Takes serious money. You're better off where you are. That house Charles and your mother have done up is an absolute beauty. Right, seen enough?'

Tilly nodded. They drove back a short way and then turned off the main road. 'This is Cap Ferrat,' said Patrick. 'Always put an equal emphasis on the syllables of Ferrat unless you want to sound like an out and out Brit. This is the haunt of the really rich who don't want to be seen spreading it about.'

He drove round the lushly covered cape, pointing out the Villa Mauresque, where Somerset Maugham once lived, the fabulous Grand Hôtel du Cap Ferrat and a couple of villas that he had been responsible for selling. 'I'm sorry, you can't see very much, everything is designed for privacy here, but we'll stop at the lighthouse where there's a marvellous view along the coast to Antibes.'

Tilly thought how Phyllida would appreciate the glimpses of expensive villas, the luxury yachts lying at anchor in the small harbours, the air of rich privilege that hung around the quiet lanes with their impressively restrained and secure entrances. 'It's all lovely,' she said politely.

Patrick glanced at her. 'But not as much fun as the markets of Nice, eh?'

Tilly felt confident enough of their relationship to say, 'Well, you can't eat pine trees or villas.'

Patrick laughed, as she knew he would. She felt a momentary satisfaction in her ability to gauge what would amuse him.

'Are you hungry again, shall we stop somewhere for tea and a *tartine*?'

She shook her head. 'Lunch was enough for me, thanks.'

Patrick drove them up to the top of Cap. There, outside a church, stood a huge statue of a madonna and child looking out to sea, standing guard over the sailors and fishermen. They stood just below the statue, where the road widened out into a small terrace, and looked through trees at the sea. The wind had died down and it was still and quiet.

'Magic,' said Tilly, looking at the sea and the yachts.

'Magic,' Patrick repeated, looking at Tilly.

Chapter Seventeen

Olivia stood watching Phyllida saying goodbye to Charles as though she was never going to see him again. She had given Olivia a brief wave of her hand and James had done little more. It wouldn't have hurt them to have said thank you, she thought a touch bitterly as James's BMW coupé roared up the drive, spraying gravel, and Tilly held tightly on to a frantically barking and lunging Juno.

'Wish I could think they'd be back soon,' said Charles, putting his arm around Olivia. 'You were great, darling. I know Phyllie really appreciated your making a proper home for her.'

'She loved that bed you bought her,' Olivia found herself saying. Already her feelings of resentment towards the girl were dying down. Like Charles, she didn't suppose they'd see her down in the South of France again for some time. 'If she can't get here, we can always go and visit her.'

They turned back to the house and went through to the terrace. 'I suppose you won't mind a little peace and quiet before your parents arrive,' Charles said.

Every Sunday, before she settled for the evening, Olivia dutifully rang her mother in Sussex. She'd suggested several times she and Thomas should pay them a visit and eventually Daphne had said they were seriously thinking about it.

'That's marvellous, Mother.' Olivia had been surprised to find that she meant it. 'Why don't we make a date? You don't want to leave it too long or you'll suffer from the weather. Apparently July can be incredibly hot.'

They were due to arrive three weeks after Phyllida and James left. Thomas would apparently have finished the first draft of his current book by then and he thought a break before working on the next stage would be an excellent idea.

'Phyllie really enjoyed her stay, didn't she?' exclaimed Charles, leaning back in his chair and tipping his hat over his head against the heat of the sun. 'We gave her quite a time.'

'We sure did,' Olivia agreed. She wondered if she would receive a bread and butter letter and decided she wouldn't hold her breath waiting. She watched Tilly throwing a rubber ring for Juno and thought that Phyllida's present for Charles seemed to have given as much pleasure to her daughter. It was Tilly more often than not who took him for walks.

With a sigh of contentment, Olivia opened her morning mail and found a letter from Margie:

Darling Olivia,

You know you said I had an open invitation to visit and see just how all those fabrics turned out? Well, business is quite quiet at the moment. Gavin has gone off to the Bahamas and he's suggested I take two weeks when he comes back. Any chance of coming down to you? If a fortnight is too much, I could easily make it just one week and go on somewhere else. At first I thought I'd drive down and be independent, then I decided it's a long way on your own and that the plane would really be more sensible.

Perhaps you'd like to ring me as I shall need to book my ticket? Do hope it's going to be all right. I can't wait to see you – and the divine Charles – and, of course, the house. What's Tilly doing? Do tell all.

Lots of love,
Margie

Olivia looked at the date of the letter and realised it had taken nearly a week to get to them. That meant that Margie was hoping to arrive the following week. Farewell her time off!

She handed the letter to Charles with a slight raising of her eyebrows.

'Of course Margie must come,' he said enthusiastically. 'Now that the house is ready, it'll be great to have lots of visitors. You'd better ring her immediately.'

Olivia reached for the mobile telephone on the table between them but before she could pick it up, it rang.

It was David Watson, Charles's best man. Olivia handed the call over to her husband.

'David, my dear chap, good to hear from you. How are you and Angela? What, you're in France? Driving down here? That's great! Don't be silly, I'm not going to recommend a hotel, not when you can stay with us. Of course you can, we've got masses of room and Olivia would love to see you both again.' He started to give directions from the autoroute.

Olivia wondered how far down France the Watsons had managed to get and hoped it wasn't too far beyond Paris. With luck they'd take it slowly and she would have a couple of days in between visitors; she felt in serious need of a battery recharge. Still, she liked what she'd seen of Charles's best man and his wife. It would be fun to see them again.

Charles put down the receiver and jumped up. 'We seem to be in business, they'll be here in a couple of hours,' he said. 'We'd better have something light to offer them.'

Olivia couldn't believe her ears. 'Two hours? You've got to be joking!'

'They stopped last night in Aix-en-Provence, suddenly realised how near they were and thought they'd give us a ring. Asked me if I could recommend a hotel near us! Well, we couldn't possibly have them staying anywhere else, could we?'

'I don't know what we've got to eat, I thought we could survive on leftovers for the rest of the weekend, what with the huge meal you took us all out to last night.'

'Oh, I'm sure you and Tilly can sort something out. We'll try and book a table for tomorrow. It's a bit short notice for a Sunday, though. I know, we'll go out tonight, that'll help, won't it?'

You couldn't say Charles wasn't cooperative, thought Olivia as she called to Tilly to check the guest bedroom and put towels in the bathroom while she rang Margie. Then heard Charles saying, 'Wouldn't it be a good idea to hold a dinner party while the Watsons are here? We owe all those people.'

Just how long were his friends intending to stay? Olivia fought a moment's rising panic as she thought of all the meals she was going to have to produce, reassured herself with the knowledge that Tilly would help, and dialled Margie in England.

By the time the Watsons arrived, Tilly had prepared an attractive salad for lunch, Charles had laid the table and Olivia had found flowers for the guest bedroom.

'My, it's better than most hotels,' Angela Watson said, surveying the large room with the brass bedstead, marble-topped *chevets*, the night tables that did duty as bedside tables, the huge Provençal armoire and the elegant dressing table.

'I'm sorry the view is towards the hills but you at least get the sun in the morning and cool for the rest of the day,' said Olivia, and opened the door into the en suite bathroom. 'Let me know if you haven't got everything you need.'

The Watsons stayed a week and had a wonderful time. They adored Tilly's cooking and the way Olivia looked after them. They loved being driven by Charles and Olivia around the region and tried to get Tilly to come as well.

The first time they asked her, she said sorry but Patrick was taking her with him on a trip to Ventimiglia, on the Italian border. She'd got up early and prepared them a picnic and now she was off down to the Ratcliffes' house.

Olivia hoped she wasn't going to be back too late. Without her help, she'd never manage to get dinner ready.

As they were finishing breakfast, Liz rang. 'Are you still looking for some-one to help in the house because I've heard of someone who might do?'

'Liz, you are without doubt the best friend any girl could have. Who is she and where do I find her?'

Liz gave a telephone number, Olivia got Charles to ring and half an hour later Maria Rivera arrived.

163

Dark and Italian-looking, Maria was working already for two families in the area but her main client had recently died. She'd helped clear the house and now needed another job. Yes, she was willing to work in the evenings and, no, she didn't need fetching, she had a bicycle and didn't live far away. Olivia took her round, explaining in halting French what needed to be done. Maria beamed at everything and announced she would be happy to work in this lovely house.

'Great,' said Charles and took over the matter of pay. Then made sure Maria would be willing to work the next evening as that was when he'd persuaded Olivia to have their first dinner party. Two couples had accepted the invitation.

Tilly arrived back from Ventimiglia with scallops to make a salad with as a starter. She followed it with roast chicken done with spices the way Jemima had taught her, then repeated her success with the *Oeufs à la Neige* and also produced a melon icecream that was another of Jemima's recipes.

Olivia thought the whole dinner was delicious and the evening a great success. After the Watsons had finally departed on the Sunday morning, though, Charles proceeded to discuss the presentation of the meal with Tilly.

Olivia resented what she saw as criticism of her daughter's efforts. 'It all looked great,' she protested.

'Sure,' Charles agreed. 'But it could have looked better. The dressing for the scallops had slopped on the sides of the plates, that platter of chicken needed something to set it off, something green or perhaps some slices of those grilled red peppers Tilly does so well, and the icecream tasted fantastic but it looked too ordinary, just piled up in that earthenware bowl. You agree with me, don't you, Tilly love? After all, you've seen the way the big boys do it, haven't you?'

Tilly nodded, her grey eyes large and serious. Far from being upset, she seemed to be considering seriously everything Charles said.

'And chicken isn't precisely the most exciting of meats these days, even done the way you produced it, which I admit was very tasty. And I think it would be nice to have some little petits fours with coffee. I mean,' he added hastily, 'bought ones. I don't expect you to make them.'

That night as they were going to bed Olivia turned on Charles. 'I really think, darling, after everything Tilly has done to help, it was the outside of enough to criticise her efforts like that.'

He looked surprised, hurt even. 'I was only trying to help. If she wants to turn professional one of these days . . .'

'Has she said she does?' Olivia interrupted him sharply.

'Well, no, but she's always talking about food and she was working in a restaurant.' Charles looked slightly bewildered.

'That's got nothing to do with it. She's never said she wants to cook professionally and I think the way you talked to her this morning was unforgivable.' Olivia, exhausted, felt near to tears on Tilly's behalf. 'You should have been thanking her for giving the Watsons such good food while they were here.'

'Which I did,' Charles said a little heatedly. 'And I think you're getting upset over nothing.'

'I could see Tilly was quite hurt,' said Olivia without thinking. Then was amazed at herself. She knew Tilly hadn't minded. It was she who was hurt. Charles didn't seem to realise they weren't running a hotel here. 'And, anyway, what's all this about professionalism? This is our home, not a restaurant, our guests don't expect there to be a chef in the kitchen!'

'Remember the high standard of the meals we've been given? How beautifully presented everything was? I just want our parties to be as good.'

'They ought to be jolly pleased they're being given a meal out! Especially with the wines you give them. Honestly, Charles, I don't understand what you're on about.' Never before had Olivia felt less in tune with her husband.

'Look, darling,' he said, sitting on the bed beside her, 'you're tired and overwrought. Leave it until the morning, it'll look quite different then.'

'I'm not tired and overwrought,' snapped Olivia.

He removed his arm and looked hurt.

She immediately felt contrite. 'Perhaps you're right,' she said. 'It really is very tiring having all these guests and we've got Margie coming tomorrow.' She got off the bed and removed her dress, bra and pants, slipping into a cotton nightie without caring whether Charles was watching her or not.

These days there didn't seem to be any time to develop her relationship with him. No time for just the two of them. No time for her to try and find out what he was like as a boy, what his hopes and dreams had been, what had happened to his marriage.

It was this remorseless necessity to keep guests happy the whole time. Every night she went to bed thinking of what she had to do the next day and every morning she woke up knowing there was no time to stay in bed for a cuddle with Charles, not when she had to be up and organising breakfast. When they'd been surrounded by building chaos, she'd yearned for the house to be finished. Now that it was, she remembered their days then as a haven of peace and togetherness.

Looking hurt, Charles stripped off his shirt and trousers, then, dressed in just his boxer shorts, went into the bathroom to clean his teeth. He said nothing and Olivia thought, We're like an old married couple already, all the excitement gone. And we've only been married a few months.

She felt tired and dispirited.

Then Charles came back, his face shiny-clean, his eyes gleaming. 'I'm an old fool,' he said contritely. 'Have I ever told you how beautiful you are and how my life would be empty without you?'

Olivia met Margie at Nice airport from the Monday mid-afternoon flight and brought her back to *La Chênais*. Charles was on the doorstep as they drove up to the house and kissed Margie as he helped her out.

She was in holiday mood, dressed in multicoloured leggings underneath an oversize T-shirt, a striped chiffon scarf trailing backwards over her shoulders. Her short black hair was as neat as ever, her face as delightfully crooked. 'My heavens, how you must have worked!' she cried, surveying the completed garage, the scrubbed stone paving round the well with its restored ironwork, the tamed Virginia creeper covering the house with green and the bougainvillaea that was already blooming in a riot over the garage. 'I can't wait to see inside.'

Olivia gave her the guided tour. She thoroughly enjoyed showing Margie everything that had been achieved. If you didn't count the Ratcliffes, Margie was the first visitor who had seen before and after. And she was someone with a designer's eye who could look at the result from a professional angle.

'I'm proud of you,' was what Margie said at the end. She sat on the guest bed, her hand caressing one of its brass knobs, her eye assessing the polished wood of the *armoire*. 'Yes, Charles has thrown money at it but you have used taste and talent to transform a wreck into a lovely home.' She flopped back on the bed. 'Oh, how wonderful to be here! I can't tell you how much I've been looking forward to this. Absolutely nothing to do but soak up the sun. I shall spend all my time sitting by the swimming pool and being absolutely no trouble to you at all. As long as I can stay in bed late in the morning, I'll do anything you say.'

Olivia went downstairs thinking that having Margie to stay was going to be a doddle. She looked forward to lots of lovely long chats, about the office, about Margie's love life and about design.

However, Margie declared office talk was out of bounds, she was on holiday, and her love life was non-existent. When Olivia protested she didn't believe that, Margie plunged into the pool and swam rapidly up to the other end.

After two days lying in the sun, Margie announced her batteries were recharged and couldn't they do some sightseeing? She'd hardly had time to go anywhere when she'd been here before. 'I'm dying to visit a scent factory. There must be one open to the public.'

'Oh, indeed there is,' Olivia said a touch grimly. She found the concentrated aromas at the perfume factory almost too much to bear. But she took Margie. And she and Charles drove her round the Gorges du Loup and had lunch in Gourdon, a tiny village that clung to the rock face. 'I feel like an eagle,' whispered Margie looking over the edge of the terrace, down into the depths of the gorge with the river running far below.

They took Margie along the Croisette in Cannes and gawped at the gin palaces moored in the various harbours. They drove up to St-Cezaire-sur-Siagne, a little town high up in the hills that had enchanted Charles and Olivia on their first visit to the area, and ate in the old restaurant they had enjoyed then.

They visited Monaco and were lucky enough to find the Prince away and his palace open to the public. It was something neither Olivia nor Charles had done before and they all enjoyed looking at the priceless furniture and delightful frescoes. 'I can quite see how Grace Kelly got bowled over by it all,' whispered Margie to Olivia as they halted by a window overlooking the splendid gardens. 'If I'd been a no-account little Irish girl, I'd have gone for it too.'

'Grace Kelly wasn't a no-account little Irish girl!' Olivia whispered back.

'Oh, I know she was a beautiful and famous film star but her father came from nowhere. I bet at rock bottom she felt like something only two steps away from the bogs,' Margie asserted.

'He made a fortune and she had the world at her feet,' insisted Olivia. Then wondered why she was arguing with Margie.

But when Charles suggested visiting the Casino, Margie said, 'Gambling in the afternoon isn't for me, it's like watching television.'

'Or reading a book when there's ironing to be done,' agreed Olivia. Then thought of Tilly back at *La Chênais* struggling with that week's batch. She'd had a go at getting Maria to do it but the results didn't meet Charles's exacting standards for his shirts or the table linen. She'd have to find a decent laundry. The answer to so many problems seemed to be money. For an instant Olivia had a vision of Surbiton's drab and dusty streets, the tiny terraced house, the constant battle to keep Tilly and herself clothed and fed.

'Let's go to the Botanic Gardens,' said Charles after lunch. 'I'm wondering whether to try cactus at *La Chênais*.'

The garden had taken hold of Charles. Any time he couldn't be found, he was trying to tame the shubbery, mowing the lawn, battling with the long grass under the olive trees beyond the formal garden, or trying to introduce new plants around the house. A garden contractor had carved out some beds and Charles was now trying to stock them with plants that would survive the cold spring Mistral winds and the hot, dry summer.

Olivia hoped they wouldn't spend too long walking the paths of the *Jardin Exotique*, she felt very tired. And tomorrow they were giving another of their dinner parties.

Tilly took Charles's strictures to heart. For the first course she produced individual spinach souffles with an anchovy sauce. She followed that with a leg of lamb that she had slowly and carefully boned, one of her cookbooks open while she wiggled away inside the meat with a small sharp knife. Then she stuffed it with kidneys and grilled red peppers.

The lamb was presented sliced on a large plate, garnished with more of the red peppers and surrounded by little bundles of haricots verts wrapped up in a thread of bacon. Pudding was the first strawberries of the season, found in Vence, accompanied by a half-frozen lemon mousse with an incredibly deep flavour. Tilly presented it standing proud above a souffle dish and topped with a ring of partially crystallised lemon slices that she'd prepared in a heavy syrup. Charles's only comment afterwards was that to have a souffle to start with and a souffle to end with wasn't the best of menu planning. Olivia felt very tired as he said this but Tilly's only comment was, 'What a clot!' as she struck her forehead with her hand. 'I should have thought about that!'

The evening had introduced Margie to the Ratcliffes. Margie had really hit it off with Liz and was invited to view her studio.

Taking her down there late the following morning, Olivia tried to explain how unusual this invitation was. 'Normally it takes ages for Liz to allow anyone in.'

'I have the kudos of being your friend,' said Margie, looking smug.

Liz met them at the door still in her painting trousers and T-shirt and with a smudge of paint on her face. 'Sorry, it's been one of those mornings, I could hardly stop,' she said with a broad smile on her face.

'Would you like us to go away and come back later?' offered Olivia.

'I hate stopping when the juices are flowing,' agreed Margie.

Liz shook her head. 'I'm mentally exhausted now. I couldn't continue any longer anyway and it's lovely to see you. Let's have coffee, I need reviving.'

'Can we take it into the studio?' asked Margie. 'I'm dying to see your work.'

Liz smiled and carried the tray into the large, light-flooded room.

Margie walked over to the easel and studied the nearly finished painting, an arrangement of triangles in various shades of green and yellow that somehow suggested a forest. Then she went and looked at a couple of the paintings leaning against the wall. 'But you're Lennox,' she said in amazement. 'I've got one of your paintings at home. It was the first original I ever bought!'

Liz flushed with pleasure. 'Lennox is my maiden name. When I left art college I thought it sounded better on its own than with Liz attached or even Elizabeth. You're the first person I've met down here who's heard of me!'

Margie made a dismissive gesture with her hand. 'How many people know anything about modern painting? Especially abstracts? But I go to all your exhibitions, though I can't afford to buy you any more.' She frowned at Liz. 'Surely you must be coming up to another one?'

'It's scheduled for September. That's why I'm so involved at the moment, I need lots more paintings.'

Soon Margie and Liz were deep into a discussion on colour values, spatial qualities and other technical matters that Olivia wouldn't have dared to ask her normally reserved friend about. But as Liz opened up, Olivia realised how much she missed being able to talk about her profession to someone who really understood.

'God, how I envy you,' Margie said, standing back and looking at the last of the paintings that Liz had arranged on cupboards around the studio. 'I'd give my eye teeth to have your talent.'

Which was another insight for Olivia. She hadn't known Margie was an abstract painter *manquée*.

'Design College was very much a second choice for me. But I knew my limitations as a creative painter.'

'Design isn't an inferior choice, merely a different direction,' said Liz, returning the paintings to their place against the wall.

'Oh, I know all that, at least my head does. It's my heart that says what it really wants is to be working like you.'

'You'd miss the business side,' said Olivia dryly. 'The discussions with clients, the marketing angles, the screwing them down on the fees bit.'

Margie brightened. 'I would, wouldn't I? An hour on my own without anyone to talk to and I start going up the wall. I think phone-in programmes were invented for people like me. And I really enjoy the financial side, it's like a game of chess.'

'I hate it,' said Liz. 'I leave all that to the gallery owner. And there aren't many people I enjoy meeting at the best of times. And never while I'm working. I put the answer machine on then and refuse to speak even to Patrick.'

'I just can't believe it,' Margie said, clapping her hands together in a gesture of delight. 'Meeting Lennox, here!'

And Liz seemed just as delighted to have met Margie.

Olivia arranged for her to come up for lunch the following day, thinking it would let her and Margie be able to chat without boring Patrick. Charles could always go and hack at the shrubbery.

Tilly wouldn't be there either, Patrick had business in St Tropez and had offered to show her Port Grimaldi on the way back. Charles's promise to take them there had yet to materialise.

Olivia felt guilty that they weren't giving Tilly enough of their time. When visitors stopped coming, she promised herself, she would devote herself to her daughter. That, though, was now going to have to wait until after her parents' visit.

The next day started badly. Margie came down and said, 'I'm awfully sorry, but something seems to be wrong with my basin, the tap won't turn off.'

'Blast. That's the second problem we've had with the plumbing,' said Charles. 'Our loo wouldn't stop flushing the other day and it took us ages to get hold of the *plombier*. Well, at least we aren't wanting to go out today.'

He got on the phone and was soon able to report that the plumber had said he thought he could make it just before midday.

'Oh, good,' Olivia said. 'Make sure you're around then, you know I'll never be able to tell him exactly what's wrong.' She was getting increasingly frustrated with how slowly she seemed to be picking up the language. As soon as the visitors stopped coming, she decided, she would take lessons. 'Oh, and, darling, why don't you take Juno out beforehand? He hasn't had a proper walk since the day before yesterday and if he doesn't get some proper exercise he'll be impossible. After all, he is your dog.'

Chapter Eighteen

Charles whistled for Juno. The dog came running into the hall, saw the lead dangling from Charles's hand and broke into excited barks, then ran round in small circles chasing his tail.

Charles decided waiting for him to calm down would take too long, waded in, grabbed the dog's collar and snapped on the lead.

'Remember to lock him up when you get back, Liz could be here by then and you know how terrified she is of him,' Olivia said, coming out of the kitchen. She was holding a raw chicken and Juno looked at it with greedy eyes.

'Is that what we're going to have for lunch?'

Olivia nodded. 'It won't be the way Tilly does it, I'm afraid, just roasted. We're having it cold with salad and some new potatoes.'

Plain roasted chicken didn't do an awful lot for Charles, especially cold. 'Aren't there some of those nice herb-marinated olives from last night? Why don't you chop them up then joint the chicken after it's been roasted and toss it in them while it's still warm? That'll give it a bit more flavour.'

Olivia looked irritated. 'What if someone doesn't like olives?'

Charles took a firm grip on Juno's lead, trying to control the impatient dog. 'I know you do,' he said patiently, 'I've seen you eat enough of them. Margie tucked into them last night and I've never noticed Liz hanging back when they're on offer. So who else is there?' Charles found it difficult to understand what Olivia was worried about. But every little thing seemed to get to her these days. 'Don't make too big a thing of it, darling, and get Margie to help you. You know guests like to make themselves useful.'

'That's not what you said when Phyllida and James were here,' Olivia shot back. 'Margie's got as much right to a proper holiday as they have and you know how helpful she was about the furnishing materials.'

Charles ran a hand through his hair and sighed. There were times when Olivia was just too sensitive. He decided he wouldn't mention that there always seemed to be too many magazines lying about the salon until later in the day. He'd cleared them away three times now and every time he looked around, they seemed to be back. Olivia and Tilly were too fond of flicking through them, that was the trouble. They'd see something that interested them, then leave the magazine lying open. He'd have to suggest they cut out whatever it was and put it in a special file in the library. That

171

was the place to have reference material. 'I'll be back in about an hour,' he said and walked out of the front door, leaving it open the way it usually stood these warm, sunny days.

Juno sprang lightly on to the back seat of the Jaguar then stood there with his head between the two front seats so he could see where the car was going, his big body looming over Charles.

He started the car and thought if Juno wasn't to break all the springs in the back seat, they needed another vehicle. Something they could throw things in the back of and transport more people than the Jaguar would take in comfort. And if Tilly was going to stay with them for any length of time, she really needed a little runabout.

Charles had had a call from his estate agent yesterday to say that contracts had at last been exchanged for the sale of his English house. Which meant he'd soon have some extra capital available. About time too, there were a number of things it was needed for apart from cars.

For instance, it was becoming plain to him that a pool house was essential. Having to run up to the house to change and shower all the time wasn't at all convenient. Sited at the north-west end of the pool, it could provide a screen between that and the drive. Then increased paving at that end with a wall behind could provide a sheltered terrace where they could eat, the gravelled area outside the salon was a bit exposed, especially in the early part of the year. And if they added a pergola with a vine, it would give shade in the height of summer. He'd been thinking about getting one of those enormous sunshades but a pergola would be a much better solution. The pool house could have a simple kitchen installed as well, that would mean they wouldn't need to carry trays up and down the lawn.

He'd get the builder in to give him an estimate. Shouldn't cost too much. The house was going to bring in more than enough to cover that and the new cars and still leave a substantial amount to swell his already generous portfolio. The stock market was steadily rising and with it his worth. Then there was the royalty agreement he'd made with the company that had bought him out. He was sitting nicely. He thought a moment how his comfortable situation must upset Veronica. She had loved the company profits.

Planning his pool extension, Charles drove up the road that led to the open hills above the house and stopped in the small parking lot. There were no other cars there. Perfect. The last thing he and Juno needed were more people. There were a sight too many of them around these days for Charles's liking.

It was ironic, he'd really been looking forward to showing off the house and his life with Olivia. Instead, he was finding there was no time for them to enjoy themselves together.

Charles got out of the car and was almost knocked over by the force of Juno's escape over the front seat. He grabbed at the dog's trailing lead and just managed to halt his headlong flight towards freedom while he checked that the meadows were clear of possible trouble from other dogs. Then he unclipped the lead and let Juno go while he followed behind and wondered when life would return to normal.

It wasn't that he didn't like Margie. He enjoyed her exuberant personality and he'd hoped she would be company for Olivia.

For the first time Charles acknowledged that he'd begun to wonder if Olivia wasn't starting to find him a little dull. He lacked the smooth talk so many of the men they'd met down here seemed to produce as naturally as they swallowed wine. Charles had watched her listening to attractive, sophisticated men at lunch and dinner parties, her head thrown back, her eyes alight, a delighted smile on her lovely face.

Veronica's bitter words came back to him, 'You never take the trouble to find out what I want! You're never interested in anything I want to do! You're boring, boring, boring!'

Was he? It had been many years since the accusation had worried him. The fact he hadn't got involved with another woman, that hectic afternoon with the long legged office copier rep apart, had nothing to do with lack of opportunity. He'd soon found out that there were any number of women eager to escort him to functions, share dinner and anything else he wanted to offer. He'd spent pleasant evenings with many of them, tried to find some reason for taking the relationship further. Had it been wariness after Veronica? Or had he really not found anyone sufficiently attractive before he'd met Olivia?

Of course there had been Phyllida, his sensitive, volatile daughter, who had made it quite clear none of the women he'd introduced her to met with her approval. It was usually then that the relationship, such as it was, had foundered.

Charles realised now that it wasn't until Phyllida had left home that he'd felt really free to form another attachment. Phyllie had needed him. The break up had affected her much more than either he or Veronica had imagined. They'd believed she was a little toughie, that she would flit between the two of them without worrying. They couldn't have been more wrong.

Charles looked around. Juno had done his usual disappearing act. His long legs had carried him into the hills. He thrust his hands in his pockets and walked at a steady pace in the direction Juno had taken.

As he had so many times before, Charles wondered how he could have been so blind as not to realise exactly what Veronica was like when she married him. For it had been her decision, no doubt about that. At the time he'd been grateful for the way she'd organised their relationship as effectively as she'd organised the office. He'd been so involved with building the business, he'd had no time for the niceties of courtship. It had been Veronica who had suggested a meal after they'd been working late. Who'd asked him home to her father's house for Sunday lunch so they could go through papers she knew he thought important. Who would produce tickets to a concert or theatre, always something light that wouldn't tax him too far, he realised long afterwards. At that stage she never seemed to worry that he almost always fell asleep before the end. He'd found her unobtrusive femininity soothing, had begun to look forward to occasions together away from business. Looking back, he could recognise the care with which she had staged his seduction. For even the final move into bed had been her decision.

It was only after marriage that it became clear Veronica's next goal was the purging of what she called his relentlessly working-class attitudes and he became aware how much she resented the fact that he never let her buy on credit, continued to drink with his old mates and preferred beer to wine. And that he hadn't a decent suit in his wardrobe.

Well, she'd educated him into the middle class all right. He'd learned to appreciate fine wine and understand what an extended line of credit could do for a business man. He'd even opened an account with a Savile Row tailor. He hadn't given up the friends he'd grown up with though, just as Veronica had remained narrow minded, snobbish and mean. If it hadn't been for Phyllida, the marriage would never have limped on for as many years as it had.

Phyllida! Charles's mouth curved involuntarily as he thought of his beloved daughter. How bright she was, how attractive! And how vulnerable under that sassy front. He wished she would show Olivia a little of her loving side.

Charles stopped walking and turned to look back towards the sea. For the first time he wondered just why he hadn't insisted on Phyllida meeting Olivia before their marriage. It had been the first time she hadn't been introduced to someone he was interested in.

Had he been blinded by his overpowering feelings for Olivia into thinking Phyllida was bound to accept her?

He recalled how he'd waited three months before contacting Olivia. Not a day had gone by when he hadn't thought about her. He'd weighed up the possibility of sweeping her off her feet by deluging her with flowers and invitations. Then he'd remembered the steady way her eyes had looked at him, heard the resolution there'd been in her voice. So he'd counted down the days, knowing she was something worth waiting for. Even during that time, he'd looked forward to introducing her to Phyllida and fantasised about the fun they would all have together.

Why had Phyllie been so reluctant to meet Olivia and Tilly?

He remembered Phyllie's white face when he'd told her he was getting married again.

'Dad, you can't!' she'd cried, her fingers gripping the table in the Grill Room at the Savoy so tightly the knuckles had become ivory pale. He'd realised then she'd had no idea he'd become so deeply involved. Had she over the years come to assume he would never marry again? That he would always be there for her?

But he always would be. Not even Olivia could come between them and it must only be a matter of time before she realised that.

She hadn't realised then; the rest of that meal had been a disaster as his daughter took in the fact that nothing she could say would deflect him from his purpose. 'Well, don't expect me to accept her,' she'd said at the end and stalked off without kissing him goodbye.

For the briefest of moments he'd toyed with the idea of postponing the wedding until she and Olivia had got to know each other. But he knew that would take too long. It hadn't been so much a hardening of his heart towards his daughter as a belief that as soon as she really got to know her new stepmother, she must come to love her. After all, Tilly seemed to have become fond of him quite quickly.

If only Phyllida had met Olivia and Tilly as soon as she knew he was engaged. If only she were living with them, the way Tilly was! Charles sighed, picked up a stick and continued up the grassy slope. He longed for them all to be a proper family.

Then he straightened his shoulders and told himself to stop worrying. It would all come in time. A slight breeze wafted the scent of thyme and rosemary past his nostrils and he stopped to drink it in. That added sweetness must be the broom. He turned again to look at the sea behind him, this time really taking in the depth of its colour beyond the still hazy blue of the hills. God, but it was wonderful! Was that Corsica he could see on the horizon? No, he decided, they'd said you could only spot it when the air was exceptionally clear and today there was this faint mistiness. Still, it was a fabulous view.

All his new found delight in life rushed back over Charles. Meeting Olivia had been like a revelation. She had brought light and joy to him. It wasn't just her beauty, it was her warmth, her sympathetic understanding, the way she responded to him. Until he met her, Charles hadn't realised he was capable of such depths of feeling or that being with the right person could make such a difference to his life.

What a contrast his present life was with a year ago. It was only now he could understand how incredibly lonely he'd been, how bleak the shuttle between work and his Essex house, how much he'd depended on his too-infrequent meetings with Phyllida.

With an exuberant rush, Juno appeared, as usual from the opposite direction from the one he'd initially taken, bounding up and demanding Charles throw the stick he was holding. A powerful thrust carried it high into the air and the dog rushed in its wake. Charles watched the swift movement of his muscular body and felt a renewed surge of love for his daughter. How wonderful of Phyllie to have given him such a fabulous present. Deep down she was a thoughtful girl.

Charles enjoyed every aspect of Juno including letting him out first thing in the morning, after which he would make a pot of tea and take it upstairs to bed. Charles frowned briefly as he remembered that Olivia never seemed to have time to enjoy the tea with him now the way they had when they'd first moved into the house, when the electric kettle was the only thing in the kitchen that worked. Then his optimistic nature asserted itself as he reflected that they would soon have the house to themselves again.

Juno rushed up with the stick. Charles laughed and tussled with him for possession, then threw it again as far as he could. Off went the dog and Charles followed.

The weather was so wonderful and Juno such fun, Charles walked for much longer than he'd intended and by the time he got back to the house it was after half-past twelve. He realised guiltily that Tilly wasn't there to help with drinks and that he'd completely forgotten about the plumber. He hurriedly drove the Jaguar into the garage, noticing the absence of a van in the courtyard. Had the plumber been and gone or was there a hope he hadn't arrived yet and would turn up after lunch?

Charles let Juno out of the car, slammed the door shut and hurried into the house. Only as he went through the front door did he remember that he'd promised Olivia he'd make sure Juno was safely shut in the study.

He went across to the salon, hoping to find the dog in his usual place.

Alas, the French windows were open and Juno had gone straight through to the garden.

Charles shouted after him but the dog went streaking down the lawn towards the group of three women standing by the pool with drinks in their hands. On the paving beside them was the ball Tilly had bought Juno and spent hours throwing for him.

Startled by Charles's shouts, the women turned round just as the dog charged the ball. Liz screamed and flung out her hands. As the dog's heavy body charged towards her, she seemed frozen by fear. Juno pushed her aside, skittering the ball into the pool with a mighty splash, and Liz's screams turned into a heartstopping shriek as she fell awkwardly and lay sprawled on the paving.

With the taste of disaster in his mouth, Charles hurried down the slope.

Juno was now doing a strong dog paddle across the pool, trying to grab the ball in his mouth. Olivia and Margie were trying to help Liz.

All around Charles could see broken glass glinting in the sun. 'Don't move, I'll get a dustpan and brush,' he said hastily.

'Don't be an idiot, we can't leave her lying here,' Olivia said irritably.

Charles hurried up the slope again thinking that if only the pool house had already been built, such essential items as dustpans and brushes would be to hand.

When he returned, Liz was sitting bent over on a lounger, cradling her wrist in her lap. She looked as though she was trying not to cry. Olivia was sitting beside her, an arm around her shoulder. Margie stood helplessly in front of them.

'Here,' she grabbed the pan and brush out of Charles's hands, 'I'll do this, you look after Liz.'

Charles hunkered down in front of the lounger. 'You all right?' he asked, concerned at her expression of tightly controlled anguish.

'Of course she isn't all right,' Olivia said shortly. 'I think she's broken her wrist. I told you to lock that dog in the study!'

'Liz, I'm terribly sorry.' Charles placed a hand on her good arm. 'We should get you to a doctor. Perhaps it's only a sprain?'

'You'd better ring him first,' Liz said through clenched teeth. 'He's probably gone to lunch now. God, Olivia, I think I'm going to be sick.' Her face became panic-stricken as her good hand went to her mouth. Olivia walked Liz to the edge of the shrub bed and held her as she bent over and vomited.

Then she helped her into the house and to the cloakroom while Charles went to ring the doctor.

When he returned to the hall, a glass of brandy in his hand, Liz was just emerging, her face white and set. 'You can't believe how difficult it is to manage with one hand,' she said bluntly. That really got to Charles.

'Come and sit down for a moment.' He took her into the salon and gave her the brandy. 'The doctor said it would be best if I took you straight to the hospital. He says you'll need an X-ray.' He watched as Liz drank the brandy in two gulps, holding the glass awkwardly in her left hand. He could see that she was in considerable pain.

At the hospital she was X-rayed and Charles waited with her for the results to come through, relieved that the pain killer she'd been given seemed to be taking effect.

'I can't tell you how sorry I am,' he said.

Liz sighed. 'It was an unfortunate accident, that's all. I panicked when I saw Juno coming down the lawn at us. If I hadn't done that, I probably wouldn't have fallen.'

'No, it was my fault.' Charles couldn't believe he had been so careless. But, then, he hadn't really believed Liz was in any danger from Juno, even after he'd seen the way she reacted when he first appeared. 'Hey,' he said, pulling out his handkerchief 'Don't cry, it isn't as bad as all that.'

'You don't understand, do you?' she said, and he was taken aback by the look in her eyes.

After a moment he got it. 'God, Liz, your painting! Aren't you working towards an exhibition?'

'The gallery is holding September for me. If this is only a sprain, I might just be able to get enough together to make it worthwhile. If it's a break . . .' She didn't finish the sentence. 'God, I'm going to be sick again.' Before Charles could help, she stumbled off in the direction of the *toilettes* and a nurse took over.

Shortly after she'd returned, looking even paler than before, the doctor appeared with the results of the X-ray. The wrist was broken. It was a nasty fracture and would require several weeks in plaster, then there would be a programme of physiotherapy to get the muscles working again.

Charles saw Liz's face close up as she heard the verdict. After she'd been led away to have the wrist plastered, he called Olivia.

'Oh, poor, poor Liz,' she said. 'That's awful! What about her exhibition?'

'She thinks she's going to have to cancel. Well, I suppose a delay won't matter very much in the long-term scheme of things.'

'I hope not,' said Olivia in a tone that suggested Charles had something to answer for.

. It was late-afternoon by the time the wrist had been set. On the way back, Charles repeated his bit about a delay in the exhibition not mattering in the long term.

Liz said nothing, just closed her eyes and leant back against the seat rest, her face expressionless.

'I mean,' Charles stumbled on, 'I'm sure it must be a disappointment but surely the gallery will give you a space next year?'

'Charles, shut up!' Liz said fiercely.

Charles did.

Olivia and Margie were sitting on the terrace when he got back, drinking mineral water. 'How's Liz?' Olivia asked. 'I thought you were going to bring her back here for something to eat.'

'She didn't feel like it,' Charles explained. 'She wanted to go straight home.'

'Well, no doubt you'd like something.' Olivia went and brought out a plate of French bread and roasted chicken. She placed it on the table beside him and said nothing.

Charles decided she was wound up about Liz's accident and the best thing was just to give the girls an account of how the hospital visit had gone. 'I know missing the exhibition must be a disappointment to her,' he added at the end. 'But she seems to be taking it very badly.'

'God, Charles, you are an idiot,' Olivia said, refilling Margie's glass. 'They need the money!'

Charles sat with a forkful of chicken arrested on its way to his mouth and gaped at her. 'But Patrick's very successful!'

'Recession hit Europe just as it did Britain, you must know that.'

'But luxury property can always find a buyer.'

'That's as maybe. Look at the way your house has hung on the market.' Olivia said, her manner thawing slightly.

'Has Liz said they're in trouble?' Charles asked, picking up the chicken drumstick to gnaw and deciding now was not the time to divulge the news about his house. Olivia would be sure to ask why he hadn't told her before.

'No, Liz wouldn't. But I can tell. They haven't given a dinner party for ages.'

'They've got a drinks party scheduled next week,' Charles said, still not quite able to accept what Olivia was telling him.

'That's one of Patrick's business affairs. I'm sure it's true, Charles. This spring Liz was talking about changing her car and the other day she told me her present one will have to do for a bit longer. And Tilly says Patrick's really hustling to sell the Villefranche development.'

'Would her paintings really bring in much money?' Charles asked doubtfully.

'Oh, yes,' Margie said positively. 'They sell for thousands.'

'Good God!'

'She's really very well known. I went to her last one and there were red dots on nearly everything. She must have been expecting six figures from the exhibition, and that would be after the incredibly high commission the gallery takes.'

'Maybe I could offer to buy one of the ones she's already completed?' Charles said slowly, wiping round the plate with a piece of bread. 'That would help a bit, wouldn't it?'

'You can try,' Olivia said doubtfully. 'Knowing Liz, I should think she'd refuse.'

'But I'd like one of her paintings,' he stated robustly. 'I was going to ask her anyway.'

'Pity you didn't, then,' Olivia shot back at him.

It wasn't like her to be so sharp.

Charles decided to change the subject, remarked that it was about tea time and made what he thought was a generous offer to go and make a cuppa.

'Ah,' said Olivia grimly. 'You remember the plumber you were supposed to oversee?'

Charles remembered. 'Didn't he arrive?'

'Oh, yes,' Olivia said carefully. 'He arrived all right. Just before midday, as promised. I showed him the tap, he grinned and waved a spanner at me. Ten minutes later he came downstairs, threw me a stream of French and left. I assumed it was OK. Until Margie and I tried to have coffee after our lunch. There isn't any water, Charles. That idiot has turned the whole system off!'

'No water?' Charles felt his shirt sticking to his body. He'd been looking forward to his bath before dinner.

'Why do you think we're drinking this stuff?' Olivia raised her glass.

Charles got up. 'I'll give the chap a ring and see what's happening.'

He was back a few minutes later. 'The answering machine's on. I've left a message but,' he looked at his watch, 'it's five-thirty and I should think he's finished for the day.'

Olivia's face said exactly what she thought of the situation. Margie tactfully wandered down to look at the pool.

'You didn't understand anything the man said?' asked Charles with a touch of exasperation.

'No, I told you!' Olivia sounded near to tears. 'He just flung a whole load of French at me and left. That's why I wanted you here. They speak so fast and in that funny accent, I haven't a clue what they're on about.'

179

'I really am sorry, darling.' Charles couldn't think of anything else to say.

They sat in silence.

Charles looked at Margie inspecting one of the new flower beds he'd just had dug. He looked at his nails. Finally he looked at Olivia. Her face was set and implacable.

'We could ask Liz if she minds us having a shower there?' he suggested hopefully.

'What, after we've ruined her life?'

Charles shrugged. There was no point in saying to Olivia that if only her French was a bit better, they wouldn't be in this mess. He was just about to suggest he found out where the nearest language courses were when there was a toot-toot in the courtyard.

The plumber had returned. With the tap that he'd had to track down to replace the faulty one in the guest bedroom. Sorry about turning off the water, he said cheerfully to Charles, but Madame hadn't seemed to worry when he told her. And it was only for the afternoon.

Charles and Olivia went down to Liz the next day to see what they could do to help.

She was dressed in a T-shirt with wide arms and a pair of shorts. She was as pale as she had been when Charles had last seen her but otherwise in control. She thanked them for their concern but said she didn't need help with anything. 'With practice, I'm sure I'll be able to cope.'

'What about shopping?' asked Olivia. 'You can't drive with that arm, surely?'

Liz closed her eyes briefly. 'Damn, I can't, can I?'

'Don't worry, I can take you or you can phone through an order and I'll get it with mine.'

Silence for a moment then Liz dipped her head in difficult acknowledgement. 'Thanks, Olivia, I'd be very grateful.'

That evening Patrick came up at about nine o'clock.

'Is it too late?' he asked.

They were all outside on the terrace, enjoying the first really warm evening of the season. Olivia had lit scented candles to keep the mosquitoes away but they didn't seem to be a problem, not yet anyway.

'Of course not,' Charles said. 'What can I get you to drink?'

'Brandy would be great, thanks.' Tilly gave Patrick a brilliant smile and he sat himself next to her.

'How's Liz?' Olivia asked.

'Sleeping. She's had a rotten day. The arm's giving her gyp and she doesn't seem able to keep anything down. I expect it's the medication they've given her.'

Charles went off to get the brandy. By the time he got back, conversation

180

had moved on to the reason for Patrick's visit.

'It's an awful cheek, really,' he was saying, 'but Liz is adamant. She won't cancel our drinks party next week and she won't hear of my moving it to the local hostelry. The thing is,' he accepted the brandy and sat cradling it awkwardly, his head bowed and an unreadable expression on his face, 'it's important for the business, especially now. I need every contact I've got if I'm going to move that Villefranche development quickly.'

Charles decided that Olivia had been right after all. The Ratcliffes did need money. 'So how can we help?' he asked.

Patrick glanced up. 'Well, Liz suggested that perhaps Tilly might be willing to help?'

'Tilly?' Olivia asked sharply.

'You mean, do the eats?' she asked. 'I'd love to.'

Patrick looked gratefully at her. 'That would be wonderful.'

'Tilly hasn't had any experience of doing cocktail parties,' Olivia protested.

Charles put a hand on her arm 'Do you think you can do it?' he asked Tilly.

She looked thoughtful. 'How many have you got coming?' she asked Patrick.

'Probably about fifty.'

'Heavens!' said Olivia.

'And it would just be canapés for drinks?'

Patrick nodded.

'It's next Wednesday evening, isn't it?'

He nodded again.

Tilly looked across at Olivia. 'We've got Grandma and Grandpa then, haven't we?'

Olivia nodded.

'Would you mind if I sort of took over the kitchen that day? And perhaps a bit the day before as well? I reckon I could do it. After all, I've been producing little eats for your dinner parties and I can easily think up some more things to do.'

Patrick looked inexpressibly grateful. 'We'll pay you, of course.'

'No,' said Charles.

Patrick protested.

'No, as Olivia said, Tilly has never done anything like this before. Your chums will understand if you say she's helping Liz out. After all, they'll see she's broken her wrist. And I'm sure Tilly will produce something they'll enjoy eating.' He turned to his stepdaughter. 'Forgive me for saying this, love, but you're going to find doing a whole party a mite different from producing a little something to get the taste buds going for eight or ten before dinner.' He turned back to Patrick. 'You just tell her what Liz would have spent on the ingredients and she'll work to that.'

Patrick was profuse in his thanks. 'You don't know what a weight off my mind it is having the party settled,' he said as he left.

As they were getting ready for bed, Charles said to Olivia, 'I shall pay Tilly to do the Ratcliffe party. I meant what I said about her being inexperienced but it will be a lot of work for her and it will be good for her to treat it professionally.' He glanced at his wife and added with a wink, 'Then I shall feel free to criticise.'

Olivia gave him a warm and beautiful smile. 'Oh, Charles, you are an old softie!'

He felt a relaxation of the tension that had been knotting his shoulders ever since Liz's accident. 'I thought you'd say it was the least I could do!'

'Well, it is but I know you didn't mean to be thoughtless. I've been really mean to you and I'm sorry.' She gave him another warm smile and drew off her cotton T-shirt dress.

He reached for her and started taking the pins out of her hair. 'We'll take your parents out somewhere for lunch that day so Tilly can have the kitchen all to herself. Then we'll help with the passing around in the evening.' He took the last pin out of her hair and spread it out over the pillow. 'And, I promise you, after your parents leave, I'm going to make sure we have some time to ourselves.'

Charles felt Olivia's arms reach round his neck and pull his head down so she could kiss him.

It was a satisfactory end to a very difficult couple of days.

Chapter Nineteen

Daphne Ferguson placed the last of her husband's clothes in the drawers of the serpentine-fronted chest in their room, then started to put her own away.

'I have to say I'm very impressed with what Olivia has achieved with this house,' she said.

Thomas looked up. He was sitting at the table by the window, in front of the first draft of his book. 'I'd say Charles has probably had something to do with it as well,' he murmured.

Daphne's lips tightened. 'Of course he has, I realise that.' She put a pile of underwear in a drawer. 'But I'm worried about how tired Olivia looks. She's lost weight.'

There was no response from Thomas. Daphne hung a couple of dresses in the *armoire* and for the first time saw what her husband was doing. She gave a deep sigh, 'I thought you weren't going to bring that with you?'

'Oh, I shan't be spending much time on it, dear. Only things keep occurring to me and I need to note them down . . .' His voice died away as he started to write something in his minuscule, beautifully formed hand. Daphne knew that by the time he'd finished the whole manuscript would be covered with notes. She continued hanging up her clothes and said nothing.

Before she'd finished the task, though, she had to visit the bathroom. She sat on the loo and looked at the view of the blue, hazy hills. If she looked at them long enough, could she manage to absorb their calm, their distant grace? she wondered. Then sighed and hoped she wasn't going to have trouble with her stomach while they were here.

'I thought we might go for a drive tomorrow morning, up into the hills. We know a nice little place where we can have lunch,' Charles said during dinner.

'Sounds a nice idea,' Thomas said looking happy.

Daphne gave a gracious nod.

'You must tell us what you'd like to do while you are here,' Charles went on. 'There are some lovely drives and we can offer you a fine selection of museums and art galleries. Or you can just relax by the pool. Whatever you prefer.'

'I prefer sea bathing,' said Thomas without a hint of apology.

'Then we can go to one of the beaches,' said Charles jovially.

'I think we should make Olivia's life as easy as possible,' said Daphne, putting her knife and fork together. 'She's looking far too tired. I just hope we won't be too much for her.'

'Nonsense, Mother, of course you won't.' Olivia pushed back a stray strand of hair.

'It's you who need the rest, Grandma,' said Tilly. 'You've come out here for a holiday and we're going to see you and Grandpa get a proper one.' Daphne saw her glance at her plate. She picked up her knife and fork again as Tilly said anxiously, 'Don't you like salmon, Grandma?'

'It's delicious, darling, just a little much for me.'

'Our elderly appetites aren't up to much these days, Tilly,' Thomas said with a hint of sardonic humour.

'Elderly? Nonsense!' Charles said with that firm joviality that was beginning to grate on Daphne. She wondered how she was going to endure a fortnight of it. How did Olivia live with it?

'You must be very pleased with the way Olivia has furnished this house,' she suggested to Charles, glancing again at the Second Empire sideboard and the superb set of walnut chairs round the dining table.

'Charles found most of the furniture,' her daughter said, a trifle sharply.

'We had a lot of fun searching for it together,' he said firmly. 'Thomas, what's your taste in wine? I've been rather pleased with this French Chardonnay, I hope you like it.'

How typical of Charles, thought Daphne scornfully, discussing his wine with his guest. He hadn't the basic manners to let its quality be taken for granted.

'Afraid I know nothing about wine, Charles. I let Daphne buy it all.'

'Ah, then it's you I should be asking.' Charles turned to his mother-in-law.

She shrugged her shoulders. 'I'm no connoisseur,' she said shortly. Wine had never meant much to her and now she was finding that even a little affected her unpleasantly. She toyed with her glass and decided she'd abandon the rest of it.

'One of the pleasures of coming to France has been extending my knowledge of French wines.'

Daphne roused herself to make an effort. 'And your study has been rewarded?' she asked courteously.

'It's been like opening Christmas stockings, treats all the way,' Charles turned to her eagerly. 'Well, perhaps not all of them have been worth drawing the cork but through talking to people and chatting up the local wine merchant, I've found some really splendid wines. Would you be interested in seeing the cellar I've started?'

Daphne nodded politely. When Charles was enthusiastic like this, she could almost understand what Olivia saw in this chunky man with his freckled face and stubborn chin. And one of the purposes of their trip out here had been to get to know him, after all. She just hoped she was up to the strain of what was obviously going to be a testing time.

Tilly announced during Sunday lunch that she needed to go into Nice the following day.

'I need various things for doing Wednesday's eats,' she said. 'I know just where to get them. I can take the train in but I have to get to the station. Is there a bus that goes there or do I have to take a taxi?'

'Why don't we all go?' suggested Olivia. 'You'd like to see Nice, wouldn't you Mother?'

'Yes, Nice might well be interesting,' agreed Daphne. She'd love to visit the Matisse Museum.

On Monday morning Thomas announced he wouldn't go with them, he wanted to work quietly on his book. Charles said in that case he'd do some gardening and they could have lunch together.

'There's not much in the fridge,' Olivia commented doubtfully.

'Don't you worry about us,' Charles reassured her cheerfully. 'There are masses of things in the deep freeze or we can go out.'

So it was her daughter and granddaughter who took Daphne to Nice. Sitting beside Olivia in the Jaguar, she was quite relieved Thomas wasn't with them; now she didn't need to worry about him being bored.

'This place is quite ruined,' she said sententiously as Olivia drove down to the coast. 'I can't believe all the development. I remember coming down here in my twenties. The coastal region was quite charming then, all open country around Nice.' She looked out of the window at a collection of shrimp-pink villas climbing up a hill. 'None of these garish estates.'

'Forty years is a long time,' Olivia commented quietly. 'The world has moved on.'

Indeed it had and not always for the better, thought Daphne. They reached the coastal road and she realised that the development on the way down had been nothing to what had taken place here. While Tilly chattered on about a visit she'd made to Nice several weeks before, Daphne gazed horror-struck at supermarkets and places selling shoddy furniture, garden ornaments, cars, boats, everything the possession-hungry modern age yearned for. Well, she shouldn't knock it, she told herself, the capitalist age had given her an excellent career and furnished her with a much-valued pension.

Then, as they drove through the outskirts of Nice, Daphne said abruptly, 'I'm sorry, darling, but I need a loo.'

Olivia gave her a worried look. 'Tilly, see if you can spot one of the super ones. You know, they're sort of a ridged oval. You see them quite often.'

Daphne clutched at her arm as she spotted a familiar pink dome. 'There, the Negresco. Stop the car, Olivia,' she said in authoritative tones.

Olivia brought the car to a halt looking distractedly at the traffic that was already beginning to snarl behind them. 'I'm not sure I can wait here more than a few minutes, Mother.' She turned round to the back seat. 'Tilly, go with your grandmother, if I'm not here when you come out, wait for me to come round again, OK?'

Daphne didn't wait for Tilly's response. She was out of the car, cursing the Jaguar's right-hand drive which meant she had to open the passenger door into the face of the busy traffic.

'Come on, Grandma, hold my arm,' said Tilly and gently slipped her hand under Daphne's so that she could grip her forearm. Daphne felt a little of her panic recede. Tilly was a dear, sensible girl.

She allowed herself to be guided across the first part of the *Promenade des Anglais* to the central strip then found herself clutching at Tilly's arm as they waited for a gap in the traffic so they could make the rest of the way across. She hated the feeling of dependency even as she gave thanks that she wasn't alone. Was this what growing old was all about?

In the quiet bustle of the Negresco, Daphne made unerringly for the Ladies. She had long ago taken the view that the only public cloakroom worth visiting was one in an upmarket hotel. Cleanliness, comfort and everything working were all guaranteed there. Though she never doubted her welcome in such places, she preferred not to display ignorance of where the cloakrooms were and over the years had developed a sixth sense regarding their location.

She walked faster, Tilly glancing curiously around as they progressed to where, sure enough, the Ladies was located.

Once in the luxurious cloakroom, Daphne let go of Tilly's arm. 'I won't be long, darling, just wait for me, will you?'

When she eventually emerged some time later and started to wash her hands, Tilly asked, 'Are you all right, Grandma?'

'Quite all right, darling. Just a little tummy trouble, I expect it's the change of diet. Don't mention it to your mother,' she added with some of her usual authority.

Daphne dried her hands then opened her handbag and found the little hairbrush she always carried. She noticed with distaste that she should have had her roots done before they came away. Keeping the grey at bay was more trouble than keeping the lawn mowed or the flower beds weeded. Perhaps Olivia could recommend a hairdresser? Cost an arm and a leg to have it done over here but she couldn't afford to let those hints of grey become a statement. Then she remembered that Olivia hardly ever went to a hairdresser.

'We'll go and see how your mother has fared with the car.' She slipped her arm back through Tilly's. She no longer needed the support but the warmth was reassuring.

'Can we see the famous chandelier?' pleaded Tilly.

Daphne smiled. 'We certainly can. I remember my first sight of it, over

forty years ago. I think it's this way, in the *Salon Royale*. Yes, here we are.'
She watched the awe in Tilly's face as her granddaughter surveyed the crystal splendour hanging from the high ceiling, the myriad facets giving off diamond-bright lights. If you gazed at it for long enough, the chandelier became a firework fall, awesome in its brilliance.

'Is it true it's Baccarat crystal?'

'It may well be. I believe it was originally designed for the Tsar of Russia. Now, come on or your mother will wonder where we are.'

Outside they could see no sign of the Jaguar.

'We'd better cross the road again and wait on the other side,' Tilly said.

'And we'd better watch it. This is where Isadora Duncan died, her neck broken when her long scarf caught in the wheels of her Bugatti.' Daphne was beginning to enjoy herself.

'Isadora who?'

'Oh dear, how young you are. She was a legend in my time and now she appears to have been forgotten. She was an extraordinary dancer, devised her own style, embraced free love, enjoyed a tragic life.'

'Can one enjoy a tragic life, Grandma?'

'Hmm, unfortunate choice of phrase perhaps. Here, let me take your arm again, this traffic is really too much.'

As they crossed the busy road, Daphne thought how Tilly had matured since she'd come out to France. Her looks had improved too. The cotton shift she was wearing was very stylish. No doubt bought over here. You could say a lot about the French but you couldn't fault their fashion sense. Her hair was glossy and hung nicely. Looked as though she'd lost a bit of her puppy-fat, too. Altogether greatly improved. Looked happy as well.

'Have you met many youngsters?' Daphne asked as they stood on the opposite pavement from the Negresco and scanned the traffic coming towards them.

Tilly shrugged her shoulders. 'Not really. All Mum's and Charles's friends are more their sort of age. They keep worrying that I'll get bored but I'm really enjoying myself. Phyllida came out for two weeks at Easter with a boyfriend, James,' she added.

'You haven't found a boyfriend yourself?'

Tilly smiled indulgently. 'You don't have to worry, Grandma, I'm not getting involved out here.'

It hadn't been what Daphne meant but she let it go.

'Look, there's Mum!' Tilly shrieked, waving wildly.

Olivia picked them up then found a parking spot near the centre of town. After that Tilly took charge and led her mother and grandmother through narrow streets to the shop where, she said, she could buy the tartlet tins, piping bags and nozzles and the cutters she needed.

'I'm impressed with the way you know your way about,' Daphne said, hurrying along behind Tilly down a series of busy little lanes.

'Oh, I spent a wonderful morning exploring here when Patrick brought me,' she explained.

'Patrick?'

'Patrick Ratcliffe is a friend of ours,' said Olivia as they reached the shop. 'It's the Ratcliffes Tilly's doing the food for. Patrick's in property. He has business all along the Riviera and sometimes takes Tilly with him. You've visited lots of interesting places with him, haven't you, darling?'

'He's been terribly kind,' Tilly agreed warmly.

'Liz Ratcliffe broke her wrist last week, you remember I told you?'

'Yes, thank you, Olivia, I'm not quite senile yet.'

'Both the Ratcliffes are coming to supper tonight.'

'I shall be interested to meet them.'

Supper was to be eaten in the kitchen, Olivia announced when they got back in the late-afternoon. 'I'm sorry, Mother,' she said. 'I know you always prefer to eat in the dining room but I'd hoped it would be warm enough to eat outside so it's a very informal meal.'

'Your kitchen is very pleasant,' Daphne said graciously. 'Quite a temple of gastronomy. I wonder how Thomas has been getting on with Charles?' she added. 'I think I'll go and see. Unless, that is, you'd like me to do something?' She waited for the inevitable denial then drifted off upstairs to make herself comfortable and find something to change into for the evening.

As she'd expected, Thomas was working at his desk. Yes, he said abstractedly, he'd had a pleasant lunch with Charles, the fellow was capable of sustaining quite an interesting conversation. What had they had for lunch? Thomas had to think about that. 'Pizza, I think,' he said at last.

'I expect you'll be interested to hear how our day went,' Daphne said as Thomas's head bent over his manuscript once again.

'Of course, dear.' The eyes never lifted from the page.

Once, many years ago, Daphne had given her husband a nonsense spiel just to see whether in fact he took in anything she said. He'd looked at her as though she'd taken leave of her senses and she realised some tiny area of his mammoth mind could absorb what she told him without its making any difference to his main activity. She hadn't repeated the experiment.

Daphne started undoing her dress. 'There are people coming this evening.'

'I know.' Thomas didn't look up. 'Ratcliffe I think Charles said their name was. Seem to be close friends.'

'I shall be interested to hear your opinion of them at the end of the evening, Thomas.'

He took off his glasses and looked at his wife. 'Any particular reason, my dear?'

'Thomas, your daughter is making a new life for herself in this place. We need to understand what sort of people she is making friends with.'

'Ah, of course.'

'And we must see if we can't help Tilly to find out what she wants to do with her life.'

'Right!' Thomas bent again over his manuscript and Daphne went to the bathroom.

The Ratcliffes were a pleasant surprise to Daphne. She wasn't sure what she'd expected but not this distinguished-looking girl with her arm in a sling and the quiet man who followed her out on to the terrace.

Olivia performed the introductions.

'I heard about your accident,' Daphne said to Liz Ratcliffe. 'It must have been a devastating blow.'

She watched Liz's tired eyes. This was a woman who was suffering, Daphne decided. The face was quite drawn, the marvellous wide mouth fiercely controlled, and there were deep lines of strain between the heavy brows. 'Sit down and tell me about your work. I gather you paint in the abstract. We had a wonderful time this afternoon at the Matisse Museum, is he an artist that speaks to you?'

Daphne felt satisfaction as Liz settled down beside her and said, 'Oh, yes. His use of colour especially. Do you paint yourself?'

'How kind of you to ask. I did, once. Then I went into advertising and found I had more of a talent for organisation.'

'You didn't keep up your painting at all?'

'No, I had no interest in producing second-rate pieces.'

'I find it difficult not to paint. If I didn't sell a single work, I would still paint.' Liz sounded driven.

'And your husband?' Daphne glanced at the tall man, now talking animatedly to Tilly, who'd arrived with a plate of small whirls of cheesey puff pastry.

'Patrick? He knows nothing about painting.' A faint smile lightened the haggard features. 'But he's tolerant.'

'As I suppose you can say I am of my husband's work,' Daphne said briskly. 'Indeed, I hope I support him in every possible way.' She knew that she did, that without her care and attention, Thomas would fall to pieces. And that it had been first the money she'd inherited from her parents and then her sizeable salary that had enabled him to pursue his academic career in a certain amount of style.

'Ah, yes, your husband is a writer, isn't he?'

'He has defined English grammar for students all over the world,' Daphne said proudly. She enjoyed telling people about Thomas's accomplishments. 'But how are you managing with your arm? Not being able to use it must make everything so difficult.'

'You can say that again,' Liz agreed in heartfelt tones. 'I never realised quite how dependent one is on one's right arm. It's not just that I can't paint – I can't dress myself, I find it difficult to wash, even go to the loo. As for

189

cooking and cleaning, apart from the simplest of things, like dusting or putting on a kettle, they are beyond me at the moment. I have to learn a completely new way of managing.'

'How brave of you to host the party on Wednesday. Thomas and I are greatly looking forward to it.'

'Ah, now that will be thanks to Tilly.' Liz looked at the girl, still talking with her husband. 'She has very nobly undertaken to provide the eats. And Olivia and Charles have promised to help serve.'

'And what can I do?' asked Daphne. 'How about dusting before the party? It's something I'm quite good at.'

Liz laughed, a genuine, ringing laugh that had Patrick looking towards her. 'How lovely of you,' she said apologetically. 'I shouldn't have reacted like that but somehow you look as though dusting was the last thing you'd be good at.'

For some reason Daphne felt complimented by this remark.

'I don't like it,' Daphne said on Wednesday evening as she and Thomas got ready for bed.

'Don't like what? I thought the evening was a great success. Everyone said the food was marvellous.' Thomas sat in the little armchair in the corner of the guestroom and started to undo his shoes.

'I'm surprised you managed to take in anything anyone said other than that Frenchman you got so pally with five minutes after we arrived,' Daphne said grimly. 'When I heard he was a writer on French prose, I knew we'd lost you.'

'His wife's into property, like Patrick,' Thomas answered the unasked question. 'Henri said she drags him to no end of parties like tonight's. He's thinking of turning to fiction, says the material on offer is so interesting.'

'I'd be interested to hear what he thought about tonight's effort, then.' Daphne pulled off her roll-on with a great sigh and scratched at her protuberant belly. The flesh was crossed with angry red creases. She wondered whether it wouldn't be better not to wear the thing tomorrow. Her dresses were all loose ones, surely it wouldn't matter? Not in this hot weather. She was unutterably glad they hadn't left it any later to come here. Everyone had been out in the garden at the Ratcliffes, it had been so warm. The sort of soft, fragrant evening that was made for romance.

'He's in love with her,' Daphne said abruptly.

Thomas couldn't follow. 'Who and with whom?'

'Patrick Ratcliffe, with Tilly.'

'Tilly? He couldn't be, she's only a child.' Thomas looked up incredulously, one sock dangling from his hand.

'Heavens, Thomas, she's eighteen! She was eighteen in March, Charles took us all out to dinner, don't you remember?' There were times when Daphne felt one more moment's obtuseness from her husband and she'd be reduced to a gibbering fool fit only for the loony bin.

'All right, there's no need to shout.'

Daphne retrieved her Marks and Sparks nightie from under the pillow and slipped into the infinitely comforting pure cotton.

'But Patrick must be twenty years older than her, maybe more.'

'He's forty-one, I asked his wife. And when has age ever stopped men being interested in young women?' Daphne still felt exasperated.

Thomas, mouth agape, sank back in the armchair. 'What about Tilly?'

Daphne sat herself in front of the brass-framed mirror on the dressing table, wound an elastic bandage round her head to keep her hair away from her face and began taking off her makeup. The years-old ritual calmed her. 'I'm not sure,' she confessed. She never liked not being sure. Daphne preferred to have life set out in ordered patterns. 'She likes him very much, you can see that. But I don't think he's made a move yet.'

Thomas moved irritably out of the chair and started undoing the buttons of his shirt. ' "Making a move?" Is that sort of talk appropriate? It sounds like, I don't know, something off the television.' He dropped the shirt on the floor and started on his trousers and pants. They followed the shirt. Naked, he wandered into the bathroom. 'I think you've allowed your imagination to run away with you,' he called back to the bedroom.

Daphne had stopped listening to him. She gazed unseeingly at the reflection of her cream-lined face. Some action would have to be taken. The question was, what? Even as she wondered, Daphne recognised ominous signs from her insides. 'Thomas, I need the bathroom,' she called urgently.

Chapter Twenty

The morning after the Ratcliffe party, checking through his mail in the study, Charles found a letter from England, the address written in the familiar round hand of John Smythe, his best friend at school.

John and he had spotted trains together, stolen apples and scrabbled for coal round the open-cast mines, taking home precious buckets. Charles had helped John with his homework and John had taught him how to mend bicycle punctures.

John hadn't wanted to go to university, which was as well because he never managed A levels. Instead, he went into his father's small electrical shop.

Back home in college vacations, Charles would down beers with John, listen to his plans for the shop and discuss how Mr Smythe could be brought to see their potential.

Eventually the combination of John's enterprise and his father's caution had built up a chain of electrical shops. John married shortly after Charles, a jolly Yorkshire girl called Meryl, inevitably known as Merry. Veronica had made sure they weren't able to go to the wedding but Charles was godfather to their first child, a boy, called Donald. Two girls quickly followed.

After Charles moved to London, contact with the Smythe family grew less and less until it stabilised at Charles's birthday and Christmas cheques to his godson, and a note Charles scribbled inside a Christmas card (Veronica always omitted the Smythe card from the huge bundle she sent off). The Christmas card from the Smythes would contain an update on the family doings and both cards always ended with the words, 'must meet next year'.

Charles opened John's letter with a happy feeling of anticipation. He didn't often write but when he did it always announced some welcome event, such as the acquisition of a new shop (six years ago), Donald's award of an exhibition to Oxford (four years ago), the landing of an excellent job by one daughter (three years ago), the engagement of the other (two years ago), followed by her marriage last year (which Charles had had to miss as it coincided with an export trip abroad). There had also been a Be Happy in Your New Home card (with 'in France' added in biro after the printed words) after Charles had sent a note of his change of address.

Dear Charles,
Long time no see! Hope the life in France is suiting you. All that *vin*

and sun, eh! Can't be bad! And the new wife! Everything must be coming up roses, and Merry and I couldn't be more pleased for you. If ever a chap deserved it!

Well, life with us is not bad either. We haven't said much but the last few years have been really bad in the trade and Jill's wedding last year was more than a bit of a strain on the old budget. But we seem to have turned the corner now and things are more hunky dory. So we thought we'd have a bit of a holiday. Merry's always wanted to see the South of France and a bit of the old sun and *vin* wouldn't do me any harm. Merry said, Why don't we look up Charles? Well, I thought, it's years since we've sunk a pint or two and it's more than time we got together again. Perhaps you can recommend a reasonable B & B near you and we could get together? Wouldn't want to be in your pocket, not with a new wife and everything. But you may just be missing old friends and, anyway, like I said, it's time we got together again. Oh, yes, we thought we'd like to make it as soon as possible, Merry has difficulty finding help to take over her craft shop in the summer holidays. So perhaps you could give me a ring fairly pronto?

Best wishes,
Your old friend, John

Charles's heart sank as he realised exactly what this letter was all about. He gave a quick sigh, hauled himself out of his study chair and went through to the kitchen where Olivia was helping to clear up after the previous day's mammoth cooking session.

'Look what's arrived for Tilly,' she said and showed him a massive bunch of flowers done up in florist's cellophane and garnished with twirls of ribbon. 'From the Ratcliffes, of course.'

'Quite right, too. Where is she?'

'Gone down to them to say thank you and collect a few dishes she left there. What have you got to tell me?' Olivia glanced at the piece of paper in his hand. 'Good news, I hope?'

'Not sure about that,' confessed Charles. 'I've had a Margie letter.'

'A Margie letter?' Olivia looked up at him with wide eyes and, as so often, he was struck by how the deepness of their blue made ordinary blues so very, well, ordinary.

He held out John Smythe's missive.

Olivia dropped the chopping board she was washing, dried her hands and took the letter.

'Ah,' she said after she'd read it.

'John's my oldest friend,' he said defensively.

'Have I met him and,' she looked again at the letter, 'Merry?'

He shook his head. 'They live in Yorkshire.'

Olivia dropped the letter on to the draining board and plunged her arms

194

into the washing-up water again. 'Well, you'd better ring them and tell them any time after the parents leave.'

Charles gave her neck a kiss. 'You're wonderful.' Then he added, 'Is your mother all right?'

Olivia straightened up and wiped her hand across her forehead. 'What makes you think she mightn't be?'

'The way she asked Tilly at breakfast if she couldn't go with us to the beach tomorrow instead of going off with Patrick to Aix-en-Provence. She made it sound as though she needed help. All that "your young legs" and "at my time of life" and "I don't know how many more opportunities there'll be to spend time with you". I mean, she's not even seventy!'

'No, but if Tilly makes her life out here, she's probably afraid she won't see too much of her.'

'It's more than that, though. Haven't you noticed how she hardly eats anything?'

'Mother never has had much of an appetite.'

'And there seems something different about her.'

'Different, how?'

'I don't know but she seems very scratchy.'

Olivia paused in her washing up. 'Isn't it awful? Over the years I've got so used to Mother's being "scratchy", as you call it, that I sort of click off.' She stood and thought for a moment. 'Her face looks much thinner but she can't be losing weight, have you noticed her tummy? I think she's just getting older and it doesn't suit her.'

Charles gave her another quick kiss and went off back to his study with a light heart. Only just over a week more of his parents-in-law and then he could look forward to seeing John. It would be so good to get together with him again. And Olivia and Merry were bound to get on. Also received in the post that morning had been a plan for a pool house that Michel Pontevrault had drawn up. Charles picked up the telephone and got through to the builder who'd been so helpful with the house.

Later that afternoon Olivia and Tilly were shopping and Charles decided to make tea. Daphne and Thomas had said they'd be downstairs from their afternoon nap around four-thirty.

Charles quite enjoyed pottering around the kitchen on his own. He found a tray and laid it with cups and saucers (no mugs for his parents-in-law) and wondered about Thomas. Was he really a cold fish who lived in a world composed of the differences between deduction and assumption, personal and reflexive pronouns, the use of the article, the importance of position, and other matters of syntax? Or had he just trained himself to ignore a wife who battered too insistently on his privacy?

The lunchtime they'd spent together had been sticky. The brief moment of contact Charles had established on their first meeting had not lasted. Not knowing anything about academic life or English grammar, Charles had soon run out of intelligent questions. His father-in-law had appeared equally stumped for conversation and, over the cheese, Charles had finally fallen back on asking about Olivia as a child.

Thomas had thawed considerably and managed to endear himself by describing a loving little girl with blonde curls and engaging smile. Only to ruin the effect when it became clear what a blow it had been for him to discover her brains were never going to carry her to his old Oxford college or into academia.

'Like mother, like daughter,' Charles had said, thinking of Tilly.

'But Daphne has a relentless intelligence, very sharp,' said Thomas.

'What do you think Tilly will do?' Charles asked, genuinely curious as to what Thomas would suggest.

'Tilly? Ah,' Thomas said with an affectionate smile. 'Such a dear girl. I should think she'll marry, settle down and raise children.'

'Don't you think that's a bit old fashioned?' Charles suggested. 'Girls need some sort of a career these days, even if they are married.'

Thomas had sighed and jabbed at the rind he'd carefully cut off his piece of camembert. 'I suppose you're right. I'm afraid I find it difficult to keep up with the modern world.'

The man was almost a caricature of the absent-minded professor, Charles decided.

He found a tin of biscuits, put some trellises of flaky gold on a plate and added that to the tray. Daphne mightn't have much of an appetite but Thomas enjoyed his food. From the odd comment that had been dropped, Charles reckoned the poor sod probably didn't get fed much at home.

The kettle boiled and he made the tea. Veronica had introduced Charles to Earl Grey and Lapsang Souchong. The tarry taste of the latter he had never managed to take to but the fragrance of Earl Grey gave him continual delight. Olivia really didn't mind what she drank but Tilly had been thrilled to find he enjoyed it.

Where on earth, Charles marvelled as he filled the warmed teapot, had Tilly got her delight in food from? He supposed it must have been her father.

Would he ever, he wondered as he put the pot on the tray and covered it with a cosy in the shape of a house, learn anything about Olivia's first husband? He longed to ask her about Peter Warboys but the keep off signals she'd given him were too strong to be ignored. Well, perhaps it would be daunting to be regaled with stories of perfect married bliss. She was no doubt sparing his feelings.

For a moment the old insecurity that had developed as he realised his marriage to Veronica was failing stirred uneasily in Charles. He remembered Tilly once telling him her father had been tall and dark and had always made life exciting. She'd only been a little girl, of course. Charles wondered how Phyllida remembered himself when she'd been that young. Would she describe him then with the same bemused enchantment?

Somehow he doubted it. Charles gave himself a mental shake. The past was the past, it was over. What he had to work at was the present. Olivia and he had a lot going for them and he wasn't going to let anything get in the way of their future together. He added a small jug of milk to his tray and checked he hadn't forgotten anything.

Daphne and Thomas were coming down the stairs as he took the tray through the hall. He was pleased to see they both looked refreshed.

'This hot weather takes a little getting used to,' he said as Daphne settled herself on the terrace and apologised for taking a rest.

'I'm looking forward to our trip to the beach tomorrow,' Thomas said, helping himself to one of the biscuits. 'My, this tea is good,' he added as he took his first sip.

'I think I've sorted out the best place to go to, one of the private beaches which has a very good restaurant attached.'

Just then the shopping party came back. And not alone.

'Look who we found sitting in the square drinking *citrons pressés*!' shouted Tilly. She sounded overjoyed.

Following her and Olivia out on to the terrace were a very tall coloured girl, a forest of braids dancing round her well-shaped head, and a young man with the wide-mouthed face of a clown.

'This is Jemima, she used to be the chef at the restaurant where I worked,' Tilly explained. 'Jemima, these are my grandparents, Professor and Mrs Ferguson, and my stepfather, Charles Frome.'

'Pleased to meet you,' said Jemima, sticking out a hand to Daphne, who shook it with a certain amount of reserve.

'And this is Rory Wilde, who pinched Jemima to run one of his father's restaurants,' Tilly went on. The young man smiled at them with great charm. 'His father owns the *Frère* chain.'

Did he indeed! Charles had heard about the growing *Frère* restaurant chain. It was rumoured the company was going to go public and he'd noted it as a promising investment possibility.

'Do sit down,' Olivia said. 'I'm sure you'd like some tea?'

'I'll get some more cups.' Tilly darted off to the kitchen and was back a few minutes later, before Charles had had to do much more than settle the visitors and ask them if they were on holiday.

'Jemima and Rory are here to search for new food ideas,' Tilly said, putting the china on the table.

'New food ideas?' asked Charles politely.

'We've been to all the three-star restaurants round Lyons,' said Rory, seated between Daphne and Charles. 'Now we're checking the places round here.'

'Aren't the *Frère* restaurants middle-price range?' asked Charles. 'I didn't think haute cuisine would be your mark.'

'Ah, but it's the ideas,' said Jemima, seated beside Thomas. 'You can always adapt dishes to suit your level of cuisine.'

Tilly started pouring tea.

'And now that the economy's improving, we're seriously thinking of adding a flagship to the chain,' Rory added. 'My father's negotiating for an established first-rank restaurant. If it comes off, we'll really be in the haute-cuisine class.'

'In fact,' laughed Jemima, 'Rory is taking it all so seriously, he's enrolled for a catering course.

'Really!' squeaked Tilly. 'You mean you're going to learn to cook?'

'From the bottom up,' he assured her gravely. 'That's the only way to know what dodges your staff can get up to to increase their take and reduce your profits.' He grinned at her then added, 'Seriously, though, I need to learn more about food and wine and the course includes marketing and promotion plus what my father calls the absolutely vital element, costings.'

'And then are you going to be the chef at the new restaurant?' asked Tilly, her eyes round in wonder.

Rory laughed. 'I won't be up to that! Be a miracle if I'm good enough for Jemima to take me on as a sous-chef.'

Tilly turned to her friend. 'You mean, *you're* going to be the chef?'

Jemima's braids danced as she laughed and shook her head. 'Not my scene, girl. I'm just being used to filter the ideas.'

'Got a really good business brain,' Rory said. 'Knows what the punters like.'

'How's the *Frère Marcus* going?' asked Tilly.

'Like the proverbial bomb,' said Rory.

'It's OK,' agreed Jemima. 'Left my sous-chef in charge whilst Rory and I swanned off down here. Should be all right, it's coming up to the quiet season.'

'Thought the summer was your busy time?' said Charles, surprised.

Rory shook his head. 'All your regulars start taking holidays and the tourists don't compensate. All most of them are interested in are the pizza houses and hamburger joints.'

Charles took to Rory Wilde. He had the sort of charm a good education and middle-class confidence gave you, the sort of charm Charles Frome sometimes wished he'd been born to. And Rory had something more: a mind that knew what it was at. The girl was interesting, too. Beautiful with that height and pale coffee skin and sculptured features but, again, with something extra, a street savvy that would keep her going in the right direction. An odd couple but very comfortable with each other. He wondered if they were an item but failed to identify any sort of sexual charge between them.

'I would be grateful,' said Daphne, putting down her cup, 'if the entire conversation didn't centre round food.'

'I'm sorry, Grandma, it must be totally boring for you,' Tilly said quickly.

'And *we've* had more than enough of it for the past ten days,' Rory added.

'Yup, we've visited our last Michelin-starred restaurant for this year,' said Jemima. 'But, boy oh boy, what a time we've had!'

'Tell you what, Jemima, come into the kitchen while I boil some more water and tell me exactly what you've eaten,' suggested Tilly. 'I can't not know.'

'Be glad to, honey.' She got up and followed Tilly into the house.

'So your trip's at an end, is it?' Olivia asked Rory.

'Just about. We ate at Roger Vergé's in Mougins last night. Marvellous meal,' he sighed then glanced at Daphne. 'But I won't tell you what we had. We were discussing where to go tonight when Tilly saw us.'

'You didn't know she was here?' asked Charles sceptically.

Rory dropped his gaze to the terrace paving. 'Actually, sir, we did. At least, Jemima had her address and we were going to ring her and ask if she'd like to join us this evening?'

'Where are you staying?' asked Olivia, carefully not catching Charles's eye.

'We've got rooms in the hotel in that square where you found us,' said Rory.

Charles let out a little breath of thankfulness, then caught it again as Olivia said, 'Any friends of Tilly's are very welcome to stay with us.' She left the sentence hanging in the air and Charles waited anxiously.

'It's very kind of you, Mrs Frome,' Rory said. 'I really appreciate the offer but I, at least, am not that good a friend and we wouldn't dream of imposing on you. My parents have friends with a house down here and I know what it's like. They say the only difference between them and a hotel in the summer months is that the hotel can hand out bills!'

Charles warmed towards the young man. 'Well, how about spending tomorrow with us at the beach?'

'What a good idea, Charles,' Daphne said unexpectedly. 'I'd really enjoy hearing more about your chain of restaurants, Rory, and about this course you're going to do.'

Charles looked at her curiously. It was the last reaction he would have expected from Daphne.

Not only did Rory and Jemima take Tilly out that evening, they repeated the invitation for the following night after a day spent with the Fromes and the Fergusons at the beach.

Everybody seemed to have enjoyed themselves.

Thomas swam far, far out, using a steady breast stroke to take him way beyond the line of the buoys that prohibited yachts from coming into the swimming area.

Charles watched his disappearing head and wondered just how strong a swimmer his father-in-law was.

'Don't worry,' Daphne said dryly beside him. 'Thomas swims regularly down in Sussex. I tell him he must be cold-blooded the way the temperature never seems to worry him.'

'You don't swim yourself?' Charles asked.

'Occasionally, when it's really warm.' She was wearing a heavily elasticated navy blue swimsuit with thick shoulder straps that was all but hidden under a floating voile shirt that exposed little more than her still excellent legs.

Olivia was in a shocking pink bikini that showed off her golden tan and lovely figure. Charles thought that the *La Chênais* pool was worth every penny just for the joy of seeing her dressed in swimsuits so much of the time.

Mind you, coming down to the beach gave you an eyeful everywhere you looked. So many pretty French girls, even though a surprising number were accompanied by tiny children. Lovely, lissom bodies they had but none more so than Jemima in her mock leopardskin bikini. Charles thought regretfully that she put Tilly in the shade. The more he got to know his stepdaughter, the deeper Charles's affection for her grew. Sometimes he even found himself wishing Phyllida could have some of her open and wholehearted attitude to life instead of so often being secretive, prickly and difficult. But then Phyllida had avoided the gaucheness Tilly sometimes displayed, and from her early teens she had always managed to look stunning. Still his stepdaughter's puppy-fat was slimming down nicely now and she did have those long legs. Give her another year or so and she'd be a right stunner. Charles could see Rory eyeing her discreetly as, wearing a well-cut emerald one-piece, she lay sunning herself on the lounger beside his.

For lunch, taken at the restaurant at the back of the beach, the girls arrayed themselves in decorative wraps and the men put on shorts and T-shirts. Charles was amused by the inconspicuous way Daphne made sure Rory sat next to her. He'd have thought she'd be more interested in sitting him next to Tilly. For Charles was almost certain Daphne had decided to do some match making.

As far as he could see, she was going to have her work cut out. Rory obviously enjoyed teasing Tilly and she him but it seemed more like the badinage of brother and sister than embryonic lovers. Charles was willing to bet that more of the previous evening had been spent discussing food and its preparation than flirting.

No, Daphne would have to be lucky to engineer much of a romance out of this relationship.

After lunch, while the rest of the party snoozed under sun umbrellas, Daphne took Tilly off for a little walk down the beach. Charles watched them as they stood by the water chatting, the long-legged teenager with hair streaming down her back and the elderly woman with her sharp haircut and the heavy body softened by the overshirt she was wearing. Just what was Daphne up to? he wondered. He couldn't help feeling irritated by his mother-in-law's relentless compulsion to control the lives of her daughter and granddaughter. Still, she'd be going home soon. Charles thanked heaven he and Olivia weren't living in England otherwise it would have been impossible to have avoided a confrontation.

Daphne showed her hand after supper that evening.

Rory and Jemima had taken Tilly off for dinner and the rest of them sat on the terrace in the velvet warmth of the evening. Olivia served coffee. Charles put on a CD of a Mozart symphony and handed round brandy. Then they settled to listen to the music drowning out the sound of the crickets. Beyond the trees, lights twinkled, their brightness increasing as the dusk deepened into dark.

The divine order of Mozart never failed to delight Charles. Replete with the sun he'd absorbed during the day and the meal they'd just finished, a brandy in his hand, his gaze resting on his beautiful wife, his dog at his feet, the perfectly crafted music blessing the evening, he felt life had little more to offer him.

There was silence as the music came to an end.

Charles rose. 'Shall we stay out here or would you prefer to come inside? Thomas, another brandy?'

Daphne got to her feet. 'Inside, I think. There's something I would like to say.'

Charles felt an instinctive alarm at his formidable mother-in-law's statement. Olivia, too, looked apprehensive.

They moved into the salon. Daphne took up a position in front of the fireplace, Juno placing himself to one side of her feet. Thomas sat on one of the sofas with a concerned expression on his face. Charles and Olivia moved close to each other on the opposite sofa.

Satisfied she had their attention, Daphne said, 'Olivia, do you and Charles realise what is happening between Tilly and this Patrick Ratcliffe?'

Charles gazed at her, dumbfounded.

'Mother, what do you mean!' Olivia gasped.

'Daphne, I don't think you should proceed without more facts,' warned Thomas.

'I think you all must be quite, quite blind,' Daphne said with a touch of complacency. 'As soon as I arrived it was quite clear to me that something had changed Tilly from a depressed, overworked girl into someone blooming with happiness.'

'She's really enjoying staying here with Charles and me,' said Olivia in a tight little voice.

'I'm sure she is,' Daphne said indulgently. 'But something more must be involved. I was alerted to what it might be by the look on her face when she was talking about visiting Nice with your friend Patrick Ratcliffe. Then when I saw the way he looked at her the night they had supper with us, it all fell into place.'

'Mother, if you're trying to tell me that Tilly and Patrick are having an affair, I'm sorry, but I just don't believe you,' Olivia said heatedly.

Charles put a warning hand on her arm. 'I have to say I agree with Olivia,' he said calmly to Daphne. Inside, though, he was thinking furiously. He had never seen any signs of great warmth between Liz and Patrick. He'd put it down to neither of them being particularly demonstrative. But Patrick was at a dangerous age. And Tilly did have a sort of glow about her these days.

'No,' Daphne said judiciously, 'I don't think matters have reached that point yet. And, to be fair, I'm not sure that either of them is aware of what is going on. But the situation is highly dangerous. A few more cosy trips like the ones I understand they've been indulging in,' her tone made a simple car journey sound incredibly suggestive, 'and we'll have a full-scale affair on our hands.' Daphne let the import of that soak in.

'Mother, I think you are building something out of nothing,' Olivia protested. Charles could feel her body beside him rigid with tension.

'What do you think, Charles?' demanded Daphne.

'Supposing there is something in what you say, how do you suggest we handle the situation?'

'Charles!' Olivia turned to him with a look of outrage. 'You can't believe this – this farrago!'

'Hush, darling, I didn't say I believed it but I'd like to know what your mother wants to suggest.' He was quite certain that Daphne had a plan all ready to put before them.

'Ah, now, that was what was worrying me, until that nice young couple arrived here yesterday. Then everything suddenly fell into place. Tilly should go back and enrol at this catering college that Rory is going to. He's given me its name and address and I'm sure you can get the telephone number. Enrolling her will not only get her out of harm's way but give her a proper training.'

'That's all you think about, isn't it?' Olivia said furiously. 'First you tried to get Tilly to retake her A levels. That didn't work so now you're trying this. You can't stand the fact that she's enjoying herself, having a bit of a break before she faces life. Oh, no, you have to interfere, like you tried to interfere in my life.'

'Olivia!' Thomas said sternly. 'I don't think your mother has anything but Tilly's best interests at heart.'

'Darling.' Charles put his arm round Olivia's shoulders and drew her closer. 'Don't you think we should ask Tilly if this isn't something she would like to do?' Olivia's body remained tense. 'It does seem to me that cooking is her thing and doesn't it make sense for her to get a proper qualification?'

Olivia said nothing.

'I think you should examine your motives in opposing what I have suggested,' Daphne said coldly to her daughter. 'All your life you have run away from painful situations.'

'Run away!' Olivia flared up. 'What on earth do you mean? Going to

202

California with Peter wasn't running away! Coming here wasn't running away! And look at how I stuck all those years with Designs Unlimited, earning enough to keep Tilly and me. That wasn't running away! And if anybody is going to examine motives, it should be you. You're the one who's always tried to interfere in my life.'

Daphne suddenly looked very tired. 'I think I'll go to bed now, if you don't mind. I'm sure what I've said is difficult for you to accept but I urge you to consider it dispassionately.' She seemed to have aged fifteen years as she moved slowly from the room.

Thomas rose. 'Your mother didn't speak lightly, my dear,' he said to Olivia. 'She has both Tilly's and your best interests at heart. I don't think you can afford to ignore the possible implications of what she has suggested.' He placed an awkward kiss on the top of his daughter's head, said goodnight to Charles then left the room.

Charles kept his arm around Olivia and waited.

He wanted to urge her not to let an instinctive prejudice against anything Daphne recommended blind her to the benefits for Tilly of the course that had been suggested. But this was something she had to decide on her own and he hoped she would realise he was there to help.

At last Charles felt Olivia start to relax. She leant back, looked up at him and said, 'Do you really think there's anything in it?'

He gave a small shrug. 'Who knows? But I think I agree with your father, we can't afford to ignore the possibility.'

'But to send her away!' Olivia sounded dismayed.

'We're not going to send her away,' Charles said firmly. 'Never that. But with Jemima and Rory on the scene, isn't this the perfect time to suggest she might think about doing something with her cooking?'

A veil of depression fell over Olivia's face. 'Oh, darling, I've been so enjoying having her here!'

He pulled her against his chest, feeling the wild beat of her heart. 'I know, my sweet, I know. But this is her future.'

After a moment or two, Olivia pulled away from him. 'What if she doesn't want to go?'

Yes, what indeed? Charles considered the possibility of an infatuated Tilly involved with Patrick, old enough to be her father and married to Liz, who'd done so much for them since they'd moved into *La Chênais*. Charles had never been one to avoid awkward situations and he knew he'd have to do something in this one. 'Then I think I'll have a word with Patrick. I might have a word with him anyway.'

Olivia laced her hands together in her lap and considered them. 'If there is any truth in it, I feel so sorry for Liz. She doesn't deserve it, especially now!' She looked up at Charles, her eyes big and sorrowful. 'And Tilly's had one unhappy relationship, I'd hate her to have another one.'

'We don't know they are having an affair,' Charles reminded her.

'That's right.' Olivia straightened up with a new determination. 'Mother just has to interfere,' she said. 'She can't let anything alone.'

'Sometimes you have to confront situations,' Charles said gently.

Olivia looked doubtful. Then she sighed deeply. 'I suppose mother's right,' she said at last. 'It can't do any harm to ask Tilly if she'd like to go to catering college, anyway.'

Charles gave her a hug. 'That's my girl,' he said.

Underneath his dismay at the unfortunate state of affairs Daphne seemed convinced existed, he felt a deep satisfaction that Olivia had been able to discuss her daughter's problem in this way. He felt closer to her than he had for some time, as close as the day they'd married when he'd been so sure nothing but unalloyed happiness lay ahead of them.

That had been Friday evening.

On Saturday morning Rory and Jemima arrived at breakfast-time to say goodbye before they started their drive back to England. Daphne and Thomas were still in bed but Tilly, even though she had come in late after their dinner together, was up and dressed.

Charles drew Rory aside and asked him about the catering college course he was going on. Was it likely to be full? If Tilly wanted to join, what were the chances?

Rory's face lit up. 'That would be terrific! Jemima says Tilly has real talent.' Then he looked thoughtful. 'I don't know about the course, though, I think it gets pretty booked up. But my father might be able to help. He knows one of the college directors and we have a work experience arrangement for some of the students.'

'Don't say anything to Tilly,' Charles warned. 'We haven't discussed it with her yet. Perhaps we could ring you if we'd like your father to put in a word?'

Rory scribbled down his number. 'Ring any time and leave a message on the machine if I'm not there. We'll be delighted to help in any way we can.'

As they said their final goodbyes, Juno circling the group with excited barks, Tilly flung her arms around both Jemima and Rory's necks. 'It's been wonderful seeing you,' she said. 'And thank you so much for those fantastic meals. I haven't had so much fun for ages.'

Charles had wanted to pay for Friday night's meal but Rory had categorically refused. 'It all comes on expenses,' he'd said. 'We really value Tilly's opinion.'

After they'd left, Charles, followed by Juno, took Olivia and Tilly into the library.

'Your mother and I have a proposal to put to you,' he said to Tilly when they were all comfortably settled.

She looked at them with round eyes.

Charles glanced at Olivia and she picked up her cue. 'Darling, talking to Rory has given us an idea. We were so impressed with the food you produced for Liz and Patrick we wondered whether you wouldn't like to go on a professional course?'

'Like the one he's going on?' Tilly said. Charles was greatly relieved to hear the note of excitement in her voice.

'Why not the actual one he's on?' he asked matter-of-factly. 'It's always a help to know someone who's doing the same thing and we'd be happier if we knew he could keep an eye on you.'

'What about it, darling?' Olivia leaned forward. 'Shall we find out what the chances are?'

Tilly looked thoughtful and Charles held his breath. Then Tilly smiled up at her mother. 'Oh, yes, I think I'd like that.' But then the excitement died out of her face as she added in something of a wail, 'But I'd have to leave here!'

'Here', Charles noted with dismay. Not 'you'. Was it her mother or Patrick she was distressed at leaving?

'You can come out and visit, there'll be holidays and things,' Olivia said quickly.

'But it won't be the same!' Tilly complained.

'That's life,' Charles said, a trifle brutally.

She looked up at him, her clear grey eyes serious and level. 'Yes, it is,' she said. 'You're right. I'm grown up now and I've got to get on with life. I've been thinking about what I should do ever since last summer and now I think I know.' Her eyes lit up again. 'It really would be great if I could get on Rory's course but any professional one would do. I'm not a baby, I don't need looking after.'

So much for Daphne's attempt at match making!

Chapter Twenty-One

'Tilly,' Daphne said later that day as they sat enjoying coffee in the garden after luncheon. 'I've been thinking that Liz Ratcliffe must be having a lot of difficulty managing with her broken wrist. I know she'd never suggest it herself but wouldn't another pair of hands be a help to her?'

'Oh, Grandma, of course!' Tilly couldn't understand why she hadn't thought of it herself. 'I'll go down right now and see what I can do.'

'Not now!' Daphne said sharply. 'I mean,' she added more gently, 'she'll have her husband to help over the weekend. Why don't you go down on Monday morning?'

Patrick had wanted to take her to St Raphael, Tilly thought regretfully but she knew she would never be able to enjoy herself there thinking of Liz struggling on her own.

So on Monday she turned up at the Ratcliffe house and cheerfully announced to Patrick that she wasn't going with him. 'I've appointed myself Liz's right-hand girl until she can manage with her wrist again,' she said. 'She needs someone to shop and help with cooking. And you'll be happier knowing she's not struggling on her own, won't you?'

Patrick looked startled. Then he gave a warm smile, 'What a little love you are! It'll make all the difference to Liz. She's still in bed, I'll tell her you're here.'

'No, don't do that, she'll only make a fuss, insist she can manage. I'll just get on with things and let her get up in her own time. Off you go and I'll make sure there's something nice for you to eat this evening.'

'I'll look forward to that,' he said, planted a light kiss on her cheek, picked up his briefcase and left.

Tilly didn't think about the fun they would have had driving to St Raphael, Patrick telling her about the country they were going through, producing little stories, making her laugh, discussing where they would have lunch, making a list of all the places she should see. Instead, she packed the breakfast things into the dishwasher, cleaned the stove, which looked as though Patrick had spent the weekend frying on a high heat, and gave the sink a good scrub. There was no movement from the bedroom. As Tilly filled a bucket and started to wash the floor, she began to feel slightly nervous about what Liz was going to say when she eventually got up and found her there. Tilly had never achieved a comfortable relationship with her, not the way she had with Patrick; Liz always seemed to be challenging her in a way she didn't really understand.

Liz wandered into the kitchen dressed in shorts and a wide sleeved T-shirt just as Tilly was finishing the floor. The plastered wrist was carried in a sling and her long hair was loose. 'Tilly! What on earth are you doing? I thought you were going with Patrick this morning!' Her tone was puzzled and something else, it sounded resentful and impatient. There were dark shadows under her eyes and her collarbones stood out starkly above the faded cotton of her shirt.

'I'm going to come down each morning and help you,' she said firmly.

'Poor Patrick, he must have been disappointed.'

'I can go with him some other time,' Tilly squeezed out the mop from the last swipe she'd given the floor.

'I suppose you will.' Liz looked around the kitchen. 'What a difference! I've learned to turn a blind eye. After all, what does housekeeping really matter?' She sat down at the table and laid her broken arm carefully along its length. 'Or are you one of those girls who is offended by a bit of dirt?'

Tilly gave her a quick grin as she took the pail to the back door and emptied the water on to the nearest flower bed. 'I'd always rather cook than clean!' She put the pail away, came back inside and surveyed her work. 'I do think it looks quite nice when everything's just been done, though. What a pity it doesn't last. I mean, when you paint a picture that's it, isn't it? You can hang it on the wall and never have to do another thing to it. It's always there, looking wonderful. I'd love to be able to create something everlasting the way you do. I cook a meal and in no time it's eaten and there's nothing left, except a load of dirty dishes that will have to be done again tomorrow.' She knew she was gabbling but Liz sitting there looking so still and stern made her feel nervous. 'Shall I make a cup of coffee then we can discuss what you'd like me to shop and cook for you for this evening.'

'You really don't have to do this, you know?'

'I want to,' Tilly said earnestly. 'I mean, it's important to help when one can, isn't it? Especially people who don't expect it.' She was saying everything wrong but it seemed important to explain to Liz just how much she wanted to be allowed to lend a hand. Not because Charles thought it was his fault or because it would make Patrick's life so much easier, she found she genuinely wanted to make Liz comfortable. There was something so brave and straightforward about her. She took the kettle over to the tap but Liz came and took it out of her hand.

'Coffee I am capable of doing.'

Tilly stopped herself saying it would be easier for her and started opening cupboards instead. 'I might as well find out where you keep things. I hate it when people put things back in the wrong place. Margie was terribly helpful but never knew where anything belonged. Grandma's much better, she leaves everything for me to put away.' She found the coffee and brought it over to where Liz was trying to take the plunger out of a cafetière, awkwardly holding the container against her chest with the plastered arm, which slipped and slid against the glass. Tilly held her breath, forcing herself not to take it away before the whole thing crashed to the floor.

Then Liz gave a great sigh. 'Here, you do it,' she thrust the cafetière at Tilly with her good hand. 'I hate people who allow stupid pride to make things more difficult for themselves.' She leant against the work surface and watched while Tilly made the coffee.

'It's very good of you,' she said after a moment; the words came with difficulty then, as though she'd got over the worst, she added in a little rush, 'I didn't want to admit it, but everything has been getting on top of me. It's extraordinary how many simple actions you just take for granted until you lose the use of a hand.'

'I should have come down before.' The kettle boiled and Tilly filled the cafetière. She took out two mugs from one of the cupboards and carried them over to the kitchen table with the milk.

Liz brought over the coffee. She suddenly looked younger and less harassed.

'After all the work you did for the party? Even you need a rest sometimes, Tilly. Tell me, are you going to become a professional cook?'

It was the perfect opportunity to tell Liz about the possibility she was going home to enrol in a catering course but something held Tilly back. Perhaps it was because nothing was settled yet. So she muttered something about being interested and, yes, she might think about it.

'I think you should. It's so important to find something you're good at. It makes all the difference to one's confidence, doesn't it?'

Tilly looked at Liz in surprise. She hadn't expected her to come out with such an understanding statement.

'It's been great cooking for Mum and Charles,' she said eagerly. 'He's awfully critical but in a nice way, you know?'

Liz laughed, an amused, friendly laugh. 'I think so. He's very direct, isn't he?'

'But he doesn't try to do you down.'

Liz looked interested, 'Have you suffered from that?'

Tilly told her about Mrs Major and the way she seemed to glory in finding fault with her efforts in the café. Then asked Liz whether she'd had much encouragement when she started painting.

'I was lucky, my father was a talented amateur painter and he took me to galleries and taught me to look, really look at everything around me, at lines, at tones, at colours. He was very supportive.'

Tilly thought about how marvellous it must be to have a father like that. Of course, Thomas had tried to encourage her but it hadn't been the same.

Liz looked as though she understood what hadn't been said, 'Yes, I've been fortunate. But my mother resented all the time he spent with me and

I never had a close relationship with her; she was jealous. I envy what you and Olivia have.'

Tilly suddenly felt very lucky after all.

'Tell me, what have you been doing with yourself down here, when you haven't been cooking or sightseeing or walking that dog? Do you read at all?'

It was, Tilly told her mother afterwards, as though Liz was actually interested in her. 'She's not cold at all.'

'I never thought she was,' Olivia sounded surprised anyone could suggest such a thing.

'Well, whenever we've met before,' Tilly traced a figure of eight on the table with her finger. 'It was as though she was being polite, listening to what I said but thinking of something else. But now,' Tilly looked up at her mother, 'we really talked. Do you think she could be shy? She told me about some books she's been reading that I might enjoy and asked me about food and growing up and what I think of the French and, well, all sorts of things.'

Tilly found she enjoyed seeing Liz each day. By Friday she still hadn't told her about the possibility of going back to England. It seemed there were several difficulties about her being accepted for catering college. She didn't have the academic qualifications they called for and apparently they were full for the coming year. But Charles had rung Rory and, true to his promise, he'd got his father working on the matter.

Word came back that the situation wasn't completely hopeless. Olivia had got Tilly's school to produce a report saying that her exam results didn't reflect her actual capabilities together with details of her ongoing assessments. And Jemima had produced a glowing reference. Then the college had said that people did drop out as the starting date drew close and that it was just possible they might be able to offer a place before the course started.

But she had to attend for an interview. Tilly suggested she should fly back to London then return to France until the start of term. Only to find her mother and Charles suggesting it would be better for her to remain in England. It wasn't that they didn't want her with them, they said hastily. But there was accommodation in London to sort out; Olivia wanted to let the Surbiton house, she thought it much better Tilly should find somewhere to stay near the college. Then Jemima rang and said she had a place available for Tilly in her kitchen. She could start working at *Frère Marcus* immediately and if, by any chance, the college place didn't materialise this year, she could stay on.

'That's wonderful,' Daphne said enthusiastically after the call had come through. 'Why not fly back to England with us on Saturday?'

Tilly felt like a train going faster and faster along rails that wouldn't allow her to change direction.

'I think I need a little more time to get organised,' she said hesitantly.

210

Daphne frowned. 'A girl like you should be able to pack up in hours not days.'

'I'm with Tilly, Mother,' Olivia broke in. 'There's not that much of a rush for her to get back to England, the course isn't going to start for a couple of months yet.'

'But what about this job?' Daphne insisted.

'Jemima wants her to start at the end of next week. I think Tilly and I need a couple of days together before she flies back. After all, if she's going to be working in London, we won't see much of her for quite some time.'

Daphne looked disapproving but Tilly was delighted her mother stood firm. It was all very exciting but the idea of a few quiet days with Olivia and Charles so she could catch her breath before coping with everything that waited for her in London sounded wonderful. Liz was getting stronger and managing better with just one hand, and the following week Tilly had only been going to do the shopping and help for an hour in the mornings anyway.

That morning Tilly told Liz what had been decided. It proved unexpectedly difficult to explain why she hadn't mentioned anything about the possibility before. 'It was all so up in the air, you see,' she stammered slightly over their morning coffee. 'I really didn't know whether it would come off.'

'And you thought if you said anything, it might all disappear, vanish like icecream under bright lights?' Liz, relaxed and smiling, seemed to understand.

'Something like that,' Tilly agreed, feeling better.

'So, tell me all about this new career of yours,' Liz invited and Tilly spent a happy time giving her all the details.

'And this Rory, what part is he going to play in your life,' Liz asked, sounding really interested.

'You mean, is he a boyfriend?' Tilly grinned, amused at the thought. 'He's a friend who's a boy.' She remembered the fun the three of them had had the previous week. Rory had been relaxed, had teased her. He'd been much the same with Jemima, like a brother. Conversation had centred round the food, they'd discussed it professionally, seriously, but there had been time for much more, for jokes, for discussions about books, music, France, for lots and lots of laughter. But nothing more. Tilly felt a moment's pang for everything she'd shared with Mark. For the way she'd given him her heart. Being with Rory didn't offer anything to set beside those memories.

'Ah, I can see there's nothing like that between you,' Liz commented quietly. 'There's someone else who's captured your young heart.'

Tilly bent over her coffee. 'It's all over with,' she muttered. There was no point in feeling anything more for someone who'd walked out on her. She wished she could forget Mark. Particularly she wished she could forget how diminished she felt by his behaviour.

'Sure?' Liz asked sceptically.

'Oh, yes. It has been for ages.' Tilly said firmly.

'The time scale of the truly young,' Liz murmured and refilled their mugs, using her left hand with increasing dexterity.

For a moment Tilly lost the sense of comradeship that had grown up between them in a sudden awareness of Liz's age, so much closer to her mother's than her own. Then Liz started discussing the shopping and the feeling vanished.

After lunch Liz went to lie down for her regular afternoon rest and Tilly cooked a coq au vin. She'd just taken it off the stove when Patrick came in.

'Hello, you're early,' Tilly said in delighted surprise.

He'd loosened his tie and taken off his jacket and looked as though the weekend had already started, which she supposed it had. 'Nothing going on in the office so I thought I'd come back and see if you'd like to take Juno for a walk.'

'Oh, that would be great!' Tilly knew that amongst everything else she was going to miss, walks with Juno held an important place. 'I'll just finish this bit of clearing up and then I'll go and fetch him. Liz is asleep.'

Patrick dried up the last of the cooking pots then they took the car up to *La Chênais* and Tilly dashed in to collect the dog.

Up in the hills where they had first walked Juno together, Patrick took deep breaths of the warm air. 'Wonderful!' he declared.

'Business going well?' she asked, watching Juno streak off in his usual bullet from gun dash after being let off the lead.

He nodded. 'Sold two of the Villefranche apartments.'

'That's terrific!' Tilly said delightedly, she knew how much that must mean to him.

'And I've been asked to handle a development in Aix en Provence. Got to go there next week. Any chance Liz could manage without you so we could go together?' he asked hopefully as they set off after the dog.

Tilly's heart fell. 'I'm off to England next week,' she said bluntly.

For a moment he didn't understand. 'When will you be back?'

She shrugged, 'Not for some time, I'm hoping to go to catering college.'

'Very sudden, isn't it? This decision?' Patrick said, looking at her sideways.

Once again she tried to explain.

When she'd finished, he said nothing, merely strode on faster and faster, his hands deep in his pockets, the sleeves of his business shirt rolled up above his elbows.

Juno rushed back from his headlong flight over the hill and flung himself at Tilly, demanding affection.

Tilly bent over him, rubbing his coat. 'Good dog, what a good dog,' she crooned at him, then glanced up to find Patrick watching her with an expression that almost stopped her breath.

'I love you, Tilly,' he said abruptly.

For an instant the hills swung crazily around her then she swallowed hard and straightened up, leaving Juno to nudge at the hand that had ceased to stroke him. 'No!' she whispered jerkily and it was a denial not only of his words but also of the way the world had behaved so oddly. 'Liz,' she added in the same trembling voice.

'I never meant to,' Patrick turned and stared out towards the incredible blue of the sea, the blue of a madonna's robe. 'One moment I was enjoying our time together, the next I knew I loved you.'

Tilly wrapped her arms around herself, squeezing her flesh tight, delight rushing through her, knowing she had no right to feel anything like this.

'I know it's hopeless,' he continued, his voice dying away. Then he turned back to her. 'It is hopeless, isn't it?'

She couldn't bear the way he looked at her, 'Patrick, I'm very fond of you,' she started, the limp, conventional words, forcing them out.

Juno, tired of the lack of action, found a promising-looking stick and brought it to Tilly.

'Oh, hell,' said Patrick. He grabbed at the stick; Juno enjoyed a brief tug of war then stood back while he threw it, hard, into the far distance. Patrick stood and gazed after the galloping dog.

Tilly laid a hand on his arm, 'There's Liz,' she said.

His serious face twisted painfully. 'I know, I know!' He paused, thrusting his hands into his pockets again. 'It's just that you, I mean, when I'm with you, you make me feel, I don't know, younger somehow, stronger, brighter; someone who could be someone.'

'You are someone!' Tilly said stoutly. His lack of self esteem pierced at her. It was so like what she'd felt since Mark had deserted her. She longed to comfort him, to tell him how very dear he was to her. But then she thought of Liz and how much she had come to like her and how she admired her courage.

Patrick smiled a smile that once again tore at her heart. 'You're such a love, Tilly. I don't know what I'm going to do without you.' Then he whistled for Juno and started to walk back towards the car. They waited together for the dog to come, Patrick staring out over the mountains towards the sea, today everything had the clarity of a stage set. 'If you hadn't told me you were going back so soon, I wouldn't have said anything,' he said abruptly, not looking at her.

For a long moment Tilly didn't say anything. Later she thought that that was when she finally grew up. At last, 'I shall always remember this afternoon,' she said. The scent of thyme was in her nostrils. From the distance she could hear the rush of Juno's return.

Patrick turned to her, his face alight. 'You mean, if things had been different?'

'They aren't,' Tilly said briefly.

But, heedless of anyone who might be passing, Patrick drew her into his arms and kissed her as hungrily as he'd eaten her meals.

213

Again, the world seemed to swing around her for a long, blinding moment.

Then, very gently, Tilly drew back.

And Juno rushed up, barking furiously and didn't stop until Patrick had dropped his arms.

'We must go back,' Tilly said gently.

Patrick opened the rear of the Volvo; Juno jumped in and stood there, still barking. Not until Tilly and Patrick were both in the car and they were driving down the hill did he quieten down.

The next day, Saturday, Tilly went with her mother to see her grandparents off at Nice airport. Daphne kissed both of them. 'It won't be long before we see you in Sussex,' she said triumphantly to Tilly.

'Look after yourself, Mother,' Olivia said, a little wearily. 'Don't do too much. You're looking much better now than when you arrived. You should take things more easily. Give up some of your committees.'

'Nonsense,' Tilly's grandmother declared robustly. 'This holiday was all I needed.'

Tilly saw her mother raise her eyebrows at her father. He shrugged his shoulders as if to say, you know Daphne, she goes her own way.

Then their flight was called and the Fergusons were gone.

Tilly and her mother made their way back to the car.

'Five days to spend together without people!' Olivia exclaimed ecstatically as she started the engine. 'I'm going to make the most of you. Are you sure Liz doesn't need you for more than a couple of hours in the morning?'

'Of course, Mum, she keeps on saying she can manage without anyone now but of course she still can't drive the car for shopping.'

'Is there anything in particular you would like to do, darling, before you go back? Somewhere you'd like to go?'

Tilly thought briefly of Aix en Provence. 'Just laze by the pool with you and Charles. That's what I'm going to miss back in England.' She wouldn't think about Patrick and his lovely laugh and his careful thoughtfulness.

'We'll have a really nice, quiet time,' her mother promised. 'I need my batteries recharged before Charles's friends arrive, Mother really is rather draining.'

'How long are they staying?'

'A week,' Olivia said gloomily.

Tilly squeezed her arm, 'You'll probably enjoy having them, I'm sure Charles only has nice friends. But I'm sorry I won't be here to help.'

'So am I,' Olivia's tone was heartfelt. 'I don't know what Charles is going to think of my catering! And he's bound to want more dinner parties.'

'Cheer up, you can always get a *traiteur* in!'

They reached the gates of *La Chênais* and Olivia stopped as a van came out. 'That's our builder,' she said in surprise as it went past them. 'I hope nothing's gone wrong with the house.'

214

As they drove into the courtyard, Charles bounded down the steps and opened Olivia's door. He looked both excited and apprehensive.

'Don't tell me,' Olivia said. 'More unexpected guests?'

Oh, please, thought Tilly desperately, not until I've gone back. It would be so wonderful to have my last few days here just with Mum and Charles.

'Phyllie's arriving on Monday!' Charles said, excitement winning over apprehension.

'Phyllida?' Olivia was astonished. 'Another holiday?'

Tilly followed her and Charles up the front steps.

'No,' said Charles. 'Well, actually, I'm not sure. She's been made redundant and she says she and James have broken up. She was in tears when she rang me.'

'Phyllida crying?' Tilly asked in awe.

'Yes,' Charles turned to her. 'You know, I can't remember the last time she cried.'

'What a shame,' Olivia said compassionately. 'Losing your job must be awful and to lose your boyfriend at the same time, poor Phyllida!'

'So I told her come on out here and forget about it all.'

'Of course!' Olivia said and almost managed to sound happy about the idea.

'She'll be able to help you, Mum,' said Tilly encouragingly.

'Exactly,' Charles said happily. 'Lose one daughter, gain another!'

On Monday Olivia suggested that Phyllida would much prefer it if her father met her on his own.

Tilly and Olivia were sunning themselves by the pool when the Jaguar swept back up the drive. They followed an excited Juno up the lawn into the courtyard.

Phyllida got out of the car and stood awkwardly. She was wearing jeans and a T-shirt, her hair needed washing and Tilly thought how different she looked from the cocky girl who had made their lives so difficult at Easter.

Olivia went and kissed her. 'I'm so sorry, Phyllie,' she said softly.

'Yeah, well,' said Phyllida tonelessly.

'I'll take your bags up, darling. Why don't you change into a bikini and come down to the pool,' suggested Charles, hefting two enormous suitcases out of the boot.

Tilly retrieved a carry-on case and a leather jacket from the back of the car. There seemed to be three times as much luggage as Phyllida had brought with her at Easter. How long was she intending to stay? Then Tilly felt mean, this house was as much Phyllida's home as hers. After all, she'd been here several months, it was only fair Charles's daughter should be able to use this gorgeous place to sort out her life as well.

But by the time Tilly had to start packing to go back to England any feelings of sympathy towards Phyllida had vanished under the onslaught of the other's sulks and selfish monopolising of her father.

215

Tilly went to the bathroom she shared with her stepsister to collect her toilet things and found Phyllida staring moodily at herself in the mirror. 'Do you mind!' she said aggressively to Tilly. 'I'd like some privacy!'

'Then you should lock the other door,' Tilly said briefly, picking up her toothpaste and tooth brushes and slotting them into her toiletry bag. She added her cleansing cream and moisturiser and was about to leave the bathroom when she thought better of it. 'Look, Phyllie,' she said nervously but standing solidly in the doorway. 'You could make life a great deal easier for yourself if you thought a bit about others every once in a while.'

'You know nothing about anything,' Phyllida said expressionlessly.

Tilly began to feel angry. All right, she was several years younger than Phyllida but she wasn't a schoolgirl any longer. 'I know that staying in bed until lunchtime every day won't help you. Losing a job isn't the end of the world but if you don't pull yourself together you really will be a failure. If you started helping around the house you could find things were a lot more fun. You might even go down and give Liz a hand, she'll be struggling with that plaster for several weeks yet.'

Phyllida gave her a look that said listening to such rubbish was beneath her and retreated to her bedroom.

Tilly took a deep breath and felt a sense of achievement. She'd been left in possession of the bathroom and that was something. Maybe Phyllida might begin to pull her weight after all.

'Look, Mum,' she said on the way to the airport that afternoon, 'you mustn't let Phyllie have things her own way all the time. Especially when you're busy with guests.'

Olivia gave a deep sigh, 'Easy enough to say, darling. There's not much I can do.'

'You can tell her she has to help,' Tilly said impatiently. 'And you should make Charles realise that it won't do Phyllie any good to mope around doing nothing.' Just at this moment she felt older than her mother.

Olivia found a place to park at the airport then helped Tilly out with her luggage. 'Being a stepmother's a bit of a thankless task,' she said when they'd found a trolley. 'And she's had a nasty shock.'

Tilly gave it up. She didn't want her last moments with her mother spoilt by discussing Phyllida.

Chapter Twenty-Two

Olivia helped Tilly check in then took her off for a last coffee before the flight was called.

They talked resolutely about what Tilly was going to do when she got to London, Olivia asking again if she had all the details that Charles had put together on the catering college and his suggestions about how to find somewhere to live.

'Mum,' Tilly protested at last. 'I'm grown up now! I can manage! Gran's going to check out the place I find to live, I've got the job with Jemima and you know Clodagh's there to give me a hand if I need one, not to mention lots of other friends. I will be OK, promise!'

Olivia gave her a wobbly smile. 'I know, darling, I'm just being a mother hen.' She hesitated then couldn't resist saying, 'I hope you're not going to miss your life here too much.' She couldn't bring herself to mention Patrick's name but she scrutinised her daughter's face for the slightest sign she might be leaving a broken heart behind her.

'London's going to seem pretty grey and depressing after here,' Tilly said blithely. 'And I'm going to miss you and Charles like mad but I'll survive. Maybe I can come out at Christmas.'

Christmas was months away! More than ever now Olivia was certain that there had been no grounds for Daphne's theory of an affair and she began to feel resentful of the way Charles had picked it up and supported the suggestion Tilly enrol at this catering college. She'd lost her daughter and it didn't seem Phyllida would be any sort of comfort.

Tilly glanced at her watch and then at the departure screen that hung in the coffee shop. 'My flight's being called, I'd better go.' She got up, put on her jacket over her denim pinafore dress and rust-coloured T-shirt and picked up the drawstring shoulder bag that bulged with magazines and a large bottle of olive oil Tilly hadn't dared consign to her suitcase.

'Sure you've got enough money?' Olivia asked as she clung to her daughter in a last embrace.

Tilly nodded; at this last moment, her eyes looked suspiciously damp. ''Bye, Mum, see you soon.'

Olivia stood looking after her for a long moment, then made her way out of the shiny glass building. The sun was blazing outside, baking into the metal of the cars waiting in the parking lot. The oleanders were blooming brightly, the sky was a singing blue. An international flight had decanted a crowd of happy passengers. Smartly dressed in varying degrees of casualness, they swarmed around the arrival area, chattering happily.

Olivia found where she'd left the Jaguar and sat for a moment, her eyes blinking behind her dark glasses. She remembered the first time she'd come to Nice with Charles. It seemed much longer ago than ten months. She tried to recapture the feeling of anticipation and fulfilment she'd had as Charles had driven down the *Promenade des Anglais*. After a moment she gave a wry little smile. So much had happened since then. She supposed they'd both changed. But they still had each other and no doubt with time and effort she could make a friend of Phyllida.

The Smythes arrived the day after Tilly left. They'd rung the night before, said they were quite near, in the picturesque hill town of Draguignon, and could they arrive in time for lunch?

Olivia went out early to shop, cursing herself for not going to the supermarket right by the airport after she'd dropped Tilly. She just hadn't been thinking straight.

Never mind, she thought, walking in the already warm air towards the greengrocer's, she liked patronising the local shops. They all knew her now and struggled to understand her poor French. What nonsense people talked sometimes about French chauvinism! Olivia had met with nothing but kindness.

Still, it was hard work finding the words that would get her what she wanted and today it seemed harder than ever. There were no haricot beans on display at the greengrocer's and she had to ask for them. As far as she could gather from his reply, the proprietor was desolated, the beans had been expected but hadn't arrived. So Olivia had to think of something else and finally got courgettes, which would be a great deal more trouble to cook and Charles didn't really like them anyway. But he disliked broccoli even more. She added tomatoes and salad to her purchases. (Charles wasn't particularly keen on salad, either, but Tilly had got him eating it with the way she did the dressing, Olivia just hoped she could remember the recipe.) Then she bought peaches and strawberries, at least they were easy and everyone liked them. Olivia handed over a two-hundred-franc note, pocketed the small amount of change, picked up her purchases and moved on to the butcher.

By the time she'd finished, she had three heavy bags to carry back to the car, her arms were aching and the day had developed into another scorcher. The Smythes would be glad they didn't have to drive too far. And that a swimming pool awaited them! Olivia opened the sunroof and buzzed down the windows. Already her blue cotton shift was sticking to her back and her feet were sweating in her sandals. If she got on with the lunch preparations, there might be time for her to have a swim before their guests arrived. Perhaps Phyllida could be persuaded to help.

Olivia drove through the gates of *La Chênais* then stopped the car in surprise. On the lawn was a small JCB-type machine that appeared to be digging up the ground at one end of the swimming pool. Just in front of her a lorry was being decanted of bags of sand, cement, breeze blocks and heaven knew what else.

For a moment Olivia sat there unable to believe the evidence of her eyes. Then she skirted the lorry, drew up in the courtyard with a screech of brakes, ignored her shopping and went to find her husband.

He was in the kitchen, laying a tray. 'I thought I'd take breakfast up to Phyllie and try and persuade her to get up before John and Merry arrive,' he said as Olivia came in.

'Somebody's digging up the lawn. A whole load of building materials has arrived and it looks as though the pool is being drained. Charles, what's going on?'

'Ah.' He dropped a couple of pieces of hot toast on to a plate and blew on his fingers to cool them. 'I meant to tell you about that.'

Olivia tapped a furious hand on the table. 'What do you mean, you meant to tell me?'

'Well, I had a meeting here the other day with Jean-Claude, you know, the builder we had for the house?'

Olivia nodded impatiently. Of course she knew who Jean-Claude was.

'Michel did me a plan for a pool house and I wanted to see how much it would cost. Jean-Claude came last week, I think it was while you were taking your parents to the airport.'

Olivia remembered the builder's van that had been leaving as she and Tilly came back from Nice. With the drama of Phyllida's arrival, she had completely forgotten to ask why it had been there.

'Anyway, we discussed it all, he took the plan away and said he'd give me an estimate. Then he rang the other day, gave me a quote on the phone and said a job had fallen through and, if I wanted, he could start today. So I told him to go ahead.' Charles looked at Olivia apologetically. 'I meant to tell you but what with trying to get Phyllie settled and saying goodbye to Tilly, it slipped my mind.'

'A pool house?' Olivia couldn't believe it. 'You got Michel to design a pool house and never showed me the plans?'

'I think I did mention something about it, a few weeks ago. You seemed to think it was rather a good thing.' Charles busied himself with pouring hot water on to a small cafetière of coffee and added it to his tray.

'You asked me if I thought somewhere to change and a terrace where we could eat beside the pool would be an idea, and I said yes, I thought so. I can't believe you took that as a go-ahead for something I had no input into and that you've landed us with a garden full of builders just when we've got guests coming!' By the time she finished this little speech, Olivia was shouting. She strode to the end of the kitchen and back again then stood in front of him, her hands placed belligerently on her hips. 'I can't believe this, Charles, I really can't believe it!'

He avoided her gaze and picked up the tray. 'I'll just take breakfast up to Phyllie and then we'll talk about it.'

Before he could move towards the door, Olivia took the tray out of his hands and put it on the table.

She raced up the stairs and threw open the door to Phyllida's room. The curtains were still closed. Olivia jerked them open. 'Phyllida, it's half-past ten and time for you to get up,' she said, her voice tight and controlled. 'Your father has made breakfast for you and it's in the kitchen. Don't let the coffee get cold.'

The figure under the bedclothes stirred and hunched itself over to the other side, pulling the duvet around its ears.

Olivia pulled the duvet off the bed. Phyllida lay curled up, her short nightie hardly covering her bottom, a teddy bear, its fur worn naked in spots, clutched to her breast.

'Phyllida, I'm waiting!' Olivia stood at the bottom of the shell bed, her foot tapping on the floor.

Phyllida groaned. 'God, what's happened? World War Three started?'

'Not yet!' Olivia ground out between clenched teeth. 'And I suggest you don't make me fire the first shots.'

Phyllida looked at her stepmother from beneath half-closed eyelids, then, rather to Olivia's surprise, got out of bed, dropping the bear on to the pillow. 'OK, if I must.' She started out of the room.

Olivia snatched the flimsy robe from its hook on the back of the bedroom door and followed her. 'There are workmen in the garden, you'd better put this on.'

Phyllida tossed her head with something of her old style. 'Bourgeois attitudes,' she said, but slipped her arms through it nevertheless.

When they reached the kitchen she looked at the tray. 'Thanks, Dad.' She picked it up. 'I'll take this back to bed with me.'

'You'll eat it down here,' Olivia said.

Phyllida took no notice and carried the tray towards the door.

'Phyllida!' Olivia said with barely concealed anger.

The girl continued on her way.

'Charles!' Olivia appealed to him. 'Tell her to bring it back here.'

'Darling,' he said placatingly, 'I don't see why it matters where she eats it.'

Phyllida tossed Olivia a triumphant glance and left the kitchen.

'Charles, are you going to let her get away with this behaviour?'

'Darling, she's going through a rough time, don't you think she deserves a little consideration?'

It was too much. 'And I don't, I suppose? I count for nothing in this house. It doesn't matter what I think.'

Charles's face creased in lines of real concern. 'How can you think that for a moment?' he started.

The front door bell rang and the dog rushed into the hall barking furiously.

Charles took no notice. 'You surely don't think . . .' he started again.

'That's probably your friends,' Olivia said in icy tones. 'You'd better not keep them waiting.'

That afternoon, Olivia took refuge with Liz.

'You have no idea what the Smythes are like,' she said, sinking into a comfortable garden chair in the shade of a large mimosa tree.

Liz put down the jug of lemonade she was carrying and carefully eased herself into another chair. 'Tell me,' she invited.

Olivia struggled with herself for a few minutes than shrugged. 'Oh, I suppose they aren't so bad, really. It's just they've got this terribly humble attitude. Their eyes were out on stalks as Charles and I gave them the guided tour. It was as though they were being taken round Buckingham Palace! Yet they can't be too badly off themselves, they've driven down in a huge great Volvo and Merry's clothes put mine in the shade.'

'Never!' murmured Liz with an ironic smile, using her left hand to pour out glasses of lemonade. She passed one over to Olivia.

'Well, today anyway,' Olivia asserted, taking the glass and looking down at the old blue cotton shirtwaister she hadn't had time to change out of. 'The whole of lunch was spent with them apologising for forcing themselves on us and Charles and me insisting it was no trouble to have them and saying how much we'd been looking forward to their visit. And I'm sure I sounded totally insincere.'

'I expect they'll settle down,' Liz reassured her. 'That house can be a little overwhelming, you know?'

Olivia let this go. 'And I haven't told you the worst thing yet.'

'Worse than the Smythes?' Liz raised a questioning eyebrow as she sipped her lemonade.

'Don't look at me like that, this really is awful.'

'Not the wretched Phyllida again?'

'It's Charles. You won't believe what he's done!' Liz listened while Olivia told her about the pool house.

'So your real objection,' she said when the story was finished, 'is that he didn't consult you?'

'That and the fact we now have a building site for a garden and can't use the pool.'

'With the Smythes staying for a week?'

'With the Smythes staying for a week,' Olivia repeated. 'Well, wouldn't you be mad?'

Liz considered for a moment. Then, 'Yes,' she said, 'I think I would.'

'Well, what do you think I should do?'

'What do you want to do?'

Olivia sighed. She looked at Liz's garden, bright with geraniums and the bougainvillaea that was wandering everywhere, pushing its magenta blooms through the branches of trees, along the wall edging the road, up the side of the house. This quiet spot was very soothing. Then the enormity of what Charles had done flooded over her again.

'It's as though I mean nothing in his life,' she complained.

'That's not true,' Liz said quickly. 'You know he adores you!'

'Does he? These days it's hard to believe. He seems to go his own sweet way without any consideration for me at all,' Olivia said sadly.

'Don't you think this pool house stuff is just because you've both been so busy he really hasn't had a chance to consult you? I'm sure he intended to.'

'Intended to? Ha! You know what they say about the road to hell! But don't you see, that's just what I'm getting at! If I really meant everything to him, the first thing he'd want to do with his ideas is share them with me.'

Liz looked thoughtfully at her. 'How long has he been divorced?'

'That's another thing, he never wants to talk about his first marriage.'

'How much have you told him about your first husband?'

Olivia shifted uncomfortably in her seat. 'Well, that's different, I'm a widow, Peter's dead. But Veronica's still alive, she's Phyllida's mother, we can't just forget about her.'

'Yes, I do see that is a little different. But haven't she and Charles been divorced for several years?'

'Six or seven, I think.'

'That's quite a long time for a man to be on his own, taking his own decisions. He can get into habits that are hard to break.'

'You mean like not discussing pool houses? But we discussed everything when we were doing up *La Chênais*. Everything,' she repeated with emphasis.

'You weren't being flooded with visitors then,' Liz said wisely.

Olivia studied her glass of lemonade and thought about this. 'You mean I should just forget about it?'

Liz shook her head. 'I think you should find the opportunity to discuss it calmly and unemotionally with him. Tell him how much you enjoy being a part of his life and that includes discussing plans for pool houses. Then ask him if you can look at the architect's plans together. You might find it isn't too late to adjust a few details if you need to. On the other hand, you could find that it's exactly what you want.'

'Well,' said Olivia slowly. 'There's no doubt that it will be very useful. No more dashing up to the house for showers and to change.'

'You see? Already you're seeing the advantages.'

'But he should have discussed it with me!'

That evening, as the Smythes settled with glasses of brandy after a meal of prawns accompanied by one of Tilly's delicious pink mayonnaises, followed by steak, and then strawberries, Olivia brought up the matter of the pool house.

'Wouldn't you like to see the plans,' she suggested to the Smythes, with what she hoped was an infectious enthusiasm.

'Yeah, Dad, if we can't swim in the pool, we might at least see what's happening,' Phyllida agreed.

Olivia felt a surprised satisfaction that her stepdaughter could be on her side. Perhaps she was beginning to feel more herself. She certainly looked good that evening, dressed in a tight mini-skirted sleeveless jersey dress that just about managed to come down to the top of her thighs. It was bright red and with it Phyllida wore matching knee length boots in very shiny and very thin leather. The finishing touch was a pair of huge transparent perspex earrings with a nut embedded in one and a bolt in the other.

'Right, Charles, let the dog see the rabbit!' said John Smythe. Somehow over dinner he and Merry seemed to have relaxed. They'd stopped darting nervous looks around and during the meal had made only two apologies for their presence.

Charles leapt up and fetched the plans from his study, unrolling them on the large coffee table.

Phyllida came and knelt beside him, slipping an arm around his neck. 'Dad, that looks marvellous,' she said, studying the artist's impression of the finished pool house. 'I really like those sliding glass doors and that pergola. It'll be great to be able to eat out there in the summer. And that vine! Think of the grapes! Perhaps you can produce a chateau bottled *La Chênais*?'

Charles looked gratified.

'That's something, all right,' John agreed, fingering the edge of the plan as it curled up.

Merry edged forward on the sofa so she could see, the skirt of her flowered cotton dress riding up over her neat knees and the shirt top falling open to display splendid breasts. 'My,' she said in an awed voice. 'You do have good ideas, Charles; I think that's wonderful,' she swallowed the last of her brandy automatically.

Charles refilled both the Smythes's glasses.

'Can we see the floor plan?' asked Olivia, shaking her head as he held the bottle poised over her glass.

'How technical!' murmured Phyllida but she reached underneath the table for the other set of plans Charles had placed there and unrolled it on top of the artist's impression. 'There, isn't that neat! Look, Merry, that's got to be a stove! He's got a whole kitchen organised here. We'll be able to have wonderful meals on the new terrace. Two showers! And, am I right, Dad, that is a loo, isn't it?'

'Sure is,' said Charles with a touch of pride in his voice. He hunkered down on the floor beside her again and looked across at Olivia. 'What do you think, darling?'

Olivia, sitting beside Merry on the sofa the other side of the table, was working out the detail, trying to visualise how the floor plan would convert into three dimensions. 'You've put a lot of thought into this, Charles,' she said. It was, she realised, pretty much what she would have designed had she been brought in at the start. Except, she drew the plan a little nearer and studied the kitchen area more carefully.

'It was really the architect,' Charles murmured modestly, looking pleased.

'I think it's marvellous,' said Phyllida with conviction. She got up from the floor, using Charles's shoulder as a lever. 'I can't think anybody would want to alter a thing.' She swayed over to the stereo system and looked through the CDs. 'Heavens, Dad, haven't you anything recorded since the stone age?'

'If what you like is anything near to the sort of thing our lot listens to, I'm damn glad Charles hasn't,' John Smythe said with a laugh.

'I shall have to find a record shop,' Phyllida declared. 'I can't possibly listen to all this geriatric rubbish.' But she sorted out one of the CDs and put it on. The overture to *Les Miserables* came through the speakers at maximum volume.

Merry and Olivia covered their ears and John laughed again, his broad face creasing into habitual lines, proving how unnatural his solemn demeanour had been ever since he and his wife had arrived. 'Right little tearaway, aren't you, love?' he said and Phyllida winced.

'Turn it down, Phyllie, we can't hear ourselves think,' Charles ordered. She pouted but reduced the volume to no more than overloud.

'Well, darling, have you any suggestions?' Charles asked Olivia.

She looked up at him and could see nothing but anxious solicitude in his gaze. 'As I said, you've really thought about everything. But perhaps if we put the oven over there and the sink here, there would be more room to stack dirty dishes and you could have a workspace between the cooking area and the refrigerator. The drains haven't been dug yet so it would be quite easy.'

Merry looked more closely at the plan. 'She's right, Charles, that would be much better.'

Phyllida swayed to the music, holding out her arms and sinuously moving her body. Without saying a word she seemed to command attention. John lost all interest in the plans and sat watching her.

'There's something else,' Olivia said quietly. Charles switched his gaze from his daughter back to the plans.

'Yes, darling?'

'This pergola covers such a generous area and it'll have that wonderful view, right across the mountains to the sea.' Olivia gestured towards the salon windows and they all looked out – but dusk had fallen and only twinkling lights could be seen. 'Neither the dining room nor the kitchen has a sea view and it seems a shame not to make the most of it.' Olivia thought of the way the mountains could vary from breathtaking clarity to shades of misty grey and blue and how the sea seemed almost to hang in the sky. 'What if we roofed over the terrace properly? Then built huge glass doors around it and linked it in with the kitchen. In the summer all the doors could be opened but that would mean we could eat there in the cooler weather as well. We could have lemon and orange trees in tubs, inside in winter, on the terrace in summer.'

'Olivia, that's brilliant!' Merry said. 'It makes so much sense. And wouldn't cost much more,' she added practically.

'But what about the vine?' Phyllida said in horrorstruck tones, ceasing her gyrations. 'What about *Château La Chênais*? Your idea isn't nearly so romantic and who wants to be out there when it's cold anyway?'

Olivia looked across at Charles, 'What do you think, darling?'

He studied the plan carefully then looked at her, his eyes twinkling. 'You're a genius, darling, that's what I think.'

Phyllida walked across to the stereo and stopped the CD in mid track. 'How about we all go out for a drink?' she asked, standing with her hand on her hip in a provocative attitude and looking straight at John Smythe.

'It's far too late for us,' Merry said quickly.

'Are you sure?' asked Charles politely.

'Oh, John's always saying he can't keep awake after nine o'clock,' Merry stated positively.

Olivia thought John looked as though he wouldn't mind going out at all but he grinned obligingly at his host, 'I'll be yawning my head off any minute,' he declared.

'What it is to grow old!' Phyllida said aggressively. 'Well, I'm going to have some fun this evening even if you're not.' Before anyone could react, she'd left the room and a moment later they heard the front door slam.

Charles looked up uneasily. 'Where's she going?' he asked Olivia.

She shrugged her shoulders. A few minutes later there came the sound of the Jaguar's engine as it roared up the drive.

Charles leapt to his feet. 'Bloody hell, I never said she could take my car!'

John laughed. 'If that's the first time, you're ruddy lucky, mate! The only way I could keep my lot out of my wheels was to lock up the keys!'

'Sit down, darling,' Olivia pleaded. 'There's nothing you can do, she's gone. I'm sure she'll be all right.'

'It's not his daughter he's worried about,' John guffawed, 'it's his precious car!'

Merry reached out reassuringly towards Charles, 'It's just a stage they all go through,' she said consolingly. 'An evening with the oldies is boring, they've got to be out and doing with their own age group.'

Olivia watched Charles's anger subside and worry take its place. She hoped Phyllida wasn't going to stay out too late because she knew Charles wouldn't sleep until he heard her return.

225

Chapter Twenty-Three

Phyllida sensed the difference in the quality of light sneaking round the curtains of her room and knew it must be heading for midday.

The night had been so warm she'd thrown off the duvet and had slept with just a sheet. She'd even thrown out her aged teddy bear who usually slept beside her. Now she drew the sheet over herself to blot out some of the light and gingerly assessed the state of her head. It felt like the Augean stables just after Hercules had started his clean-up operations, what with the hammering and the unpleasant sensations that were rising from her stomach. She'd never thought teeth could itch; ache, yes, itch, no. Now she believed it. And the state of her tongue she preferred not to think about.

Phyllida let out a soft groan, a louder one would have hurt too much, and slowly struggled into a sitting position. This activity was almost too much. She picked up the worn teddy bear that James had objected to so forcibly that she'd brought herself to leave him behind at Easter, hugged him gently and carefully thought of nothing very much until her stomach recovered its equilibrium. After a little while she reckoned she could make it to the bathroom where she remembered seeing a supply of Alka-Seltzer. Olivia, her stepmother, the perfect hostess! Was that why her father had remarried, to gain a rather superior type of housekeeper? Phyllida couldn't see any other reason. She recognised that Olivia was attractive in an anaemic sort of way but why marry her? Phyllida and her father had been doing very nicely, just the two of them. Now everything was spoilt.

The Alka-Seltzer were in an unpleasantly noisy box and the effort needed to rip open the foil packets was almost too much. Phyllida sat down on the loo seat and waited once again for her insides to settle.

After she'd drunk the medicine and a couple more glasses of the mineral water that had also been provided by the perfect hostess, Phyllida returned to bed. The half-light that came through the curtains said that today was going to be as relentlessly hot as yesterday.

Then Phyllida realised that the hammering came from outside the window. The wretched workmen were hard at it on the pool house. And until they'd finished the pool would remain empty.

How could Dad have been so asinine as to allow the work to start now? Phyllida had to admit she was at one with her stepmother on this. Not that she would dream of saying so, of course. She had to support her father.

The Smythes had been pretty impressed by his plans. Well, they would be, little nobodies from Yorkshire. God, but her mother was right about the provincialism that she had rescued Phyllida from. It was no wonder she'd had to find something more entertaining.

When she and James had come down at Easter, they'd found that one of the cafés in the square was used by quite an amusing collection of young people.

Phyllida didn't actually want to think about James now. For a time there she'd really thought he might be the one. He'd laughed at her witty remarks, acknowledged she was more intelligent than he was but hadn't seemed threatened by it, and his performance in bed had been more exciting than any of her previous boyfriends. Why then had he suddenly said thanks for the ride but he was going to get off now? And then become an item with a stupid little girl who hung on his every word? He'd be bored with her within a couple of months. All Phyllida had to do if she wanted was to wait around. But that wasn't her way. She could replace James with someone better in half a minute. Which no doubt she would do when she got back to England. In the meantime, it would be fun to see what the French could offer.

She had strolled into the café wearing her mini dress and boots to match and watched the effect. It had only taken a moment for a couple of the young men gathered there to recognise and invite her to join them.

They were all local, between, she supposed, late-teens and early-twenties. Thought themselves really sophisticated but were in a minor league so far as Phyllida was concerned. Then a dark-haired, dark-eyed young man called, she thought, Jean-Pierre (so many of them were called Jean something), had discovered she had a car. He'd whispered to her that there were more amusing things to do than knock back wine or Ricard all night and why didn't they go off to the Casino at Cannes? He didn't speak English, of course, but her French was more than adequate. She found when they got there that she was expected to pay, he'd wanted to drink whisky and they had, of course, lost all their chips. Afterwards it turned out he didn't have a place of his own and she couldn't see Dad being overjoyed about a strange young Frenchman in his daughter's bedroom, so that left the car. Not the most accommodating of places. If she was going to spend any time here, Phyllida thought, she was going to have to organise something. Perhaps there was a certain merit in the conservatory idea.

Feeling a little stronger by now, she went back into the bathroom and had a shower. She let the water run all over her for a long time, gradually decreasing the heat until the shower was icy cold and sent little slivers of sensation pulsing into her skin and muscles. Gradually she felt the worst of the hangover release its grip on her.

She towelled herself down then dressed in a violently striped pair of shorts and a mauve singlet top that matched one of the stripes. She placed round her neck the single diamond suspended from a platinum chain that her father had given her for her twenty-first birthday present (together with a neat little Volkswagen Polo car). She considered her reflection for a long moment then added a pair of big silver exclamation mark earrings, brushed her still wet hair into place and went downstairs.

Everyone was in the kitchen making lunch. At least, Olivia and Merry were preparing food, Charles and John were sitting at the kitchen table drinking beer, and Maria, the daily help, was polishing silver.

'Well, well,' said John when he saw her. 'Woken up at last, have we? Something of a late night, was it?' His leer was positively lascivious.

She ignored him and helped herself to a glass of mineral water, found a lemon in the fridge, cut herself a couple of slices, slipped one into the glass and added several lumps of ice from a tray she took from the freezer section.

'I'd be grateful if you could refill the ice tray and put it and the lemon back where they came from, Phyllida,' said her stepmother pleasantly.

She ignored this and started sucking the other lemon slice. She sat down beside her father, leant against his shoulder and watched Maria deal with both the ice and the lemon while she sipped her drink.

Charles smiled down at her. 'Who took the car last night, then? Don't you think you should have asked?'

She gazed disingenuously up at him. 'But, Dad, you've always said I can have anything I want!'

John Smythe gave a shout of laughter. 'Got you there, hasn't she, Charlie?'

'Do you realise, Phyllida,' asked Olivia, slicing up a cold chicken, 'that the French laws on drinking and driving are pretty strict?'

Merry, putting together a salad, launched into a story of some friend of theirs who'd been stopped by the French police the previous year. 'Ted says he thinks he can't drive in France now. Mind you, he said he wasn't any too sure of what was happening except it cost him a deal of money! And John won't touch a car in France or England if he's had any alcohol at all now.'

Phyllida thought how incredibly boring it all was. She edged closer to her father. 'What I need is a car of my own,' she said in a sweet voice, the one that always got her what she wanted from her father.

He gave her a concerned look. 'Really? What's happened to your Polo?'

Phyllida drew back just a little and started moving her glass of mineral water in circles on the table. 'Ah, well, Dad, I was going to talk to you about that. There was this accident, you see. It wasn't my fault, it really wasn't, this chap almost jumped the lights just as I was coming across them and, well, the insurance company said it was a write off.'

'And when did this happen?' Her father looked quite stern.

'Just over a month ago.' Phyllida looked at him steadily.

'Presumably they are going to pay up its value?' Charles said.

'Yes, but, you see, there's the mortgage on the flat to pay, I'm not earning at the moment and I had to pay off my credit cards, so there wasn't really enough left to buy a car with,' Phyllida said, still sweetly, but beginning to think that she would have been wiser not to have raised this matter until they were on their own.

Then she could hardly believe her ears as Olivia said, 'I think it sounds a very good idea, I can't think how we've managed with only one car so far.'

As Olivia lined up large slices of chicken on a plate edged with frilly lettuce, Phyllida waited for her to add something about Tilly's not being one to beat up the surrounding countryside (what a dull girl she was, Phyllida was really pleased she'd gone back to England, they would never have got on) but instead her stepmother said, 'And a left-hand drive car isn't the most sensible thing for Phyllida to be driving out here anyway.'

'You're right, of course, darling,' her father said. He smiled at Phyllida, 'Why don't we go and see what we can pick up this afternoon?'

Phyllida threw her arms around him and gave him a big kiss. 'That's wonderful, Dad!'

Always thank men when they give you what you want, that was what her mother had dinned into her. It's the only thing they're good for, Veronica always added. Phyllida's mother had a very low opinion of men. Too conceited and too stupid for their own good, most of them, she said. A clever woman can run rings around them, that's why men don't actually like women very much. What they do like are our bodies; women have to realise that and use it for their own advantage.

Another thing Veronica was fond of saying: If women didn't have to take time out to have babies, they would be running the world.

It had been a terrible shock when her mother announced that she'd asked Charles for a divorce. Phyllida had thought they had a reasonable relationship. Not an overfond one, perhaps, and her mother had never been one to hold back from criticising Dad for everything from the way he held his knife and fork to his taste in pictures. But then she'd made sure his opinion on anything didn't count so Phyllida had imagined her mother had things organised her way. She'd been aware, though, that they had little in common, that her mother despised her father's Yorkshire background and cultivated what he designated as 'smart friends who wouldn't know sincerity if it hit them in the face'. A second shock had come when her father hadn't fought to save his marriage but had almost seemed to welcome the break.

What he had fought for was the house. Veronica hadn't wanted it but she'd said it should be sold. There was too much of her in it, Charles shouldn't be able to install anyone else there, she said. He had accused her of total selfishness. He'd had the house built and he was damned if he was going to give it up. As long as he made Veronica a reasonable settlement, one that recognised her contribution to the company as well as to the marriage, he couldn't see what she had to complain of. And it would mean that Phyllida wouldn't lose the security of her home.

For what seemed to Phyllida like the first time, her mother lost a battle with her father.

The divorce had coincided neatly with her O levels and she had been sent to boarding school to do A levels, with the holidays being split between her parents. Which had meant that for at least some of the time she had had her familiar bedroom. The posters of pop stars varied with the years but the basic decor – the thick white carpet, mirrored built-in cupboards and polished elm furniture, her array of soft toys – remained the same. Her father had wanted to redo the house but after finding the settlement money, there hadn't been the funds. So it remained as it had been designed by Veronica, austere modern furniture in a minimalist style.

Charles's mother had come down to live with them. Somehow, Phyllida hadn't minded her Yorkshire accent or the nursery food she'd cooked because from her grandmother she'd had total, uncritical love. When Phyllida's mother tried to make fun of old Mrs Frome, Phyllida had flared up at her so effectively, she hadn't made the mistake of doing it again.

The worst part of her father's remarriage had been his putting the house up for sale. Phyllida hadn't really lived there for several years but it had been home. Now she had nowhere she could go back to.

Veronica had remarried so soon that Phyllida had realised there'd been something else behind the divorce other than a sudden decision by her mother that she could no longer stand life with Charles. Richard Hughes was an austere businessman, widowed with two daughters. There was no love lost between them and Phyllida; all they cared about was who your father was, they were dead between the ears and had no idea about style. She failed equally to get on with her stepfather, who regarded her as a price that had had to be paid to acquire her mother. Phyllida thought his ideas positively neanderthal. Her mother liked his background, though, and the large Elizabethan house not far from London that had been in his family for generations. Phyllida hated the house. It was dark with heavy furniture and rich fabrics, which she found stifling. Her father's French house, with its graceful furniture and charming colours, had been a wonderful surprise.

Phyllida's life with her stepfather had been made supportable by the fact that he spent a lot of time travelling and his daughters had moved out to share a flat in London soon after Veronica's arrival. Not that Veronica spent much time at home. She'd taken Charles's generous settlement and founded an extremely successful employment agency. Not, unfortunately, dealing in Phyllida's line of work. Veronica specialised in computer aspects of the engineering industry. She had suggested to Phyllida that she train in computer programing. 'With your brains, Phyll, and charm, I could set you on course for a career that would take you to the top.' But the one favour her stepfather had done her when she announced she wasn't going to go to university was to find her a job with a chum of his in a merchant bank. She'd soon discovered the heady excitement of the money markets.

Computer programing could never provide the same adrenalin, the sense of danger, the euphoria that came with a big killing.

After lunch Phyllida and Charles went down to Antibes and found a dear little Peugeot diesel. Not the sort of thing to catch a gendarme's eye but capable of quite a nice turn of speed. 'We'll take it,' said Charles.

Of course, they couldn't drive it away immediately, all sorts of boring paperwork was necessary, but it looked as though Phyllida could count on having her wheels by Monday.

Until then she was grounded. Her father had taken all the Jaguar keys into his possession and said he needed the car. He told her she was welcome to accompany them on their sightseeing expeditions but wasn't to take the car herself.

Phyllida could see very little profit in spending her time with the Smythes. The way her father and John reminisced about their Yorkshire boyhood, and Merry and her stepmother chatted about the knitting wool and embroidery shop Merry apparently ran in Leeds, set Phyllida's teeth on edge. To someone who had been used to making six-figure profits on the turn of a fraction of a percent, in minutes, it was all just too incredibly provincial.

But then Phyllida found a new form of entertainment as she discovered that baiting her stepmother could be developed into a fine art.

From the start Phyllida had taken every opportunity to flout any instruction from Olivia, despising her for offering such an easy way to have her authority as Charles's wife undermined. But quite soon these simple targets started disappearing and Phyllida realised it was much more subtle to appear to respect Olivia's wishes while using them to sideline her. Phyllida's father was such a dear old bear and so happy to have his daughter staying with them, he'd never realise what was going on.

And now the Smythes proved useful. When Charles proposed a visit to the Gorges du Loup and Olivia suggested a visit up to the mountains instead, Phyllida had only to remark to John hadn't he said he'd love to see the Gorges and that darling little village on the side of the rock face, and he was pushing for them to go there.

And then John insisted he wanted to take the Fromes out to dinner and proposed the Carlton at Cannes; to his mind, he said, a really classy hotel was the place to eat. Olivia murmured something about going to Mougins, it was so charming and had a number of excellent restaurants. Merry seemed quite keen on that idea. Phyllida jumped in with, 'But the Carlton is *the* "in" place and wouldn't it be fun to visit the Casino afterwards? Bring back those days John was telling us about the other night, when he and Dad used to go betting on the greyhounds?' And that settled that. Her mother was quite right, men were stupid.

Not that Olivia was. It didn't take her long to see what sort of game Phyllida was playing. She stopped making suggestions, which suited Phyllida fine. She racked up her charm an extra voltage and became the life and soul of the party, highlighting Olivia's hurt withdrawal.

Charles started asking what was wrong with her. Which didn't help Olivia's good humour at all.

With all the rising tension, it was a relief for Phyllida to have her own car and be independent. Not that it was actually hers. The Peugeot was a second car for the household, Charles had said. After all, he'd added, she would at some stage be off back to England to look for a job. Not that he wanted to suggest she wasn't welcome to stay with them as long as she wanted. But she didn't want to be out of work permanently, did she?

Phyllida didn't know what she wanted.

She'd made one or two enquiries in the money markets before coming out to France but it didn't seem as though anyone wanted Phyllida Frome on their workforce at the present time.

To get the right job she really needed to be on the spot, to keep up her contacts, follow up any hint of a possibility. She was good, she knew that. All right, maybe she had put some people's backs up. But only because they were so much less intelligent than she was. If she really tried, it would only be a matter of time before she was in there again, making it with the best of them. Meanwhile, she had to admit it was something of a relief not to be under constant pressure.

But it was a bore not having the sort of money she was used to spending. Her father couldn't be persuaded into making her anything like the allowance Phyllida felt she needed for life to be supportable. However much she wheedled, all he would do was promise to give her enough to cover the mortgage on the flat for a few months. 'You've got everything paid for here with us,' he told her finally. 'If you can show me you really need something, of course I'll get it for you. All you need otherwise is a bit of pocket money.' Phyllida recognised when Charles couldn't be charmed and that at some stage she would have to find herself another well-paid job. Meanwhile she arranged for her flat to be let on a short lease to help her cash flow.

She soon built up a retinue of young French men who seemed more than happy to show her the 'in' places: the little bars, the discos, the night clubs, the casinos. Some of them were even prepared to pay for her as well. All in all, life was not bad.

She couldn't get on with Liz and Patrick Ratcliffe, though. They gave her an uncomfortable feeling. Phyllida could sense Liz disliked her, however hard she tried to be polite. Patrick was less antagonistic but not at all interesting. All in all, Phyllida preferred to be elsewhere when Charles and Olivia were entertaining the Ratcliffes and she never accepted an invitation to their house. As for helping Liz the way Tilly had suggested before she left, forget it!

It was a relief when the Smythes left and Phyllida could spend more time alone with her father. She got him to take her down to the beach and along the coast in both directions. And she found it was quite easy to suggest that Olivia was exhausted after all the entertaining and would probably appreciate some quiet days on her own.

Then there were always new ways of getting at Olivia.

For instance it was quite fun to offer to prepare a meal and then to produce some almost inedible concoction and laugh it off by saying maybe both of them should take cookery lessons.

There was the fun of playing Olivia one way and her father another. Like the time her stepmother couldn't stand it any longer and took her to task over the state of her room. 'It's not fair to leave it all to Maria to clear up, she has enough to do keeping the main part of the house clean.'

'I don't see why not,' sulked Phyllida, safe in the knowledge that Charles had taken Juno for a walk. 'After all, it's what she's paid for.' Olivia had looked grimly at Phyllida but said nothing more.

However, she obviously had a word with Charles because when they were on their own later in the day, he said, 'Honestly, poppet, do you think you could manage to keep your room halfway tidy? You may not think so, but Maria has more than enough on her plate without having to clear up after you. It's not as though you have much else to do with your time.'

Phyllida looked contritely at her father. 'Of course, Dad. As I said to Olivia, cleaning my room is only a job to Maria, not a lifetime's mission. She deserves a little consideration.'

'I knew you'd understand, poppet.'

Phyllida gave what she thought of as a sphinx-like smile.

Then her father enjoyed having her walk Juno with him. Sometimes Phyllida would ask Olivia in a pretty voice why she didn't come too but the offer was seldom taken up.

Then, just as Phyllida was beginning to feel bored with all this, diversion came by way of a call from some girlfriends of hers who'd come down to the South of France on holiday. They were wondering, Anna said on the phone, if they could take her up on the open invitation she'd extended before she left England.

Phyllida couldn't remember giving any such invitation but she was delighted. She persuaded Charles to organise the building work so that the pool could be refilled. Surely the whole point of this property, she wheedled, was being able to swim without leaving the grounds!

A word with the contractor resulted in a temporary screen being erected between the construction work and the pool and the water turned on again.

Anna, Sarah and Becca were delighted with the facilities. Anna and Becca were in the guest room, Sarah in Tilly's room, which meant Phyllida had to share the bathroom again but it was a small price to pay for the company.

At first the girls were punctilious about helping to clear the table after meals and offering a hand with the food preparation. But Phyllida soon got them out of that. Olivia was happier on her own, she told them, confident that her stepmother wouldn't start ordering guests about.

The girls spent hours sunning themselves and swimming and talking. Phyllida introduced them to the young men she'd met. They patronised all the local hot spots and saved money by asking the chaps they liked for meals at *La Chênais*.

Charles loved having the young around. 'That's what this house is all about,' he said jovially when Sarah said how absolutely splendid it was of him and Olivia to have them. Olivia said nothing. Non-confrontational, that was her style, which certainly made things easier for Phyllida.

Then one morning Phyllida and the others were sitting on the terrace with Charles, under the big umbrellas that shaded them from the heat of the midday sun. The delightful silence that meant the builders had broken for lunch had fallen, the white wine was crisp and cool and no doubt Olivia would soon be back from her morning's shopping and would prepare something for them all to eat.

Phyllida had her back to the long windows leading out from the salon and the first she was aware that something strange had happened was when Charles's jaw dropped open. Then Anna said, 'Wow!' and Phyllida turned to see Olivia standing in one of the windows, her blonde hair shorn into short curls.

'What the hell have you done?' roared Charles. It was so unusual for him to raise his voice, even Phyllida was taken aback.

Olivia gave him a level look. 'I was fed up with long hair, what with all the swimming and the hot weather.' She gave a little shake to her head, making the chic curls dance from side to side. 'This is going to be so easy to wash and manage.'

Charles's eyes narrowed. 'I can't believe you did this without asking me if I minded.'

'It's not your hair,' retorted Olivia shortly.

Charles turned to his daughter. 'Don't you think it's a pity Olivia's cut her hair off?'

Phyllida thought that, actually, the curls suited Olivia and took several years off her age. They had a style that the chignon, classic though it might have been, completely lacked. She put her hair on one side, contemplated her stepmother then nodded sadly. 'I always thought how beautifully your long hair suited you,' she said sweetly. 'And I know Dad loved it.'

Olivia sent her a look that contained a wealth of understanding. 'I'm glad there was something about me that met with your approval,' she said.

'If I had hair like yours, I'd never cut it,' said Sarah, tossing her long dark tresses. 'I always wanted to be a blonde.'

'Actually, I think it looks great,' said Anna, which earned her a nasty look from Phyllida. Becca, whose short hair, like Anna's, was cut with

235

boyish precision, hastily said she, too, thought it was a shame that Olivia had had her crowning glory cut.

All Olivia said was, 'Well, I can always grow it again.'

'But it'll take ages,' Charles sulked.

'And in the meantime you can see if this isn't a look you could get used to,' Olivia suggested sweetly, turning to go back into the house. Then was stopped by the sound of the telephone ringing.

Charles picked up the mobile receiver. 'Hi!' he said. 'How are you?' Then he handed it to Olivia. 'It's your friend, Clodagh.'

Olivia took the receiver and went into the house.

When she rejoined them she had a triumphant gleam in her eye. 'Wonderful news, Clodagh's had a novel accepted!'

Charles expressed his congratulations.

'And she's decided to celebrate by coming down here,' Olivia added.

'Ah,' said Charles guardedly as the girls exchanged glances between themselves. 'When does she want to come?'

'I suggested next week. You did say, Anna, that you thought you had to get back to England this weekend, didn't you?'

'Oh, absolutely, Olivia,' Anna said hastily. 'And Sarah has to go, too.'

What finks, thought Phyllida, leaving me alone with one of Olivia's boring friends. She fixed her eye on the third member of the trio. 'But Becca thought she'd say on for another couple of weeks, didn't you, Becca? Because your new job doesn't start until the end of the month, does it?'

'But only if it's no trouble?' Becca said with a conciliatory smile at Charles.

'Of course not,' Phyllida said quickly. 'You can move into Tilly's room when the others go, that will mean Clodagh can have the guest room. That's fine, isn't it, Olivia?'

She smiled weakly. 'I can see you've got it all organised.'

When Clodagh arrived, Phyllida found that, first, she was actually a lot of fun with a good line in repartee and, second, that she'd picked up a quite sensationally good-looking man on the plane out and spent as much time with him as at *La Chênais*.

'This place gets more and more like a hotel here,' Phyllida heard Olivia complain to Charles one day. 'Clodagh's been here four days and I've hardly seen her.'

Two days later, Phyllida and Becca had oiled themselves and taken up their customary morning positions on the loungers by the pool when Clodagh came and joined them.

'Becca, Olivia would be really grateful if you could help her in the kitchen for a bit,' she said pleasantly, sitting down on the lounger next to Phyllida's. She was wearing a voluminous wrap in gold and red over a one-piece costume in black that looked sensational with her pale skin and red hair.

Becca got up from her lounger with a certain reluctance. 'Of course,' she murmured, glancing at Phyllida.

She closed her eyes and thought how sensible it had been of Olivia not to suggest that she be sent to help her.

Then heard Clodagh say softly, 'Now, Miss Frome, I think it's time we had a little talk.'

Phyllida opened one eye. Clodagh had spread a towel on the lounger, settled herself under a large umbrella and was applying a total sun block to her exposed limbs.

'I could beat about the bush, start a sympathetic chat about the difficulty of finding jobs in today's market, perhaps a discussion on financial matters – oh, yes, I know quite a bit about them, my ex-husband is Managing Director of a merchant bank,' Clodagh said conversationally, rubbing the block over her feet. 'Or I could get you talking about your father, tell you how I can see he's devoted to you, perhaps slip in a bit about his worries about your future now that you appear to have lost interest in a career.'

Phyllida slowly raised herself until she was sitting upright.

'But,' Clodagh continued in the same pleasant tone, 'I've never been one for the subtle approach. I prefer to shoot from the shoulder, or is it the hip?' She appeared to consider the question quite seriously for a moment, pausing in her lotion application, bottle held arrested in the air. Then she started on her arms as she continued, 'No matter. I'll just come out with it. What, Phyllida, makes you quite such a poisonous bitch?'

Phyllida felt as though she'd had the wind knocked out of her. For a moment she was unable to say anything.

Clodagh appeared happy to wait all morning for a response.

'I suppose Olivia has been complaining about me,' she finally shot out furiously.

'Olivia is a kind and loyal person. Far too loyal to slag off her stepdaughter. The only thing she has said to me is that she feels she's failed you,' Clodagh said in the same pleasant tone.

'How presumptuous of her,' Phyllida said without thinking.

'Now that's an example of just the sort of thing I've been wondering about. Here you are, an apparently intelligent girl, certainly attractive – when you manage a smile that is – adored by your father, with a stepmother who has been anxious to make friends, and all you can do is practise making her life a misery.'

Phyllida felt a surge of savage satisfaction that she had been so successful.

'I see by your smirk that I have indeed hit the mark. What a shame your undoubted talents should be directed towards such a contemptible target.'

Phyllida found herself flushing at the acid in Clodagh's voice.

'You don't know how lucky you are with Olivia,' she continued dispassionately. 'If you were my stepdaughter, you'd have been sent home with a flea in your ear long before this. We'd have had a right old barney!'

'Olivia can't send me home, this isn't her house,' Phyllida ground out between clenched teeth.

'Really, that's your attitude, is it? My poor girl, you are deluding yourself. I had a very interesting conversation with your father last night. I know something about French property laws, you see, and how difficult it can be for widows when their husbands die if they don't have a legal interest in the property.'

Phyllida felt her attention caught.

'Charles very kindly explained to me that he had arranged for this property to be bought by an English company of which he and Olivia are the sole and equal shareholders.'

'I don't believe you, he never told me that!' Phyllida burst out.

'I don't suppose he realised you would be so deeply concerned,' Clodagh said levelly. 'So, you see, this is as much Olivia's house as your father's.'

Phyllida decided attack was her best weapon in this unexpected engagement. 'I don't think much of a friend who comes to stay then spends all her time going out, treating the place as an hotel.'

'Ah, then you *do* understand basic good manners, I was beginning to wonder,' said Clodagh softly. 'Yes, you're right, I've been very selfish. And I've apologised to Olivia and Charles. I shan't be going out for the rest of my stay here.'

'I suppose your friend's got tired of you?' Phyllida offered.

'That's no more than I've come to expect from you. He hasn't, actually, nor have I tired of him. In fact, after my stay here, we're going to take a trip into Italy together.'

There was suddenly such a glow about Clodagh that Phyllida caught her breath and felt deeply envious.

'Olivia has been a really good friend to me,' she continued after a brief pause. 'I shan't suggest you could gain by accepting her friendship. Instead I'll say that if you aren't careful, you'll lose your father's respect. I'm sure he'll never stop loving you but is that really all you want?' She put down the bottle of sun lotion, lowered the backrest of the lounger, lay down and closed her eyes.

She had apparently said everything she intended to.

Phyllida too lay back. An uncomfortable cocktail of emotions and thoughts whirled around in her mind. For once in her life she wasn't at all sure what to think.

Chapter Twenty-Four

The summer wore on. Clodagh went off to Italy with her man, and a week later Becca flew back to her new job.

Phyllida moped around *La Chênais* during the day then spent most evenings out, mixing, as Charles put it, with heaven knew who.

Not having anyone staying, though, meant Charles thought they could throw dinner parties. He was worried about all the people they owed. Invitations had slowed down in the summer, their friends were also involved in having guests to stay, so you asked one couple and found you'd invited four or more. Trying to remember all Tilly had taught her, Olivia managed to put together two menus Charles approved of and served one or other at a series of supper parties.

When she had time to think about it, Olivia realised with a faint surprise that she was getting used to Phyllida and her war of attrition. It was like enduring constant toothache without being able to visit a dentist. If only Charles realised what was going on. But Phyllida was too clever, she reserved the worst of her attacks for when he was elsewhere.

The summer, though, was coming to an end and perhaps then she would start looking for a job and the seemingly unceasing stream of visitors would end. Not yet, though. Two more of Charles's friends had invited themselves.

Olivia was in the kitchen preparing supper a few days before the next invasion when her father rang.

Charles found her sitting at the table, turning a tea towel over and over in her hands, a curious, twisted expression on her face.

'What's happened?' he asked, a note of apprehension in his voice. 'Not more visitors?'

'It's my mother, she's in hospital, she's had an operation,' Olivia said, and two tears started down her face.

He came and sat beside her and took her hand, gently removing the tea towel and tossing it on the table. 'How is she?'

'As well as can be expected, Father said.' Her face worked convulsively. 'I can't take it in, Mother's never been ill. The most she's ever had is a cold, not even 'flu! She's always said it's mind over matter.'

She felt as though the world had shifted on its axis. However much she'd resented her mother's interference in her life, the fact that Daphne had been

239

there had provided a firm foundation whose existence, even while she fought against it, had been taken for granted. Now rock had turned to shifting sand and nothing in her life seemed sure any more.

'What's the matter with her?'

Olivia clasped Charles's hand tightly. 'It's cancer!'

'Oh, darling, I'm so sorry.' He put his arm around her and drew her against him.

Olivia burrowed her head into his shoulder and he caressed the short hair. 'Father said she hasn't been well for some time, since before they came out here.' Her voice was muffled. 'Apparently she thought if she ignored it, she'd get better. Then she finally had to go to the doctor and he sent her for all sorts of tests.'

Charles stroked her back. 'Where is the cancer?'

Olivia raised her head, her cheeks streaked with tears. 'In the stomach, Father said. He was too upset to give me much detail.'

'Has the operation been successful?'

'Father said the surgeon was very optimistic.' Olivia tried to wipe her eyes with the back of her hand.

'That's good!' Charles said encouragingly and fished out a handkerchief.

'But he's asked if I can't go home and help look after her when she comes out of hospital.' She blew her nose on his handkerchief and looked at him.

Charles said nothing.

'Father says he can't manage.'

'Isn't there anyone else?' Charles asked.

Olivia shook her head. 'It's my job, that's what daughters are for.' She released herself gently from his embrace and sat back in her chair. 'I'm sorry about your friends but you must see I haven't any alternative,' she said, rather stiffly. 'But you can take them out to meals and I'll see if I can get Maria to come more often. At least we haven't got any parties organised at the moment.'

'Damn the Roberts,' Charles said vehemently. 'It's you I'm worried about! I know how difficult you find your mother.'

Warmth flooded Olivia. 'Darling, she's ill!'

'Why didn't she tell you before?'

Olivia sighed. 'Father said she didn't want to worry me. She said it was nothing very much. Even when she knew it was cancer and they were going to have to operate, she still made him promise not to tell me. Darling, I've got to go.'

He put a hand to her cheek. 'Of course you have. Only I'll miss you.'

It wasn't until Charles said that that Olivia realised she'd been hoping he'd come with her. That he would cancel his friends or tell Phyllida she would have to cope with them. It wasn't just that his support and his company were important to her, she wanted to know that she came first with him; that her feeling they were gradually drifting apart was an illusion.

'What about a flight?' he asked.

She sighed again as she recognised there was no hope of his cancelling his friends or telling Phyllida she'd have to cope on her own. 'I told Father I'd try and catch the afternoon plane the day after tomorrow, Thursday. Mother comes out on Wednesday but he thinks they can manage without me for a day or two. Oh, if only he'd rung before! Then I could have been there before she got home.'

'She's a very proud woman,' Charles said slowly.

Juno pushed open the kitchen door, loped across to Olivia and pressed his big body against her leg. He rested his handsome head on her knee and looked up at her with soulful eyes, as though trying to offer comfort.

Olivia caressed his red coat and felt the muscles ripple under the skin. At that moment she would have been glad to have been able to take him back to England with her.

'Dad, how about taking Juno for a walk?' asked Phyllida, coming in behind the dog.

'Phyllie, Olivia's had some rather bad news. Her mother's very ill and she's got to go home to look after her.'

Phyllida stood stock still, her face quite expressionless. Olivia waited for her to show how pleased she was that she would be left alone with her father now, give or take the odd visitor.

'That's rotten for you,' Phyllida said abruptly. 'I'm sorry.' She turned and went out of the kitchen.

The next afternoon Olivia went down to see Liz. Sometimes she thought it was only Liz's friendship that had kept her going this long summer.

Poor Liz still had her arm in plaster. The fracture hadn't healed properly and the wrist had had to be broken again and reset. It had been a dreadful blow to her and Olivia hadn't been able to help nearly as much as she had wanted, guests having continually got in the way. Somehow, though, Liz had not only overcome the disappointment and become more and more adept at managing with one hand, she had developed a technique for working on new ideas for paintings. She'd started sifting through the hundreds of photographs she had taken whilst they had been in Provence, identifying shapes, sketching them crudely with her left hand, getting Patrick to cut them out, then juxtaposing and shifting them around. The final stage was to experiment with splashes of colour on bits of paper. Then, confident she knew exactly how the finished painting could be created, she slipped everything into a plastic bag and started working on another.

'Olivia, I'm so sorry,' Liz said after Olivia had broken the news about her mother. 'Come and sit down. I'll fetch you a drink, you look as though you need one.' She managed to sound sympathetic and brisk at the same time, a combination that Olivia found curiously bracing.

'Charles gave me a brandy, I don't think I'd better have any more alcohol!'

'So, how about a *citron pressé* instead? Come into the kitchen while I squeeze the lemons then we'll go and sit outside.'

'Any more news on when you'll be rid of the plaster?' Olivia asked.

'In about ten days, they think.' Liz tipped the pure lemon juice into two glasses and went to the fridge for ice and soda water.

'About time too!'

'They've warned me the muscles will need exercising before I've got full control again. Lots of physiotherapy and clutching of rubber balls. Now, tell me exactly what your father said.'

Olivia repeated what she'd told Charles. 'Father said the outlook is very good but he sounded really worried,' she finished.

'People are about cancer,' Liz said gently.

'Poor Mother. She's always been so strong.'

'The strongest people are often the most afraid when it comes to something they've got no control over.' Liz added a little sugar to each glass, gave it a good stir and put both drinks on a small tray. Then she opened the fridge again and took out a vacuum-packed plastic bag of olives marinated with olive oil and herbs. She laid a bag of flour on its side, balanced the bag of olives against it, snipped it open then upended the olives into a bowl and placed that on the tray as well.

'Could you possibly carry it for me?' she asked. 'It's too heavy for one hand. I usually put things in that,' she waved her hand at a round, shallow wicker-basket with a flat bottom, 'it's ideal for carrying things, but glasses filled with liquid are always a hazard.'

'Looks very practical,' Olivia said, glancing towards the basket as she picked up the tray. 'Is it new?'

'Patrick got it for me.'

'That was thoughtful.'

'Wasn't it!' Liz walked swiftly out into the garden; instead of being plaited, her dark hair was secured by an elasticated holder, giving her face a softer look. Olivia followed, placing the tray on the table under the mimosa tree at the bottom.

'How is your father coping?' Liz brushed fallen leaves off the cushions of a pair of garden chairs.

'Punch drunk, I think. He's so used to Mother running everything for him, he seems lost.' Olivia took a sip of the astringent, mouth-puckering, sense-tingling drink and leant against the back of the chair, trying to let the peace of the garden soothe her.

'Then this is going to be a difficult time for him as well.' Liz slipped on the big straw hat she kept underneath the table.

'That's why I know I've got to go home,' Olivia agreed, running a hand through her short hair, enjoying the still novel lightness and freedom.

242

'Is Charles very upset? Will he go too?'

'Heavens, no, he's got Phyllida here, not to mention his friends coming out on Saturday. No doubt he and Phyllida will manage,' Olivia said tartly.

'Ah, the foul Phyllida. How is she, being as dreadful as ever?'

Olivia felt tears pricking at the back of her eyes. 'Liz, you have no idea. I think she hates me.'

'She's just jealous, you mustn't allow her to wind you up.'

Olivia didn't reply for a moment then she burst out, 'If only Charles would understand what she's up to. But he just indulges her on everything. I'm the one who's always in the wrong.'

'He was all hers until you came along.'

'Oh, Liz, stop being so bloody sensible! Next thing you'll be telling me it's only a matter of time!'

Liz sighed. 'Sometimes even time doesn't help in that sort of situation.'

'Now you're being really cheerful! Look, I don't want to talk about Phyllida. Tell me about yourself. How's the work going?'

Liz smiled. 'I've got so many ideas, Olivia, I can hardly believe it! Sometimes I think this period of not being able to put paint to canvas was the best thing that could have happened to me.'

'Charles will be thrilled!' Olivia said, only slightly ironically.

'Really, I mean it. I feel as though my creative mind has been on holiday and some sort of clearing out has been taking place. Now it's refreshed, with new ideas, new ways of looking at things. It's incredibly exciting!'

Olivia looked at her more closely. Yes, it was true, Liz did look excited. More than that, there was a new repose in her face, a sort of contained happiness that hung like an aura around her. Surely all that couldn't be due to a reviving of her creative processes? 'What's happened?' she asked. 'There's something, I don't know, something different about you.'

'Yes?' Liz looked smug.

'You're glowing, like . . .' Olivia hunted for the right words and found them '. . . like someone who's fallen in love.' The words shocked her. 'Liz, you haven't!'

'Why should you be upset?'

'I . . . well,' Olivia floundered. 'I never thought you'd be the one . . .'

'The one to what?'

'Have an affair!'

Liz let out a peal of laughter, a soft, amused laughter that rang with happiness. 'I haven't fallen for another man, don't think that.'

'Just a minute, Liz, I'm not very bright at the moment. You're not telling me you're having an affair with a woman?'

Liz laughed and cradled her broken wrist in her lap. 'No, lesbianism may be all the rage but I've never felt I had to keep up with fashion.' Then she smiled her secretive smile again. 'Can you really not guess what's happened to me?'

Suddenly Olivia knew. Maybe it was the softness that seemed to

243

surround Liz, maybe the way she was holding her arm against herself.
'You're pregnant!'

Her eyes dancing with delight, Liz nodded. 'At last!'

'But, how did it happen?'

'The usual way.'

'Oh, don't be an idiot, you know what I mean.'

'And I can't answer you. The doctors never found any reason why I didn't become pregnant before so I suppose it was old Mother Nature. Perhaps I just wasn't ready to have a baby before this.' Her face grew serious, 'It's going to make an enormous difference to my life, to *our* lives.'

'Patrick must be thrilled!'

Liz's smile deepened to tenderness. 'Oh, he is. I got the confirmation from the doctor yesterday afternoon and I told him last night. Tonight he's taking me out to a dinner *à deux*. I was going to ring and suggest we all got together for a meal on Friday so we could break the news.' Liz looked at Olivia, her lips slightly parted, her eyes shining. 'It couldn't have come at a better time. He's been wonderful over this arm business, helped me in so many ways. Sometimes it's almost been like it was when we were first married. I feel like I'm giving him a present to say thank you.'

'When's it due?' Olivia asked.

'Middle of February.'

'But,' Olivia said, astonished, calculating on her fingers, 'that means you're . . .'

'Four and a half months,' Liz sounded amused. 'I know, but I've never been regular and I thought all the trauma of breaking my wrist had made it even worse than usual. It never occurred to me I could be pregnant until I realised my trousers were getting so tight.' She was wearing a loose-fitting, floaty dress, very different from her usual jeans or tailored slacks. 'Then I remembered how terribly sick I'd been when I first broke my wrist and everything sort of fell into place. So I went to the doctor.' She smiled. 'I did feel a bit of a fool but I'm so glad I took so few of the painkillers they gave me. I thought it was those that were making me feel so unwell.'

'I'm very, very pleased,' Olivia said warmly. 'And Charles will be too. I can tell him can't I?'

Liz nodded. 'Of course. I'm just sorry we won't be able to get together on Friday.' She glanced apologetically at Olivia. 'Do you think Charles would like to come anyway – and Phyllida if she's not doing anything else?'

'I'm sure he would. As for Phyllida, you'd better ask her yourself.' Olivia heard bitterness in her voice. She could see Phyllida and Charles together with the Ratcliffes, her stepdaughter delighted to have her father alone again. Then she felt guilty. Phyllida had been sympathetic about her mother in a way that seemed sincere. For all her surface sophistication, she was little more than a child. Olivia was the one who was mature, who should have been able to handle the situation more successfully. She hardly

244

realised she was using the past tense in thinking about her relationship with her stepdaughter.

Olivia put down her empty glass. 'Liz, I must go, there's such a lot I've got to do before I leave.'

Liz rose too and kissed her. 'I'll keep an eye on Charles for you. Don't worry about what's happening here, look after your mother, she's the one who'll need you most.'

Yes, thought Olivia as she walked slowly back up the hill to *La Chênais*. Charles didn't really need her. He had his house and his daughter.

She tried to fight a depression that had been slowly growing throughout the summer and now seemed to clamp down on her. Everything she'd thought she had seemed to be slipping through her fingers and she felt powerless to prevent it happening.

Once before in her life she had felt like this. Then nothing had been able to stop a remorseless slide towards disaster. It had taken years to recover and reach the point where she'd been able to accept Charles's love. Surely she couldn't now be in danger of losing everything for a second time?

Olivia stood with Charles by the check-in desk. Her case had been sent on the conveyor belt and no doubt she'd be reunited with it when she arrived in England. At the moment she didn't care very much whether it went off to Timbuctoo instead.

'You're sure your father's meeting you?' Charles asked.

'Yes, I spoke to him last night and told him my flight details and he promised he'd be there.'

'He won't have forgotten?'

'Charles, he's not that absent-minded.'

'And you'll ring me tonight?'

'As soon as I reach Mother and Father's, I promise.' Olivia looked at Charles. She took in the fair skin, now so tanned that the freckles hardly showed, the sandy hair that gleamed gold at the tips from the sun he'd been enjoying all through the summer, at his blunt mouth that now looked so tense. He'd taken off his sunglasses and she could see the white creases at the corners of his eyes where he'd screwed them up against the sun. She wanted to fling her arms around him and say she'd be back just as soon as she could.

'Give my love to Tilly when you see her.'

'I will.' Olivia thought that the fact that she'd be able to see her daughter was the only bright spot about returning to England.

'Dad!' Phyllida was back at her father's side brandishing a fashion magazine. 'I want to see if we can find a dress on the way home.'

'Just a minute, Phyllie!' It was the closest Olivia had ever heard him come to irritation with his daughter. 'We're saying goodbye to Olivia.'

Her eyes flickered then she turned to Olivia with an expression very like contrition on her face. 'I do hope you'll find she's all right when you get there, Olivia. And don't worry about Dad, I'll look after him for you.'

Olivia scanned her face and couldn't find a hint of the ironic smile that so often said her words couldn't be taken at face value. Something made her give Phyllida a sudden hug. 'Thanks, Phyllie, I know you'll do a good job.' The girl turned away and Charles drew Olivia to him and gave her a swift, hard kiss.

'Come back soon,' he said.

'I will, I promise.'

'Remember, I'll be waiting for your call.' He turned to his daughter. 'OK, Phyllie,' he said gruffly. 'We'll just watch Olivia go through then we'll have a look for your dress.' He put an arm around her shoulders.

Olivia gave them one last, brief look and went into the departure lounge. They were staying here and she was returning to England. She thought they looked content with each other as she left.

246

PART THREE

England

Chapter Twenty-Five

Olivia was shocked when she first saw her father at the airport. If it hadn't been for his height and extreme thinness, she mightn't have recognised him. He looked ten years older than when she'd seen him last, a scant three months before. Lines had deepened in his face, his shoulders were bent and his hair had turned from a brindle grey to white. He was scanning the passengers with desperate urgency as they came out through customs.

'Father,' Olivia called, 'I'm here!'

'Olivia!' He came towards her and took her hand, she felt his tremble. 'Thank heavens you've come.' Then he began fussing over her luggage, hiding eyes that had filled with tears. 'The car's three floors away, I hope we can manage all your stuff.'

'Of course we can, Father. You lead the way and I'll push the trolley. How's Mother?'

He paused irresolute, as though he couldn't remember where they should be going. Olivia gently steered her luggage trolley in the direction of the car park. 'This way, I think, Father.'

Again there was that helpless glance around him then Thomas followed her. Olivia increased her pace slightly, then had to slow down again as she realised he couldn't keep up. 'How's Mother?' she repeated.

Thomas tried to straighten his shoulders. 'Fine, just fine.' He spoke loudly, above the background clatter of the other people crowding the terminal.

Olivia understood that there wasn't much point in trying to conduct a conversation.

'Would you like me to drive?' she offered when at last they reached the dark blue Rover and, after an increasingly frantic search, Thomas had finally found the keys.

Relief lit his face. 'Would you?'

Olivia took the keys, released the doors, popped her case in the boot then slid into the driving seat and adjusted it forward.

Thomas leant his head back and closed his eyes with a sigh. But it wasn't the usual remote sigh of an academic wishing he was back with his books, it was the sigh of a man who felt that a burden he could hardly bear had been lifted from his shoulders.

Once safely on to the M25, Olivia tried again. 'Tell me about Mother.'

Thomas opened his eyes and turned slightly towards her. 'She'll be so pleased to see you,' he said gently.

'What exactly did the hospital say?'

Thomas appeared to take a grip on himself. 'The surgeon expressed himself very satisfied. He said he thought they'd got everything they could and the prognosis was extremely hopeful.'

'Well, that's good.' Olivia felt immensely relieved. From the guarded way Thomas had talked on the telephone, she had expected to be faced with the fact that her mother faced a very doubtful future. 'You must both be delighted. How's she feeling?'

Thomas's shoulders slumped again. 'Difficult to say. She's very depressed. The hospital sister says she has to be allowed to come to terms with her condition.'

'But you said the surgeon was very hopeful?' Olivia felt there was something she wasn't quite understanding here. She tried to concentrate on what her father was telling her. But it had started to rain, the traffic was heavy and she needed to give attention to her driving as well. At least on the motorway there was no chance of not keeping to the right side of the road. But how dismal everything looked after the bright sun of Nice. Around them the traffic became thicker and thicker until the car had to slow to a crawl. Olivia quelled her feelings of impatience at the delay. At least the slower speed gave her a chance to have a proper discussion of her mother's condition. 'Father, what aren't you telling me?'

'Nothing, really, darling. It's perfectly true, the hospital believes she has every chance of a very good recovery and years more life. It's just that your mother is finding things rather tough. Part of it is the shock, never having had an operation before, do you see?'

'Poor Father, you must have had quite a time trying to feed yourself and then looking after Mother,' she said as they turned off the traffic-bound M25 and headed down the A3.

'Well, you know, people are very kind. So many casseroles have arrived, not to mention flans and things, I don't think we need to cook for days.' Now that they were off the subject of Daphne, Thomas seemed to cheer up. 'And Betty says she will come four mornings a week, including Saturday, instead of her usual two. I really haven't had much to do.' Everything sounded so under control, just for a minute Olivia wondered why it had been necessary for her to dash back. But she knew these were mere details. The real trouble must lie with Daphne herself.

'I suppose you haven't told Tilly, either?'

Thomas shook his head. 'She came down to see us just before Daphne went in, said she thought her grandmother looked very tired. Sweet girl, she seems to be working very hard in that restaurant.'

Olivia waited for him to suggest Tilly should be doing something else. Instead he added, 'Not that it's doing her any harm. She looked very well, she's lost a bit more weight. Almost slender these days. And she does seem to be enjoying her work.'

Which reinforced Olivia's opinion. Tilly's telephone conversations had been ebullient, full of what she was learning even as a lowly commis-chef, preparing and cooking vegetable orders. And she'd found a house near the restaurant that needed an extra person to help with the rent. She was sharing with two girls and two young men. Because of her hours, she didn't see much of them but said they seemed a nice enough bunch.

'Now, tell me about Charles and life in that lovely house of yours,' Thomas urged her.

Olivia tried to give him an expurgated account of the summer. 'And Liz is pregnant,' she added as they drew near the house. 'Isn't that wonderful?'

Thomas agreed but as they drew closer to home, he seemed to grow more and more tense. Olivia felt her nervousness increase. What exactly was her mother's condition? If she'd been shocked by how her father looked, how was she going to feel when she saw Daphne?

When they arrived, Olivia dropped her suitcase on the hall floor and went straight up to her mother's room.

It took a moment to take in just how changed Daphne was. It wasn't the fact that her face had got shockingly thin. It was the blank look in her eyes as she stared out of the window. Heavy rain was falling and battering a few pink roses that nodded at the window. Beyond them could be seen the fragile, yellowing leaves of a weeping willow.

'Hello, Mother.' Olivia bent and gently kissed Daphne. 'I brought you some nice smelly stuff.' She laid a matching talcum powder and toilet water she'd bought in the duty free on the bed.

Daphne made no response.

Olivia looked around the room. There was an arrangement of florist's flowers perfuming the air, a bowl of grapes and a jug of what looked like barley water sat on her bedside table together with a selection of magazines. Lying on the bedcover was a copy of the latest bestseller. It seemed she had everything needed to be comfortable.

Olivia sat on the edge of the bed and took her mother's hand; she felt bereft as she took in the changes in her appearance. This wasn't the woman who had raised her, bullied her, loved her, strengthened her.

Daphne's facial flesh seemed to have melted away beneath a skin that was, curiously, both taut and flabby at the same time. Sunken eyes stared out of their sockets as though trying to hide themselves. The mouth drooped like a disappointed child's. Her hair showed grey roots and needed cutting; it wisped unattractively around her ears and the nape of her neck. The woman of business, in control of her life, had vanished.

'Olivia.' Daphne's gaze slid over her daughter's face without expression, then returned to staring blankly out of the window. Olivia involuntarily tightened her grip on her mother's hand.

Daphne gave a small whimper and drew it away.

'I'm sorry, Mother, I didn't mean to hurt you. It's just that I'm so pleased to see you, especially looking so well.' The lie slipped out involuntarily.

The eyes swivelled back to Olivia's face with something of their old snap. 'Don't try and molly-coddle me, Olivia. At least treat me as someone who has not yet slipped into total senility.'

Olivia drew a deep breath of relief. This was undoubtedly her mother.

'You should have told me you were going into hospital, I'd have come back at once.'

'No need for that.' Daphne, with infinite care, pulled herself up slightly in the bed.

Olivia moved to help her, only to have her hand knocked away. 'I'm not a total invalid,' Daphne snapped at her.

'Of course you're not.'

'Nor yet a total idiot. I might have known your father would have told you to approach me with caution.'

Olivia brought over a chair, sat down beside the bed and told herself that patients are always at their worst when getting better. 'The only thing Father has said is that the surgeon was very pleased with the result of your operation,' she said gently. 'But I'm sure it's going to take time for you to feel like your old self.'

To her horror, Daphne started to cry. Her mother made no attempt to wipe away her tears, just lay on her pillow and allowed them to spill out.

'I'm sure you'll soon feel much stronger and can start doing all the things you did before the operation.'

Daphne's mouth tightened mutinously and her chin trembled. With her right hand she pounded at the bedclothes. 'Don't talk to me like that. You know nothing about it.'

Behind Olivia the door opened and Thomas brought in a tray. 'Look, darling, here's some lovely chicken which Betty prepared for you. I've reheated it in the microwave just as she told me.'

Olivia was amazed. Never before had she seen her father tending to Daphne, it had always been the other way about. And if anybody had asked her, she'd have said it would have been beyond him to be so patient.

Daphne picked up the fork and prodded bad-temperedly at the chicken in its white sauce with plain boiled potatoes. 'You'd better go and have your meal,' she said to Olivia. 'I expect there's something for you.'

'A very nice beef casserole Mary brought over yesterday,' Thomas said soothingly. 'Really, we are very lucky in our friends.' He looked at Olivia. 'Shall we go down and have it?'

Olivia rose. 'I'll come back and see you again later,' she told Daphne. She hovered for a moment, feeling she'd like to kiss her mother, do something to show her concern. The implacable expression on Daphne's face stopped her.

'Is she like this all the time?' she asked Thomas once they were

252

downstairs. There were two places laid at the small kitchen table.

He placed a little dish of salad on the table and opened the bottom oven of the Aga. 'She's only been home a couple of days,' he said defensively, taking out a casserole dish. 'Sister warned me she'd take a little time to adjust.'

'Adjust to what?'

He put the casserole on the table and stood twisting the oven cloth in his hands. 'We're all so frightened of cancer,' he said at last. 'The big "C", isn't that what John Wayne called it?'

Olivia looked in astonishment at her father. When had he ever seen John Wayne? Had he sneaked off to watch Westerns instead of holding tutorials in college? She almost laughed at the improbability of it and felt her depression lift slightly. 'Can we hold supper for a few minutes, Father? I promised to give Charles a call.'

'Of course,' he said promptly and put the casserole back in the oven. 'By the way, I like your hair short.'

Olivia wasn't surprised it had taken so long for her father to notice her new hairstyle but the fact that her mother hadn't taken in her changed appearance was almost more worrying than anything else.

Charles sounded relieved to hear from her and full of concern. 'Really rotten,' he kept saying in a way that could refer to either Daphne or Olivia. But Olivia eventually put down the phone feeling that Charles and their life in the South of France were so distant that they could be on the other side of the world. She hadn't been able to bring herself to ask after Phyllida and Charles hadn't mentioned his daughter. Somehow, though, her presence in the background had been almost tangible.

Olivia took breakfast up to her mother in the morning and found a changed woman.

As she took in the tray, Daphne looked up at her with bright eyes. 'How nice to see you, darling. So good of you to come for a few days. And you've had your hair cut! What an improvement!'

Olivia put the tray on the table and swivelled it across Daphne's legs.

'Oh, look, a boiled egg, how lovely. I shall enjoy that. I hope you slept well?'

Thomas had shown Olivia to the small room she'd occupied as a child. 'I'm sleeping in the guest room at the moment, I'm afraid. I hope you'll be comfortable in here.'

The wallpaper was exactly the same and the bookshelves held her pony books and her set of Georgette Heyer. Olivia had felt the years rush backwards.

'I slept beautifully,' she said to her mother.

'And the newspaper! I am being spoilt.' Daphne picked up the *Independent* and started to read the lead story.

Olivia gathered that the previous evening's behaviour was to be ignored.

'Will you be getting up?' she asked tentatively.

Daphne glanced up from the paper. 'Of course,' she said with just a touch of sharpness.

Downstairs Olivia relayed this news to Thomas.

He sighed with relief. 'That's good, that's very good,' he said.

Olivia rang Tilly, catching her before she went off to the restaurant. Her daughter sounded in great form but was shocked to hear about her grandmother. 'She looked awful the last time I saw her but she swore she was just tired. How is she?' she asked anxiously.

'Getting on all right, I think,' Olivia said cautiously.

'Do you want me to come down? I've got some things arranged for the next couple of Sundays but I can always cancel them.'

'No, it's not necessary. I'll try to come up and see you,' Olivia said; just talking to Tilly made her feel more cheerful.

Daphne appeared downstairs at eleven o'clock, dressed in one of the loose frocks she'd adopted during the summer. It was another overcast and chilly day. 'Will you be warm enough, Mother?' asked Olivia anxiously.

'Of course, don't fuss,' Daphne said waspishly.

'Come and sit down, dear.' Thomas hovered around her, his tall, thin figure contorting itself as he tried to offer a hand and plump up a cushion at the same time.

'Don't fuss, I said,' Daphne repeated, her mouth beginning to adopt its mutinous mode. She looked at the chair her husband had prepared for her. 'I think I shall take a stroll round the garden, see what's been happening since I went into hospital.'

'Let me come with you, give you an arm to lean on,' Thomas offered, springing round to her side from his hovering position by the chair.

'I shall be quite all right on my own, thank you,' she said frostily. 'I'm sure you have work to do, Thomas.' She walked slowly but surely through the garden door and down the path.

Thomas and Olivia watched her as she started to inspect the flower beds: the tall stands of Michaelmas daisies, the bright, flat heads of sedums and the red-hipped sprawl of shrub roses.

'I'll just go and give her room a tidy,' said Olivia after a moment. 'I shouldn't think she'll want to be out there very long. Perhaps you could offer her a cup of coffee if she looks like getting cold?'

She went upstairs, stripped the clothes back from the bed and opened the window, then was held by the view. The trees were just starting to turn and a patchwork of green and gold alternated with the brown of newly tilled fields, sweeping up to the roll of the Downs. It was almost exactly a year since she and Charles had spent that incredibly happy day walking up there. It seemed much longer. Olivia felt she'd lost touch with the person she'd been then. Then she'd seemed to be entering on a new, more confident phase of life, she thought she'd learnt enough to accept happiness and give joyously.

Now everything seemed hopelessly complicated.

Olivia sighed and went into the next-door bathroom.

'What are you doing?' Daphne's voice said harshly from behind her.

'Just giving things a little clean,' Olivia replied gently. 'I thought you'd be downstairs for a while. Isn't Father getting you some coffee?'

'Don't want any,' Daphne said irritably. 'And there's no need for this, Betty can do it tomorrow. You know I don't like my things messed about with.'

'I'll just make your bed.' Olivia moved out of the bathroom suddenly aware that her mother probably needed to be alone.

The door was closed firmly behind her and she heard a tap being turned on. Olivia pulled and tugged the bedclothes into position as quickly as she could, wishing her mother could abandon blankets for a duvet, then went down to the kitchen.

Daphne spent a long time upstairs. She came down in time for lunch. Her meal was more of Betty's chicken in white sauce while Thomas and Olivia ate a bacon and cheese flan produced by another neighbour. Followed by fruit.

Daphne's hand hovered above a peach then slowly withdrew. She said nothing but her mouth drooped in the way it had the previous evening.

'Won't it do you good, Mother?' Olivia suggested. 'You know how you love peaches.'

'Perhaps later,' Daphne said abruptly and rose. 'I'm going to have a rest now. I feel quite tired after all my activity this morning.'

'Shall I bring you up a cup of coffee, my dear?' offered Thomas, opening the door for her.

'When I want coffee, I'll ask for it.' Daphne's tone rose irritably.

'Just give your bell a ring if you need anything,' he said gently.

Daphne almost pushed her way past him. She hauled her way up the stairs, pulling at the banister rail as he watched her anxiously.

Olivia observed her parents with wonder. Where had her father found these reserves of patience and how long would they last?

She cleared up lunch then read the paper while Thomas worked on the final draft of his book. Unusually, he didn't retire to his study but brought his manuscript into the living room and they sat companionably together.

At half-past three Olivia slipped upstairs and quietly opened her mother's door. Daphne was asleep, breathing quietly and evenly, her mouth open, one arm flung across the side of the bed where Thomas usually slept.

Olivia closed the door again and went back downstairs.

She made tea at half-past four and was preparing a tray to take a cup and a biscuit up to her mother, when Daphne came down.

Her mood was depressed, the flash of her old self she'd shown in the morning had disappeared again. She sat silently in her chair, sipping tea and watching the fire which Thomas had lit.

The doorbell rang. It was one of Daphne's old friends. 'Gave her a couple of days to settle after the hospital then thought I'd just pop in and say hello,' Elizabeth Spratt said conspiratorially to Olivia. 'How is she?'

'Getting on, I think is the phrase,' Olivia said holding open the door. 'Come in, we're just having a cup of tea. I'm sure Mother will be delighted to see you.'

That proved over-optimistic but Daphne at least made an effort to say hello.

Elizabeth produced a small packet of smoked salmon. 'I thought you'd like that better than chocolates,' she said, handing it over.

Daphne looked at it for a long moment then put it on one side and thanked her friend in a gracious voice that Olivia knew from long experience meant the gift was the last thing she wanted.

Elizabeth noticed nothing, though. She directed a laughing look at Thomas and said she hoped there would be enough for him.

'Oh, Thomas is doing very well,' Daphne said dryly.

'And so are you, my dear,' he added quickly. 'The surgeon's very pleased with her but she does get tired,' he said to Elizabeth. She took the hint, chatted brightly for ten minutes then left.

'I'll pop back in a few days,' she whispered to Olivia as she showed her out. 'We'll all play our part. Lots of little visits is the thing, isn't it?'

Olivia returned to the living room to find Daphne looking exhausted and sunk into a deep depression. Nothing Thomas or Olivia said seemed to reach her.

Olivia picked up the packet of smoked salmon. 'I'll put this in the fridge. I expect you'd like a little for supper. Shall I bring it up to you in bed?'

'Don't bring it near me,' Daphne snapped. 'What an idiot the woman is! I'll have a little scrambled egg for supper.'

Olivia took the delicacy to the fridge without comment. She came back and said firmly that she was going to help Daphne upstairs. 'You've done too much; you'll have to learn to pace yourself,' she scolded gently and placed a hand behind her mother's back to ease her up the stairs.

Daphne concentrated on negotiating each step.

'Shall I help you undress?' Olivia offered, taking hold of the cardigan to ease it from her mother's shoulders.

Daphne clutched the heavy wool fronts firmly to her chest. 'No need for that!'

At least she wasn't completely sunk in depression! 'Sure you can manage all right?'

Olivia almost welcomed the tart response she got.

As she said to her father when she went back downstairs, 'As long as she can still get annoyed, I think she's on the mend.'

'I'll take her up a whisky before supper,' Thomas said. 'Perhaps she'll feel like having a chat.'

Olivia stared at her father. When had he ever wanted to chat before?

Usually it had been a case of Daphne laying down the law on some subject and Thomas giving half an ear, if that. Rarely had he been in the habit of instigating a conversation.

'How was it when you and Mother were first married?' she asked curiously.

'What on earth do you mean, my dear?' It was Thomas's turn to be startled.

'Did you have lots of silly, lovey-dovey conversations, or did you have long, intellectual discussions, or were you just happy together?' That was what she and Charles had been, at the beginning anyway. Yes, they'd told each various things but Olivia was conscious now of how much they had left unsaid. The vast areas of both their first marriages had been untouched. Had it been sensible, she wondered now, to have said so little? Should she have brought herself to open the doors she'd so firmly closed on her time in California?

Thomas lay back in his chair and regarded his daughter with amusement. 'What strange things you ask. I remember as a child you'd come out with the most curious questions. Wondering whether animals minded being eaten or if it was a good thing to have blonde hair.'

Yes, Olivia remembered too. Remembered how such questions never produced the sort of answers she wanted. Either her father gave her a learned treatise on the subject of vegetarianism or he retreated into a technique that analysed her form of questioning and reduced it to a matter of syntax.

'I thought at the time it was a sign of maturity when you gave up asking them but I wonder now whether it wasn't my fault. I wasn't very encouraging, was I?'

'They must have seemed very silly to you.'

'I don't think I've given enough importance to communication in my life,' Thomas said sadly. He got up and went over to the drinks table. 'I'm going to have a whisky, how about you?'

Olivia accepted. She felt she could do with a strong drink and it was after six o'clock.

'With soda or water?'

'Water, please.'

Thomas brought two generously filled glasses over and gave her one. 'You asked about your mother and me in our early days,' he said, settling himself again in the chair. 'Do you know, I regret to say that I think I was as bad at communicating with her as I was with you. There was so much filling my mind, you see,' he said apologetically. 'My work overflowed into every area of my life, I couldn't find room for little conversations about this and that.' He regarded his drink ruefully. 'It was a great mistake.'

'What made you get married?' Olivia had no trouble understanding Thomas's difficulty communicating with wife and daughter, what she found hard to understand was how he'd acquired them in the first place.

Thomas leant back and ran a hand through his thinning, silvered hair. All at once he looked younger, less careworn. 'Your mother was so sparkling, so attractive,' he said simply. 'I couldn't believe she could be interested in me. It was like being bowled over by, by – well, by the whole of the *Oxford Dictionary*.' He fell silent, back in those days. 'We met at some sort of academic thrash on the banks of the Cherwell. I'd just got my doctorate and had had my first book accepted by the University Press. I was on top of the world that day and there Daphne was. Girls hadn't formed a great part of my life up until then, I'd always been working too hard.'

'You mean you hadn't taken anyone out?' asked Olivia, amazed at her father opening up in this way to her. But then there hadn't been much opportunity before. She'd left for California with Peter when she was twenty; at that age you never asked parents about their love life. And after she'd come back to England, she'd been far too guarded to start this sort of conversation.

Thomas smiled. 'Not quite that! But my fumbling attempts at pleasing girls up until that time had been doomed to failure. I didn't know how to talk to them, you see. I had a few brief encounters with girls who weren't interested in conversation but they hardly held the promise of lifelong happiness, however satisfactory they might have been in the short term.' He grinned reminiscently and Olivia realised with deep shock that her father was a sensual man.

But why not? The fact that Olivia had never noticed any outward sign of physical attraction between her parents didn't mean it didn't exist. Just that they believed such moments were private, not for display even to their daughter.

Had that sense of privacy been donated to her along with her genes?

'But Mother was different?'

'She was . . .' He hesitated, seeking exactly the right word or words. 'She was a revelation,' he said with awe. 'A marvellously attractive girl who seemed actually interested in my work. Intelligent and sympathetic, too. It was almost too much for me. I was trying to pluck up courage to ask for her telephone number when she suggested I join an expedition that had been organised for the next day; she and some friends were to visit Blenheim. Somehow after that one thing led to another and within three months we were engaged.'

Olivia recognised the relentlessly organising hand of Daphne. Left to himself, Thomas would undoubtedly have taken years to get to that point.

'I'm so pleased you told me this, Father.' She went and gave him a kiss.

He held her briefly. 'I'm very worried about Daphne,' he said as he released her. 'I've never known her like this. She's always been so strong, so in control.'

'I'm sure it's just a matter of time. A major operation is an enormous shock to the system. We can't expect her to bounce back into her old self immediately.'

'I suppose not,' he muttered, flipping the pages of his manuscript as though his frustration needed some outlet. 'I think I'll go and see if she needs anything.'

He was lost without Daphne to guide his every footstep, Olivia thought. Then told herself that was unfair. Actually he seemed more organised than she had ever seen him before. Concern for Daphne had taken him out of his rarefied world and he was making a valiant attempt to come to terms with being the sort of support for her she had always been for him.

But Olivia, too, was worried about her mother.

Betty Foster came the next morning. Small and spry with amazingly ginger hair that never had a line of grey along its roots, Betty had been helping Daphne ever since the Fergusons had first bought the Sussex cottage as a week-end retreat. In those days she had come in one day a week to keep an eye on the place, together with the occasional Saturday morning. After Daphne and Thomas had moved down permanently, Betty had agreed to come two mornings a week. She was incredibly fast at whisking her duster and vacuum cleaner around, never mind scrubbing floors or cleaning dustbins; her only faults as far as Daphne was concerned were her insistence on calling her employer by her christian name and her constant stream of chatter.

'I suppose I'm old fashioned but I just can't get used to being "Daphne" to the home help,' she said. 'But as for her chatter, as it never seems to get in the way of her work, I let it all flow over me.'

Olivia supposed Betty must be getting on now but whether it was getting on for sixty or seventy she had no idea. The energy seemed as inexhaustible as ever. Betty thought nothing of the three miles she had to ride on her bicycle to the cottage.

'Sight for sore eyes you are, Olivia,' she said as she arrived. 'You'll do Daphne no end of good. Proper down in the dumps she is. Well, poor thing, no wonder. I'd be too in her shoes, so to speak. So how is she this morning?' she asked as she took off her jacket and put on a flowered sleeveless overall. 'Sleeping better, is she?'

'I think so,' Olivia said cautiously. 'She seemed quite bright when I took in her tray.'

'Good, that's good,' Betty announced vigorously, going to the cupboard where the cleaning aids were kept. 'Getting up, is she?'

'She hopes to.' Olivia cleared away her and Thomas's breakfast things from the kitchen table.

'Right! Well, I'll get on with the main room, then. When she's down, I'll do her room and bathroom. OK?'

'Betty, you carry on exactly how you think best.'

'Right! Awful weather, isn't it? Splashes all down my stockings this morning!' Betty showed a surprisingly well-shaped leg whose thick stocking was indeed spattered with mud. 'Shocking them drivers are. Never think about anything but themselves. 'Alf a mind to report some of them. But,

259

then, who'd I tell? The police don't want to know. Mind you, terrible time they have these days. All those youngsters out of jobs, no wonder they're up to no good. Thomas in his study, is he?'

'I think he's working in the living room but I'm sure he'll be happy for you to carry on. Oh, Betty,' she added as the woman hefted up the vacuum cleaner under one arm and took the box of cleaning items by its handle with her other hand, 'I tidied up my mother's bathroom yesterday and there was a rather curious odour. I couldn't find out what was causing it.'

Betty stood poised in the doorway, hung about with the cleaning items, and her small features under the tight ginger curls assumed a slightly shifty expression as her round blue eyes flicked rapidly between Olivia and her path to the living room in a rare moment of indecision. 'You leave that to me, I'll sort it out,' she said finally, moving off at top speed.

Olivia collected Daphne's breakfast tray and enquired if there was anything she could get her mother.

She received no answer. Daphne's head was turned towards the window, where rain was once again streaming down, and the blank expression was back on her face. The composure with which she'd woken up seemed to have disappeared.

'Would you like me to brush your hair for you?' offered Olivia gently.

There was no answer and the eyes never moved from the window.

Olivia picked up her mother's hairbrush and lightly dressed Daphne's hair. 'As soon as you are a little stronger, we'll make an appointment for a cut and shampoo,' she said as she worked. 'A visit to the hairdresser always makes one feel so much better, doesn't it?'

'I'll thank you not to address me as though I was some patient in a geriatric hospital,' Daphne said wearily, her gaze still fixed on the rainy day outside. 'You can't imagine how much worse it makes me feel.' There was a hopelessness in her voice that removed any sting from her words. Olivia wished the old, tart note back. She returned the brush to the dressing table, took the breakfast tray outside then came back to empty the linen basket that stood by the bathroom door.

'Put those back!' commanded her mother.

'But I'm going to do the washing,' said a startled Olivia.

'Betty will do that.' Daphne's sunken eyes now blazed, all her old authority in place.

Olivia dropped the clothes back into the basket. 'I'll go and see about lunch, then,' she said quietly.

Someone rang the bell as she came down the stairs.

Olivia put the breakfast tray in the kitchen then came and opened the door.

It was the District Nurse, a slender woman dressed in a dark blue uniform, with brown hair swept back into a bun and lively dark eyes. Her only makeup was a soft pink lipstick and Olivia guessed she must be in her mid-thirties.

260

'Do come in.' Olivia held the door wide open. 'I'm Mrs Ferguson's daughter, Olivia. I've come to help my mother for a few days.'

'That's splendid! I'm Terry Barker,' the nurse said, removing her coat.

Olivia hung it up on the line of hooks behind the front door. 'Can I get you a coffee?' she offered.

'After I've seen my patient I'd love one. Up here, is she?' The nurse headed for the stairs carrying a small leather hold-all bag. 'How's she doing?'

Olivia hurried behind her but had little opportunity to say much more than that her mother didn't appear very strong and seemed rather depressed.

'Normal,' said the nurse briskly as they approached the bedroom door.

Olivia opened it and announced Daphne's visitor in the bright voice she had now adopted when speaking to her mother.

Daphne's face took on a militant look that cheered Olivia. 'How kind of nurse,' she said with the air of a general welcoming some minor officer from an opposing side. 'Perhaps you'll be kind enough to organise coffee?' she said to Olivia.

Interpreting this to mean her mother wanted to be private with the nurse, Olivia went back downstairs and put the kettle on.

Ten minutes later the nurse reappeared in the kitchen. 'Mrs Ferguson seems to be coping well,' she said briskly.

'I've made coffee. Can you just wait a moment while I give a cup to our help and ask my father to take this up to my mother? Help yourself to coffee and a biscuit, I really do need a chat with you.' Olivia whisked out of the kitchen and was back again a few minutes later.

The nurse had sat at the kitchen table and was sipping her cup of coffee.

Olivia sat opposite. 'I'm really worried about my mother's depression,' she said. 'At the moment she seems OK, just as she did yesterday morning. But suddenly she seems to lose all interest and gets very depressed.'

Terry Barker put down her cup. 'Colostomy patients quite often have a difficult time when they first come out of hospital,' she said gently.

Olivia stared at her. 'Colostomy?'

The nurse made a small tutting noise. 'You didn't know?'

Olivia shook her head, so many things were falling into place.

'Nothing to get worried about.' Terry Barker was brisk. 'The modern bags are very discreet. No odours and the procedure is quite simple.'

She carefully outlined what Daphne's operation had entailed and how she was going to have to cope in the future.

It seemed that the facts were tedious but needn't interfere much with a normal life.

'It's most unlikely other people will be aware of your mother's condition,' Terry said reassuringly. 'The important thing is that she maintains a positive attitude.'

'Easy to say,' Olivia commented. Daphne's present attitude was anything but positive.

A little later she closed the door behind the nurse and walked rapidly

261

into the living room. 'Father, why didn't you tell me about Mother's colostomy.'

He glanced towards Betty, clearing out the grate from last night's fire.

'It shouldn't be a secret,' Olivia said gently.

Betty banged the brush against the edge of the hearth and her ginger curls bobbed as she glanced up, her small features belligerent. 'Don't mind me, Daphne told me as soon as she came 'ome.'

'My wife told you about her condition?' Thomas was amazed.

'Poor thing had to tell someone, didn't she?' Betty ran a damp cloth vigorously over the hearth. 'Wouldn't want her smart friends to know, would she?'

And obviously didn't want her daughter to know either!

'But why didn't you tell me, Father?' Olivia repeated.

Thomas cleared his throat a little nervously. 'It wasn't my decision, your mother made me promise not to.'

'But why?' Olivia burst out, hurt and almost offended.

'I, well, I think she's ashamed.' Thomas, eyes down, shuffled the pages of his manuscript.

And he didn't feel at all comfortable with the fact, either, Olivia realised. Her compassion for her mother increased.

'Well, it's a fact of life and we all just have to come to terms with it, Mother included,' she announced baldly. 'I'm going up to have a word with her.'

'Do you think that's wise?' asked Thomas, alarmed.

'I think it's essential,' Olivia declared. For once in her life she had no doubts about going against someone's wishes.

Chapter Twenty-Six

Tilly trundled her trolley round the fruit and vegetable section of her local supermarket, expertly assessed the freshness and weight of the red peppers, chose one, followed it with a packet of mange tout, added a bunch of spring onions and some oyster mushrooms, picked out a ripe mango and a bunch of fat white grapes and moved on to the meat section.

It was Sunday and Olivia was coming to lunch. Tilly hadn't seen her mother since she'd arrived in England three weeks earlier. There'd been no time to go down to Sussex and Olivia had been unable to get up to London.

Not that Tilly's working hours made seeing her easy. She was only off for a few hours in the afternoon and on Sundays. The previous Sunday she'd been invited to the Wilde home for lunch and the one before that Jemima had wanted them both to visit a new restaurant. Olivia had refused to let her cancel the arrangements. 'Why don't you join us?' Tilly had suggested.

'No,' her mother said quickly. 'I think I'm needed here. We'll get together soon enough.'

'How is Grandma?' Tilly had asked, not quite able to grasp that strong, independent Daphne hadn't been able to bounce back after her operation.

'She's getting her strength back slowly but it's her mental state I'm worried about.' Olivia had sounded really concerned. 'I've tried to have a talk with her but it was hopeless. She told me I didn't understand and then clammed up.'

'Are you sure you wouldn't like me to come down? I could help cheer her up,' offered Tilly.

'Maybe in a little while, darling. How are things going with you?'

'Fine, Mum, fine,' Tilly said hastily. 'But what's happening to Charles? When are you going back to France?'

'Not until Grandma's much, much better. I've told Charles, he understands.' Olivia sounded unusually decisive but, far from reassuring Tilly, she left her with the distinct impression she didn't want to discuss her relationship with her husband. Which worried Tilly even more.

Casting her eagle eye over breasts of chicken, Tilly wondered, as she had each time after she'd spoken to her mother recently, just what was going on between Olivia and Charles.

'I say, do you mind if I make a reach for those thighs over there?' asked a well-bred and oddly familiar voice.

Tilly drew her trolley aside with an apology, then did a double take. 'Mark!'

He turned round and stared at her. 'Tilly!' he said at last. He looked her up and down, like a judge at a dog show, she thought, amused rather than resentful. 'Good heavens! What on earth are you doing here?'

'Much the same as you, I imagine,' she said, looking pointedly at the contents of his trolley, which appeared to consist of much the same items as her own, except that instead of the fruit, he had a frozen cheesecake and a carton of cream. 'Lunch?'

'I've got someone coming,' he said, a trifle awkwardly.

'So have I,' said Tilly composedly, thinking how tired he looked. If anything it increased his attractiveness; the shadows under his eyes emphasised their deep blue and threw the aquiline strength of his nose into relief. The heavy dark hair needed cutting but he was wearing a very smart navy sweatshirt over a blue and white striped poplin shirt and dark green cords. He seemed even taller than she remembered. 'I'm doing a chicken stir fry followed by a hot fruit salad with sweet white wine. Haven't reached the alcohol section yet. What about you?'

He looked slightly startled, 'Chicken thighs in mushrooms and cream with mixed vegetables, and cheesecake for pudding.'

'So you've got stuck into the cooking?'

'Why not?' he asked, a trifle defensively.

'I thought you said the only males who should approach the kitchen stove were professional chefs?'

The navy blue eyes narrowed. 'Did I really? What a memory you've got!'

'It's amazing the useless bits of information that stick,' she said sweetly.

His expression sharpened into interest. 'You've changed!'

'Well, it's been over a year, hasn't it? Time for a lot of growing up.' Tilly put the first packet of chicken breasts she could find into her trolley. 'Nice to see you Mark, perhaps we'll run into each other here again one of these days. Must get on now.' She gave him as sparkling a smile as she could produce and started to wheel her trolley on to the next section.

He was beside her in an instant. 'I say, you can't just walk away like that. Not when I've only just found you again.'

Tilly wondered how he could manage to sound as though she'd been the one to disappear and said nothing.

'I've nearly finished here.' He glanced at his wrist watch, a heavy gold number. 'And Caroline, my guest, isn't arriving for at least an hour. What say we have a drink? I know a good little pub not at all far from here.'

'You may not want to do any preparation beforehand but that's not my method,' Tilly said tartly, trying to control the faint trembling of her knees.

'Oh, come on, a quick one, for old time's sake,' Mark wheedled, smiling at her with all the charm she remembered so well. 'I'll drive you to wherever it is you live afterwards, make sure you're not late.'

It was the offer of the lift that did it. 'All right,' Tilly agreed, 'I've just got one or two more things to get. Meet you at the end of the checkout section.'

'Shan't be more than a few minutes,' he promised her.

He was leaning against the wall, two plastic bags on the floor beside him, when she finally came through her checkout, five bags full with not only her luncheon ingredients, including wine, but also toilet rolls, cleaning materials, foil, cling film and other staples that needed backing up. 'How kind this is,' she beamed up at him without the slightest hint of apology. 'Having a lift makes all the difference.'

'I can see it does,' he said sardonically and led the way to his car.

Trust Mark to have a Porsche, Tilly thought derisively as he opened the boot and put both lots of purchases inside.

The pub he took them to was relatively empty. At eleven-thirty in the morning the lunchtime drinkers had yet to appear and the polished mahogany fittings, dark red carpet and sporting prints gleamed in a low-key but inviting way.

'What'll you have?' Marked offered after selecting a corner table.

'Oh, I think a white wine spritzer,' Tilly said with aplomb.

'Right!'

He went over to the bar and placed his order, then leant against it, half-turning towards her and giving her a smile that said he was enjoying the view she offered.

Tilly gave him a small, dulcet smile in return and crossed her ankles. Over the last year she had met a number of young men, both in France and England, but she had to admit that Mark was more attractive and sophisticated than any of them. She was deeply grateful that her long hair was freshly washed and that she'd put on a pair of designer jeans and an attractively knitted, loose-fitting sweater (both bought with some of her Casino winnings). She looked, she knew, very different from the gauche schoolgirl he'd seduced last summer.

'Have you completed your finals?' she asked after he'd returned with their drinks.

He nodded, taking a deep draught from his pint of bitter. 'I've now joined a city firm of solicitors for two years articles.'

'And after that you'll no doubt command a high salary?'

He gave a small, satisfied smile. 'If I don't, something will have gone badly wrong. I'm certainly working hard enough.' He replaced the smile with a look of earnest interest. 'Now, tell me what's been happening in your life, Tilly. I've thought about you so often since we last met.' Just as though he hadn't dropped me like an old sock, she thought as she told him about her work at the restaurant. 'I'm hoping to go to catering college shortly but, because I applied late, I've got to wait and see if they've got a place.'

'You always were a splendid cook,' he said, looking pleased with himself. 'I remember every one of those meals you prepared for me.'

Tilly just smiled at him and waited.

'And what have you been doing with yourself since we last met? School?'

'No, I left last summer.' He couldn't even remember she'd been working for her A levels! 'Then I worked in another, much smaller restaurant for six months. After that I joined my mother and stepfather in the South of France. They live just outside Nice now, you know.' She enjoyed his expression of surprise.

'Really? That sounds very nice.'

'Oh, it is. They've restored a lovely old house that has an amazing view of the Mediterranean and wonderful grounds. You know, gardens, swimming pool, an olive grove and . . . things,' Tilly ended vaguely, trying to give the impression of size. Then wondered if she hadn't overdone it as Mark looked at her closely.

'You know, you really are very different,' he said slowly.

'I am?' Tilly began to enjoy herself. 'How?'

He looked at her for a moment, a slight frown between his dark eyebrows. 'I suppose you've grown up. Become a woman. You're even more attractive than you were before.' His gaze travelled over her face and figure and Tilly felt herself grow hot as she remembered their passion the previous summer. 'You've lost weight,' he said, his voice slower and darker in texture. 'And it suits you. I like a girl with curves and yours are now quite delicious.' He dropped his voice and moved closer to her. 'Sweet Tilly, you were lovely before but now you're beautiful.' He put a hand on hers, picked up his glass of bitter and raised it in a toast. 'I'm so glad we've found each other again.'

Tilly took a look at her watch. 'I'm sorry, Mark, but I think we shall have to go in a minute, I really do have things to do before my little luncheon party.' She drank deeply of her spritzer and allowed her gaze to move lightly over his face.

'Perhaps I shall be invited to one of your luncheon parties one of these days?' he suggested. 'Before that, though, we must get together. How about one night next week?'

'Sorry,' she said sweetly. 'My social life is rather restricted at the moment, I work at the restaurant in the evenings, you see.'

'Every evening?' he asked, startled.

She nodded. 'Afraid so. But if I get into college, things could be a little different.' She finished her drink, picked up her shoulder bag and rose.

'I'll keep my fingers crossed that you get your place,' Mark said with his easy charm. 'OK, Cinderella, your coach awaits.'

She told him her address and he drove her straight to one of the smarter parts of Clapham, drawing up outside a large semi-detached house. 'This yours?' he asked, his voice respectful.

'I share it with four others.' She managed the difficult exit out of the low-slung Porsche with a certain amount of grace. 'Charles, my stepfather, has been very generous to me,' she said with deliberate intent to mislead. She had no intention of telling Mark the house belonged to Gina Murray, an extrovert journalist who'd been left it by a godmother. Anyway, Charles *was* being generous, insisting on subsidising her rent.

'Are you going to invite me in?' Mark asked, hauling her shopping out of the Porsche's boot then carrying it up the steps.

'Not today,' said Tilly, checking the contents of the bags to make sure she had everything of hers and none of his. 'Thanks for the drink. You've done me a big favour.'

'Bringing you and your shopping home, you mean?' He gave her another of his charming smiles. 'That was a pleasure.'

'No, I didn't mean that.' Tilly unlocked the door and rapidly transferred her shopping over the threshold.

Mark stood on the doorstep with the air of a man about to take matters into his own masterful hands and insist on coming in.

'You see,' Tilly said quickly, 'I thought you broke my heart last summer.' His expression combined regret and satisfaction in equal measure.

'And today I found out it had only been very slightly dented and I won't need to waste any more time thinking about you!' She gave his startled face the sweetest of smiles, gently shut the door in his face then leant against it, feeling her heart beating rapidly, her face flushed with heat, and, above everything else, an overwhelming sense of relief.

She didn't love Mark, she'd never loved him. She'd been taken in by his charm and his good looks and never realised how shallow and selfish he was. What a marvellous morning's work to have been able to explode her memories of him into tiny fragments that could be blown by the wind wherever it pleased.

By the time Olivia arrived, Tilly, singing under her breath, had unpacked her shopping and prepared the lunch.

When the doorbell rang, she ran to open it, flinging the door wide. 'Mum, how wonderful to see you!' She was enfolded in a close embrace and for a moment it was as if they had never been parted.

'Come into the kitchen,' Tilly said when, breathless and laughing, she detached herself. 'That's where we eat.'

She led the way past the stairs and through a narrow passage to a large, cluttered, old-fashioned but comfortable kitchen. An antique Aga was fitted where once a range had stood. A tall mantelpiece displayed a collection of pottery jugs. Under the far window was a china sink. Near to it a modern fridge looked out of place beside some old cupboards topped with formica, so that all the business part of the kitchen was concentrated at the end of the room. An ancient, green-painted dresser covered with assorted china, empty wine bottles, old letters and odd books, ran along one wall. In the middle of the room was a large kitchen table with a red check tablecloth, two places laid for lunch, and a pot of white chrysanthemums. The table was surrounded with a selection of wooden chairs with patchwork cushions. On a rocking chair, bathed in sunlight from a wide sash window, sat a large marmalade cat, fast asleep. A noticeboard by the door was festooned with notes and postcards.

'My!' said Olivia, taking it all in.

'The whole house is like this,' Tilly said cheerfully. 'Gina's godmother was eighty-four when she died and she'd lived here most of her life. We think all the furniture and decorations belong to the thirties, when she married and first moved in here. Gina says she was widowed in the war and hardly changed a thing after that. She was a historian, wrote lots of books, they're all in the living room. Gina now has her study as a bedroom, says she thinks the walls will drip inspiration on to her.'

'You get on well with, what do you call them, your housemates?'

'Can't very well say flatmates,' agreed Tilly, getting out a bottle of white wine from the fridge. She fetched two glasses from a corner cupboard, also painted green, opened the bottle and poured wine for them both. 'I don't see an awful lot of them. Caroline's in advertising, Paul works in the city and Michael's articled to a firm of accountants. Occasionally one of them is here at weekends but mostly they're all off somewhere. Gina's hours tend to be as odd as mine and we sometimes meet in the morning or afternoon. She's fun, we get on well together.'

'I'm glad. And very happy to have seen seeing where you're living.' Olivia took her glass of wine and studied her daughter. 'You look well, darling. I do like that sweater.'

'I'm in great form!' Tilly went to the fridge and sorted out a container of olives. 'Now that I've decided what I want to do, everything seems to have fallen into place.'

'Are you seeing a lot of Rory Wilde?' her mother asked.

Tilly smiled. 'No doubt you think that's a perfectly logical follow-on but you're way off beam,' she said. 'Rory and I are just good friends. I told you that when you rang on Monday wanting to know how Sunday went.'

It had, in fact, been great fun. The Wildes had a large house in Highgate, furnished with opulence in what her grandmother would no doubt consider nouveau-riche style, with lots of brass trimmings to the furniture, gold taps in the bathroom and huge mirrors everywhere. Mrs Wilde was warm and homely and Mr Wilde autocratic and intelligent. Rory appeared to be on excellent terms with both his parents, teasing each of them remorselessly. They obviously loved having him there and had treated Tilly with great kindness, asking her exactly what she thought of the restaurants in the chain that she'd eaten at. They'd been equally interested in her experiences in the South of France.

'Ah, the Hôtel de Paris,' Mr Wilde had said. 'Do you remember that weekend we spent there, darling?' he asked his wife.

It was clear it had been a highlight for them both.

When she and Rory were leaving, Mr Wilde had held her hand. 'I've done what I can about a place for you at the catering college but who knows what happens in life?' He'd shrugged his shoulders, turning out his hands in a helpless gesture. 'But if the place knows what's good for it, they'll take you. Then you'll be able to keep this boy of mine on the straight and narrow. Keep him from thinking he knows it all and doesn't need to complete the course, eh?' He'd given Rory a gentle cuff around the head. Rory, a good eight inches taller than his father, pretended to be mortally hurt.

His mother had stood in the background, beaming at her two men and Tilly realised that Rory's wide mouth came from her.

'I like your parents,' she'd told him as he drove her back to Clapham.

'Good, so do I,' he'd said with one of his broad grins.

He'd come back to the house with her and they'd played a double Patience together that she'd taught him and discussed various ideas Rory was thinking about for the new flagship restaurant his father had just added to the chain. Later a couple of the others had come back and they'd had an uproarious time playing Racing Demon, then Tilly had cooked scrambled eggs for them all. It had been a pleasant end to a very enjoyable day. But Tilly had no intention of letting her mother think any serious sort of relationship was developing between the two of them.

'I like Rory very much,' she said, decanting the olives into a small china dish. 'But there's nothing between us. Now, tell me all about Grandma.' She put the dish of olives on the table and took the chair opposite her mother.

Olivia sighed. 'Physically she's making a very good recovery but she refuses to come back into the world. She spends most of the day up in her room, even after I've bullied her into getting up. She has a constant succession of visitors and most of the time says she isn't well enough to see them. She just doesn't seem able to cope mentally with her condition. It took me days of gentle persuasion to get her to the hairdresser's.'

'I can't imagine Grandma not being able to cope!'

'I know, I feel the same. I think it's losing control over her body when she's always been used to keeping a tight hold on everything connected with her life.'

'Poor Grandma, I'll come down and see her next Sunday,' Tilly promised.

'Oh, she'd love that, darling.'

'How's Grandpa coping?'

'Amazingly well, really. In a way I think he likes being able to do things for her, except he's so worried about her.' Olivia paused then added, 'I never realised just how fond of her he was. Isn't that awful?'

'I know what you mean.' Tilly nibbled on an olive, savouring the oily bitterness. 'I used to think his work was a way of escaping.'

Olivia gave a small sigh. 'I did, too. And I think it was. But he's always 'been grateful to her for organising life so that he could work without being worried by all the little things.'

'Like money, and where the next meal was coming from?'

'Exactly.' Olivia reached for an olive as well and looked at her daughter. 'When I was your age, I bitterly resented Mother.'

'Really?' Tilly was amazed. Her mother was such a gentle soul and had always seemed so accepting of what life handed out.

'Oh, yes. I resented the way she tried to control me just as she did Father. I swore to myself she wasn't going to force me into anything I didn't want. We had several minor battles about clothes and friends that I wanted but that she didn't think were suitable but nothing major until I met your father.'

'That must have been a battle royal,' Tilly said gently. 'I wish I remembered him better.'

'So do I, darling.' There was a moment's silence then Olivia asked, 'Just what do you remember?'

'Only that he was very, very tall and had a pony tail and everything was, well, sort of *brighter* when he was around. And that he spent lots of time away.' For the first time in her life, Tilly realised that there was something odd about her father's frequent absences. A longlost memory suddenly slipped into her mind. A brilliantly sunny day, a car driving up, her father getting out, shouting: 'I'm home,' the way he did. Tilly herself dashing out, short legs negotiating the big steps from the house down to the dirt drive, then being swept up in his arms and swung around. Her mother running out too, laughing, her long blonde hair loose and blowing about, wisping across her eyes and mouth. Then she'd stopped and her face had become quite blank. And Tilly had seen there was somebody else getting out of the car, a tall girl with short blonde curls and laughing eyes.

'So this is Tilly?' she'd said, bending down to say hello. 'I've brought you a present.'

Tilly could remember her excitement at the beautifully wrapped box and taking it off to open, only to be called back sharply by her mother and told to say thank you. Then she had indeed run off to her corner of the terrace and found her present was a large doll with a sequined dress and elaborately arranged blonde hair. She'd wanted to show the pretty lady how much she liked it but both the lady and her father had left. Back over the years came the desolation that had washed over Tilly as she stood on the front steps and realised that the driveway was empty. In the far distance, she could see clouds of dust following her father's car as it headed back to Hollywood. She couldn't remember anything after that.

'Were you and Dad really as happy as everyone says?' she asked her mother.

Olivia's gaze dropped and she played with the stem of her wine glass. 'The first few months we were together were sheer bliss,' she said slowly. 'I couldn't imagine being happier. Perhaps it was too much to expect it to

270

last like that. And there were other times, like when you were born.' She smiled at Tilly. 'We both adored you! I went back to waitressing quite soon so your father could work at his scripts and he looked after you. Changed your nappies and brought you to the restaurant when you needed feeding. The charm I had to employ to keep the owner sweet and get him to allow me the time off each evening when it was your six o'clock feed! Thank heavens you never went to sleep. Even in those days you treated food as a serious business.' Olivia smiled reminiscently. 'Your babyhood was such a happy time.'

'But it didn't last?' Tilly probed delicately.

Olivia sighed and looked again at her wine. 'I think things started to go wrong when Peter had his first script accepted and was offered a contract. That was when we bought the house on the edge of the desert.'

'That's the one I remember?'

Olivia nodded. 'I asked Peter, wasn't it too far away? Wouldn't it be difficult to commute? But he said, no, it would be much better than getting too involved with the Hollywood set. But, of course, he soon organised himself a room near the studios so that he had somewhere to stay when he had to work late, which seemed to be more and more often.' She drank her wine and said sadly, 'I shouldn't really be telling you all this. I always swore I'd never spoil the picture you had of your father.'

'I'm a big girl now, Mum,' Tilly said. 'You can't protect me all my life.'

'That's what I've tried to do, I suppose. And I always swore I wouldn't try and control your life, the way my mother tried to control mine. Always from the best possible motives, of course.'

'Nobody's perfect, are they?'

Olivia tried to smile. 'I suppose not. And your father was wonderful in all sorts of ways.'

'I wish he hadn't died,' Tilly said bleakly.

'I know, darling.' Olivia smiled mistily. Then her expression changed, became lively and cheerful. 'Look at us, we should be happy, not getting all depressed, we'll get as bad as your grandma.'

'Tell me about Charles,' Tilly suggested, topping up their glasses. 'Then I'll start lunch. It's a stirfry so it'll only take a few minutes. Is the wretched Phyllie still out there?'

Her mother nodded gloomily, her sparkle gone. 'I should be pleased for him, I suppose. Apparently she was a great help when his friends stayed with him. Instead of which I keep thinking that perhaps they're better off together without me.'

'For heaven's sake, Mum!' Tilly felt exasperated. 'What a wimpish thing to say! I expect they are having fun together but a little of that will go a long way for both of them. I bet Phyllie's eyeing every young man on the Côte d'Azur and Charles is getting fed up with her not looking for a job. Not to mention wanting you back.'

'Oh, Tilly, I don't know! I spend all day trying to cheer your grandma

271

up and keep your grandfather from getting depressed as well. Then I ring Charles and he tries to be sympathetic but I know he hasn't a clue what the situation is really like.' She gave a strangled laugh. 'At first he kept asking when I was coming back and I'd get upset and say I didn't know. Now he's stopped asking, and instead of being relieved, I'm worried he doesn't want me back!'

'Mum! Charles adores you, of course he wants you back.' Tilly got up and went across to the stove, so cross with her mother she hardly knew what to say. 'What's happening between you two?'

Olivia slumped back in her chair. 'I don't know, darling. I used to think it was just having so many visitors and never having time to talk properly. Now I think perhaps we wouldn't know what to say to each other anyway.'

This was much worse than Tilly had imagined. 'I've never heard of anything so ridiculous,' she said crossly. 'You didn't seem to have trouble talking to each other before you got married. It's just having all those people and Phyllida around so much.' Olivia said nothing.

Tilly put the wok on the Aga and added oil. She took the sliced vegetables and chicken out of the fridge and brought them over to the stove. 'You know what your trouble is?' she said, looking straight at her mother. 'You've taken not interfering in anyone else's life to ridiculous lengths. You always think everyone else knows better than you, I don't think you've got any confidence in yourself.' She flung the chicken into the wok and began stirring it vigorously, wishing she could shake some sense into her beautiful, insecure mother.

'That's what Margie always says,' Olivia murmured.

'And she's right. Look at you now! Why aren't you telling me I don't know what I'm talking about?'

Olivia stared at her daughter. 'You really have grown up, haven't you?'

Tilly flipped her hair back over her shoulders, removed the cooked chicken into a colander placed over a plate, wiped out the wok, added more oil and tossed in the vegetables. 'Guess who I met today shopping?'

'Can't imagine,' her mother said.

'Mark!'

'Good heavens! What did you do?'

'Said hello, of course.'

'And what did he say?'

'You're beginning to sound like a game of consequences,' Tilly said severely, stirring the vegetables and beginning to feel a little happier. 'After he got over his shock, he was sweet as cane sugar, took me out for a drink.'

'Tilly, you didn't go?'

'Why not? Perfect opportunity to find out what I really thought of him. *And* he had a car so I was able to buy all the bulky stuff that's so difficult to carry home.'

'Tilly, you're incredible,' Olivia said faintly. 'I had no idea you could be so decisive.'

'It's quite easy, all one needs is a little practice.'

'And what happened?'

'Oh, he tried to pick up where he left off and I told him no thanks. When I think how I fell for his smoothie charm and couldn't see what a jerk he really was, I'm ashamed of myself.' Tilly bit through a piece of vegetable to test its degree of doneness. Compared with Rory, she thought, Mark was superficial. Very sophisticated, no doubt, but being with him was like eating *zabaglione*: lots of froth and sweet flavour, very little substance. While Rory was, what? Roast beef served with a zingy Thai sauce.

'So you've got over him?' her mother asked.

'Who, Mark? I'm glad to say, yes! Absolutely!' Tilly put back the cooked chicken and stirred it together with the vegetables, letting the chicken reheat. Then she added the sauce and stirred that in. 'I'm now well and truly heart whole.'

She got the serving dish and a couple of plates out of the warming oven, piled in the stirfried chicken and vegetables in their shiny, tangy sauce and brought it all over to the table. 'Why are you looking at me like that?' she demanded.

Olivia ducked her head, obscuring the hard stare that had been fixed on her daughter.

'Don't you believe me?' Tilly pressed, handing her a plate and placing the serving dish beside it.

'It was just something your grandmother was suggesting.' Olivia helped herself to the dish. 'This looks and smells delicious.'

'What was she suggesting, that I was pining away for Mark?' Tilly demanded half-jokingly as she sat down at the other place.

'No, she thought you'd fallen for Patrick. And he for you,' Olivia added quickly.

Tilly took the dish her mother handed across the table and said nothing.

'Well, did you?' her mother asked, half-apologetically.

'No, I didn't,' Tilly said quietly. 'I'm very fond of him, he's a lovely person, but he's far too old for me.'

'Lots of girls fall in love with older men,' Olivia stated reasonably.

'Not me. Anyway, he's married.'

'That's what worried your grandmother, and us when she told us.'

'Is that why you suddenly hatched up the idea of my coming back to England and turning professional cook?' Several pieces fitted themselves together for Tilly and she felt a certain amount of awe for how rapidly everything had been organised. What a formidable person her grandmother had been. Still was, she told herself fiercely.

'Well, Charles and I had been wondering what you wanted to do with yourself,' her mother said, a little defensively. 'And he was sure it would be the best thing for you, whether Mother was right or not.' Olivia went on to say how much Charles admired her cooking and Tilly realised that her mother had been safely deflected from asking whether Patrick had been in love with her.

Dear Patrick. He'd been a life saver for her in those early weeks in France when Phyllida had been throwing her weight around. She'd really enjoyed their days out together. She hadn't seen him alone after their walk on the hill. She had said a final goodbye to him and Liz together.

'Don't forget us,' he'd said, holding her hand just a little too long.

'Never,' she'd said, equally cheerful. Then she'd given Liz a big kiss. 'I look forward to your next exhibition. Then we can meet in London.'

And Liz had given her a little smile. 'I shan't know what to do without you,' she'd said.

Patrick had put his arm around his wife. 'You'll still have me.'

She'd looked up at him. 'So I shall.' Her voice had sounded odd to Tilly and she'd wondered if Liz had guessed.

And now Tilly knew that Liz was pregnant. She'd written to her, telling Liz how glad she was for them both and saying she hoped she could come out and see the baby in the spring.

To have had someone like Patrick declaring he loved her was, Tilly thought, the best gift she could have been given. It had made nonsense of the way Mark had dropped her, had given her back her self-esteem and enabled her to face the future with confidence.

To have met Mark again and found what she'd felt for him had been no more than calf or puppy love had been a bonus.

Having steered her mother off the subject of Patrick, Tilly kept the conversation firmly focused on how much she was enjoying the challenge of working in Jemima's restaurant and how she was phoning the catering college regularly to check whether a place had come up yet.

'The thing is not to let them forget my existence, or allow anybody else to slip in front of me,' she said. 'You've got to show them how determined you are.'

'I'm sure you're doing that, darling.' Olivia sounded amused.

Tilly wondered if she should say something else to her mother about making sure she didn't allow Phyllida or Daphne to interfere with her happiness with Charles. But you couldn't bludgeon people and she reckoned she'd said enough already.

It was late afternoon by the time Olivia left, saying she'd promised to call in on Margie before she returned to Sussex.

'I'll come down next weekend,' Tilly promised as she said goodbye.

Then she went and cleared up the kitchen, enjoying the thought of the free evening in front of her.

When the front door bell went just before six o'clock she went to answer thinking it was probably one of the others having forgotten their key.

On the doorstep stood Rory.

'Hallo!' exclaimed Tilly. 'I wasn't expecting to see you.'

He jingled his loose change in his trouser pocket and gave her one of his wide grins, 'I've been to see some friends in the country for lunch and as I was coming back into town, I thought I'd see if you were doing anything or if you'd like to go to a flick.'

Tilly felt incredibly pleased. Of course, as she'd told her mother only that afternoon, there wasn't anything between them but she did enjoy being with Rory and he'd never asked her to go to the cinema with him before. 'Lovely idea,' she said. 'I'll get my coat.'

They went to an American comedy/romance that had received rave reviews. Rory bought an enormous carton of popcorn and they shared that with the laughs. It was only nine o'clock when they came out. 'What about something proper to eat?' suggested Rory.

'Why don't you come back and I'll see if I can find something for supper, since you didn't let me pay for my ticket?' The atmosphere of the film floated around them and she felt warm and light hearted.

'I won't argue with that, you have a rare touch with scrambled eggs,' Rory tucked her hand through his arm as they went to find his car.

None of the others seemed to be back yet and they had the kitchen to themselves. Tilly made a quick pasta dish with the remains of the vegetables from lunch and the trimmings from the chicken breasts. Rory leant against the sink, drinking a glass of wine and chatting happily about things he'd been doing over the past week, stretching out every now and then to pinch a bit of half-cooked vegetable.

The third time he tried it, Tilly slapped his hand with her spatula, 'Stop that, otherwise there won't be anything to go with the pasta!' and gave him some cheese to grate into a small bowl. Then suggested he lay the table as she drained the pasta, at the same time warming two plates with the cooking water.

As Rory found forks, placed them carefully on the table, added the dish of grated cheese and poured more wine into their glasses, she tossed the pasta in olive oil and the mixture of vegetables and meat. 'I'm sorry if a saucepan offends your carefully educated sensibilities but I forgot to warm a serving dish.'

'Makes me feel at home,' he grinned at her.

'Your mother would have a fit if she could hear that,' Tilly said severely as she dried the warmed plates and picked up the saucepan. 'Right, à table.'

'I'm just about ready to do murder for this.' Rory sat down and looked expectant. 'My, what a girl with talent can do with left overs,' he said after demolishing half of his supper. Then ducked as Tilly made a mock swipe at him with the wooden spoon from the saucepan. 'No, seriously, the sky's the limit after you've graduated from that course we're going to do.'

'If I ever manage to get on it,' Tilly all at once felt profoundly depressed at the idea that Rory could be going to college on his own. Suddenly the prospect of continuing to work with Jemima instead of absorbing everything a structured course could offer her while studying alongside someone who'd become a real friend was almost more than she could bear.

'We'll take our coffee into the living room,' she said, getting up and putting on the kettle.

The living room was comfortable with well worn furniture, shelves of books and odd ornaments and photographs, all belonging to the thirties. Tilly lit the gas fire and placed the coffee pot and cups on a low table then went over to the one modern item in the room, a music centre, and chose Sergeant Pepper's Lonely Hearts Band, an old recording of the Beatles that she'd recently fallen in love with.

Rory sat on the well stuffed chesterfield and poured the coffee. Tilly came and sat beside him.

They heard the front door open, the sound of people coming in and then footsteps going straight up the stairs. 'No racing demon tonight, then,' murmured Rory, adding milk to his cup.

'Do you want a game of cards?' asked Tilly. The standard lamp she'd switched on threw a pool of light round them, the gently flaring fire contributed welcome warmth, the big sofa with its soft cushions cradled her nicely beside Rory and she was quite happy just listening to the idiosyncratic, oddly hypnotic music.

Rory put his cup on the coffee table and turned towards her. 'Certainly not,' he said. 'I don't want to share you, and cards are the last thing I'm interested in.'

Tilly was held by the look in his hazel eyes. There was a softness she hadn't seen there before, quite different from their usual derisive expression. He put out a hand and smoothed back the long hair that had fallen in front of her shoulder. 'You're so beautiful these days, Tilly. What have you done with yourself?'

Tilly caught her breath, 'Nothing, nothing at all.' Inside she felt her stomach turn to liquid.

The hand that had been smoothing her hair slipped behind her head and drew it towards his mouth, then the long lips gently closed on hers and her heart rose, threatening to stifle her as her mouth opened under the soft pressure.

She didn't feel the heady excitement Mark had aroused when he'd kissed her. Instead there was a marvellous feeling of completeness as the kiss deepened until shivers ran down her spine and she found her arms reaching round his neck to draw his head closer to hers.

Then they drew apart and looked at each other in amazement.

'When did it all happen?' asked Rory, looking at her with startled delight. 'I knew you were different from other girls but I had no idea . . .' He started to draw her towards him again but Tilly resisted.

'Don't, please, Rory. I'm not ready. It's too soon. Can't we just stay good friends?'

'Too soon? What do you mean?' He looked hurt and puzzled and a little

276

pulse beat at the right hand corner of his jaw.

Tilly thought of the relief she'd felt this morning when she realised she had never been in love with Mark. Had some part of her known then that this was waiting for her? 'Well, if we're going to have all that studying ahead of us, we shouldn't get involved,' she stammered.

Joy surged back into his face. 'Silly Tilly, is that all that's worrying you? We'll enjoy working together all the more! And we can help each other. It's all going to be so much fun, you'll see. What a team we'll make!'

The door opened and a head was thrust round, 'Hi, Tilly! Thought you must have the coffee pot, any to spare?' Michael came in, then stopped as he realised what he'd interrupted. 'I say, sorry! Hope I haven't disturbed you.'

'Not at all,' Rory looked up, his arm tight round Tilly's shoulders. 'Take the coffee pot, take everything, we don't need anything else.'

Tilly giggled and buried her head in his chest as Michael darted forward, lifted up the pot and disappeared muttering apologies.

'Oh, Tilly,' said Rory, leaning back and taking her with him. 'I don't think I mind what happens as long as you stay just like this for ever and ever.'

Chapter Twenty-Seven

After she'd left Tilly, Olivia went round to Margie's flat in Chelsea for a late tea that turned into supper.

She received another lecture from Margie about being more assertive.

'You sound just like Tilly,' Olivia said. 'She spent most of lunch telling me to stand up for myself.'

'Bully for her! As long as I've known you, you've let people walk all over you.'

'Pax!' Olivia held up a hand, laughing. 'I've got the general idea, promise! Now, tell me what's been going on in your world.'

Margie cleared away the remains of the generous amount of smoked salmon they'd been helping themselves to and placed a cheeseboard on the round, black glass table that stood in the corner of her chic living room. She grinned mischievously at Olivia. 'I've handed in my notice.'

Olivia stared at her. 'Why?'

Margie placed a basket of biscuits beside the cheese and sat down again looking pleased at Olivia's surprise. 'Just what Gavin asked. He couldn't believe his second most valuable employee wanted out. It was bad enough when you left. I tell you, Olivia, you have no idea how much he relied on you. You could have named your price for staying. But to lose me as well!' Margie never underestimated her worth.

'But what are you going to do?' demanded Olivia.

Margie paused in the act of cutting herself a slice of brie. 'Start my own company,' she said without prevarication.

'Congratulations!' Olivia toasted her in the glass of mineral water she'd insisted on. 'You always said that was what you wanted. And now really is the time?'

Margie nodded. 'We're coming out of recession, I know the work's there and I've got the contacts. I found some lovely premises the other day; the rent's affordable, the location is right and my plans are all ready. So I told Gavin on Friday that I'd work my two months' notice then be off.'

Olivia was fascinated and wanted all the details of the new company, the business Margie was aiming for and how she intended to market her services.

Margie was full of ideas and produced a portfolio of sketches for the offices she'd taken together with designs for her letterhead and various brochures, pushing aside the remains of their meal to make room for them on the table. Olivia studied them all, then borrowed a pencil and produced a couple of alternative sketches for Margie's logo. She also made some suggestions on how the main brochure could be angled that Margie immediately made notes. 'You've not lost your touch, I see, Olivia.' She paused for a moment, shuffling through the various papers she'd spread out, then looked up at her friend and said, 'Quite a few of my main contacts are in Switzerland and Italy, and one is actually in Nice. I wondered if you'd like to come in with me, run a French branch, so to speak.'

For a moment Olivia was so astonished she couldn't think of anything to say. Margie waited, her eyes bright, her fingers playing with her pencil.

'I wouldn't be any help to you at all, Margie. I hardly have time to think down there, let alone work on designs for exhibitions and conferences. Anyway, there can't possibly be enough business in our part of the world to justify having me on the payroll!'

'You could handle Italy, Switzerland, Austria, all within a few hours travel of Nice Airport. Plenty of scope there. And do you really like being treated like a hotel?' demanded Margie, getting up to make coffee.

'It's not that,' protested Olivia, bringing through their dirty dishes to Margie's minute kitchen, her mind performing gymnastics. She was aware part of her wanted very much to get back to her career, just that brief contact with a pencil and a few ideas had made her fingers itch for more and she'd always been good with clients. But another part of her clung to the vision she'd had when she married Charles of a life spent with a loving companion, building a home and enjoying life together. 'This summer has been exceptional. We aren't going to go on living like that.'

'Oh no?' Margie said sceptically, watching the water filter through her machine. 'Face it, Olivia, with a house like that you're always going to have visitors pounding on the door.'

'All the more reason not to be trying to do a job as well,' retorted Olivia, stacking the last of the plates in the dishwasher.

While they drank the coffee, Margie attempted to get Olivia to change her mind without success.

'Look,' she said at last. 'Think it over, there's no need for hasty decisions. I shan't be setting up shop for at least two months. "London and Nice" would look good on the letterhead, wouldn't it? But I can understand if you want to go on enjoying life with lovely Charles in that beautiful house – plus all your friends!'

Olivia laughed, kissed her and promised to keep in touch.

As she drove away, though, she knew that her real reason for refusing Margie's offer was not that she didn't want to spoil her married life with the distractions of work. She wasn't at all sure if she still had a married life.

The relationship between her and Charles that had started so ecstatically had already drifted into stagnant waters. They had become two people

280

sharing little more than a house. Recently they had been too tired at night to do more than exchange a quick kiss and put out the light. Even more serious, they hardly seemed to talk any more. Was it just because they'd been so busy?

Olivia picked up the main A3 arterial road and felt her panic increase with the speed of the car. Had she made a terrible mistake in marrying Charles? Had she done so because she'd been more than a little fed up with the way Gavin seemed to take her for granted? Fed up with the constant struggle with money, with not being able to give Tilly all the things she wanted to? With fighting her mother's attempts to rule both her daughter's and granddaughter's lives? Had she looked on Charles as some sort of a fairy godfather and the move to France a means of getting away from all her problems?

Then, as she pushed her mother's Metro up to top speed and the London traffic was left behind, Olivia remembered the joy of being with Charles on that first trip to the Riviera. The delight of sharing experiences with him, the fun of planning the French house.

For a brief moment she wanted to drive to the coast, take the first ferry and keep on driving right down France until she reached him and home.

But she couldn't leave her mother at the moment and there was Phyllida. While Charles had achieved a marvellously successful relationship with Tilly, Olivia had completely failed with her stepdaughter. Every time she thought of Phyllida, Olivia could feel her stomach contract and a dead weight of despair fill her heart. The effort of fighting her animosity, of trying to defuse what Olivia could only see as malice was so wearing, so destructive. Particularly as Charles appeared to be oblivious of the situation. Even Tilly didn't seem to understand the battle that was going on, she thought her mother was being weak and spineless.

The truth was, Olivia had no idea what to do to save her marriage.

Even if she could leave Daphne and Thomas, she couldn't see returning to *La Chênais* while Phyllida was still there was going to help matters. A real showdown would only alienate Charles.

And he hadn't exactly sounded desperate to have her back during their telephone conversations these past couple of weeks. On the contrary, Olivia had gathered an impression of life proceeding for him and Phyllida very happily without her. Perhaps Charles was trying to spare her the pressures of a husband demanding her return but it would have been nice to be told that he was desperately missing her.

Olivia pressed on into the darkness, her thoughts in a turmoil.

One thing she was sure of, Tilly and Margie were right when they said she had to make more of an effort to control her life. She had to fight for what she wanted. But what was that? And how was she going to achieve it?

It was almost midnight by the time she reached her parents' home.

She found Thomas sitting beside a dying fire, his manuscript on the table beside his chair and looking untouched, a glass of whisky in his hand.

He looked round as she came in and his expression pierced her through.

'Father, what's happened? Is it Mother? Has she had a relapse?' She hurried towards him, took the hand he held out to her and crouched on the floor beside him.

'No, nothing like that,' he said quickly but his voice sounded exhausted.

'So, what's the matter?'

'She's been hoarding sleeping pills,' Thomas said, his breath coming out in a long, dying sigh.

Olivia drew up a chair, her own worries forgotten at the implications of what he'd said. 'How do you know?'

He gave another deep sigh and rubbed his eyes. 'She was complaining she couldn't get comfortable; I gave her a sleeping pill and saw there weren't many left in the bottle. I didn't think she'd been taking them, several times I've noticed her light on when I've gone downstairs to make myself a hot drink. I've taken her one up as well but by then the light's always been off and she's seemed asleep.'

'Judging by how she looks in the morning, she never appears to have had a really restful night,' Olivia said slowly. 'But she swore to me she took one every night.'

'Exactly what she said to me. So when I saw how few were left, I told - her they obviously weren't strong enough and I'd have a word with the doctor, get him to prescribe something more effective.' Another rub at his eyes. 'She told me very sharply, you know how she can be, that I was to do no such thing.'

Yes, Olivia could hear her mother saying it.

'So I assured her I wouldn't mention it and then went up later and saw that she really was fast asleep. At first I was just relieved that tonight, at least, she was getting a proper rest. Then something made me go through the bathroom cabinet. And I found those,' he nodded towards a bottle labelled Paracetamol sitting on the table beside his manuscript.

Olivia picked it up, unscrewed the cap and spilt several of the pills on to her hand. Definitely not Paracetamol, equally definitely her mother's sleeping pills. She tipped all of them on to the small table beside her chair. Yes, all sleeping pills. Over two dozen of them. Almost one for each night she'd been home from the hospital.

Olivia looked at her father. 'But why?'

'Don't be an idiot,' he said roughly. 'She's obviously amassing enough to ensure her exit from this harsh world, as Hamlet had it.'

'She can't be!' Olivia was horrified.

'Why not? She obviously finds living in her present state insupportable.'

'You have to tell her she mustn't!'

Thomas wearily dragged down the skin under his eyes. He looked despairing. 'If I haven't convinced her over the last few weeks how much she means to me, I won't have any effect now. Perhaps I have to respect her decision?'

'For heaven's sake!' Olivia began to feel very angry. 'A colostomy is not the end of the world. Lots of people live with much worse handicaps.'

'I think in all honesty she would have preferred to have lost a leg or an arm.'

Olivia stood up. 'This is nonsense. I shall speak to her in the morning.' Then her father's misery got to her. She kissed him. 'Don't worry, together we'll shake her out of this.'

Next morning Olivia carefully laid her mother's breakfast tray and added a late rose from the garden.

'Here we are,' she said cheerfully as she went into the bedroom. She placed the tray on the bed table then drew the curtains. Sun poured into the room. 'Look what a beautiful morning it is,' she said.

Daphne hauled herself sleepily up the bed, with no sign of her usual morning alertness.

'I've made you a boiled egg and soldiers.' Olivia arranged the pillows behind her mother, checked that she was sitting up properly, then pulled the table across the bed.

Daphne unwrapped her napkin and spread it across the sheet. She surveyed the tray, picked up a small knife and attacked the top of the boiled egg, revealing deep yellow liquid yolk. 'Perfect,' she said.

Olivia sat on the side of the bed and watched her mother eat with a growing gusto. She poured her a cup composed equally of freshly made coffee and hot milk. '*Café au lait*,' she said cheerfully. 'Don't you think the French way of doing it the best?'

Her mother finished her egg and pushed away the shell regretfully. 'I always enjoyed the way you did it at *La Chênais*.' She eyed her daughter keenly. 'Isn't it about time you returned there?'

'I can't leave you yet,' Olivia said pleasantly.

'Your Charles will grow tired of waiting for you,' Daphne said waspishly.

'I hope not,' Olivia said in the same pleasant tone. 'But it's a risk I'll have to take until you start behaving sensibly again.'

Daphne put down her cup of coffee. 'What's this? I've never behaved anything but sensibly all my life,' she said belligerently.

'How sensible is it to hoard sleeping pills?' Olivia demanded.

Daphne's eyes blazed. 'That is my business,' she said harshly.

Olivia was pleased that at least she didn't try to deny it. 'Suicide is never just the business of the victim. It hurts all those left behind. How would Father live knowing you preferred death to keeping him company when he loves you so much? What about me? What about how I love you? How could I live with my sense of failure?'

'It's nothing to do with you,' Daphne insisted but with rather less force.

'Oh yes it is. We love you, we want to see you enjoying life again. And there's absolutely no reason why you can't.' Olivia paused, drew a deep breath, wished she'd been able to practise assertiveness before this and said, 'I never thought I'd see you a coward.'

Daphne's eyes narrowed. 'You can't get me that way,' she grated.

'Can't I? What else is it? I can't see it as anything but cowardice. There are thousands of people out there.' Olivia waved a hand at the window where the sun was still pouring in, lighting the carpet and falling across the bed. 'Tens of thousands of people,' she added sternly, 'who are managing with bags like you. Except that they aren't complaining the way you are. They are just getting on with it. Why can't you do the same?'

Daphne lay back against her pillows and stared at her daughter. 'Turning into a bully, are you?' she asked unpleasantly.

'If that's what it takes to bring you to your senses, yes!' Olivia asserted. 'I'm not going to run away from this. I'm not going to run away from anything. You were right when you accused me of not facing things this summer.'

Daphne folded up her napkin, making turn after turn until it was a thick bundle. 'You took that to heart, I see.' She threw the bundle of linen on the tray with a triumphant gesture.

'Eventually,' Olivia admitted ruefully. 'It took Tilly to tell me I had to stand up for myself. Now I'm telling you, you have to stand up for yourself. You have to tell fate you're not going to let it beat you. What are people going to think if Daphne Ferguson can't handle this? Because if you take those sleeping pills every detail will be all over the district. Everyone will know how you couldn't cope.'

Olivia watched her mother stiffen and take this in. At last she'd got through to her. 'If you won't live for Father, me and Tilly, live for the sake of your reputation,' she suggested. She picked up the tray. 'Now I'm going to take this downstairs and I suggest you get up.' She stood staring at her mother, willing her to respond.

Daphne stared back, her eyes dark and angry. At last, slowly, reluctantly, she nodded. Olivia put the tray back on the table, bent and kissed her. 'Put on your glad rags, I'm taking you and Father out for lunch,' she said. 'It's time you started going out so I've booked a table at that nice pub down the road.'

She picked up the tray again and swept out of the bedroom, using a foot to close the door behind her.

Outside she took a deep breath and waited. There was silence from inside the room. Then there was the sound of bedclothes being flung back and the rustle of her mother slowly getting out of bed.

Olivia took the tray to the kitchen. She wouldn't know if she'd won until her mother came downstairs but at least there hadn't been outright protest.

Olivia spent the next hour and a half helping Betty to turn out the larder

284

and making a list of staples that needed restocking, listening with half an ear to her account of her husband's prostate operation and with the other half for the sound of her mother coming down the stairs.

It was as Olivia was taking coffee through to the living room that Daphne appeared, dressed in a smart knitted suit, her hair newly washed and makeup in place. She smiled at her husband and daughter. 'I understand we are going out for lunch,' she said magisterially. 'It sounds a lovely treat.'

Thomas looked at her with astonishment.

'Perhaps you'd like to come with me for a little trip round the garden before we go?' Daphne continued. 'We shall need to be planning for next year.'

'It will be my pleasure,' said Thomas eagerly as he offered her his arm in a courtly gesture.

Olivia watched them go through the door to the garden, wondering when she had ever seen her parents planning things together before.

Lunch was a considerable success. The pub was pleasantly full and Daphne met an old friend who joined them for a drink and appeared delighted to see her so much better. Daphne didn't eat much but seemed happy to chat and even suggested she and Thomas plan a trip to Jersey in the near future. 'I'm sure it would do me good and we once had a most enjoyable week there, do you remember?' she asked her husband.

'Indeed I do,' he said, smiling at her in a way that suggested it had been a special time for them. 'I'll go into the travel agent in Chichester this afternoon and see what they can suggest.'

For the briefest moment Daphne hesitated and Olivia waited for her to tell him to leave it to her. Instead, 'What a good idea,' she said.

When they returned, Thomas dropped the two women and said he'd go straight into town and look into trips to Jersey.

'I think I need a little rest now,' Daphne said as she and Olivia entered the house. 'Would you like to bring me up a cup of tea in about an hour? I don't suppose Thomas will be back by then, he's bound to visit that bookshop he always goes to and he never gets out of there until closing time.'

Olivia watched her mother go upstairs then went into the living room, sat down and picked up a magazine. For the first time since she'd returned to England, she felt free to flip through articles and relax. The sun still poured through the windows and it was pleasant to let her mind wander. She knew she should be thinking about her own future but it was such a relief that Daphne appeared to have regained an appetite for life, she was content to doze for a few minutes.

With a start, Olivia woke and realised that well over an hour had passed and that Daphne would be wondering where her cup of tea was.

But when she took a tray up a little later, Daphne was still dozing herself. She woke as Olivia drew back the curtains. 'What a nice little rest,' she said, hauling herself up in bed and looking at the tray Olivia had placed on her bedside table. 'And you've brought a cup for yourself, that's nice, I hoped you would, come and sit down,' she patted the space that was Thomas's side of the bed.

'Do you remember the teas we used to have at Fortnum and Mason when you were a little girl?' Daphne asked as Olivia poured for them both then settled on the bed.

'After we'd done the dentist and then John Lewis for my school uniform?' Olivia could picture vividly the visit to Harley Street for her regular checkup, the delight when there were no holes to be drilled and filled, then trotting across Cavendish Square to John Lewis, trying on pleated skirts and blazers, her mother tut-tutting at how she'd grown since the previous year. Then they'd emerge through the other side of the store, into Oxford Street, always so busy and bustling, and walk down Bond Street, Olivia gazing into the shoe and dress shops, wishing that instead of the dull school uniform they were buying her the sort of clothes she saw in the windows of Fenwick's, and shoes with stirrup trimmings instead of buttoned sandals. It was Asprey's that her mother would walk more slowly past, sometimes pausing in front of a choice piece of furniture. But soon they'd reach Piccadilly and the soft green front of Fortnum and Mason's with its mouth watering windows.

'I used to love the hot crumpets and the ice creams,' Olivia smiled reminiscently. 'It was always a great treat.'

'You were such a lovely little girl,' Daphne lay back against her pillows and smiled at her daughter. 'So solemn with your long plaits and big eyes. I can see you now, looking at other tables and wanting to know who all the people were. Did they live in the country? Did they have children? Had they been shopping in John Lewis? Had they taken the afternoon off work as well?' Daphne took a sip of her tea then leant back against her pillows. 'I wish now that I'd taken more days off work but I did try to have what I liked to think of as quality time with you.'

'You mean those visits to the art galleries and museums?' Olivia asked quietly.

Daphne looked sad, 'Yes, I don't think you enjoyed them all that much, did you?'

Olivia refilled her tea cup. 'Tea at Fort's was much more fun,' she acknowledged, 'but I did enjoy our visits to the National Gallery and the Tate. I loved looking at the pictures and being able to ask you questions knowing you'd be able to answer.'

'Yes,' said Daphne sadly, 'I was very good at that. But I don't think I was good at just talking to you. Having silly little conversations that meant we got to know each other.'

Olivia couldn't help laughing. 'Mother, have you ever had what you call a "silly little conversation" with anyone in your life?'

'No,' said Daphne even more sadly. 'I don't think I have. That's why I'm

286

such a good chairman, I keep everybody to the point. Though I do allow others to have their say, that's most important. But I've never been one for gossip or just social flim flam. It's always seemed a waste of time to me. Now I wonder if I haven't missed out.' She reached across and put her hand on Olivia's thigh. 'I'm so grateful to you, darling. Not only for coming home and looking after me but never losing your patience even when I was at my most beastly. And I know how difficult I can be, believe me. But thank you most of all for making me see how much I still have to be grateful for.'

Olivia was overwhelmed. She'd never seen her mother humble herself before, it was touching but unnerving. 'I'm afraid I bullied you more than you ever did me,' she laughed uncertainly.

'You're a very kind girl, I don't think I've realised before just how important kindness is in this world. You're like your father and I'm afraid I haven't been very kind to him lately.'

Olivia leaned over and gave her mother a kiss. 'He's just been so worried about you, we both have.'

Daphne blinked hard. Perhaps it was the result of her rest but Olivia thought her face looked younger, more relaxed than it had done for longer than she could remember.

'I'm glad you've found someone to look after you like your Charles. He may not be what I would have chosen for you but I know now that the sort of man I thought you should marry wouldn't have been right for you at all.'

'Mother!' Olivia gave a wholehearted laugh. 'Are you sure you're feeling well? Should I call the doctor?'

Daphne looked pleased but said severely. 'Show me a bit more respect, girl! For once in my life I'm acknowledging I could be wrong and all you can do is laugh at me!'

Olivia gave her a warm hug. 'You're wonderful, Mother, don't let anyone ever suggest any different.'

Daphne touched her face briefly. 'Well, I think I shall get up now. They'll be throwing your father out of that bookshop soon and I expect he'll have some details about Jersey to discuss, that is, if he remembered to go to the agent before succumbing to the lure of literature.' Then, as Olivia put their tea cups on the tray and picked it up, she added, 'You should be starting to think about getting back to that husband of yours but I hope you can manage to stay just a few more days?' There was a sudden note of pleading in her voice that was irresistible.

'Of course, Mother, I'll be here until you're properly on your feet again.' Olivia wanted to add that Charles had probably got used to being without her by now but restrained herself. It was too soon to suggest to her mother that her marriage might be in difficulties. But, ironically, now that she had achieved this unexpected rapprochement with Daphne, she felt more lonely than ever. As she carried down the tea tray, she couldn't help wondering just what Charles and Phyllida were up to.

Chapter Twenty-Eight

Charles drove back into the courtyard of *La Chênais* and let Juno out of the car. He put the Jaguar in the garage then followed the dog into the house. He stood in one of the open salon windows and looked out at the still uncompleted pool house construction.

It had been a wonderfully sunny day, almost as warm as high summer, too warm to take Juno for a walk earlier, but with a lovely softness in the air. It was turning into a splendid autumn and they'd recently had one or two heavy downpours of rain so that the garden was looking fresh and green. Beyond the hills, all shades of purples and dark blues, the Mediterranean was a dramatically azure blue.

Charles sighed. He should go down and check what the builders had done today. He'd hoped that the pool house would be finished by the time Olivia came back but completion still seemed several weeks away.

He sighed again as the depression he'd managed to keep at bay while he energetically exercised Juno settled around him like a sea mist. Olivia didn't look like returning for some time.

He ran over their recent telephone conversations in his mind. Oh, she'd said she was missing him but he could tell that she was so deeply involved with her mother's problems, she found it difficult to get inside what he was thinking. Even when she said she loved him, he thought he could detect a note of uncertainty.

Charles thrust his fists into the pockets of his shorts and walked irritably down to the construction site at the side of the pool thinking of how he and Olivia had supervised the renovation of the house. It had been such fun checking the progress of the builders together, even when the work had seemed to be going frustratingly slowly. There had always been so much to talk about and discuss.

Charles entered through the terrace space where patio windows would eventually be placed and kicked moodily at the protective covering that had been placed on the marble floor as he went through to the kitchen and changing area. Sink, stove and dishwasher had been delivered that day, they were still in their packaging, fitting was scheduled for tomorrow. He gave another sigh as he realised that the fridge hadn't arrived. He'd better call about that first thing in the morning. But the shower and loo fittings were in place and the plastering had been done. He supposed things could be worse.

Outside, the barbecue had also been built. Charles tried to feel more cheerful as he imagined presiding over sizzling steaks and pouring jugs of Pimms on an evening like this. But with Olivia there.

Just how long was it going to take before she could leave her mother?

Charles remembered Daphne Ferguson during her holiday with them, every inch the dominant matriarch. However much Olivia resented her interference in her life, Charles knew she found it difficult to go against her wishes. He knew Daphne would have prevented Olivia's marriage to him if she could have. He wasn't sophisticated enough, hadn't been brought up to know which was the right knife for what, hadn't been to a public school. He might have built up a successful company but he was still too blue collar, too northern, too ordinary. Thank heavens her daughter wasn't the same sort of snob.

Charles started up the slope of the lawn again. It was time for his evening drink. He wondered where Phyllida was.

Phyllie had driven off to Monte Carlo this morning saying she wanted to do some shopping. She'd wheedled several thousand francs out of him. She hadn't bought any clothes for ages, she said, and she'd been asked to a dinner party by one of the young French chaps she'd taken up with. It was going to be terribly smart, she'd told him, and nothing in her wardrobe was suitable.

She'd chosen her moment well. Maria was there and the builder was waiting to discuss the choice of handles for the shower room. When he'd protested that she couldn't possibly need another dress, Phyllie had pouted prettily and pointed out that they hadn't found what she'd wanted after Olivia had flown off from Nice airport, when he'd said he'd buy her something. He hadn't felt up to arguing so he'd given her his smart card, which only needed a validation code, told her what it was and threatened dire retribution if she spent more than five thousand francs.

Charles found the whisky and poured himself a generous finger then took the glass into the kitchen, where he found ice and added a splash of water. He wandered through the salon and into his study, where he switched on the evening news. Juno padded after him and settled with his head on Charles's feet. Charles liked the feel of the heavy head on his instep, it removed a little of his loneliness.

He tried to concentrate on understanding the newsreader but found his thoughts returning again and again to Olivia. Gradually over the last ten days or so he'd begun to fear that she wouldn't come back. He tried to tell himself it was only the distance given by the telephone and his inability to communicate without being able to see and touch her. But he couldn't help remembering how little they were talking to each other before her father rang and she returned to England.

He finished his drink and went and got himself another, bringing the whisky bottle back with him.

Olivia had been enjoying herself out here, hadn't she? She'd seemed so alive early on. Particularly when they started going out and meeting people.

Charles tried to avoid the thought that she had begun to get bored with him but it nagged at him.

Then there was her difficulty in getting to grips with French. He'd been going to suggest she went on a course in the autumn. Perhaps they could go together. This newsreader, for instance, was far too fast for him. There must be somewhere that could offer an advanced course for him as well as something more basic for Olivia. Was her difficulty in coming to grips with the language one of the reasons she hadn't seemed to settle the way he had? Or was it all those damned people that kept coming and staying? They'd hardly had any time to themselves since the house had been finished.

She would have missed Tilly when she went back as well. Phyllida couldn't have been much of a substitute. As so often before, Charles told himself it would take time for the two women he loved best in all the world to get used to each other.

As he once more refilled his glass, Charles realised it was seven o'clock, time he called Olivia.

The moment he got through, he could hear a new note in her voice. She sounded happier, more relaxed. 'Darling, how lovely to hear you. How's everything going with you?'

Feeling slightly happier himself, Charles launched into a long grouse about the time it was taking the builders to finish the pool house. Not much came back to him down the telephone wire. He could see Olivia leaning back in a chair, the receiver held to her ear, her attention wandering, to what? Her parents? A magazine? Charles finished abruptly. 'That's enough of that,' he said, 'how's your mother?' The standard question and he waited for the standard answer while taking a sip of his third drink.

'Great news,' Olivia's enthusiastic voice suddenly hit him. 'Mother's really turned the corner!'

Charles hastily swallowed his whisky. 'Fantastic! Then you'll be booking your flight back here!'

There was a pause at the other end of the line. 'Well,' said Olivia hesitantly, 'I'm not sure how soon I can get away.'

'But you said your mother's better,' Charles said, almost shouting. He couldn't understand how she could hesitate. That is, unless she really didn't want to come home.

'I said she's turned the corner,' Olivia said, rather coldly to Charles's ear. 'I didn't say she was completely better.'

'Well, how much better does she have to be before you can leave her?' Charles heard his belligerent tone with despair but could do nothing about it.

'I don't know!' Olivia sounded harassed. 'Look, I can probably tell you more in a couple of days.'

Which meant she wasn't going to be back for five or six days at the earliest.

Charles signed off feeling less in tune with his wife than ever before. She just didn't seem to be considering him at all. He swallowed the remaining few drops of his drink and reached for the bottle again.

Where the hell was Phyllida? She should have been back hours ago! It was more than time he had something to eat.

Not that Charles expected his daughter to cook for him.

At first he'd had high hopes of her ability to look after him. When his friends, the Roberts, arrived, she'd got up early every day and prepared breakfast for them. Most days they'd had every other meal out but she had managed to assemble a couple of salads. And she'd charmed Richard and Yvonne, friends from his early days in London, a doctor and his physiotherapist wife. Like everyone else, they had enjoyed staying at *La Chênais*, the only dark spot being the absence of Olivia.

'I'd really been looking forward to meeting your new wife,' Richard said after Charles had explained the situation to them. 'You should have told us, we'd have put our visit off.'

'We didn't want to spoil your holiday,' Charles apologised. 'And this way you've got to come back and see us again. Phyllida is here and delighted to have a chance to look after you.' That was stretching the situation but she had appeared happy to go around with them while Charles showed off some of his favourite spots. The Roberts had been charmed by Phyllie and by everything they had seen.

Then they left and life had taken a deep dive. Phyllida disappeared more and more often. No longer did she go with him to walk Juno. Asleep until late morning, by lunchtime she'd driven off in her little Peugeot and often didn't return until Charles had gone to bed. When he asked what she got up to, she would look at him under her eyelids and give him a slow smile. 'Dad, weren't you ever young?' she'd enquire in dulcet tones. 'I'm just making the most of life.' Then, after several days when he'd hardly seen her, she came downstairs and twined her arms around his shoulders and said, 'Isn't it time we spent some time together? Why don't you take me out to lunch? Let's go to *La Bonne Auberge*, I just adore Philippe Rostang's cooking.' Charles was too happy to have her spending time with him to ask when she'd been there before.

They'd had a superb lunch and she'd asked him about the early days of his company.

'I don't know why Mummy wasn't happy with you,' she said at one point, sipping her glass of Chablis, looking into his eyes, her own clear but narrowed. 'You're so much more man than that prat she's married to now.'

He'd laughed at that.

'When's Olivia coming back?' she'd asked then.

'When her mother's better,' he'd said briefly.

She'd played with the remains of her bread. 'I wish I could be sure I'd be able to leave all this and go and look after Mummy like that.'

'You would, my darling, if she needed you.'

Phyllida didn't look convinced.

'And it won't be for very long. She'll soon be back here.'

Phyllida gave him a smile that had a touch of insecurity about it. 'You do like having me around, don't you, Dad?'

'Phyllie, how can you ask that? You know I love being with you. I just wish you were around more often.'

'If ever you need me, Dad, I'll be there. I'll come back from anywhere for you.'

For a moment it was enough for Charles.

But that was one lunch. He'd hardly seen her after that.

He wandered out to the kitchen and found some cheese in the fridge and a salad that Maria had left. He ate it at the kitchen table, reading a copy of *Love in the Time of Cholera* that Olivia had been in the middle of and forgotten when she went back to England. He'd asked if she'd wanted it sent. 'No, you read it, then we can talk about it when I get back,' she'd said. He'd mentioned the other day that he was halfway through it now and was loving it but Olivia had made no comment. What would he do if Olivia decided not to return?

The front door banged and Juno ran barking into the hall.

Charles followed, in time to see Phyllida running upstairs, laden with carrier bags.

'Do you want supper?' he called after her.

'I'm going out. Michel is calling for me in half an hour.' She leaned over the bannisters. 'Got the most heavenly dress, Dad, you'll love me in it. And I met the most divine man. He took me drinking, I could hardly drag myself away.' She gave a delightful laugh and disappeared.

Charles abandoned the rest of his supper, poured himself a brandy, took it into the study and fell asleep watching an old film.

He woke at ten to one in the morning, his mouth sour, his head aching. Phyllida still hadn't returned. He left the light burning in the hall and went to bed, stretching out his arms towards where Olivia used to lie.

Phyllida was still in bed by half past eleven when the fridge arrived for the pool house and payment was required.

Charles went upstairs and knocked at her bedroom. There was a groan from inside. He put his head round the door. 'Can I have my smart card back, Phyllie, please?'

His daughter muttered something incomprehensible, waved a hand towards her dressing table and pulled the duvet over her head.

Charles went over, found the card in its holder and tiptoed out.

As he removed the card from its plastic case to give to the delivery man, he found the payment slips for Phyllida's purchases the previous day. While the card details were being taken, he flipped idly through them, then stopped and studied them more carefully.

'Monsieur?' Numb with shock Charles signed the payment slip held out to him then took his copy automatically.

He saw the delivery man off the premises then went back to the main house.

Phyllida was in the kitchen, still in her nightdress, squeezing oranges in the electric juicer. 'Hi, Dad,' she said, lifting the full glass and downing it in one go. 'Wow, that's better.'

'Phyllida,' Charles said grimly. 'It's time we had a word.'

'Dad?' she said questioningly. He hardly ever used her full name.

'Get dressed and come to the study.'

'But I haven't had breakfast yet.'

'It'll be time for lunch in a minute. Do as I say.'

She gave one look at his face and disappeared.

He went and sat behind his desk. Before him, on the smooth, dark, polished surface, he laid out the slips that had been with his charge card.

Phyllida saw them the moment she came in. She'd showered, her hair was wet, plastered against her scalp, and she'd put on a pair of jeans and a scarlet T-shirt. Her feet were bare. 'Ah!' she said.

'Ah! indeed,' Charles said grimly. 'Perhaps you can explain, Phyllie?'

The use of the pet name appeared to give her confidence. 'It was just that I found these heavenly mix and match ensembles. The sort of thing you never see in England. They were just perfect and I knew you'd say I could have them if you'd been there, so I bought them.' She ended with a touch of bravado and sat on the corner of the desk, looking at him with the little girl expression that had never failed to get her what she wanted.

'You promised you wouldn't go above five thousand francs.' He picked up the slips. 'These amount to nearly fifteen thousand. That's around two thousand pounds. How can you spend two thousand pounds on clothes?'

'Come on, Dad, you know how much nice things cost these days. And you can afford it.'

'Phyllida, if you want to spend this much on your wardrobe, you must earn it.'

'I bet Olivia spends much more,' Phyllida muttered sulkily.

Charles was so angry he could hardly speak. 'What Olivia spends on her clothes is nothing to do with you. But I can tell you that she'd never go over her budget. As far as I can see, the word hasn't entered your vocabulary.'

Phyllida rose. 'Well, if that's all, I'll see what I can find for lunch.'

The offer to provide a meal did nothing to placate her father. 'Sit down, Phyllie, I haven't finished.'

She gave him a quick look and did so, choosing the chair in front of the desk this time.

'It's time you did something about getting back to work.'

'Dad! I thought you liked having me here.'

'I do but not like this. I'm not giving you any more money and I mean that. It's no good you're giving me those looks, it won't work. You must get a job. I've always been prepared to help you but not so you can swan around doing nothing but be far too familiar with any young Michel, Jean or Pierre who crosses your path.'

'God, Dad, you're old fashioned!'

'I've decided to go and see Olivia. I'm booking myself on tomorrow's plane and I suggest you come with me.'

Phyllida exchanged her sulky look for one of astonishment. 'Why, Dad?'

'Because I want to see my wife, that's why.'

'But why do I have to come too? I can stay here and look after Juno.'

'And fill the house with your friends? No, thank you, I'd like to see some whisky left when I return. Juno can go to kennels.'

'But I've got nowhere to go,' Phyllida said with a touch of desperation.

'You've got a perfectly good flat.'

'It's let,' she said without thinking.

Charles stared at her. 'Let? But I'm paying the mortgage on it for you.'

'Come off it, Dad, I have to have some money, you hardly give me enough for petrol.'

'Right, Phyllida, that's it! You're coming back to England with me and the first thing you'll do is look for a job.'

For a long moment father and daughter looked at each other, Charles implacable, Phyllida openly pleading.

Then she shrugged her shoulders. 'Well, I better start packing, I suppose.'

'You'd be better off seeing to some lunch for us,' Charles said, not relaxing for a moment.

With a flash of her old style, Phyllida retorted, 'If you want a decent meal, you should take us out but I'll see what I can find.'

As she disappeared, Charles sagged in his chair. He didn't know when anything had left him so drained. Then he reached for the telephone and booked two seats on the following day's plane. After a little thought he made another call. Then he rang the Ferguson number in Sussex.

Olivia answered, 'Charles! Is something wrong? I didn't expect to hear from you until this evening.'

'I'm fed up with waiting for you to come back,' he said without preamble. 'I'm coming over tomorrow.'

'Oh, darling!' Olivia sounded overcome. 'I'll meet you at the airport.'

'That'll be great,' he gave her the flight details. 'Phyllie and I will be counting the minutes until our plane gets in.'

There was a small silence at the other end of the phone. Then Olivia said in a colourless voice, 'Right, I'll see you both tomorrow then,' and put the phone down.

Some of the excitement Charles had felt telling her of his plan faded. Maybe it wasn't such a good idea after all. But he'd done it now. And it was the right thing to do, he was sure of that. He had to find out where he stood in their marriage.

Chapter Twenty-Nine

Olivia's pleasure in hearing Charles was coming over to see her had been destroyed. Couldn't Phyllida have stayed in France? What sort of reunion could they have in front of her? Then she wondered if Charles was expecting her to stay with them. Olivia was sure she'd heard Phyllida tell one of her friends that she'd let her flat. With Thomas in the spare room, where would everyone sleep?

The last question was answered the following morning. Charles's arrival provided the perfect excuse for Daphne to invite her husband to return to her bed. Thomas flushed with pleasure and Olivia was delighted.

She spent the morning making beds with Betty, who was full of Daphne's new spirit. 'I just knew she was going to buck up one of these fine days,' she said, hauling blankets back from one of the spare beds. 'Time, that's the great healer, isn't it? Time and love, that's what we all need in life, lots of love.'

Olivia agreed wholeheartedly.

Dressed in a skirt and polo neck sweater under a leather jacket, Olivia set out in gloomy weather that afternoon to drive to the airport.

Traffic was thick, it always seemed worse when rain threatened and she began to worry that, having started early, she would be late. How dreadful if she wasn't there when they came out from customs! Despite all her forebodings about this meeting, she realised she was desperate to see Charles again. And perhaps the trouble with Phyllida had been her fault. If only she'd discussed the situation with Charles, made him understand how threatened she'd felt. If only she'd been firmer with Phyllida but also more loving. After all, she was Charles's daughter, she must be likable. Perhaps it was just a matter of searching for her good points – even if that meant a jungle-type expedition! She pressed her foot down and the little Metro speeded up. But it was no use, the traffic on the M25 had slowed almost to a halt.

Olivia drove into the airport and parked the car with no time to spare.

She hurried through the crowds to the arrival hall, only to find that the Nice flight was late and she had to stand watching wave after wave of passengers come through and be greeted.

As she waited, all her doubts and insecurities jostled her as badly as the crowds. She ran nervous fingers through her not-quite-as-short hair. The other day she'd let the hairdresser cut off just enough to reshape the growing ends and they'd begun to wave around her face. What would Charles think of it now?

Someone bumped their trolley into her back and was gone without an apology. So much discourtesy on display in this airport, so many people in too much of a hurry.

Then she saw them. Charles wheeling a luggage trolley, Phyllida walking beside him.

But Olivia hardly noticed her stepdaughter, her eyes were on her husband and she was suffused with a wave of love. He looked taller than she remembered, his face stronger, the eyes a deeper brown. How could she have forgotten the contagious warmth of his smile, the way his eyes lit up when he saw her?

'Charles,' she shouted and ran towards him, pushing past the flimsy barrier and the other passengers, flinging herself into his arms, feeling the familiar comfort of being held by him as he closed his arms around her.

Then she drew back, flushed and laughing, and turned to her stepdaughter with sincere goodwill. 'Phyllida, how lovely to see you. You're looking great!' It was a small lie, Phyllida was actually looking depressed and far from her usual jaunty self.

'Yah,' said Phyllida awkwardly. She slipped an arm through her father's and stared at Olivia with her old belligerence.

Well, thought Olivia resignedly, I should never have expected an immediate breakthrough. 'What are your plans?' she said brightly. 'We have a bed for you if you want to come back with us? My parents would love to meet you.' Would Phyllida realise Olivia didn't want to shut her out of her father's life?

Phyllida's eyes were scanning the waiting crowd of people. Then her face lit up. 'There she is,' she said excitedly. Coming towards them, moving swiftly but without any sense of hurry, was an extremely smart middle-aged woman of medium height, her lithe figure dressed in a dark trouser suit that had to be a designer model, her straight fair hair precision cut, immaculate makeup making the most of a classically chiselled face with determined nose and chin.

'Charles!' she gave him a brief nod, ignored Olivia and turned to Phyllida. 'Not got your own trolley, then?' she asked crisply, taking in the heavily laden luggage carrier Charles was pushing.

Phyllida flushed and looked disconcerted.

'It's all right, Veronica, only one case is mine, the rest is all Phyllie's.' Charles removed a flat foldover suit carrier from the load he'd been pushing. 'Let me introduce Olivia.' He put an arm around her to bring her forward and Olivia found herself shaking hands with Charles's first wife.

Veronica looked her over carefully. Tilly would have said like a cook inspecting a cut of meat, thought Olivia, with an inward gasp of amusement.

'It's nice to meet you,' Olivia said as the remorseless inspection continued.

'And you,' Veronica said briefly as she seemed to make up her mind her husband's new wife could be acceptable. 'This is the most ghastly place, isn't it?' She turned to her daughter. 'Right, darling, let's go. I have a host of things to do and a dinner party this evening. Why do you always organise your life so badly? Grab that trolley and follow me,' she ended briskly, starting towards the car park.

Phyllida clung to her father. 'Thanks for everything, Dad,' she said. 'See you soon?'

'You bet.' He gave her a warm hug. 'Just remember what I told you.'

She smiled uncertainly at him and then turned to Olivia. 'Thanks for inviting me, perhaps I can come some other time?'

With genuine feeling Olivia hugged her stepdaughter. 'Any time, Phyllie, anywhere.'

Phyllida started off after her mother then turned back. 'Hope you enjoy your evening,' she said with one of her old grins.

'Phyll,' an autocratic voice called above the hubbub.

Phyllida's smile faded as she started pushing her trolley away from them.

'Wow!' said Olivia as she watched the girl's disappearing back. 'Was Veronica always like that?'

Charles grinned. 'Looking back, I can recognise the first shoots but the full flowering came slowly over the years. Personally, I would say she is now well past her sell by date.' He picked up his case. 'Now, darling, do you have a car or should we hire one?'

'Mother is letting me drive her Metro, I've promised no speeding and to go easy on the clutch.'

'If I promise to abide by the ground rules, any chance of my doing the driving?'

Olivia fished out the car park ticket and money for the pay machine. 'I'd love you to, if you're sure you're not too tired?'

'One short hop across France? Have pity on me, I'm not on the scrap heap yet.'

Charles started the engine. 'Mustn't forget to drive on the left,' he muttered under his breath as he put the car in gear and carefully negotiated his way out of the car park.

Olivia sat beside him, her hands neatly folded in her lap, her heart thudding. She controlled her instinct to put her hand on his thigh, the way she had when they were engaged and first married. Faced with his powerful presence, she wondered how she could have let the hassles of the summer come between them. Then she saw he'd taken the wrong road out of the airport. 'Charles, Sussex is the other way!'

He paid no attention but moved rapidly up through the gears until the little Metro was bounding along in the direction of London.

'Where are we going?' Olivia asked, a little sharply.

'Worried?' He turned to look at her with an unreadable expression, his shoulders straight and tense.

More doubts gnawed away at her. So, Charles, too, wanted somewhere neutral where they could talk. Perhaps he had no intention of coming back to Sussex with her?

She couldn't continue to sit beside him in silence and he obviously had no intention of telling her where they were going. 'Tell me how Liz and Patrick are,' she suggested.

His shoulders relaxed just a little. 'Ah, now, all's well there, as I told you on the phone the last time you asked.'

'But I want some detail. Has the baby started to show yet; how's Patrick adapting to the idea of fatherhood; has Liz been able to start painting again? Don't just fob me off with an "all's well" bulletin,' she insisted.

He glanced at her with a slight smile. 'Getting demanding now, are we? Well, where shall I start? First, no, unless she's wearing something close-fitting, you still can't tell Liz is pregnant. Two, I'm beginning to get just a tiny bit bored with Patrick's plans for the baby. Fond fatherhood is all very well but when I start being shown brochures for baby buggies and asked to go comparison shopping for cots, that's it!'

'Poor Charles, no wonder you've hot footed it over here,' murmured Olivia.

'As to Liz's painting, she hasn't got back to it yet. Her wrist is out of plaster, though, and she's having physiotherapy and doing lots of exercises. Is that a complete enough answer for you?'

'I'm almost back there with them,' Olivia assured him, feeling nostalgic for her friends and life in France.

'Now tell me about your mother. I've found the bits and pieces you've told me on the telephone difficult to put together.'

The full tale of her mother's condition took time. 'The final tonic was her meeting a friend when we went out to lunch,' Olivia finished. 'Within two minutes, they were pulling to shreds some committee they both sit on! Margaret's husband had to drag her away. But I think it finally showed Mother there is life after a colostomy.'

'What a relief for you.'

Olivia nodded. 'For Mother most of all.'

They'd entered London proper by now and he was heading down the Cromwell Road extension, towards Knightsbridge.

'What about Clodagh?' asked Charles as the Metro dived into the underpass to Piccadilly.

'Oh, I've had several chats with her on the phone. She's deep into her next book, she's already got a contract for it. And she's still seeing that gorgeous man she met on the plane out to us. I have hopes something may come of it.'

The car turned right at Fortnum and Mason's, wound its way back towards Piccadilly and came to a stop outside the Ritz.

'Good heavens,' said Olivia, her heart sinking. She didn't want to try and talk to Charles over a drink surrounded by all the splendour of one of the world's greatest hotels.

A tall, magnificently uniformed porter opened the car door and helped her out.

'Can you dispose of this?' Charles took out his suitcase and waved a hand at the Metro.

'Certainly, sir.'

Charles tossed him the keys, slipped his arm under Olivia's and helped her up the steps and through the revolving doors, easing her left into reception.

She could hardly believe it. 'Charles, we can't stay here.'

'Why ever not?' he asked reasonably, then gave his name to one of the tail-coated receptionists.

'Well, I haven't got anything with me,' she said weakly.

'I've brought everything you'll need,' he assured her, filling in the form that had been placed in front of him. 'There, I think that's everything.'

'Splendid sir. Now, if you will come with me? A porter will bring your case.'

The room they were taken to was so spacious and beautifully furnished, Olivia was reduced to silence. She walked over to the window by the seating area and looked out at Green Park, the leaves on the trees golden and falling in the last of the setting sun. She hardly heard what the charming receptionist said as he showed Charles where the bathroom was and how the lights and television worked and which bits of the panelling opened to show where you could arrange your clothes.

The receptionist disappeared.

'Charles,' Olivia began.

There was a knock on the door and the porter appeared with Charles's suitcase. He found some money to tip him and showed him out of the room. 'Now, my darling,' he said and took Olivia in his arms.

It was a highly satisfactory kiss. During it, Olivia felt the weeks of their parting and the difficulties of the summer slip away and it was as though they were back in the early stages of their marriage. 'Charles,' she said as he reluctantly lowered his arms. 'This is all very romantic.'

'I hope so,' he said.

'But I shall have to ring Mother and Father and say we won't be coming home.'

'I think you should.'

So Olivia made her call, assured her mother that the car was being properly parked and not left to the tender mercies of vandals and said she'd let them know when they'd be returning.

'Just remember that without my car I'm stranded,' Daphne said. Then she added, 'But your father says I can use his if I need to go out, or he'll drive me. Oh, and Tilly wants you to ring her. She said she'd be at home until six o'clock.'

Olivia severed the connection convinced that Daphne had made the necessary breakthrough and was facing life with her old courage. Then she glanced at her watch, it was after six but she dialled the number just in case. Tilly answered so quickly she must have been standing by the phone.

'Oh, Mum, thanks for ringing, you've just caught me. No, nothing's wrong. How's Charles? You're at the Ritz? That's awesome! Give him my love. What it was, I wanted you to know I've got a place on the course. The college rang today! Isn't that wonderful? Look, I must dash, talk to you later.'

Olivia was left holding a disconnected line. 'Tilly's been accepted for the course,' she said to Charles.

He looked up from placing his change of clothes in one of the wardrobe units. 'I was sure she would,' he said, 'once Rory got on the case. We must try and take both of them out for a meal.'

Then he placed on the bed a brand new midnight blue silk dress, a pair of patent leather shoes, the satin nightdress Margie had given Olivia before their first trip to France, slippers and a negligee, plus change of underwear and a toiletries bag.

'Phyllie helped me choose the dress and pack everything,' he said, a trifle nervously. She had to take something back to a very smart shop in Monte Carlo and we chose it there. She said she knew exactly what you'd like. Then she sorted everything out from your wardrobe and dressing table.

'Phyllida?' Olivia gasped. She unzipped the toiletries bag and found toothpaste, two brand new toothbrushes and a selection of the makeup she'd left behind, including the lighter tinted foundation she'd abandoned for the summer, eye makeup, a moisturiser and cleansing milk. The last two she looked at in wonder. 'But I brought these with me.'

'I know, we stopped on the way to the airport so Phyllie could get them. They are the same make as your cosmetics so she hoped they'd be all right for you. She also bought the dental stuff.'

'She's done very well, the dress is beautiful and I've got everything I need here.' Olivia zipped up the bag and went and placed it in the marble bathroom.

When she returned, Charles was undoing the neck of a bottle of champagne.

'My word, did you organise all this from France?'

'Amazing things, telephones and fax machines.' He grinned at her as the cork popped out. He started to fill two glasses. 'I thought this would be perfect before we had a small rest, then a bath, then dinner. I've booked a table for two for nine o'clock, in the restaurant. Does the programme suit Madame?'

Olivia swallowed hard. If she wasn't careful, she was going to allow being surrounded by luxury to distract her from her purpose. The trouble was, Charles made it too easy to forget about the important things of life.

'Charles,' she said determinedly as he put a glass of champagne in her hand. 'We've got to talk.'

'I know,' he said cheerfully. 'But we've all the time in the world.'

'No, we haven't. That's the mistake I made before. I thought if I didn't worry about anything, it would all work itself out.'

Charles started to look uneasy.

Olivia took a hasty gulp of champagne and continued, 'I always swore I was never going to be like my mother, bullying people, being assertive, always questioning their motives. I thought if you tried to make life pleasant for everyone, everyone would be happy.'

'One of the things I love about you, darling,' Charles said quietly, 'is how restful you are. Veronica was always challenging me, trying to pick a fight, wanting to "wake me up", as she called it. I hated that. I'm a man of peace.' He sat down on a small sofa at one end of the room and put his glass on the coffee table. 'Come and sit down.' He patted the sofa beside him.

Cautiously Olivia settled herself down on the blue damask.

'Tell me exactly what's worrying you.'

Now that it had come to the point, all Olivia's carefully prepared phrases deserted her.

'Well, there's Phyllida,' she started clumsily.

Charles picked up her hand and held it to his face. 'My poor, stupid little daughter,' he said sadly.

'I wanted to love her, really I did,' stammered Olivia. 'But right from the start she made it impossible.'

'As you saw today, her mother's a difficult woman,' Charles said elliptically. 'I've always seen my job as being a steadying influence in her life. I loved the way you were so patient with her in France.'

Patient? Had he seen nothing of the war that had gone on between them?

'I know she's bloody difficult and I know I spoil her too much but she doesn't get much love in her life, mostly her own fault.'

'She really needs to get another job,' Olivia said boldly. If she wasn't assertive now, she never would be.

'I've told her that,' Charles said to her surprise.

'And is she going to?' asked Olivia sceptically.

He looked rueful as he told her about the ultimatum he'd given Phyllida.

'After that Phyllie rang her mother, said she was coming back with me to look for a job and could she stay with her until she got her flat back? Veronica will soon see that she gets organised,' Charles said with a certain satisfaction in his voice.

Olivia reckoned that leaving the two of them together had to have been the smartest thing she could have done. Some day she'd tell Daphne there'd been a credit side to her illness after all. Then she remembered Phyllida's sweet grin as she'd said she hoped Olivia would enjoy her evening. She thought of the care with which she had chosen the new dress, how it was exactly her style. Perhaps they could both start afresh now and build a proper relationship.

Still holding fast to Olivia's hand, Charles topped up their champagne glasses, 'Darling, these last three weeks have been amongst the most miserable of my life. I was going mad out there without you. If your mother needs you any longer, I shall insist on parking myself in Sussex as well. Your father and I can surely find something to talk about.'

Olivia gently released her hand and moved slightly away from him. 'There are certain things we have to get straight,' she said with determination.

Charles looked worried.

'I am not running some kind of luxury hotel that never hands out bills.' Olivia looked up at him sternly. 'I know you're proud of our house and I am too but surely we want to be able to enjoy it, not feel exhausted the whole time?'

'My feelings exactly,' he said eagerly. Then his gaze dropped. 'The only thing is, how do we choke the visitors off? I mean, it's not as though we invite half of them. And we can hardly say to our friends that they aren't welcome.'

'I've thought of that and I've got the answer. I'm going back to work.'

He looked at her, appalled. 'But that will merely compound the problem. I want to have you in France, not commuting between London and Nice.'

'Nothing like that,' Olivia assured him and outlined Margie's offer. 'Why don't you come in as well and handle the business side of things?'

Charles looked thoughtful.

'It wouldn't be full-time, at least not to start with. But, don't you see, if we were running a business, we'd have the perfect excuse to turn visitors down.'

'Or at least limit them to one night.'

'Charles!'

'Well, there might be some people we'd *like* to have – for one night, that is,' he added hastily.

'Well, what do you think?'

'I think I'd like to meet Margie and have a discussion about it all. There's a lot that would need to be thrashed out.'

'You mean, you might think about it?' Olivia was thrilled, this was more than she'd dared to hope for.

'Tell me, would you go ahead and work for her even if I didn't want to come in?'

Olivia looked straight at him. 'That's what we've got to talk about. We should have discussed it much earlier. You just assumed I'd give up work when we got married.'

His worried look was back. 'Didn't you want to?'

'I didn't say that. But it's niggled that you never realised, even though we worked together, how much it meant to me. You never even suggested I might try to be a part-time consultant, you never even raised the subject!'

'I thought we wanted to share things together.' He sounded injured.

'I know, darling. That's what I thought too. I just didn't realise . . .' She hesitated.

'Didn't realise what?' There was an edge to his voice. 'That it wasn't going to be enough?' He got up and walked to the window where he stood, his hands jammed into his pockets, looking at the park. 'You're not going to turn out like Veronica after all, are you?' he asked without turning round.

'Heavens, I hope not. From what I saw today, I would hate to share life with her. But, don't you see, we should have discussed it? And there are other things we've never talked about.' Charles looked back towards her, his face apprehensive.

Olivia took a deep breath and said, 'For instance, I've never told you about my first marriage.'

That brought him back to the sofa. 'No,' he said. 'I haven't asked you because I thought you'd tell me in your own good time.'

Olivia sipped her champagne nervously. Now that the moment had come, she found it difficult to begin.

'Do I gather your first marriage wasn't the unalloyed bliss I'd been led to believe?'

Olivia flushed. 'I didn't mean to mislead you but – oh, it's so difficult to explain.'

Charles waited.

'It started with my parents being so against Peter. When . . . well, when things started coming apart, I found I couldn't tell them.'

'And have them say, "I told you so"?'

'False pride, that's what it was. I was so stupid but I used to write letters to them saying how wonderfully happy I was. Peter had sold his first script, was earning what seemed like huge sums of money. Everything *should* have been wonderful.' Her voice cracked.

'So why wasn't it?'

Olivia lifted her shoulders in a helpless shrug. 'I don't know. That was the awful thing. I could only think it was something to do with me. Peter started seeing other women, he never tried to hide it. When I asked him why, he'd say things like "sugar's all very well but not as a daily diet", or "don't be such a bloody martyr". I told him if he wanted a divorce, I'd give him one. I couldn't stand the sort of life we were leading, hardly seeing him, stuck out in the back of beyond, no friends, no job, only Tilly for company.'

'But he didn't want a divorce,' Charles hazarded.

'He adored Tilly, we both did. He said we were a family and a family we were going to stay. He was providing me with enough money to have anything I wanted, why couldn't I be happy?' Olivia felt the old tears coming to her eyes. 'I felt such a failure. We'd been so much in love, at least, I thought we had; I adored him and I couldn't seem to make him happy. The more I tried, the less I saw of him.'

'Bastard,' Charles said savagely.

'I asked him once why he'd married me if he thought so little of me? Do you know what he said?' Olivia tried to brush the tears away from her eyes.

Charles shook his head, his gaze never leaving her face.

' "I had to beat your mother. I couldn't let her win." I'd just been a pawn in a battle between them!'

'No wonder you didn't want to let Daphne know how right she'd been,' Charles said softly and took her hand.

'I was a complete and utter mess. The only thing I was any good at was looking after Tilly. When it was just the two of us, I managed to keep myself together. And while she was around, Peter and I could manage to pretend we were a happy family. Real Hollywood stuff,' she said bitterly. 'But as soon as she'd gone to bed, it would start. I'd try to pretend everything was all right between us and he'd taunt me with details of who he'd been sleeping with. He'd drink too much, smoke pot, try and make love, fail, curse me for being such a "poor lay", reduce me to a quivering heap of self-loathing, then disappear in the morning for another few weeks. We seemed to be locked into some terrible cycle. And the awful thing was, I still loved him! Even when he came to me straight from some other woman's bed – and I always knew, I could smell it on him, see it in the shift of his eyes, hear it in the excitement in his voice – even then all he had to do was smile and give me a kind word and I was all his.' Olivia's voice was full of self-disgust. 'When I think about it now, I can't understand how I could have stood it. I should have left him, taken Tilly and gone back to England. No matter what my mother said.' Tears were falling freely now.

'God, if I could only have got hold of him,' Charles got out through clenched teeth. His hands formed themselves into fists. 'What an unmitigated bastard.'

'It's only recently that I realised I made everything worse. If I'd told him to stuff it, stopped acting as a doormat, he might at least have respected me. We might have been able to be friends. Maybe if he hadn't died . . .' Her voice drifted away as she remembered that last occasion.

'He'd never brought a woman to the house before. But that day . . .' Olivia was back under the Californian summer sun, the desert landscape hard and shimmery, the heat bouncing off the hard earth, the only green and succulents planted round the drive, their dark emerald dusty and subdued. She could smell again the scent that wafted round the tall girl with the curly blonde hair, Diorella, the same scent that Peter had given her; afterwards she'd never been able to smell it without feeling sick.

And Peter had had that look in his eyes and his hand was on the girl's shoulder as she gave Tilly a gift and Olivia could see the caress he gave her.

Tilly had run off to open her present and Olivia had controlled herself long enough to call her back to say thank you properly. Then she'd waited until Tilly had gone out to the back terrace before turning to them both and telling them in a low, furious voice, to leave immediately and not to come back, ever.

The girl hadn't minded, she'd grabbed Peter's hand and told him to come, now. But Peter had cursed her, told her to get in the car. Then he'd tried to sweet talk Olivia, told her he'd be back that evening and that everything would be all right.

For once his voice had done nothing to her. She'd looked at him and seen only the way his body was now too thin, eaten by dissipation and hard living, the cruel twist his mouth had acquired over the years, the bloodshot eyes with pin-prick pupils and a tic that twitched and twitched beside his left eye.

There'd been no emotion at all in her voice as she told him he wasn't to come back, that everything was over between them.

He'd refused to believe her, said again that he'd take the girl back to Hollywood and return immediately.

Olivia knew it was because he hated losing anything and that he would fight to the death for Tilly. She bored him, she knew that. Her body could still excite him but she, the woman, was no longer of any interest.

Still protesting, he'd got into the car and gunned it up the stony drive; the bumper had caught the big boulder at the entrance and the car swayed on the dirt road, the girl screaming and clutching the open window. Then he'd revved the engine again and soon the car was just a cloud of dust travelling towards the horizon and Tilly was crying because her father and the pretty lady had gone.

He'd never made it back to Hollywood. Both he and the girl had been killed in a head-on collision with a lorry. The other driver had survived. He'd said he'd had no chance, Peter's car had driven straight at him. The autopsy revealed not only a level of alcohol well over the limit but also heroin. Olivia hadn't realised he'd graduated to hard drugs.

'Everyone in England assumed I was heartbroken – and I was,' Olivia finished her story. 'It seemed easier to let them assume the fairytale had continued right up until the end.'

'Instead of which, a nightmare was over,' Charles said gently.

'Something like that,' she agreed. 'Well, you know the full story now. How useless I was at sustaining a relationship, how boring I turned out to be as a wife.' She tried to keep her voice level and ironic but failed.

'Olivia, darling.' Charles drew her to him. 'It wasn't your fault, he was sick!'

She let him hold her. Solid, reliable Charles, so very different from the mercurial man who had been her first husband.

After a long moment he said, 'Poor darling, what a rotten time you had of it. No wonder you lived a nun-like existence for so long.'

307

Olivia drew back and ran a finger under both her eyes, wiping away the traces of tears. The worst was over now. 'When I first came back, all I was concerned with was the struggle to find a job and a house so I could look after Tilly. I was far too battered and bruised to want any sort of relationship. It was only when I met you,' she smiled at him, her eyes huge and soft, 'that I realised everything I'd been missing for so long.'

Charles squeezed her hand and would have drawn her to him again but Olivia resisted.

'I've told you this for two reasons. Firstly because it's something I should have done right at the start. I had no right to let you go on thinking my first marriage had been idyllic. I was badly damaged and it was totally unfair not to let you know that.'

'You're not damaged as far as I'm concerned,' he said gently, his hand resting warm over hers.

'I thought you were so different from Peter, I didn't need to worry about being treated the same way. But now I realise I've been in danger of allowing exactly the same thing to happen again.'

'You're not trying to compare me to that – that *sadist*!' Charles was outraged.

Olivia smiled faintly. 'Of course not. But I was so worried that you were going to be disappointed in me, the way Peter was, I've given in to you all the time instead of realising that if I abandoned the sort of person I was, I could hardly blame you if you became bored.'

'I'll never be bored with you,' Charles objected.

Olivia said nothing and after a moment he said, 'Is this your way of explaining why you want to go back to work? That you're somehow going to lose your personality if you don't? Because if it is, I think it's a load of rubbish.'

'Which means you don't want me to?' Olivia's shoulders slumped. It seemed Charles hadn't understood anything of what she'd been trying to tell him.

Then she straightened up and decided to fight.

'Look, you can hardly call me the world's greatest housewife,' she said with a laugh. 'But I am an extremely good exhibition designer. Margie and I could have something really great going, especially if you were to come in on the business side. But you must see, we can't go on with you acting as chairman and treating me as the company secretary any longer.'

He looked affronted. 'That's not fair. I've never treated you like that.'

'You are far too fond of assuming that whatever you decide, I'll agree. Look at that business over the pool house. How's it coming along, by the way?'

'Oh, you're going to love it,' Charles said, his expression lively again. 'And it's going to be such an asset next summer.' Then, semi-seriously, he added, 'But if we do start this design company with Margie, are we going to have time to enjoy it?'

Olivia put her head on one side and looked at him. He was the most darling man. She didn't think she'd ever properly appreciated him. Why hadn't she told him about Peter before they married? It was the most cathartic thing she could have done. She felt light now and whole. Poor Peter, he was the damaged one, unable to handle success and fatherhood and being a proper husband.

'If you really hate the idea,' Olivia said slowly, 'I'll find some other way of fulfilling my creative instincts. The house really did turn out well, didn't it? Perhaps I can take up interior decorating and use *La Chênais* as an example of my work.'

'Well, that at least would mean you'd keep everything tidy,' Charles teased her. 'No, darling, I do understand what you're saying. To be honest, even before you had to come back here, I was beginning to feel at a loose end. And since you've been away it's been hell. Nothing to do and rattling around with just Phyllie for company. I'll confess, I've been seriously thinking I'd like to start another business. And it would be wonderful to work with you. We didn't have any problems working on that exhibition stand together, did we?'

'Not once we'd got the budget sorted out,' Olivia said with a grin, excitement beginning to fill her.

'Well, let's talk to Margie and see exactly what she has in mind.'

'Oh, Charles.' Olivia gazed at him, relief and love overflowing from her eyes. 'We'll be a real partnership, sharing everything.'

He put a hand to her face. 'That's all I want to do, for the rest of my life, share everything with you.' Then he took her into his arms.

After a moment he drew away and said, 'This is a damned awkward sofa. Would you think me too masterful if I suggested the other end of the room offered more comfortable accommodation?'

'I don't think we need take a vote on that one,' murmured Olivia, leading the way towards the bed, her hand linked with his.

Cloud Cuckoo Land

Peta Tayler

Life has been kind to Laura Melville. She has a beautiful home in a picturesque Sussex village; a happy marriage with Edward; and three loving and supportive friends nearby. She has only one regret, that she has never been able to have a child, but at forty-two she feels she has come to terms with this. She is very attached to her friends' children – in particular Daisy, a teenager who is just beginning to grasp the complexities of adult emotions – and her life appears to be satisfyingly full.

Then Edward comes home with shocking news. Her loving husband has been keeping a secret from Laura for almost fifteen years – a secret in the shape of a son. Edward has never seen the boy, but now Mark's mother wants Edward to take charge of him while she travels abroad. Suddenly Laura's peaceful existence is turned upside down and she finds herself looking with new eyes at her relationship with Edward, her childlessness and even her own sense of identity. Laura's life will never be the same again . . .

0 7472 5012 X

HEADLINE

Country Affairs

Jennifer Rennick

'Sharp, witty and, in parts, achingly moving'
Yorkshire Evening Post

Every woman needs an indulgence – something to look forward to, something to savour. And once a year Kate Hopegood has hers – a secret rendezvous in a plush London hotel with Patrick Bray-Smith, the man she loved before she met her husband, the man who, despite almost two decades of marriage and family, still sets Kate's heart racing.

But one year it all goes desperately wrong, leaving a shattered Kate to reassess what she decides is her own unsatisfactory existence. What she needs is a change and, refusing to accompany her husband on his new job abroad, she answers an advert for a housekeeper to an elderly colonel in the depths of the countryside.

But fashionable Gloucestershire is not the idyll she imagined. Colonel Beamish is a bully, the picturesque countryside threatened by developers and, worst of all, the Colonel's daughter, doyenne of the fast-living hunting set, turns out to be the woman who, only weeks ago, was haranguing her in the lobby of a London hotel – a certain Mrs Patrick Bray-Smith . . .

'A lovely combination of escapism and realism . . . a rollicking rural read. Thoroughly enjoyable' Katie Fforde, author of *The Rose Revived*

0 7472 4915 6

HEADLINE

A selection of bestsellers from Headline

LAND OF YOUR POSSESSION	Wendy Robertson	£5.99 ☐
DANGEROUS LADY	Martina Cole	£5.99 ☐
SEASONS OF HER LIFE	Fern Michaels	£5.99 ☐
GINGERBREAD AND GUILT	Peta Tayler	£5.99 ☐
HER HUNGRY HEART	Roberta Latow	£5.99 ☐
GOING TOO FAR	Catherine Alliott	£5.99 ☐
HANNAH OF HOPE STREET	Dee Williams	£4.99 ☐
THE WILLOW GIRLS	Pamela Evans	£5.99 ☐
A LITTLE BADNESS	Josephine Cox	£5.99 ☐
FOR MY DAUGHTERS	Barbara Delinsky	£4.99 ☐
SPLASH	Val Corbett, Joyce Hopkirk, Eve Pollard	£5.99 ☐
THEA'S PARROT	Marcia Willett	£5.99 ☐
QUEENIE	Harry Cole	£5.99 ☐
FARRANS OF FELLMONGER STREET	Harry Bowling	£5.99 ☐

All Headline books are available at your local bookshop or newsagent, or can be ordered direct from the publisher. Just tick the titles you want and fill in the form below. Prices and availability subject to change without notice.

Headline Book Publishing, Cash Sales Department, Bookpoint, 39 Milton Park, Abingdon, OXON, OX14 4TD, UK. If you have a credit card you may order by telephone – 01235 400400.

Please enclose a cheque or postal order made payable to Bookpoint Ltd to the value of the cover price and allow the following for postage and packing:

UK & BFPO: £1.00 for the first book, 50p for the second book and 30p for each additional book ordered up to a maximum charge of £3.00.
OVERSEAS & EIRE: £2.00 for the first book, £1.00 for the second book and 50p for each additional book.

Name ....

Address ....

....

....

If you would prefer to pay by credit card, please complete:
Please debit my Visa/Access/Diner's Card/American Express (delete as applicable) card no:

Signature .... Expiry Date ....